STAR-CROSSED LETTERS
FALLING FOR FAMOUS SERIES

SARAH DEEHAM

WWW.SARAHDEEHAM.COM

Copyright © 2023 by Sarah Deeham

All rights reserved.

No part of this book may be reproduced in any form or by any electronic or mechanical means, including information storage and retrieval systems, without written permission from the author, except for the use of brief quotations in a book review.

This book is a work of fiction. Names, characters, places, and incidents, other than those clearly in the public domain, either are products of the author's imagination or are used fictitiously. Any resemblance to actual events or locales or persons, living or dead, is entirely coincidental.

www.sarahdeeham.com

Cover by: Cover Ever After

❋ Created with Vellum

For my husband for being endlessly patient and always supporting my dreams.

They slipped briskly into an intimacy from which they never recovered.
 — F. Scott Fitzgerald

CHAPTER 1

hase

    To the new owner of my fabulous writing machine,
    If you're reading this, it means you bought my grandmother's typewriter. This old Remington may be worn, but it's wonderful, as most worn things are. The A key sticks. Be gentle with the hard return. I'll miss the soft K and the sound of those keys. Because I'm sentimental, I'm also giving you the first story I wrote on this typewriter. I wrote it twelve years ago, at the ancient age of eight. Save it as it may be worth money when I become a famous novelist. If you aren't too busy, perhaps you could tell me how you and this Remington get along. You can write to me at the consignment shop where I sold my typewriter.

    Sincerely,
    Typewriter Girl
    C/O Antiques Around the Corner
    49 Cherry Blossom Lane
    Noe Valley, San Francisco

It all started with a typewriter.

A vintage Remington, to be exact.

The therapist in my first and only session said to think of something that brings me peace in moments like this.

So as I sit in the back of the limo, trying not to freak the fuck out, I close my eyes, focus on my breath, and think of something good. I think of the typewriter. I think of that first letter. I think of her.

I'm not sure how long it takes. Seconds? Minutes? Time is marked only by the rhythm of my deep inhales and slow exhales. Eventually, my balled-up fists loosen, and the nausea begins to subside. I can't put this off any longer, so I steel my jaw, swing open the door of the limo, and step out into the sticky New York City air.

A thundering wave of sound slams into me as three thousand people shout my name. A velvet rope holds the crowd back, barely. There are autograph peddlers and paparazzi, reporters and fans. All looking to take away some part of me to keep for themselves.

I blink against the flashes. Over the last several years of unfathomable fame, I've learned that the crowd has its own all-consuming energy.

A girl hurtles past the rope and grabs my coat.

"My God. It's really you." Tears stream down her face. Her words are a prayer, a benediction to the gods of celebrity.

My main bodyguard, Duncan, is there in half a second, prying the fan away. He's always patient and ever watchful, a soldier in a suit with a buffed-up body and close-shaved head.

"He's so hot. My ovaries are gonna explode!" a girl cries.

Duncan barks out a laugh. "Not the ovaries again. What is it with the ovaries?"

My lips quirk as humor wars with nerves.

"You ready?" Duncan asks, his face rearranging into its usual sternness, any expression of levity tucked away.

Four more oversize men surround me.

I nod. Over time, Duncan and I learned to communicate through looks and gestures, forming a secret language between us. He's been my constant shadow since this insanity began. A wall of stoic muscle and steady confidence who comes between me and the world.

Up ahead, I see my costars already working the crowd for the premiere of the third movie in *The Wanderers'* franchise. The small indie movie that launched my career was never meant to be a blockbuster. It was a time-traveler adventure that somehow struck celluloid gold, and I became an A-list movie star overnight.

I force myself forward, ignoring the sweat that crawls down my neck. I remind myself that most guys would kill to have thousands of girls screaming their names.

Making my way toward the red carpet, I stop to sign autographs and pose for selfies. I hate this part, but fans have been waiting for hours, some even days, camping out just to meet me. So I sign, and I smile.

Once my duty is done, I stride toward the protected space that separates me from them.

The star versus the crowd.

After all this time, I still can't reconcile that this is my life. None of it makes sense because, in reality, I'm the opposite of special. Before, I was nothing but a statistic. A foster kid and runaway with shit luck—until that luck finally turned.

My phone buzzes, and I pull it out of my pocket.

It's a text from her.

The crowd chants, "Chase, Chase, Chase."

But the girl on my phone is the only one I'll answer.

The only girl I want.
The only girl who really knows me.
And she doesn't even know my name.

CHAPTER 2

livia

Dear Typewriter Girl,

I'm the new owner of your typewriter. After I read your letter, I wrote all night, thanks to the magic of the Remington—soft K and all. It unlocked words in me I didn't even know were there. I liked your story, but I hope your spelling has improved in the last twelve years since you wrote it, and that you now use far fewer exclamation points. Since you sent me your first story typed on this machine, I'm sending you mine. Maybe you can write back and tell me more about yourself. But not too much. Sometimes a little mystery is good.

Sincerely yours,
Remington
PO Box 143
Malibu, California

It all started with a typewriter.

My grandmother's typewriter, to be exact, when I sold it at my neighborhood antique store.

I typed that first letter on a whim and left it in the typewriter for the new owner to find. Then, the unexpected happened.

The new owner wrote back, which somehow sparked a five-year friendship I could never have imagined. For the first year, my mysterious pen pal sent me letters to Mr. Jensen's antique store. I hoarded every one, rereading them over and over. And I wrote him, as well. Our words filled my lonely days.

Back then, I only had to walk into this antique store and hear the jingle of the bell to make my heart full of anticipation and hope, as if it were tethered to a helium balloon, wondering if there would be another letter from him waiting. The rising thrill when there was. The deflating disappointment when there wasn't.

But today, five years later, there's no buoyant rush when I walk into the shop. There are no letters anymore, at least not the typewritten kind. We'd switched to texts long ago.

So much has changed since that first letter. Yet the shop remains the same. The familiar cluttered surfaces of antiques and artifacts passed down through time. The fine layer of dust in the air that never quite dissipates, giving the afternoon light filtering through smudged windows an otherworldly character. As a child visiting the store with my grandmother, I'd twirl in that light-filled mist on our frequent visits, making up stories about the past lives of the furniture and jewelry, tchotchkes and treasures.

Now, Mr. Jensen sits at his long mahogany desk in the front of the shop as he always does, a welcoming smile on his weathered face.

"Olivia! I've missed you, my girl."

"I was just here three weeks ago," I remind him with a grin. I set a cardboard box on his desk with a loud thump and brush the bangs back from my eyes.

"Exactly. It's been almost a month. You used to visit every day. But that was so you could collect correspondence from your beau, not chat with an old man."

I shake my head, smiling at his grumping and choice of words. *Beau. Correspondence.* I've had this conversation with Mr. Jensen countless times. At almost eighty, his mind is like a record player stuck in a groove. But I play my part in our dialogue, as frayed and familiar as the items in his shop.

"He's not my beau." *I wish.* "He's just a pen pal." *And I don't even know his name.*

"You two still writing?"

I blush. "We text now."

He shakes his head in disapproval. "Texts. Bah. They don't last. Now, letters are forever." He turns his attention to the large box. His frown deepens the lines of his brow.

"More from home?"

I nod and swallow the lump in my throat. "Some of Nanna's jewelry. A few first edition books. And this." I hold up a framed black-and-white print.

"Your grandmother's Adam Reynolds!" He reaches for the photograph, his hands shaking with age and eagerness. I will myself to let go of the photo that has been in the landscape of my life for so long. A picture of a naked woman lying amid sweeping sand dunes. Light and shadows stark, flowing curves sensual. The woman is my grandmother, taken when she was in her twenties. She had an affinity for photography, bohemian artists, and getting naked back in the day. It was her kind of luck that she modeled—and possibly more—for Adam Reynolds, one of the most celebrated American photographers. He gave her a few prints over the years, but this was the first and most famous of the photographs from their collaboration.

"How much do you think it's worth?" I swallow.

"This is way out of my league, my dear. But I do have a friend who might be able to appraise it and find a buyer if that's what you truly want. He owns one of the best galleries in San Francisco."

"Thank you. That would be great." I smile, pretending not to care that I'm talking about selling my legacy. Bartering the last tangible threads that connect me to my family piece by piece.

While I busy myself by carefully stacking the jewelry and the books on the counter, Mr. Jensen evaluates each item for consignment and makes notes in a leather-bound ledger.

She would have wanted this, I remind myself. My grandmother would have wanted me to keep our home in our beloved neighborhood, even if it means selling a few things. She left the house for me, and it's my job to make sure I keep it up and don't lose it. The photograph could pay to fix the leaking roof. Or the iffy plumbing. Or make a dent in the taxes. If I'm really lucky, maybe all three.

Just a few weeks ago, I graduated with my master's degree in creative writing, a process that took years longer than planned as I cared for Nanna through her long battle with cancer. All our savings had gone to medical bills.

Guilt stabs me. I probably should do the practical thing and take a job that pays better than working at a local bookstore. A former classmate offered me a position as a technical writer. If I took it, I could afford the upkeep on the house without selling my grandmother's things.

But I think my soul would die writing software instructions all day, and I fear it would be the end of my dream of becoming a novelist. My job at the bookshop doesn't pay much, but I love it. It gives me the time and mental space to write, and I'm surrounded by inspiration all day.

I don't have to decide my future now, I remind myself. By selling the photo, I can buy more time to write and live the life I want.

This shop had been lucky for me in the past.

Five years ago, I sold a vintage typewriter.

In return, I got a pen pal, a best friend, and a hopeless crush.

It was as if this dusty store somehow knew I needed a little magic, so it brought me Remington.

Now, here I am again, needing another miracle.

Mr. Jensen's eyes twinkle as he pulls an envelope from a drawer. "Did you think I forgot your birthday?"

"Thank you, Mr. Jensen," I say, both embarrassed and touched. "But you shouldn't have gone to the trouble."

"It's not from me," he says as he passes me a letter.

If it's not from Mr. Jensen, it must be from Remington, which is a surprise since we haven't exchanged an actual letter in years, but maybe he remembered my birthday and sent me a card. I look down at the envelope, and my breath catches.

"But—how? It's from…" I trail off in confusion.

"Your grandmother gave this letter to me for safekeeping shortly before she passed. She wanted you to read it on your twenty-fifth birthday. I'd planned on visiting you later today, but you saved me the trip."

I take the envelope with one hand, careful not to wrinkle it. With my free hand, I trail a reverent finger over Nanna's elegant script, tracing the familiar loops and curls. A wave of longing to hear her voice cuts through me.

Grief is a funny thing. It's not linear. I'll be fine, just making my way through my day, and then a small detail that reminds me of her will grip my heart. Tasting her favorite tea. Hearing a beloved song on the radio. Seeing her familiar scrawl on an envelope.

"I can't believe it," I say, holding the letter tight to my heart. Part of me wants to tear it open now, to share this moment with

Mr. Jensen. But another part wants to be alone when I do. I'm sure there will be tears. A fountain of them.

Mr. Jensen seems to sense my dilemma. "Open it at home, in the place your grandmother most loved," he says. "Happy birthday, sweet Olivia."

I say goodbye, push my way out the door in a daze, and walk the block back to my house in that lingering moment before dusk turns to twilight. Streetlamps flick on, while the last bit of light hangs stubbornly in the air.

When I get to the corner, I wait for the light to turn green and try to view my house across the street from a stranger's perspective. What would they see? In the soft glow, the faded pink Victorian I grew up in looks like a genteel lady of a certain age, one who was once the toast of the town, but now has few prospects. Its pale-rose paint and white trim are dim and peeling, the steps sag to the left, and the large bay window in front is in need of a wash. It feels out of place now among the impeccably restored Victorians around it, a vibrant mix of family homes and locally-owned shops.

When I was young, Nanna made our house bright with laughter, a gathering place for her artist friends. They'd knock on our door at all hours, stumbling in, drunk on wine and life. She'd get to work, cooking a midnight feast. At some point, hearing the tinkle of glasses, the strain of music, I'd creep downstairs, hair in a braid, feet bare, pajamas on, and curl up in my favorite window seat in the living room, letting the voices and guitar strumming wash over me.

Now, it's just me in the old, cluttered house echoing with too many memories. The elegant bar cart is always filled and ready, though no one comes for a party anymore. The pie cupboard with green glass and delicate china, the baskets and books, the collection of cameras and typewriters that line the built-in shelves. It's all still there, minus the things I've had to sell.

I shake my head clear of the memories and cross the street.

My phone rings, and I dig into my bag as I reach my front steps. I look at the number. Despite my contemplative mood, I smile when I see it's Daisy, my exuberant neighbor who adopted me as her friend years ago.

"Hey, Daisy," I say into the phone.

"It's your birthday, bitch. You better be out at the clubs already, having drinks and flirting with boys."

"Um, it's like you don't even know me," I say.

She snickers. "It's your twenty-fifth birthday. You should be partying. Please don't tell me you're not going out?"

I don't want to admit that I have no plans. That makes me sound way too lame. "How's wine country?" I ask, changing the subject. Daisy owns the vintage clothing shop next door to my house and spends most of her weekends traveling to estate sales like the one she's currently at.

"It's amazing, Olivia." Daisy lets out a dreamy sigh. "Mrs. Vanderpool has the closet of my dreams. Rare Pucci prints. Yves Saint Laurent dresses from the seventies. Everything is in perfect condition. I have online buyers just waiting. You know how my shop has been struggling? I think this might turn it around. But I'm so sorry to be missing your birthday."

"It's fine, Daisy. I'm a big girl."

"What are you doing tonight? And don't say staying home."

"I'm going to stay home," I admit.

She groans. "Olivia! Guys would fall all over you if you gave them a chance. I'd kill for your rocking curves and long black hair. You've got that Snow White thing going on, if Snow White only wore baggy jeans and oversize sweaters. So squeeze into something sexy and hit the town."

"I don't feel like it."

"You never feel like it. Are you going to spend the night texting your mystery *lover* instead?"

"There's no lover."

"Fine, call him what you want. Your mystery text boy, then.

At the very least, you two should've moved on to sexting by now."

"It's not like that. He's just a friend."

"Tell him he needs to give you a birthday orgasm."

"Daisy, stop." I laugh.

"You deserve all the special things," she says slyly.

"I did get something special. I saw Mr. Jensen today, and he had a letter for me. From Nanna."

"Wait, what?" Daisy had known and loved Nanna. Sometimes I think the reason she worked so hard at being my friend after moving next door was because she loved hanging out with my grandmother. They could talk about photography for hours.

"Before she died, Nanna gave Mr. Jensen a letter. She wanted me to open it on my twenty-fifth birthday."

I swallow past the lump in my throat and touch my jacket pocket containing the letter, as if to assure myself that it's real.

"Oh my God, Olivia. That's amazing! But I wonder why Nanna gave it to Mr. Jensen. She could have given it to me to keep."

"Do you think you could have kept that secret?"

She bursts out a laugh. "Good point. Probably not." She pauses. "What does it say?" she asks, tentative now.

I finger the edges of the envelope as I take the steps up to my house in slow motion. "I haven't opened it yet. I want to be home and alone when I read it. So, I guess that's what I'm doing for my birthday." My stomach dips at the thought.

As excited as I am to read what she wrote, I know it will bring a new wave of grief, a feeling I've been fighting this week as I got closer to my birthday. Nanna died eleven months ago, and this will be my first birthday without her, my first birthday with no family left in the world. I never felt like an orphan while I had my grandmother. But now, I'm truly alone.

Except for Daisy. And my boss, Audrey.

And Remington, I remind myself. I have Remington.

"Oh, honey. Do you want me to come back early from Napa?"

"And give up Pucci?"

"To hell with Mrs. Vanderpool and her fancy closet. You're more important."

"Thank you, but I don't mind being alone. I'm the not-so-friendly neighborhood introvert, remember?" Daisy gave me that nickname because of my reluctance to go out with her. Daisy was the party-loving extrovert to my book-loving introvert.

"Hmph. So you say. Well, let me know if you change your mind. Love you, babe."

"Love you," I say automatically, feeling grateful for her friendship. "And thank you."

"I left a bottle of champagne and a double chocolate fudge brownie cupcake in your fridge before I left because I knew you would never buy something special for yourself. You can toast your nanna while you read the letter."

"How did you get into my house?"

"The key you hide in your flowerpot. You really do need a better hiding spot."

I laugh and say goodbye, digging into my bag for my key. Once inside, I flick on every light to make the dark old house feel more cheerful, though the emptiness still echoes across my soul.

CHAPTER 3

hase

SHE STANDS BEFORE ME, her body trembling, breath coming in gasps.

My female fans do that, responding to me as if they're in the throes of sex, even when all I've done is glance their way.

"She's hot and begging for it." Sebastian Blake, my costar from *The Wanderers*, nods toward the hyperventilating girl.

Her large blue eyes widen at having two of Hollywood's hottest stars focusing on her. I turn away, fearing she might pass out if I keep watching.

"Not interested," I say and down the shot in front of me.

The shots have been arriving all night, though I haven't ordered any of them. It's dangerous. I've lost count of the number I've tossed back.

Sebastian is right; the girl is pretty. Twentysomething with a good body and a cute face from my quick glance at her. I could ask her to take off all her clothes right here, in this crowded club, and she would. Not that I'd ever do that, but the power of my celebrity unnerves me. I don't need to make a move to have a willing woman in my bed. But the more willing they are, the less I want them.

There's only one girl I want to hear from tonight.

What's she doing now? I wonder. Is she with some guy? Just the thought makes acid churn in my stomach. The years of writing to each other, first in typewritten letters and then in texts, and she's never mentioned a hookup or a date.

"James, every chick in this place is panting for you, but you're like a fucking monk. What the hell is the point of all this" —Sebastian gestures around the bar to the women staring at us —"if you don't enjoy the spoils?"

"Like you do? Not all of us want to whore it up every night," I say, bored with this conversation. It's one we've had more than once.

"Being a manwhore is underrated," he slurs, downing another shot of Patrón. "It's the Hollywood way of life."

If there's one thing Sebastian knows, it's Hollywood. Sebastian's parents are movie-star royalty, a legacy they passed down to him. Sebastian had his first TV role as a three-year-old, his first movie role at six, and a Disney contract by eight. With his blessed genetics, he'd gone from cute kid to teen heartthrob with zero awkward phases and a perfect reputation.

That all ended when he turned eighteen. In the time-honored child-star tradition, he made up for lost time with a free flow of women, gambling, drugs, and liquor that ended in wrapping his car around a tree. A long stay in rehab, swearing off drugs, and a starring role in *The Wanderers* gave him a second chance to rebuild his career. But lately, the edges around his carefully constructed comeback have been fraying.

I shift uncomfortably and pull my hat down lower. Sebastian loves attention, while all I want is to blend into the crowd. My black cap isn't much of a disguise, but it serves its purpose. It hides my hair and shades my eyes, both of which are the subject of an endless array of articles, memes, and fan-made videos.

A group of girls giggle and point their phones toward us. They're trying to be subtle, but spotting an iPhone at a thousand paces is a skill I've honed over the years. Photos will appear on social media in minutes, and a crowd of fans will arrive soon after. A story will trend in the morning. We frequent this bar because of its exclusivity and no-picture policy, but this shit still happens.

Sebastian remains oblivious to the cameras. "We just finished filming after six gnarly months of freezing our asses off in Canada. You need to relax and enjoy the ride, bro. It doesn't get better than this. If you don't want to bang the fangirl, what about Layla?" Sebastian turns his attention away from the starstruck blonde and nods toward a tall brunette across the bar. She makes eye contact, a standout among her almost-as-beautiful friends.

"You can trust her." Sebastian nods as I eye the famous model. "Her parents don't want her in the tabloids. She won't risk losing Daddy's trust fund."

Sebastian's right. Since Layla's the daughter of a famous billionaire known for his privacy, she knows how to be discreet. I've never heard of any drama or scandal attached to her name, which is rare. I tilt my head, and her lips curve into an inviting smile.

I should feel something, but I'm numb, barely interested. I already know it will be like all the others, just another casual fuck with someone who likes me because I'm famous, a bragging point to friends. Regardless of who her daddy is, after we hook up, I'll spend the next week worrying if it'll come out in the tabloids. I don't need any more stories about my technique or the size of my dick, no matter how flattering they are.

I throw back another shot and look at my phone again, at

the last message I'd left my... What is she? Long-distance friend sounds weak. She's so much more.

It may seem fucked up that my best friend—the first person I think of when I wake and the last I text before bed—doesn't know my real name. But that's precisely why our relationship works. I never have to worry if she's friends with me just because I'm a celebrity. She doesn't go starstruck and get me confused with my character from *The Wanderers*.

And if I just keep my distance, she won't get ravaged by trolls, ambushed by paparazzi, splashed over the tabloids. And I won't have to face the terror of wondering when she'll get her first death threat. All that happens to any woman who enters my orbit.

My Typewriter Girl exists outside all of that.

We work precisely because of the rules we drew up, like lines in the sand for boundaries.

No real names.

No real-life meetups.

No dick pics. (That was her rule.)

But those lines can erode with time.

Too often lately, I find myself just as I am tonight, wondering where she is, who she's with, and fighting the overwhelming urge to tell her the truth, to hell with the consequences.

But I can't do that to anyone who hasn't signed on for my kind of crazy. If I really care about her—and I do—I need to stay the hell away.

As much as I hate to admit it, Sebastian is right.

I need perspective. I need to get laid.

Using the intense stare I've perfected in *The Wanderers*, I make eye contact with the model. It's a mask I put on for photographers and fans—and women in clubs, apparently.

Layla responds with her own sexy, come-hither stare. I'd be

willing to bet also perfected for the cameras. We could film a perfume advertisement on our way to the bedroom.

She does a hair toss and laughs with her friends, looking back at me with a flirtatious glance. She's putting on a show, but it's a good one.

"Why the hell not?" I say, as much to Sebastian as to myself.

I'm overanalyzing. It's been too long since I accepted one of the invitations that's thrown at me like so much confetti.

One last shot for good measure, and my world is hazy around the edges. Her smile glitters in the dark, smoky room in a silent invitation.

"Finally!" Sebastian laughs, patting me hard on the back and shoving me in her direction.

She propositions me within five minutes, and then it's all about logistics. Not romantic, but necessary.

Avoiding the paps involves evasions worthy of secret agents, but we make it to my place undetected.

She follows me to my bedroom and strips before me, her body tanned, sleek, and clad in black lace. There's nothing soft about her.

"My friends bet me I couldn't sleep with you."

I raise an eyebrow. "Why?"

"You turned down Avery Woods," she says with a shrug. "No one turns her down. We thought you were gay. Or secretly dating someone else."

Avery Woods is the most famous singer in the world. She has a string of hits longer than the list of men she's supposedly dated. We met at an awards show years ago, but I've never even had a conversation with her, despite the rumors.

I don't want to talk about some singer, though. And I sure as hell don't want to be told that Layla only wants to sleep with me to win a bet, or as an ego boost for besting a bigger celebrity. I pull her flush against me with a little more force than usual.

Something behind her eyes flares to life. So, that's how she likes it. Noted.

"Are you sure you want this?" I ask her. "I don't do anything besides casual."

She laughs. "Don't flatter yourself. I'm not looking for some guy to put a ring on it. I'm at the top of my career right now and having way too much fun. Casual is how I like it." She rubs her hand up and down my dick through my pants.

I kiss her hard and deep. One of my hands roams her firm, angular body as the other wraps in her hair, pulling her head back. She moans. Yeah, she likes it a little rough—and a lot dirty, I'll bet. If anyone could get my disinterest to dissolve and carnal pleasure to take over, it should be her.

I kiss her again, trying to lose myself in it, in her. But I can't. Being with her feels wrong, like I'm cheating. Which is ridiculous. But the woman in my arms is not the one I want.

Finally, I pull back. "Fuck, I'm sorry. This isn't right," I say. She looks at me like I'm crazy, which I must be. I try my best to let her down easy with an excuse she probably doesn't buy.

A few minutes later, she's gone, muttering, "Gay, I knew it."

All I want is to shower off her lingering perfume. Loneliness claws at my gut as I step into the shower, wishing the strong jets of water could wash away my unease as well. I drank too much, or perhaps I didn't drink enough. I'm too heavy, too itchy, too hollow, too horny—all at the same time.

The robe I throw on after drying off is an elegant designer dressing gown, a gift from my foster sister. I laughed when she first sent it to me. It doesn't fit my jeans-and-a-T-shirt style, but I wear it more often than I'll ever admit to her.

The living room's minimalist decor seems more bare than usual in the moonlight. I prowl the darkened room, not able to settle. I nurse a whiskey and watch the way faint moonlight plays across the shimmering depths of the Pacific Ocean.

I could have had sex with a woman lusted after by millions.

But I can't shake the thought that I have more fun texting with Typewriter Girl. I hoped someone else could cut her from my mind, like surgery. But it feels impossible.

The more we write, the more I want to know her in every way possible. And, worse, the more I want her to know me.

I wish I could tell her about my secret dream of being more than just a pretty face on a billboard, of going back to school to get my GED and then college to study screenwriting and filmmaking so I can tell my own stories, not someone else's.

But I can't, just as I can't share with her my bone-deep fear that this unrelenting fame will never fade, the cold, hard certainty that the door to any normal life is closed forever.

The fame I've somehow fallen into is beyond anything I ever imagined. The crowds I attract are Elvis-worthy. I am Justin and Brad at their peaks. And I have no idea why, because I'm the same person I was in my teens. Back then, I was just another street punk, invisible to most people. Now, I can't walk down the street without drawing a crowd.

During our all-night conversations, I imagine telling Typewriter Girl who I am. How would she react? Would she hate me for lying to her? Perhaps most aren't outright lies; I'm careful about that. But I lie by omission and redirection constantly.

And then there's this small part of me that thinks she'll change if she knew. Friends morph to leeches all the time, seeing me as their ticket to Hollywood.

Even good people change around me. They might try, but they can't see past the celebrity, as if I'm more an icon than human.

I worry she'll stop seeing the real me. And then I'll lose the real her.

But that fear is nothing compared to the rest of it—that, if I'm found out, photographed with her, if the paps get ahold of our friendship, then her life will be thrown into the chaos of mine. I once almost destroyed the life of someone I cared about.

I won't ruin hers. After what happened a few years ago, I'll never again risk getting close to an ordinary girl who hasn't already chosen the life of fame.

Grabbing my phone off the nightstand, I click open my text messages. Few people have my personal number, and she's the only person I text regularly. I've always considered texting a waste of time. But with her, it's different. There's row after row of our messages, laying out years of our relationship that's based only on words. A river of them.

I should close my eyes and hope for sleep to come. Instead, I stare at my phone, debating. Like always, I tell myself to be smart. Every conversation only pulls me in deeper. The right thing would be to put distance between us, to not text as often, to pretend we have a simple friendship we can just let go.

But then loneliness extends its claws, and I know tonight isn't going to be the night when I finally do the right thing. Tonight, I won't build the dam and stop the flow of words.

I have to message her, I rationalize, because it's her birthday. I sent a text in the morning, but there's been nothing since then. This is her first birthday since her grandmother died. She must be sad. Maybe she needs me. I latch on to that excuse and start typing, feeling a sense of relief as my fingers hit the keys.

CHAPTER 4

livia

I SIT in bed with a glass of champagne, make a toast to myself and my twenty-fifth year 'round the sun, and open Nanna's letter. I read slowly, savoring every word. Tears build in my eyes because it feels like she's here with me. I can hear her voice. Smell her Chanel perfume.

> *My dearest Olivia,*
> *I wish I were with you to celebrate your twenty-fifth birthday. I want to see it all. You growing from a girl to a strong, sure woman. Your first novel published. Your first love. Marriage. Family. All those firsts that I will never be able to hold your hand through. I don't have a letter for every occasion. Just this one.*
> *You'll be graduating soon, after taking care of me for all those years while studying and holding down a job. Even as a small girl, you always had an old soul—too serious and cautious for your age. But this is your time to be young, free, and have fun.*

Once upon a summer, I ran away from a fiancé and a life that had become too small for me. I vowed to take a risk a day, and it changed everything. I shocked everyone modeling—nude! I discovered my passion for photography, for men, for everything life had to offer. During one glorious summer, I did all the things I shouldn't, and I loved every minute of it. It was my summer to be wild, my summer of risks.

I want that for you, my dear. Make this your summer of risks. Risk, so you don't regret. Take a risk a day, like I did so many years ago. Step out of your comfort zone and see where your wild will lead you.

PS: I am your dead grandmother, so you have to do as I say. Love always, Nanna

I'M A MESS. Maybe drinking a bottle of champagne by myself while reading a letter written by my "dead grandmother"—her words, not mine—was not such a great idea. After a long crying spree, I sniff and wipe my nose on the sleeve of my cardigan. Then, deciding that's too gross even for me, I pull it off and toss it on the chair closest to my bed.

A risk a day. It's just like Nanna to direct me from beyond the grave. She always pushed me to be bolder, to take more chances.

But I know firsthand what being bold does. My mother sped through life recklessly—and died that way as well. Luckily, I had Nanna. And I had the lessons of my mother's life to use as a cautionary tale. Any feelings of restlessness, I firmly squash. I always thought the safe, sure path was the right one, but I wonder if I haven't gotten it a little wrong.

I look around at my bedroom. It retains the vestiges of my childhood. The twinkle lights I put on my headboard in ninth grade at Christmastime are still there. My bookshelf is a timeline of my life, from *Black Beauty* through to my favorite mystery writers.

My phone buzzes on the nightstand. It's late, past 11:00 p.m., so I know it's Remington. He says he travels for work, so he's often in a different time zone. And even when he isn't traveling, he's a night owl like me. Our conversations regularly occur in the midnight hours when the rest of my world is asleep.

Grabbing my glasses, I stare at the screen, concentrating so as not to make any embarrassing champagne-fueled typos.

REMINGTON:
You awake?

TYPEWRITERGIRL:
I'm here.

REMINGTON:
HAPPY BIRTHDAY.

TYPEWRITERGIRL:
Sheesh. Don't yell.

I try to downplay how pleased I am that he messaged again for my birthday. We don't usually exchange personal information, but I'd accidentally let my birthdate slip a few years ago, and he's remembered every year.

REMINGTON:
So what'd you do tonight?

I roll over on my stomach, get comfortable, and flex my fingers. These night texting sessions often run long.

TYPEWRITERGIRL:
Oh, you know… Two guys at once. They just left.

Brave words from the single girl with no birthday plans or

dating prospects. Dots appear and disappear, indicating typing and deleting. Finally, after long minutes, his answer appears, short and to the point.

REMINGTON:
Bullshit.

TYPEWRITERGIRL:
It could be true. There's a lot I haven't told you.

REMINGTON:
...

TYPEWRITERGIRL:
And there's a lot you haven't told me.

REMINGTON:
But only the unimportant stuff.

TYPEWRITERGIRL:
Like your full name. Where exactly you live. Who you work for. Whether you have a dog. And, if so, what its name is.

REMINGTON:
No dog, no name.

TYPEWRITERGIRL:
No name for you or the dog?

REMINGTON:
If I don't have a dog, how can it have a name?

TYPEWRITERGIRL:
Is this a philosophical question? Like what came first, the chicken or the egg? You could have a name picked out for your hypothetical future dog.

As I feared, my typing is slower than usual from being tipsy. My fingers feel too clumsy with my phone, and I keep having to correct mistakes.

TYPEWRITERGIRL:

Wow. That took me a long time to type. My fingers are like sausages tonight.

REMINGTON:

Have you been drinking?

TYPEWRITERGIRL:

Maybe. I had a few glasses of champagne. Or maybe most of a bottle.

REMINGTON:

And did you share that bottle with someone?

I'm embarrassed to admit I didn't. I don't want him to think I'm pathetic. Or an alcoholic. I debate lying, but he'll know. I'm terrible at it, and he has some kind of built-in lie detector when it comes to me.

TYPEWRITERGIRL:

Just me.

REMINGTON:

Good. I mean, no more drinking alone. I'm here now.

My heart warms. Even if he's only online, he's the best friend I have. He may not know my name, but he knows my heart.

Not for the first time, or even the hundredth, I wonder what he looks like. What color is his hair? How wide is his smile? He could be anyone. He could be an octogenarian, married with ten kids, or a former mobster in the witness protection program.

But even though I know those are all possibilities, I doubt them. It might be wishful thinking, but I believe we're similar ages and live a similarly lonely life.

TYPEWRITERGIRL:

I'm glad.

REMINGTON:

Just face it, you're stuck with me.

TYPEWRITERGIRL:

This from the guy who won't tell me his name.

REMINGTON:

I can't help it if I'm better at following our rules than you.

TYPEWRITERGIRL:

I suck at them. You know almost every detail of my life. You know my birthday, when I don't know yours. I even told you where I work. I'm just really bad at being mysterious.

REMINGTON:

Cheer up. You haven't broken all the rules. I don't know your name. And you've never sent me a dick pic.

TYPEWRITERGIRL:

That's because I don't have a dick.

REMINGTON:

Thank God.

TYPEWRITERGIRL:

Maybe I do know more than you think.

REMINGTON:

What do you think you know?

TYPEWRITERGIRL:

Well, it's all your LA stories. It's like getting my own personal episode of Entourage typed into my phone. You've got to be a personal assistant to someone rich or famous. It explains so much. The travel. The parties. So? Who is he? Or she?

REMINGTON:

Who are you talking about?

TYPEWRITERGIRL:

Don't play dumb. Who's your famous boss?

REMINGTON:

Not everyone who lives in LA and goes to parties works in the industry. I'm not telling you anything. I respect the rules even if you don't.

TYPEWRITERGIRL:

Spoilsport.

I want to keep grilling him. But I know from experience that he's a vault. The things I learn about him are by accident. Details he lets slip in the stories he tells. I decide to change the subject.

TYPEWRITERGIRL:

So what'd you do tonight?

REMINGTON:

I went to a friend's party.

TYPEWRITERGIRL:

See! Another party. Were there balloons? A piñata?

REMINGTON:

It was at a bar.

TYPEWRITERGIRL:

You're making my case for me, Mr. Entourage. I bet somewhere swanky with bottle service. Did you drink too much?

REMINGTON:

I had a little too much of everything.

TYPEWRITERGIRL:

Does that include girls?

My text is meant to be playful, but his slowness in responding has me holding my breath. Shit. I love hearing his stories about the crazy things he encounters in LA. But him telling me about hooking up with a girl? Not so much. It's been months, maybe even a year, since I recall him with someone. But maybe it's only because I rarely ask.

REMINGTON:

One girl. Not multiple.

At his admission, my lungs deflate. Feeling sick, I type.

TYPEWRITERGIRL:

And did you hook up?

Why am I doing this? I'm picking at a scab. Or, more accurately, exploring an open wound, one that's raw and deep.

REMINGTON:

Fuck. I don't want to talk about this shit. Not with you. Not tonight.

TYPEWRITERGIRL:

A simple yes or no, please...

REMINGTON:

Yes. Sort of. Happy?

Just a simple *yes*.
For him.
Yes, the sky is blue. *Yes*, I'd like a cup of coffee. *Yes*, I hooked up with a girl tonight.
But for me, the answer is no. No, I'm not happy to hear this.

TYPEWRITERGIRL:

Where is she now?

I have an incurable curiosity when it comes to Remington. Every little tidbit he drops, I hoard. They're breadcrumbs to his soul. I gather them all, even the sad, dirty, trod-on crumbs that make me sick when consumed.

REMINGTON:
She's gone.

TYPEWRITERGIRL:
So you hook up with a girl, sleep with her, and she doesn't even stay the night?

Oh, hello jealousy, my old friend. I shouldn't hate this anonymous girl who apparently doesn't mind being a one-night stand. She isn't less than me. In some ways, she's more. What would it be like to feel that free? To seek pleasure or comfort in someone else? I only seek comfort between the pages of a book while tucked safe and sound alone in my bed.

REMINGTON:
We didn't have sex.

TYPEWRITERGIRL:
Oh. Why?

My heart is in my throat.

REMINGTON:
It didn't feel right with her. The whole time I wished I were with someone else.

Is it possible he could be talking about me? His words make my heart race. I want his touch to do the same. I want to know if his hair is soft, his body hard. What would it be like if we were more than just words behind two screens?

My gaze falls on Nanna's letter and her words. *Risk, so you don't regret.* I can't even tell a guy I like him or show him what I look like. And all at once, I get what Nanna is saying. Remington is out there every day, meeting other girls, hooking up with them. What if the next girl he meets becomes his girlfriend, and she doesn't like us being friends? I could lose him.

I'm still not sure what makes me do it. Maybe it's his words.

Maybe it's Nanna's letter. Maybe it's being tired of always playing it safe. Maybe it's that, at twenty-five, I've never had a boyfriend, unless you count book boyfriends.

Maybe it's just the bottle of champagne.

I pick up my phone, adjust a few camera settings, point it at me, and click.

I'm not glamorous. My hair is in a loose braid with tendrils escaping, my reading glasses are on, and I'm wearing a white "Write Drunk, Edit Sober" T-shirt, part of my ever-growing collection of writerly shirts. Though, given my champagne consumption tonight, it's probably an apt choice of clothing.

I evaluate the picture, delete, and try again. Apparently, selfies are an advanced art form that I've yet to master, but eventually, I take one that I can live with. My face and chest are partially covered by my hair, which is probably why I like it.

Then I start typing.

I type for a long time. When I'm done, my hand hovers over the picture and message.

I'm poised on a cliff, and with one click of a button, I step over that edge.

The free fall is scary. Will there be a parachute? A tandem jump? Or will I hit the ground alone, with all my broken pieces shattering in the dark?

Dots on my screen appear almost instantly.

I wait. And I wait.

And as I'm waiting, it strikes me. Perhaps I shouldn't have listened to my dead grandma after all.

CHAPTER 5

hase

TYPEWRITERGIRL:

I'm sorry, Remington. I need to break our rules. You see, I received an unexpected birthday gift. It was a letter from my grandmother, which she wrote before she died. She advised me to take risks, so this is my first. Tonight, when I blew out my candle, I wished for you. I want to know your name, see your face. But I'm tired of wishing. So, I'll go first. My name is Olivia Evans and this is my photo. Make my wish come true. Give me anything. Your name, your photo, the hope that we can be real.

ALL I CAN DO IS stare at her selfie. *Olivia.*

The image, taken at an angle, shows a portion of a girl. Pretty in a delicate, natural way. Her skin is like milk—pure cream, with a dusting of freckles across the bridge of her nose, a contrast to the smooth fall of jet-black hair. Her arching black brows disappear into bangs cut straight across. Black-rimmed glasses frame eyes that appear gray, though it's hard to tell exactly. Looking at her lips makes me want to trace their shape.

And that's just her face. She's wearing a white T-shirt with a saying that makes me smile and no bra. I can see the outline of generous curves. I admit it, I look closer. Nipples. She might be cold. Or turned on. She appears softer than the girls in LA, in a way that makes me ache to touch all that creamy skin, that makes me want to follow those curves and lose myself in her.

I can't look away.

This is my Typewriter Girl. My pen pal. My best friend. This girl with pale skin, midnight hair, and haunting eyes.

Her photo is a punch to the gut, but her message is an even more direct hit.

She wants me to give her my name.

If I do, I'll risk this house of cards we've built.

It only takes one push, one detail too many. And this safe space we've constructed between us will crumble.

I can't even send a selfie. She'll recognize me immediately.

She thinks she wants to be together but dating me could destroy her. I know she's strong. She's known death and loss, and like me, she has no family. But despite her survivor's strength, she's sensitive. She tries to hide her vulnerability, yet it's evident in every message and conversation. The tabloids would rip her to shreds for clickbait.

Our relationship, *she*, is too special, too precious, to risk. In my experience, caring for someone only leads to loss or pain. I can't lose her too. What we have now, friendship from afar, is safer.

I want to explain. Apologize. I try to type a few responses. But I delete each one before sending.

Finally, I type out a quick response, dread weighing down my heart.

REMINGTON:

> I'm so damn sorry. I wish I could give you more than just friendship on a screen. But I can't. This is all we can ever be.

I hit send.

There's nothing else to say.

I drop my phone like it's a snake ready to attack. I'll pretend this never happened and hope she can too. I'm good at forgetting things, such as the feeling of hunger scraping my belly when I was eight, or the dread of walking into a new foster home.

I step onto my deck to put space between me and my phone, when what I really want is space between me and my thoughts. The wood is cool beneath my feet as I stare at the water below, watching it shift in and out, ever-changing.

I've already forgotten my first life. Or at least rewritten my part. I'm now Chase James, superstar. I have a whole fake bio that doesn't mention anything about dead mothers or runaways. This message is one more thing to pretend didn't happen in a lifetime of pretending. I guess that's why I'm so good at acting. I've had a lot of practice.

It's better this way. If I tell myself that often enough, I just might begin to believe it.

CHAPTER 6

livia

THE NEXT DAY, I pour my third cup of coffee and will the pounding in my head to stop. Thank God it's slow in the bookstore today. Audrey is taking advantage of the quiet to organize inventory, so I'm keeping an eye out for customers at the café and trying hard not to puke.

Champagne is evil. The happy bubbles are deceptive and make people do stupid, stupid things. I'd never been a big drinker. My mom had been overfond of alcohol, so I've always avoided drinking too much, and now I know why.

But it isn't just my headache, exhaustion, and upset stomach causing the regret.

It's what I did last night.

I close my eyes, my head hitting the counter. I look at my phone for the hundredth time that morning.

I sent a selfie to my pen-pal crush. And not just any selfie—a sexy selfie. I hadn't realized my nips had been in full view in that white shirt. I broke our main rules and smashed through the wall we'd erected. I asked him to tell me his name, send me a photo back. And he turned me down—hard—then went radio silent.

I'm humiliated. Does he think I'm hideous? Does he have a girlfriend? Is he secretly a creepy sixty-year-old man living in his mama's basement? Has he broken both hands so he can't type?

Fuck. My. Life.

Remington never indicated he wanted anything more than a virtual relationship with me. The guy ignored every subtle hint I made over the years to become more than online friends.

Tipsy Olivia decided subtle hints were overrated. There was nothing subtle about what I'd done last night.

I cringe for the hundredth time today.

I ruined everything.

The door jingles. I look up to find Daisy strolling toward me. She's sunshine personified in flared vintage jeans, a white top, and a crocheted green beret that should look ridiculous, but is adorable. Her curly blond hair rebels from two thick braids.

"Happy birthday, babe!" she cries. "Mama's back!"

Her smile fades into an expression of concern. "Whoa. You look rough."

"Thanks."

My forehead collides with the counter again.

"I don't mean to pry, but what's that fabulous pink Formica ever done to you?"

"I'm hoping if I hit my head long enough, I might lose my short-term memory of last night. Champagne is evil."

Daisy grins. "Damn. I missed it. I wanted to be the first to see Drunk Birthday Olivia!"

"Trust me, no one should ever see Drunk Olivia," I say. "Drunk Olivia is going to crawl back from where she came and never again emerge."

"And you call *me* dramatic." Daisy saunters behind the

counter and helps herself to a cup of the brewed coffee, adding a load of sugar and milk to it. Daisy doesn't work here, but she might as well since she spends more time at the bookshop than at her own store. I keep telling her she needs to hire someone because, while Daisy is great at sourcing designer vintage clothes, she's crap at the day-to-day running of a business.

"Drinking is the devil. It made me…"

"What? What'd you do?" She sets down her coffee and leans against the counter, all chipper eagerness. I should've known she would appreciate my bad decisions.

Telling her might not be the best idea I've ever had, but I need to unburden myself to someone. "You know how I was going to text my friend last night?"

"Of course. Your text-should-be-sext guy from your nerdy forums."

"I'm not on nerdy forums. I'm on mystery writer forums. We help each other with research. Like how to murder someone and leave no trace. Or how to get rid of a body."

"You're kind of proving my point here. And also, you're freaking me out."

"Okay, fine. Maybe I am on nerd forums. But I didn't meet him there. It's a long story." I've never told Daisy or Audrey about how I met Remington. I never even told Nanna. I'm not sure why, other than it felt too personal.

Our relationship is just between Remington and me. I also don't want their judgment. They'll tease me about being catfished. I know our relationship is weird. But it works for us. Or at least, it did, before I messed everything up.

I look down at my hands. "The problem is, we've been messaging each other for years, and I've sort of developed feelings for him."

"I knew it! You like him. So, what's the problem?"

I sigh. "From the beginning, we agreed not to get too personal. No names, photos, not even phone calls. But we got close. So last night, I took a chance, probably because of your champagne and Nanna's letter."

"Oh, my god! I forgot to ask. What did Nanna's letter say?"

"She said I needed to start taking more risks."

"Go, Nanna. I miss her." Daisy's smile is a little misty.

We exchange wistful looks. "Me too."

I know that Daisy, like me, didn't have much in the way of parents. Nanna took Daisy under her wing and cared for her as well. When she died, she left a hole in both of our lives.

Daisy shifts, as if shaking away the memories. "So, continue. Last night, you were drunk, lonely, and horny."

"I didn't say I was horny! Well, maybe I was a little. But anyway, I sent him a selfie and wrote that I wanted to be with him."

I pass her my phone, and she reads my message, then grins.

"Honestly, I kinda dig Drunk Olivia. You really put it out there. You're smoking hot in that photo you sent him. So? Are you two an item now?"

I watch as she scrolls down to read the message he sent me back, and she inhales sharply.

"Shit, I'm sorry, honey," she says softly as she passes the phone back to me with a frown of concern. "Maybe he'll change his mind after he thinks about it." She reaches to touch my hand. "He might have just been caught off guard."

I shake my head. "He made it pretty clear that he doesn't want anything more than an online friendship. He hasn't messaged again, and I'm too humiliated to text him back."

"I hate to tell you this, Olivia, but this might be for the best. You can do better. He's probably texting you from his mother's basement."

"I knew you'd think that. But he doesn't come across as a creep."

"Eh." Daisy shrugs. "I'm not sure if you can tell. There are a lot of online catfishes. You probably dodged a bullet. Besides, he's an ass if he isn't running here to meet you. And as for drunken mistakes, welcome to the real world. We all do stupid shit when we drink. I've done way worse. It's why I never drink cheap vodka anymore." She shivers. "Only the top shelf for me."

"It's not all his fault. I changed the rules on him."

"Oh shit. What if he's married?" Daisy gasps, as if the idea just occurred to her.

My stomach churns. "He's not. I've thought about it. But I don't believe he is."

I shove the coffee cup away, sick from more than just the alcohol. "Did I ruin everything, Daisy? I don't want to lose him. He's my best friend."

"Excuse me. Aren't I your BFF?"

I can't help but smile. "You're my best *girl* friend." I sigh. "In her letter, Nanna encouraged me to take more risks. Problem is, this photo and message were my first risks, and it didn't end so well."

Daisy leans forward. "That doesn't mean you should stop. This is the best thing you've done in ages, no matter how it ends. Think about it. You never took the time to get to know anyone real because you've been hung up on a fantasy. Now, you can find someone who can actually seal the deal."

I raise an eyebrow. "Seal the deal?"

"Oh, do you prefer, bang you till you scream? Take your V-card?"

I laugh, but it's rueful. "I have to admit you're right, even if I don't want to hear it. I'm scared of waking up in five years, alone and still afraid to go after what I want." My face heats. "Still a virgin."

"Heaven forbid," Daisy says, making the sign of the cross. "Well then, what *do* you want?" She rests her head in her hand and watches me.

I stare at my now half-empty coffee as if it holds the answers to her question. "I want someone to love and to care about," I say slowly. "I want someone I can watch movies with and cuddle, not just text reactions to each other. I want someone to hug when I wake up and make breakfast with, and someone who will hold my hand when we walk down the street."

"You want a boyfriend, babe."

I bite my lip and nod.

"And you aren't going to find that with a guy who won't even tell you his real name." Daisy points accusingly at my phone.

I wince because I know she's right.

"Drunk Olivia knew what she was doing. You may not be happy with the results, but at least you did something. Going after your dreams isn't easy, and it can be messy."

At seeing my expression, Daisy leans over and gives me a hug. "I'm sorry, hon. Is that too harsh? What do I know? Maybe he's not texting because he's going to fly to your side and surprise you."

I side-eye her because, *hello*, reality.

She shrugs. "Or not. Regardless, Aunty Daisy will make it all better. What you need is a guy who's real. You're just hung up on this online dude because you're afraid to take a chance on a real man, someone who could really hurt you." She grins. "Someone who could fuck you."

It isn't the first time Daisy has told me this. And she's probably right. Since Nanna first got sick all those years ago, when I wasn't working at the bookshop or in class, I was home, caring for my grandmother and writing.

It was easier to have a guy friend who was on the other side of a screen. I never had to put on cute clothes, do my hair, feel self-conscious, or even leave the house to hang out with him. I was bullied and harassed when I developed early as a tween, so I've never felt completely comfortable around boys. With Remington, I never had to be vulnerable or go outside my comfort zone.

But I also never got a full-fledged relationship either. Or swoon-worthy kisses. Damn, I wanted those. So much.

In some ways, I'm old beyond my years. But in others, I have no experience. I feel like an awkward kid with a crush.

I'm still thinking about what Daisy said when I finish my shift in the afternoon. I wave goodbye to Audrey and step outside, breathing in the crisp June San Francisco air. Despite the bright blue sky and sun, I wrap a scarf around my neck against the wind.

I take out my phone to check my messages for the hundredth time today. Nothing from Remington. *Fuck it*. Drunk Olivia may have been a fool. But Sober Olivia will guard her heart better. And find a man I can kiss who wants to kiss me back.

With that vow, I step off the curb to cross the road. I turn and freeze as a bike messenger speeds around the corner, straight at me. Our shocked gazes meet for a split second before I register a screech of tires. My phone flies out of my hand as I brace for a crushing impact. The world switches to slow motion. Images of my life flash one after another. A high-pitched scream engulfs the air as I hit the pavement. Searing pain splits my skull. Something warm and wet seeps through my hair at the back of my head.

This can't be the end. I haven't even lived. Or had sex.

Shit. I can't die a virgin. It's my last desperate thought. And then there's nothing.

CHAPTER 7

livia

My eyes open to a bright light. I immediately close them against the glare. *Did I die?* Was the light I saw *the* light? The one I'm supposed to walk toward at the end of my life?

Then my other senses kick in. The sounds of traffic, honking, someone yelling. The noises become clearer, like a camera coming into focus.

And that's when I know. I won't die a virgin. I'll live another day to hopefully, someday, somehow, get laid.

"Olivia! Olivia! You can do it. Open your eyes, honey."

Daisy?

I squint one eye open and a searing pain splits my skull, but I force myself to open the other eye. Everything floods through me in a rush of sensory overload. The sun overhead, two faces peering down at me, warm, rough…pavement? I groan.

"Thank God you're awake. Olivia! Stay with me. You gave us a scare."

I try to sit up, but my head only lifts a fraction before my body screams at me in pain, so I flop back down on the ground. *Ouch. Shit.*

"Don't move. You've been in an accident." Daisy's worried face stares down at me.

I sift through my memories. It all comes rushing back.

"Bike?" I croak out.

"That would be mine."

I turn my head with a wince.

A man in a bike helmet is kneeling next to me. He's about my age, with concerned golden eyes, smooth brown skin, and curly hair. I'm not so out of it that I don't notice he's cute.

"Next time you cross the street, you might want to look away from your phone long enough to make sure no one is coming," he says. His attractively wry smile softens the douche factor in his little speech.

"Next time you ride your bike, you might want to make sure you don't almost kill anyone," Daisy snaps. I turn back to Daisy with another wince. She's glaring at the bike guy, but she isn't fooling me. She's noticed he's hot because her dimples flash through her glare.

I close my eyes. I'm not well enough to be subjected to hate-flirting between my friend and the guy who almost ran me over a few minutes ago.

I sit up slowly. Daisy helps me rise into a sitting position. It takes a few minutes, but the world gradually stops spinning.

"He's right, Daisy. It's my fault. I wasn't paying attention. I shouldn't have stepped out onto the road. I was distracted by—"

My eyes widen in horror. "My phone!" It had gone flying. *Shit. Shit. Shit.*

I look around wildly, ignoring the dizziness.

"Stop, you're going to hurt yourself. It's fine. It's right there. It's barely scratched, I bet." Daisy points to my phone in the middle of the road.

We all watch as a car drives by, giving us a wide berth by edging toward the yellow line and my phone.

"Nooooooooo!" I cry.

Crunch.

The bike messenger gallantly runs into the road to grab my device; the screen is shattered and the case is dented. He hands it to me.

"Um. I'm sure it can be fixed," Daisy suggests with forced brightness. "It didn't *completely* get run over. Just a little. Maybe they can replace the screen. Anyway, the SIM card might be fine. That's what matters."

"Besides, I'm sure you do regular backups," the bike dude says.

Backups. Everything in me slumps. I've never been very good at technology. I'm an analog girl in a digital world. I like typewriters. Record players. Even my television is old-school. Every time I tried to back up my phone, it asked me for a password, which I couldn't recall. I always meant to figure it out. It was on my to-do list. The problem is, as much as I love making lists, I'm not so good at actually following them.

And then I remember Remington. All our texts are in my trashed phone. And nowhere else. I want to throw up, and it's not only because of nausea from the accident. I try to recall his phone number. I can't. I'm not a numbers girl, just like I'm not a technology girl. I like English, not math.

Do I have his number written down somewhere? I wonder in increasing worry. Maybe, if he sent me his phone number first. But I realize that he didn't. I sent my number to him in a letter. I remember, because I was so worried about taking that step, afraid he wouldn't want to go from letters to calls. In the end, he didn't call me. But he'd texted. And now, all those years of texts might be gone, wiped away with one accident as if they never existed.

"What matters is that we're both okay. A phone can be replaced, but people can't," the bike messenger says.

I turn my phone over. An edge crumbles in my hand.

"Great, hit-and-run dude is a philosopher," Daisy says.

"I didn't hit and run. I'm here. I hit and stayed. And this whole hitting situation isn't my fault. You may be cute but did anyone tell you that you're obnoxious?" he asks Daisy.

"All the time," she says. "So, you think I'm cute?"

A loud pounding sound drowns out their voices. I put my head in my hands, hoping it will go away. But the sound is coming from inside my brain.

"Olivia, are you okay? Olivia—"

And for the second time, it all starts to slip away—the hard ground, the voices, the music of the city, the feel of cool air on my body, the smell of asphalt. I vow, if I can get the world to come back, even for a minute, I'll do things differently. I'll go after my dreams. I'll find a boyfriend and actually have sex. I'll change my life one risk at a time, so when I finally do die, it won't be with regret. And I'll get better at numbers and technology, so I can back up my damn phone.

* * *

"I CAN'T BELIEVE a hot bike messenger ran you over and then you got Dr. Heartthrob to care for you. You have the best luck." Daisy lounges in the chair next to my bed, looking fresh and pretty. In contrast, I feel like I've been run over by a bike. That sounds lame. A truck would be far more dramatic.

"I spent the last few nights in the hospital and had my phone destroyed. I don't have good luck," I counter.

"Don't be so negative. You could have been seriously hurt. The universe works in mysterious ways. Besides, Doc Hotty said you can leave the hospital today."

I adjust the bed to sit up higher. Bruises still mar my body, and though the pounding in my head has lessened, it hasn't gone away entirely.

Daisy is right, though. I'm lucky and should feel grateful. After I passed out on the street, I woke up in the hospital with a painful headache, balance issues, and the worry that my brain could be irreparably broken. Luckily, my broken brain proved temporary, and the doctors finally proclaimed me fit to go home.

It wasn't exactly a near-death experience, but it shifted something in me. When I was in the hospital, it occurred to me that there would only be a few people who would care if I disappeared tomorrow, and one of them was behind a screen with no intention of ever meeting me. I wanted something different from my life, something more.

Speaking of screens…

"I hate to ask you, but were you able to take my phone to the repair shop?" I ask Daisy.

"Do you want the good news or the bad news?"

"The bad news." If she gave me the good news first, I wouldn't be able to enjoy it, because I'd be worrying about what bad news would follow, canceling out the good.

"The repair guy said your phone is fucked."

"Shit," I whisper, closing my eyes against the tears that threaten. The truth is, I don't care about the phone. All I care about are my texts with Remington. And his contact number, which I still can't remember.

A sense of loss settles over me. His old PO Box is no longer valid. I tried to send him a Christmas card a few years back, and it had come back to me as undeliverable. I only hope that he'll wonder what happened and write to me at Mr. Jensen's shop. But after our last messages, when I stupidly broke our rules, I'm not sure he will. He might think I'm ghosting him, and maybe he'll be happy about it. Maybe he'll be relieved I stopped texting.

"Hey, you look like you lost your entire Agatha Christie book collection. It's okay. Daisy to the rescue. Surprise!"

She holds out a small paper bag. I peek into it and pull out an iPhone, a far newer model than I'd had.

"Daisy! I can't accept this. There's no way I can afford it." Especially after I get the bill for the hospital. I have insurance, but it's not a great plan and my co-pays are ridiculous. *How am I going to pay for more medical bills?*

I could, if I accept the job offer as a technical writer, I can't help thinking. I'd make double what I make at the bookshop and have better benefits. *Ugh.* I got my master's in creative writing, not software manuals.

Daisy waves a hand. "Oh, this old thing? I just had it lying around."

I raise an eyebrow.

"Stop looking at me that way. You deserve this. You never ask for anything. Just think of it as a birthday present. It's unlocked, so I bought you a temporary SIM card with data."

"I can't accept it, Daisy. That's too much."

She blows out a breath. "You're so stubborn. You need to get better at accepting gifts. If it makes you feel better, think of it as a loaner until you can get yourself a replacement."

I don't want to accept it, but I need a phone. "Thank you, Daisy. I'm grateful for the loan. I'll give this back to you when I get a new one." I try my best to give her the cheerful smile she deserves for being so amazing, but it wobbles a little.

"Hey, what's wrong? I thought you'd be happy with your new phone."

"No, I am. I'm just tired. And maybe a little sad about everything in my phone I've lost."

She grins impishly. "Which is how I come to the good news."

"Wasn't the phone you gave me the good news?"

"Nah. That's just a bonus. The good news is that even though your phone is fucked, I flirted with a repair guy, who is some genius phone specialist, and he's going to do us a solid by trying to fix it or at least recover all your data. He can't get to the job right away, but he said he's confident he can do it."

"Daisy!" I squeal. "Thank you, thank you!" This time, my smile is real.

"You can thank my teeny tiny but perky boobies and see-through shirt. He stared at my tits the whole time I was trying to convince him to help."

"Thank you, Daisy's boobs!" I say with enthusiasm.

"You know, it might not be a bad thing that you lost your phone. To be honest, I was tempted to let your phone stay broken."

"What? Why?"

"To start fresh without your text buddy as a distraction. You can have your own summer of risks—just like you said Nanna wants you to have."

"I'm not going to model nude for a famous photographer like my grandma did. Not that anyone would want me to." I look down at myself.

"Of course they would. You're hot, even if you insist on hiding your assets. But you don't have to do exactly what she did. Just take a risk a day, any risk. It can be something small. Like getting on Tinder."

"Really? Tinder?"

"Well, any dating app. There are plenty. Or what about speed dating, then? Bungee jumping? We'll think of something. But the point is to take some risks."

I gnaw on my lips, which are chapped after two days in the hospital.

I nod. "Okay. Let's do this. The summer of risks."

"Yes!" Daisy pumps her fist in the air as if she's Rocky Balboa at the end of a fight. "But you need a plan, or you won't do it. You need to take one risk a day for the entire summer."

"Okay," I agree. "But I get to choose the risks, not you."

"You have to seriously consider the ones I suggest."

"Fine," I say, because sometimes it's easiest to just agree with Daisy.

"This is going to be fun," she says. "And I think your first risk should be finding someone new to crush on."

A new crush.

My relationship with Remington, if you could even call it a relationship, was supposedly risk-free.

Except "no risk" is just a mirage. There's a risk in everything, even the things we think are safe, like stepping off a curb. Maybe my phone breaking is the universe sending me a message. I almost died because I was preoccupied with my phone, and that's basically the way I've lived the last few years. When Nanna got sick, it just felt easier to retreat. But hiding isn't safety. It just means I don't get all the good stuff along with the bad.

I feel a glimmer of excitement for the summer. *The summer of risk.* And Daisy is right. My first risk should be falling for someone real.

CHAPTER 8

hase

"Chase, darling, get your head out of your ass. I said look brooding. I didn't say look like someone pissed in your cereal. Good gracious."

Glaring at Emma, I give my profile to the camera. I'm backlit by the large window of the fancy suite that's designated press central for the day. I've done enough photo shoots by now to sense the image the photographer is going for and to offer myself up, in character, with the variety of expressions and angles I've perfected over the years—my tilted smirk, my profile in silhouette.

The three leads of *The Wanderers* have been holed up here all day, alternating between interviews and photo shoots. The studio expects us to keep the fandom machine fed.

"That's the face, sugar. A little more pout, a little less pain-in-my-ass." Our personal assistant, Emma, keeps the insults flowing with her slight Southern accent. She can be mean as hell, but with her accent and sassy smile, you're more likely to thank her than curse her as she bulldozes in and gets her way.

Which is why she's such an effective personal assistant to Sebastian. And why I convinced her to work for me as well. She can make any publication print a full retraction and have them apologize to her for the inconvenience. Emma is magic in getting people to do what she wants. Usually.

But her tricks aren't working with me today. My costars and I just did a full day of press, being polite to reporter after reporter, answering the same mind-numbing questions dozens of times, all the while trying to sound charming and humble. I have to be confident, yet pretend that I don't realize I'm famous for my abs and face.

Doing press is never my favorite activity, but I try not to be an asshole about it because it beats being broke, jobless, and homeless like I was when I was a teen. Today, however, I'm over it.

I take a deep breath and will my patience to return as I turn back to the photographer who's been snapping away for the last thirty minutes. "We good? Please tell me you got what you need, man." I don't want to be rude to the guy. He's only doing his job, and it's not his fault the publicists booked us so solidly I can't breathe.

The photographer checks his camera one last time and nods. "We've got it. Thanks, Chase. It's been an honor." We shake hands before he turns and packs up his equipment. He already shot Sebastian and Ronan, my co-leads in the movie.

"No more, Emma. I'm fucking done here," I growl.

Emma taps long, painted nails on her clipboard and rolls her eyes at me. "You may be extra feisty today," she drawls, "but I don't have time for it. We've got three more interviews to go."

"Sorry, bro, but Emma's right. You're being a pain in the ass. What gives?" Sebastian asks from the corner of the room as he sprawls out on the sofa in the hotel suite.

"Boys, we don't have time for a deep discussion. You have reporters waiting to interview the two of you. After that, y'all can braid each other's hair and talk about your feelings," Emma says.

"Why is she like this?" Sebastian whines.

I shrug. "She's your assistant. It was your idea to have her help with PR for this," I point out, cracking a smile.

Emma stalks over to Sebastian and fusses with his collar. "I'm like this because you boys need to get your work done, and I make it happen." She narrows her eyes and gives him a once-over, patting his chest. "You'll do, darling. You both have a ten-minute break, and then we're calling in the next reporters."

When Emma leaves in a whirl of skirt and clipboard, Sebastian calls over the girl who's guarding the door. "Hey, gorgeous, can we get some beer? Or vodka?"

"Oh my God, Mr. Blake. I'm such a fan of yours," the girl gushes with wide-eyed admiration. Sebastian grins back at her, then winks at me, apparently thinking this is going to be a slam dunk.

"But Ms. Emma said you'd ask, and she told me to tell you." The girl frowns and flips through the papers on her clipboard. "Oh yes, here it is. She told me to say, and I quote, 'Remember what happened on your last junket.'" The girl's eyes get even bigger. She looks up. "What happened on the last junket?"

Sebastian shuffles his feet. "Nothing. Never mind," he mutters.

The girl turns to me. "Mr. James, would you like a drink? She said you're allowed."

I smirk at Sebastian. "I'm good. Thanks"—I try to recall the girl's name from when she introduced herself earlier in the day—"Ashley."

I'm not sure if I remembered it correctly, but when her smile widens like I've served her up Thanksgiving dinner on a platter, I figure I did. Remembering names is something I promised myself I'd do when I first made it. I spent so many years as a nameless nonentity to most people, I vowed I'd never treat anyone else that way.

"Dude. You could have at least gotten me a beer," Sebastian says.

I ignore him, so he sighs and tilts his eyes up to the ceiling. "I swear Emma does this to torture me. It's like having a babysitter."

Emma, who started working for Sebastian years ago, never puts up with any of his shit.

"Admit it," I say. "She has a point about the last junket. You got hammered and made out with that reporter. In the middle of the interview. On camera."

"I was bored, like I am now. Bad things happen when I get bored." He sits up, his leg bouncing up and down.

I check my phone for the hundredth time today. Still nothing. It's been four days now since I've heard from Typewriter Girl. *Olivia*. Four days since she sent me her photo and I shot her down.

All my messages since have gone unread. She must hate me. But what if something happened to her? She could be hurt, and I'd never know, all because of the damn rules.

I try to be discreet in checking my phone.

"What's wrong? Your mystery girl ghosting you?"

For a selfish idiot, Sebastian is surprisingly astute.

"Why do you say that?"

"You keep checking your phone, but you're not texting and staring at the screen with that stupid-ass smile you get. You've been a miserable prick instead. It's not hard to guess."

That's the thing about *The Wanderers*. There is zero privacy on or off the set.

Fuck it. Maybe Sebastian can give me advice. I'm that desperate.

"You're right. She ghosted me." I run my hand through my

hair, messing up the casual style that took my stylist an hour to create. My "groomer," the girl whose job it is to make sure I'm camera-ready at all times, won't be happy.

"Did you fight?"

"Not a fight," I hedge.

Sebastian leans back, drumming a hand against his knee. "If I'm going to help you, I need to know more details."

I grit my teeth. "There's not much to tell. She's an online friend. She lives in San Francisco."

"Dude. She could be some stalker fan."

"She doesn't know who I am, so she's not a stalker."

"She doesn't know you're famous?"

"No," I clip out.

Sebastian cracks up. "Whoa, so this chick thinks you're just some random. That's *sick*."

"It's not funny, asshole. I'm worried. I haven't heard from her in days, and we usually text constantly."

I can't even articulate all the things I'm worried about. And I miss her more than I thought possible.

"You're in deep. So, find her."

"What if she doesn't want to be found?" I need to be sure she's okay. I swallow past the lump in my throat.

"Do you know anything about her? Besides San Francisco?"

"I know the name of the bookshop where she works."

"Ooh, I dig the hot librarian thing. So, what the fuck are you waiting for, an invitation? You're Chase fucking James. Go get her."

The door opens, and Emma is in the doorway. "Boys, two minutes. Ronan is on his way back up to join you for this interview." Emma glares at me. "Chase, your hair is all crazy again." Her tone is half accusation, half resignation.

"Leave it," Sebastian says. "Chicks dig the sex hair. So, Emma, you're a girl…"

"Woman, but glad you noticed," she drawls as she saunters into the room, her attention on the papers in her hand.

"As a *female*, don't you agree Chase needs to get off his ass and find his woman?"

Emma looks up, interest in her eyes now. "The sexting girl?"

"We don't sext," I snarl. "What happened to privacy?"

"Privacy is a myth for people like you," Emma retorts.

"Sexting Girl disappeared. Don't you think he should grow some balls, go to San Francisco, where she lives, and find out why?"

"We. Don't. Sext. We text. That's it. And I won't be some stalker who chases after her just because she doesn't answer a few messages."

"Pussy. A few texts, my ass. You've been blowing up her phone all week. Emma, tell him he needs to man up."

Emma purses her lips and tilts her head, her sharp eyes darting from Sebastian to me and back again.

"I think a guy who is smart enough to recognize a good thing and go after it is rare," she says slowly with a quick glance at Sebastian. She shrugs. "So, stop pitching a fit and go after her."

I run my fingers through my hair again in frustration, garnering another glare from Emma.

"Find her," Sebastian says. "Go now. I'll cover your last interviews."

"Hold on. I didn't say to go now. You're not leaving early." Emma's scowl is now at DEFCON 5. "But if you're real nice, Chase, I'll help you. Jake Edgerton has been looking for leads in his latest movie. And your name is topping the list."

I frown. "I hadn't heard that." Edgerton is one of the best directors in the business. "How do you know?"

Emma smiles smugly. "I've done a few favors for the casting agent."

"And?"

"I also happen to know that Edgerton lives in San Francisco and is there now. I'd be willing to bet that he'd be happy to see you. A meeting would give you a non-stalker-y reason to visit San Francisco for a few days and check on your girl."

"God, you're scary good," Sebastian says in admiration. "How do you do it?"

"I work at it." Emma's smile is smug. "I understand work is a foreign concept for you, but try it sometime."

"Always throwing shade. I work. I work hard!" Sebastian protests.

"Fine. Let's do it." I nod to Emma. "Can you help set it up?" I can be in San Francisco tomorrow. And I can find Olivia. Anxiety shoots through me. I'd be betraying our rules by doing this.

But she broke the rules first, I remind myself. I'll see her, make sure she's okay. Then, I'll leave.

"I can arrange it." Emma types into her phone. "Make sure you take Duncan. You've had more freaky fan letters lately."

"What about *my* fans?" Sebastian asks. "I have creepy fans too, right?"

"Seriously? You're mad because I get more stalkers than you?"

He tilts his chin up. "Please. I had my first stalker at eight months. Before the Olsen twins, even. You could never keep up."

Emma rolls her eyes. "Face it, Sebastian. The crazy girls love you, but they love Chase more."

"It's his hair, isn't it? He has great hair." Sebastian turns to me. "So, go use that great hair and get your girl."

Emma nods. "You're the king of the pretty boys. She won't be able to resist."

"I told you, it's not—"

"Like that. I know. And I don't care. Now, let's get back to work."

* * *

THE NEXT MORNING, I stare out the window of the black SUV cruising through the streets of San Francisco. The sunrise is a pink bruise in the sky. My eyes are gritty, and I need a shave.

"I have one stop to make before the hotel, Duncan."

Typewriter Girl once told me she works the morning shift at Books & Buns, a bookstore and café. I confirmed that the bookstore doesn't open until 9:00 a.m., but the café's portion opens at six. When I looked up the address before I left New York, I discovered it's just a block from the antique shop in Noe Valley where I wrote to her that first year. Does she live in the neighborhood, as well as work there?

I scrub a hand across my face and gaze at my tired reflection in the car window. Guilt gnaws at me for breaking the confidentiality I insisted on, but I'll check on her this one time to make sure she's safe, and then I'll be gone. I'll never have any peace until I know she's fine.

"It's a little early for a stop, isn't it, Mr. James?"

"I want to get some coffee. There's a café around the corner from the hotel." I reserved a room at an exclusive boutique hotel a few blocks from the bookstore. It's reasonable to stop for coffee. Nothing too stalker-ish about that, right?

"Are you sure that's wise, sir?"

"I just want some coffee. And stop calling me 'sir.' I'm Chase, and you damn well know it."

"I can't call you Chase. It doesn't keep the appropriate professional distance." He sounds affronted.

I snort. "And does appropriate professional distance also include giving me unsolicited advice?"

"Consider it a bonus of my protection duties, *Mr. James*."

I tell Duncan the address of the café, and he enters it into his phone. The quiet streets and colorful houses whir by as excitement builds. I'm getting closer to her.

"We're almost there."

I take a deep breath. What I'm about to do is stupid. But that knowledge won't stop me. Not at all.

CHAPTER 9

livia

I ARRANGE THE MUFFINS, cinnamon buns, and breakfast sandwiches in the display case and pour myself a giant cup of coffee from the first pot of the day.

Audrey comes to work when the bookshop opens at nine, so it's only me in the café with the early birds. It took a while for me to get used to the hour, but I've grown to love the quiet morning rituals of readying the shop for opening as soft music plays in the background and the city wakes around me.

When Audrey took over the bookshop from her aunt, she expanded the café hours to take advantage of the regulars from the neighborhood who want to fuel up with expensive caffeinated drinks and our famous cinnamon buns before heading to work. With Noe Valley rent, an indie bookstore isn't easy to keep afloat, even one with a rich history in the neighborhood. Audrey is always thinking of ways to bring in extra revenue, from hosting poetry slams and book clubs to renting out the space for special events.

I sip my coffee and gaze out at the still-dark morning. My free hand feels empty, like a phantom limb, without my old phone resting in it. During this quiet time, in the break between getting the café ready and the first customers, I would often text with Remington, depending on the time zone he was in. Now that he's not on the other side of my phone, I realize how much he filled the spaces of my life. And how much I need to find new people and activities to fill those old voids. People I can see and touch.

The door jingles as I'm pouring a second cup of coffee, and a tall guy in a hoodie walks in. He isn't one of our morning regulars. I shiver a little, watching him. His face hides in the shadows of his hood, except for the thick scruff on a strong, aggressively masculine jaw. His body is rangy but powerful, and that, combined with his obscured face, makes me apprehensive. The mystery writer in me is already coming up with plots for him as either the hero or the villain.

I set down the coffeepot and wipe my hands on the café's apron, tamping down my fears and pasting on a smile. I remind myself that this is a café and he's a customer looking for a fix of caffeine. The soothing sounds of Adele play over the speakers. Nothing bad can happen when Adele is singing in the background, right?

As the man approaches the counter, he looks up, his hoodie falling back.

Oh. My. God.

My brain struggles to compute what I'm seeing.

Chase James stands in front of me.

I've never been the type to get all woozy from some celebrity. Daisy and Audrey love to tease me because I don't know the latest bands and movies. I'm more about all things classic. But this isn't some random celebrity. Justin Bieber leaves me cold. The One Direction dudes? Meh.

But Chase James? He's in an entirely different league. In fact, no other league comes close, I think in awe.

Now that I see his face, I can say the hype surrounding him is deserved. I've always thought that a star's good looks must be exaggerated on-screen or in magazines, that they are enhanced by good lighting, makeup, and a liberal sprinkling of Photoshop. But this man, though scruffy this early in the morning, is almost unearthly beautiful with rich auburn hair and deep green eyes.

His eyes rake over my face, my body. Perhaps his questioning look is because my hand still holds on to the pot of coffee and I've yet to say anything. I stand frozen. My mouth opens, but no sound emerges.

My brain is stuck on trying to solve the conundrum before me. How is it possible for eyes to be so green, lashes so long?

He runs a hand over his face, looking up in a way that's almost shy. "A very large black coffee, please. Your regular brew, nothing fancy." His voice is low and deep. It's familiar. But not.

Of course, I've heard him speak in *The Wanderers*, but in that movie, he has an English accent and not this American drawl I can't quite trace.

When I don't react right away, he tilts his head, his eyes shifting toward the pot.

I'm expected to pour coffee into a cup. There's no way.

He's just a customer, I remind myself. "Um, s-sure. Will that be all?" My voice is about three octaves too high.

I close my eyes in embarrassment, silently forming the word *shit* as I turn to grab a to-go cup, rather than a mug for here. I figure Chase James isn't going to sit in my café and sip a cup of coffee. As I pour, I peek at him through my too-long bangs. This is my fatal misstep.

He's watching me, as if trying to solve a puzzle. Our eyes meet, and my heart stops.

Until scalding liquid burns my hand and splashes onto my white shirt and apron.

"Oh crap!" I realize I overfilled the cup, and coffee runs down the side.

Before I react, he grabs a cloth from the counter and dabs at my hand and then my shirt. He gets dangerously close to my breast. I'm not complaining. But I can feel my cheeks on fire. One of the worst things about having such a pale complexion is that I blush easily. I hate having my flustered emotions broadcast on my face.

"Are you okay? That had to hurt," he says. His eyes wander from my chest to my shocked gaze and back down to my name tag. His mouth quirks in a private smile before forming my name, as if testing it out. "Olivia."

My hand smarts where the coffee burned it, but the heat from his touch affects me far more. *Damn.* He's lethal, which shouldn't come as a surprise, considering he was voted the Sexiest Man Alive last year.

I step back to gain some equilibrium.

"I'm fine, just feeling clumsy, but that's not unusual." Nervous laughter bursts from me as I swipe at the spilled coffee on the counter. I breathe in and will my overactive heart to chill out. As good-looking and famous as this dude is, he's a guy, like any other.

What do public speakers do to help them when they're nervous? They imagine the audience naked. Yes, I'll do that.

I sneak another glance at him, which is a huge mistake. *Nope! No! Abort!* Imagining him naked makes it even worse because, in my imagination—and I'm absolutely sure, in reality—Chase James naked is one hundred times hotter than Chase James clothed.

I whirl away to grab another paper cup. After taking ten calming breaths, I attempt to pour his coffee again. This time, I pour the dark, steaming liquid in without spilling a drop.

I put the lid on, check it twice, and only then do I have the guts to turn back to him, my cheeks red, I'm sure. Heat turns to goose bumps when his hand brushes against mine as he takes the coffee.

"Um, anything else?" I ask, pleased I got that out smoothly. Then I ruin it. "We have some lovely buns. They're hot." *Why did I say that so creepy?* "I mean cinnamon buns," I rush out. "We have all kinds. It's our specialty. We have pecan buns, maple buns, apple buns, even peach buns." I bite my lip to stop the flow of words.

He watches me with a crooked smile, as if I amuse him.

He shakes his head. "Not today."

That sounds as if he'll be back. No, that's wishful thinking. What's he even doing in San Francisco? I wonder. Shouldn't he be in Hollywood? Or New York?

"That will be four dollars," I say.

He bends his head to his wallet, pulling out a crisp twenty-dollar bill while I memorize everything about him.

His hands are strong, with long fingers that make me want to know what he can do with them. His gray hoodie isn't a normal sweatshirt. The material seems softer, more luxurious. The sleeves are pushed up to show muscular forearms. His hair is longish and thick, a unique shade of brown with shots of red and gold running through it.

I punch in the amount, and the register opens. I count his change, doing an awkward exchange of money with him. Our hands brush again, and this time, I don't think it's my fault. His fingers trail over mine as he takes the change. His touch is electric.

He drops the bills I gave him into the tip jar.

"That's too much. You don't need to—"

The rest of my words die in my throat because he flashes me a smile that feels like a promise. It's a smile in slow motion, beginning in his eyes and moving to his mouth. A tilt of his lips, a quarter smile, a half-smile, then the twinkle in his eyes. Next come the quirk of laugh lines, the slash of a manly dimple, and finally, a full grin.

And just like that, I'm his forever. Only as a fan, of course. Because he's Chase James, movie star. There's not any possibility of anything more.

CHAPTER 10

hase

I CHANGE my mind with each step that slams into the pavement.

I should. I shouldn't. I will. I won't.

The right thing would be to run back to my hotel and stay the fuck away from Olivia. But I keep pushing myself in a rhythm as steady as my thoughts are chaotic, letting my legs carry me farther and farther from my hotel, until I find myself in front of her café once again.

Sweat drips down my back. Cold air rasps through my lungs. The light is just a promise in the foggy morning, weak as my faltering will. I swore that yesterday would be the first and only time I'd visit her. Yet here I am again.

I'm a shadow in the dark as I watch her, bright and glowing, through the café window. Inside, she shimmies as she fills a row of containers with sugar packets.

This is wrong. I shouldn't be here, in front of her shop. I shouldn't even be in San Francisco. I came to make sure she was okay, and she is. She isn't lying in a hospital bed or a ditch somewhere. She ghosted me, not because she was hurt or in danger, but because she doesn't want to talk to me anymore, and I don't blame her after our last messages. Which means being here is all kinds of creepy.

Stepping away from the warm scene inside, I turn in the opposite direction, determined to leave her and head back to my empty hotel room. My feet are anchors now, but I have to walk away. For good. Forever.

"Wait! We're open!"

I whip back, and there she is in the doorway, out of breath and blushing. My Typewriter Girl. My best friend for years. The girl I know better than anyone and whose name I only just learned last week. *Olivia.*

Would I have noticed her if we met by chance? With her black fall of hair and her pale, serious face, she's the opposite of the LA girls who usually surround me. Her body is more lush than thin. She's pretty, but in a librarian-next-door way. Shier than I imagined.

In our letters and texts, Typewriter Girl has a bold confidence and a wicked sense of humor that can eviscerate me with a few sentences. She is wise and knows exactly who she is, with no apology. In contrast, the girl standing before me seems uncertain and has trouble meeting my eyes.

She holds the door open, flips the sign from Closed to Open, and gifts me a timid smile.

"Are you here for coffee?" she asks. Today, she's wearing a gray shirt that brings out the color of her eyes and a pair of black jeans that skim over her curves. I'm thankful she hasn't put on the jaunty yellow apron she wore yesterday that hides her body.

I stand there like an idiot. Her presence does that. She shifts under my intense scrutiny, adjusting her midnight bangs. She tilts her head, opening the door a little farther in silent question, and bites her bottom lip, which makes me want to take a nip at it as well.

Is she bashful because I'm famous, or has she, like me, hidden more of herself than she let on in the letters? The girl I always considered to be an open book is turning out to be more mysterious. It's wrong, but at this moment, the need to find out if she's the same person I thought I knew is a compulsion.

She stops when she gets to the counter. "Up early for a morning run?" she asks, taking in my athletic pants, my damp hair, and the trickle of sweat that runs down my neck.

I shrug. "I like the streets when they're quiet." This is the truth, at least. Otherwise, I'm running, not just to keep in shape, but to get away from a crowd of fans.

She nods. "A large brewed coffee again?" She holds up the pot. Her hand shakes, the coffee sloshing from side to side.

She sets down the pot when she sees I notice the shaking, and I avert my eyes so as not to embarrass her. I hate that she's nervous around me. Typewriter Girl was always comfortable with me, to the point of glibness. I spend my life surrounded by varying levels of deferential and fawning. Our relationship had been free of those constraints.

I want that connection I had with the girl behind the screen. I long to peel away the layers of us to get a glimpse of the real her before I walk away for good.

"Can I have a mug for here?" I ask, with a nod to the large cup of coffee on the counter, which I assume is hers.

Her eyes widen in surprise, but she grabs a turquoise mug from a shelf behind her. She pours the coffee and pauses to look up as it nears the top. I nod, and she keeps pouring until the coffee reaches the brim.

She pushes the cup toward me. "Anything else?"

I shake my head.

When I pay, she takes my money and gives me back my change, and just like yesterday, our fingers brush, igniting a spark. She yanks her hand back as if burned. I put the money in the tip jar and consider her.

"Actually, I would like something else."

I'm already breaking the rules. I might as well go all in.

"I knew you couldn't resist the buns. No one can."

My mouth quirks. "I'm tempted," I murmur. "But not today."

I'm as nervous as a teenager asking a girl out for the first time. "Sit with me if you have a few minutes." I incline my head toward the empty tables in the restaurant and hold up my coffee. "I hate drinking alone."

Her hand freezes on the register. Startled eyes meet mine. Again, slight pink tints the cream of her skin. I want to make her blush daily. Hourly. Always.

Her eyes widen as she stares at my face, and I can see the fangirl glaze to her eyes. It isn't fair for me to judge her. My fame freaks everyone out. But I don't want her to be everyone. I want her to be my sweet, snarky best friend who makes me feel like a real person, not some caricature of a celebrity.

"You want to have coffee? With me?" she squeaks. "Aren't you busy? Are you making a movie in San Francisco?" she asks, looking down into her coffee as she says the word movie, like a dirty secret.

The one girl who liked me for me, and not my fame, is now asking about my movie schedule with a starstruck look in her eyes.

It's a thousand times fucked up that I'm jealous of Chase James. When Chase James is…me. This is getting complicated. This is why I should never have come.

I run my hand through my hair in frustration and clasp the back of my neck, massaging the tight muscles bunching there.

I must have waited a beat too long to answer because Olivia frowns.

"Never mind. I shouldn't have asked. It's your business."

"No, it's fine. I'm here for some meetings." I evade, guilty now. None of this is her fault. I'm to blame for making a mess of everything. "I'm staying at the Heights."

She shifts her feet and tilts her head with a hesitant smile of her own. It's small, but it gives me hope that maybe—just maybe—we can have a normal conversation.

"The Heights, huh? Pretty fancy. Don't they have coffee?"

I'm sure they do. The small boutique hotel is world-famous for its history, discreet service, and wealthy guests. But I chose it not for those attributes, but because it's one of the few hotels near here.

I meet her eyes. "Not like yours." And there's her blush again. I want to explore how far it goes down her body.

I walk to the nearest table. "Will you sit with me?" I ask again.

She looks around the empty café. "I'm supposed to be prepping for the morning rush, but…"

"Please," I say. It would be ironic if the one time I want to get to know a woman, she blows me off. What good is the dubious title of Sexiest Man Alive if I can't gain the attention of the only girl I want?

Olivia's confused gaze meets my hopeful one, and my heart flips over. Her beauty isn't flashy, but she has a fresh-faced loveliness that's riveting to me. A long black braid falls over one shoulder, her straight bangs framing the deep gray of her eyes. If she's wearing makeup, I can't tell.

She nods and comes out from behind the counter, mug in hand, and pulls out the chair opposite me. I don't even realize I've been holding my breath until it whooshes out of me at her assent.

"So," I say when she's seated.

Since becoming famous, I've rarely needed to work at conversation with women. They throw themselves at me with no effort on my part. As a result, I find I have no game. As

Remington, I have a thousand things to say to her. But as Chase James, it's all blank.

"Sooo," she says, drumming her fingers against her coffee cup. She makes a slow show of taking a sip.

"How long have you worked here?" I ask a little desperately. I already have the answer, but at least it fills the silence.

"Melody, the former owner, hired me when I was fifteen, and I've been working here ever since," she says, warming to her subject as I hoped she would. "I live in the neighborhood and worked my way through high school and college here. When Melody passed away a few years ago, Audrey, her niece, inherited the bookshop."

Her eyes shine with mischief. "Melody was a big fan of the first *Wanderer*s. She would've freaked out that you're here."

I shake my head. "And you? Are you a fan?" The question just slips out. Damn, I sound as arrogant as Sebastian. But suddenly, I'm dying to hear what she thinks of Chase James, the actor. Maybe it's weird to think of myself in the third person like that, but the Hollywood version of me is a persona I put on, another part I play. Remington is closer to the real me than the movie star partying on a yacht or walking a red carpet.

"I-I don't know you or your movies well enough to say. And that's a rather forward question for a first coffee." Her smile softens her words. "But I'm sure 99.9 percent of all girls would faint if you smiled at them, so stop fishing for compliments."

There's the sassy attitude I know so well.

Relief sweeps through me. She's still Typewriter Girl, even when I'm Chase James.

I look around the shop. Old photos crossing decades clutter the walls. Beyond the small, bright room of the café is an arched doorway that leads into the darkened interior of the bookshop itself. It's just light enough to make out leather chairs and shelves of books from floor to ceiling. There's a feeling of history, of permanence.

"This shop is great."

She looks around, as if she's enjoying seeing the store through my eyes. "I love it here. I love imagining all the people who have come through its doors over the years. All their stories, the lives they've lived, and all the stories that live within the pages of the books we sell." She shrugs and gives a self-deprecating laugh. "Sorry, I don't mean to get carried away. I guess you could say I'm a bookworm."

"I am too," I admit with a grin, our eyes meeting, holding.

"I'm not sure I believe you."

"Actors can read too," I tease.

"Sorry. I don't mean to sound like a jerk. It's just that you must be so busy. I can't imagine you have spare time."

"There's a surprising amount of downtime on set and between projects. Being on location can get boring and a little lonely. Reading helps."

"You?" She arches an eyebrow. "Lonely?"

"Sometimes." I shift in my seat. "I've always loved books. Believe it or not, I was at a library when I was first scouted. I was hanging out on the steps reading when an agent walked by, saw me, and handed me his card. At first, I thought it was bullshit, but a modeling gig led to a TV commercial, which led to a part in a small movie, which led to *The Wanderers*. But it all started at a library."

I don't tell her that libraries were a haven for me when I was a homeless teen. They're warm in the winter, cool in the summer, dry in the rain, and a free way to escape to other worlds.

"What's your favorite book?" she asks, taking a sip of coffee.

I'm focused on her lips, so it takes a few seconds to break my gaze enough to concentrate on her question. "I have too many to name just one. But when I was young, it was *The Catcher in the Rye*. The only teacher who ever believed in me gave me a copy. I read it so many times, it eventually fell apart."

"I have a friend who loves that book."

Shit. I forgot to be on my guard. Of course, she knows that's one of Remington's favorite books, which is why this was such a bad idea.

"I can imagine. It's a bit of a cliché for a guy to like that book," I say, playing it casual. "What's *your* favorite?" I deflect.

She laughs. "Guess."

I run my hand along my chin. Another moral dilemma. I already know her favorite. Or at least, I know Typewriter Girl's favorite.

"Is it by Jane Austen? Or maybe you're a Hemingway girl. Or Edith Wharton?" I ask, knowing they're all wrong.

"I do love Edith Wharton, but no."

"I give up," I say with a grin.

"It's not really one book. It's a series. Encyclopedia Brown," she says with a laugh. "I was obsessed. Do you remember them?" she asks.

My lips curve into a smile. "Boy detective. I loved trying to solve the mysteries."

"Right?" she says. "I fell in love with mysteries. Then, I got into Nancy Drew, The Hardy Boys, Sherlock Holmes, Agatha Christie, but it all started with Encyclopedia Brown."

I watch, fascinated, as her face loses any speck of self-consciousness while she discusses her favorite books.

She blushes when she realizes how closely I'm observing her.

A honking horn and a yell sound from the street, and I jerk back, pushing up my hoodie. It's getting busier outside our little oasis.

My eyes meet Olivia's concerned gaze. A wrinkle forms between her brows. "It must be weird to always be worried about being recognized."

It's a classic Typewriter Girl observation. This is her, seeking, curious, looking under the surface of things to what's below. This is my one chance to get a little closer to the truth with her, as I never could before. But I'm not used to sharing my feelings, especially on this. It's hard to explain the effects of my celebrity without sounding like an ungrateful, entitled jerk.

"I'm sorry. That's another intrusive question," she says, misinterpreting my silence. "You can ignore me. I'm way more awkward than I need to be."

"No. It's fine." I look up, trying to come up with words that ring true.

I lean toward her, speaking with a soft intensity that belies the fact that we've only just met, at least for her. There's so little time left to explore this connection between us.

"My life is ridiculous. A dichotomy of privilege and constraint. I live on the edges of things. I enter through back doors and sneak out the same way. I dress to keep people from seeing me." I gesture to my hood. "I get whisked to places in a dark car with tinted windows and then swept away again."

Another car horn honks. Sunlight filters in brighter now. The day has awakened. At any moment, someone will walk through the door and break the peace.

"But you're here, sipping coffee in a café."

I want to inhale her sweet sincerity.

"Yes, just after dawn in an empty café. I can't do this in half an hour. Hell, in five minutes, it will probably be too late. Three months ago, I tried to go to a bar in New York City. Someone tweeted that I was there, and thirty minutes later, a stampede of people was trying to get in. They had to call the police." I shake my head. "That was the last time I tried to do something normal like that, to be someone normal."

She looks concerned. I said too much. I want to bare my soul to a girl I've liked for years. But for her, she's having an oddly serious conversation with a stranger she's just met.

"Sorry, didn't mean to get too deep. I understand how lucky I am." I throw her my devil-may-care smile, trying to lighten the mood.

The door jingles as it opens. I adjust my hood. She turns to the new customers, and her expression brightens.

"Morning, Joe," Olivia says with a broad smile that causes my breath to catch. She hops up from her chair and makes her way back behind the counter. "What are you in the mood for today?"

"One large coffee, and do you have any blueberry muffins?"

"We always have blueberry muffins for you."

Olivia's warm reply does something to my heart. The man is homeless. I saw him on my run over here earlier, huddled in the corner of a stoop with his dog. But Olivia treats him as a valued customer. People like her are rare, I know firsthand. But they make all the difference.

She pours a large, steaming cup of coffee and shoots me a look from under her lashes. She seems nervous to find me watching.

Joe grins. "Always flattering this old man."

He pats his pockets, as if looking for money.

Olivia leans over the counter, staying his hand. "Joe," she admonishes, "it's on the house."

The man puffs up with pride. "I can pay today, thanks to this guy." He points at me.

I sit up straighter. I hadn't realized he'd noticed me.

Olivia shoots me a curious glance.

"Handed me a nice, crisp one-hundred-dollar bill. Complimented Lady and gave me this jacket." He gestures to the designer leisure-wear jacket I was given for free. It costs more than most people make in a month, and it makes me grin to see it on Joe.

"It made my day."

When I passed him on the street, he asked for change with polite cheer, a sweet lab mix sitting by his side. Though the man wore an incongruous bow tie, his clothes were threadbare. But his dog was clean, with a makeshift coat draped over her. When you're homeless, rain and cold are your nemeses. June in San

Francisco is surprisingly cool, with a fierce wind. He needed my coat more than I did. I try to donate to as many charities as I can, usually focusing on at-risk youth and the homeless. I might not be able to save all those kids I met years ago in foster homes and the streets, but I can do some small part to help now. But even with my huge movie paychecks, it never seems to be enough.

The smile Olivia bestows on me is a gift.

I tip my head to Joe in greeting. Olivia adds two large muffins bursting with blueberries in a carrier bag.

"I also threw in some treats for Lady and some water," she says as she hands the bag to the homeless man. "We missed you last week. We worry when you don't come in for a while."

"Lady thanks you, and so do I." The man gives a courtly bow before leaving the shop, the door jingling behind him.

"That was nice of you," Olivia comments as she wanders back toward the table. "Joe and Lady have been fixtures on this block for as long as I can remember. We try to watch out for him, and he watches out for us. I wish I could help him more. I've tried over the years to get him into shelters, but he says he prefers the streets, and I think he fears they'll separate him from his dog. She's his only family now."

Olivia stands next to her recently vacated seat, as if she can't decide whether to sit back down with me.

I want nothing more than to drink coffee all morning, watching her kind, expressive face as she tells me all the things I already know about her, and all the things left to learn. But the light is glowing in the windows. It's only a matter of minutes before customers fill the shop.

Besides, there's the whole stalker thing—and me not wanting to be more of one than I already am. It's ironic how the tables have turned since I'm usually the one being stalked.

I stand, pulling a pair of shades out of my pocket.

"Your disguise?"

I flash my smile that breaks hearts. I don't want her to remember me as the star who complained about being famous. I'd rather leave her thinking I'm a cocky asshole than some whiny, overprivileged celebrity.

"I'm a ninja. A ghost. I could be a spy."

"You're a real badass, superstar," she says dryly.

"Thanks for the coffee and the, um, conversation." I shift my weight from one leg to the other. Real smooth, James.

"So, this is goodbye." It's neither a question nor a statement; it just is. She offers her hand.

I wrap my large one around hers, engulfing her warm fingers. I don't shake her hand. Instead, I just hold it, reveling in her soft skin and the electricity that flows between us. I lightly brush the inside of her palm with my fingers and take in the heat of her, the hitch of her breath.

It makes it that much harder to walk away, but I need to do it. It's the right thing. This is goodbye.

Laughter sounds outside the café, breaking the connection between us.

I lean into her and tell myself I'm doing this for her, for this unexpectedly shy girl to understand beyond any doubt that she's desirable. Remington may have rejected her, but Chase James is going to give her the kiss she deserves. At least, that's what I tell myself.

But the truth is, it's selfish. I've dreamed about this moment for years of sleepless nights. I want her lips on mine more than my last breath. She's my best friend. My everything.

Her mouth opens in surprise as I move toward her. I touch her cheek and let my fingers follow a path down her face to her chin. When I reach that soft curve, I tilt her head up. Our eyes meet. Hers are confused. I pause for a moment, asking silently.

She leans closer, as if magnetized, and I let that be my yes.

Lips brush lips in a touch that's as electric as it is gentle. It's meant to be soft and swift, but she stands on her tiptoes and melts into me. Her full breasts against my chest make me ache. I trace her face with my hands, then I smooth her hair back, following the line down to her braid, which I tug on, as I've wanted to do all morning.

At that light tug, she makes a small sound, something between a squeak of surprise and a groan of longing. The kiss deepens into something frantic, our mouths seeking each other with quiet desperation. It's hot and wild, and it leaves me breathless. The door jingles again. That damn door. We break apart, panting, in the middle of the cheerful café.

Voices filter to us. Being discovered by fans or the paparazzi in a coffee shop would be bad enough. Being discovered in a lip-lock with Olivia would be a disaster. I try to get my body under control.

She touches her lips, looking shell-shocked. "Why did you…" She shakes her head. "Why me?"

"Because you're perfect, and you don't even know it," I say. I don't tell her the whole truth. She's perfect for me. I want her to understand before I leave, but there isn't enough time.

"Goodbye." It's all there is to say, my voice rough with unexpected emotion.

"Goodbye," she whispers back, her finger still on her lips.

Not see you later, like last time.

This time, it's goodbye.

CHAPTER 11

livia

IT'S BEEN two days since The Kiss, and my mind is still a mess.

When I should've been getting ready for work this morning, I snuggled under the covers, replaying The Kiss. And earlier when I was working in the café, I should've been concentrating on taking people's coffee orders, but my mind was one-tenth on remembering their skinny caramel macchiato and nine-tenths on The Kiss.

Even now, sitting at the bookshop's customer service desk, I keep replaying it over and over in my brain.

Let's be real; nothing can compete with The Kiss. I'm worried that I'll be stuck forever in this daydream of lust and pointless longing. This is just a fantasy. It's not as if I'll ever see Chase James again. An international movie star coming into my empty café two mornings in a row is just a weird and wacky coincidence. His kiss meant nothing. The guy probably kisses girls all the time.

I don't follow the tabloids carefully, but I've seen enough

covers at the checkout line to know that this heartthrob isn't a stranger to women. I remember reading that he even dated Avery Woods. *The* Avery Woods! And there's his costar, who everyone believes is his secret love. Perhaps, in between those ridiculously beautiful ladies, he goes around making random, average women swoon by kissing them stupid. That's the only explanation I can muster.

There's no way he likes me. I'm not saying I'm a troll or anything. I'm kind. I'm smart. My hair, my best feature, is sort of nice—long and black and shiny. I have a truly kick-ass collection of records featuring everything from classical to blues to '80s pop. And I'm a loyal friend, even if I don't have many of them.

I'm just not the kind of girl who inspires movie-star kisses. That's reserved for magical unicorn girls who sing in sold-out stadiums and star in blockbuster movies, who are waif-thin and classically beautiful, who skip the bread, go to the gym daily, and are no strangers to the red carpet.

I'm not that girl.

Just saying.

I'm entirely ordinary. But maybe he kisses ordinary girls as a matter of course to keep his fan base happy. It's fan outreach, similar to posting on social media.

Speaking of social media…

I drum my fingers on the desk, debating. It's a slow time at the store, so I'm editing Audrey's blog post on great beach reads. Instead of wrapping up the article, I let my fingers wander, pulling up a search engine and typing the words *Chase James*.

I kissed the Sexiest Man Alive. Of course I'm going to internet-stalk.

I feel a little hot when I type in his name, though I don't know why. The guy is one of the most-searched men on the planet. Checking his social media accounts is no big deal.

Maybe he's even tweeting about the crazy fangirl he kissed this week.

Only.

Huh.

I stare at my computer screen, reading an article lamenting that Chase James isn't on social media. Apparently, he's low-key and private like that. My opinion of him goes even higher. I click a few more links and find that, though he's not on social media himself, he does have a lot of fan accounts devoted to him. My heart stops when I click on a red-carpet photo. He's staring into the camera like he knows all my secrets. I've been on the receiving end of that stare, and it's even more devastating in person. *He's* even more devastating in person.

Next, I click on a timeline of his relationship with his costar. It says, despite rumors, they broke up years ago amid much drama and tears—hers, not his. He's single.

I'm glad. At least he's not a cheater who goes around kissing random girls.

I touch my lips, still feeling the imprint of his kiss. With my other hand, I touch the screen, tracing his lips.

Slowly blowing out a breath, I continue clicking on images. Him arriving at an airport, surrounded by paparazzi, and at a hospital, visiting children. I smile at the hero worship in the eyes of the kids. He's dressed in his *The Wanderers* outfit, an Indiana Jones look that works for him, big time.

I click again, and there's a video of him walking down a New York street. My eyes get big as I take in the five bodyguards walking with him. Girls break away from the crowd, trying to grab any piece of him they can. He walks fast, eyes down. The bodyguards close in, forming a human shield, as the women follow. I click off, feeling guilty for even viewing the recording. I'm stalking him as well.

At the café, he approached me warily, as if he was uncertain of my reaction. He hesitated before letting his hood fall back and revealing his recognizable face.

The video leaves me disturbed; I have to wipe the icky feeling away. I manage that with a photo of Chase from a magazine shoot, looking far more comfortable in front of the camera, even shirtless. *Damn, he has abs for days.*

"Busy working?" A familiar voice breaks through my thoughts.

I jump, almost falling out of my chair. Daisy looks down at me with a grin. I'd been so focused on the screen—on Chase James's abs—I hadn't noticed Daisy walk up next to me.

"No! Yes! I mean, I didn't see you come in. Are you on your lunch break? Audrey's around somewhere." I lean forward, subtly trying to block the screen.

Confession time: I'm a bad friend. I haven't told Daisy about my close encounter of the celeb kind. I plan to tell her. It will be fun to talk with someone about it, especially Daisy, who gets so excited about everything. But I want to keep it to myself for just a little longer, like a delicious secret.

I take a deep breath and exhale. I almost got caught ogling Chase James on a computer screen.

How mortifying.

"Whoa, easy, girl." Daisy laughs, leaning against the side of the desk. "You're all pink and breathing hard."

"I was…doing exercises in the back a few minutes ago."

"Really?" Daisy looks skeptical.

I can't blame her. I never work out, and I certainly wouldn't start in the stockroom at work. I'm the worst liar ever.

"Yes. I need to get more fit," I babble, doubling down. "I read an article about how you should break up exercises into short segments throughout the day. Improves your mood and circulation."

"You know what's great exercise? Dancing." Daisy swivels

her hips in a slinky move. "I'm going to the Red Room tonight, and you're coming with me!"

The Red Room is actually not red. And it's not a room. It's a nightclub. I usually resist when she tries to drag me out, choosing to stay in and text with Remington, watch old movies, read, write—anything that doesn't involve getting dressed up and mingling with strangers, especially not in a crowded bar with too-loud music.

Though I did like mingling with Chase James, especially that part when our lips mingled.

My eyes glaze over as I remember The Kiss once again.

"Olivia!"

I startle. "Huh? Sorry. What did I miss?"

"Oh, nothing. You agreed to go out with me tonight."

"I did not. Don't you have a store to run?"

She shrugs. "There were no customers, so I got bored."

"There will never be any customers if every time they try to call or stop by, you're always closed in the middle of the day."

"I'm just popping in for a few minutes. I deserve a break. Why are you trying to get rid of me?" She leans over the counter until she can see the computer screen and lets out a laugh.

I sigh. *Caught. Damn.*

"Chase James. Well, well, well. I didn't know you had the hots for him."

"I don't!" I blush. "I mean, I'm just, um…" Yeah, I have nothing.

"Don't worry. I won't spill your secret." Her eyes twinkle. "I'm just surprised. I've never heard you talk about him before. You only seem to like those old mysteries and film noirs."

"Hey, old movies are the best." Audrey strolls up to the desk, carrying a stack of books. She drops them on the table next to me with a loud thud. "They don't make heroes like Gregory Peck anymore," she says with a sigh.

"Love the outfit. You channeling Audrey Hepburn today?"

"Well, we do share the same name. And taste," Audrey says with a grin. Audrey is obsessed with, well, Audrey. And Marilyn, Grace, Ava, and the rest of the classic movie stars. All her outfits are inspired by her favorite movies. Today, she's wearing cropped pants and ballet flats paired with a black turtleneck, her hair in a cute pixie cut.

She takes in my flushed face and Daisy's grin. "What's going on? What did I miss?"

"We're talking about how Olivia is a superfan of Chase James." Daisy slaps a hand over her mouth in an expression of horror. "You won't get a cardboard cutout, will you? Those are weird as fuck."

I frown. I should tell Daisy and Audrey about Chase coming into the bookstore's café. If they met someone famous, I'm sure they'd both tell me. But I still hold back. Maybe it's because of that crazy video I just watched, the one where he can't even walk down the street without being accosted.

It feels wrong to share, as if I'd be betraying his ability to have private moments without them becoming fodder for the gossip mill. So, feeling guilty, I decide to keep our meeting just for me. And especially our kiss. That's for me and my dreams.

"Don't tell me you've never Googled a celebrity."

Daisy grins. "Of course I have. Just not Chase James. He's not my type."

"He's everyone's type," Audrey argues. I mentally high-five her.

"Not mine," Daisy insists.

"Then who *is* your type?" I want to get dirt on her, just in case she keeps teasing me for my crush.

She hesitates and then leans over, types on my keyboard, and clicks.

A photo of rock legend Ryder Black fills the screen. I'm not surprised she has the hots for him. Most girls do. But it surprises me she has a crush she's never mentioned. I always think of Daisy as an open book with no filter.

"I didn't know you liked him. You never even listen to his music."

She shrugs. "I do. But it's a private thing."

Audrey smooths her hair. "The problem with celebrity crushes is that they're pointless. It's not like he would ever meet and fall in love with a regular girl."

"True." I've had enough of unrequited love with Remington.

Daisy crosses her arms and frowns. "Celebrities aren't gods. They're just people. They would be damn lucky to go out with one of us." She turns to me. "But don't change the subject. Start mentally preparing for our night out. I want to meet Drunk Olivia in person."

"I'm still recovering from the last time I got drunk. I made an ass out of myself and lost a friend." The one good thing about The Kiss is that being preoccupied with it has helped distract me from missing Remington. But even with the excitement of Chase James, I ache when I think of Remington. I miss our friendship deeply. A dozen times a day I think of things I want to tell him and then remember I can't.

"We'll find you a *real* man tonight."

"Where are you going?" Audrey asks.

"I'm dragging Olivia to the Red Room for dancing. You up for it?"

Audrey laughs. "Not in a million."

"I'm not sure this is a good idea, Daisy," I hedge.

"Aren't you supposed to be taking a risk a day?" Audrey asks. "This can be your risk."

I knew I shouldn't have told Audrey about Nanna's letter. Now the two of them are going to gang up on me.

"I already took a risk," I defend, crossing my arms. "I had one of our new banana scones."

"In what world is eating a scone a risk?"

"You know how much I hate bananas." I shudder. "That mushy texture."

"If that's what you consider a risk, then you are definitely coming out with me. Just don't drink champagne, and you'll be fine."

Famous last words.

* * *

LATER THAT NIGHT, we're in an Uber on the way to the club.

Daisy's phone rings. She looks at the screen and smiles as she answers. "Hey, big bro."

I've never met her brother, but I know Daisy talks to him frequently. Audrey and I both suspect he's a silent partner in her vintage shop, or he at least helps her financially. With her haphazard approach to business, it would amaze me that she's been able to keep it open completely on her own.

"Ooh, a surprise for me? Well, can you give me a hint?" She laughs at his response.

"Okay, I'll be patient."

"We're here," the Uber driver says, pulling up to the curb.

"Hey, I gotta go. We just arrived at the club. I resent that. I'm always good. Okay. Can't wait for your surprise. Talk to you tomorrow. Love you." She clicks off.

"Sorry," she says. "Just my brother."

I look out the window at the tall, old, narrow building that houses the Red Room. Each floor has a different theme and music. I've only been here once before, and it was early and quiet on a weeknight. The topmost floor was set up like a speakeasy, with deep velvet chairs, bluesy music, and a skilled bartender. It was intimate and felt like stepping into another era. I plan to hide out there while Daisy gets groovy dancing.

We wave goodbye to the driver and link arms, walking down the street. A giddy feeling overtakes me. The air feels electric, as if anything is possible. Maybe Daisy is right; maybe I've gone so far into my rut I forgot what fun a night out can be. I'm young. I shouldn't waste my twenties staying home alone. Even introverts need people sometimes.

We walk toward a long line of club kids dressed to party. A beefy bouncer wearing all black is checking IDs.

As always, Daisy leads us straight to the front of the line.

The bouncer's face is a scowl until he sees Daisy. He goes from scary to welcoming in a flash. "Hey, tiny dancer. Where've you been?"

She leans over to give him a hug. "Oh, you know me, here and there. Juan, this is my friend Olivia."

I give him an awkward wave and try to pull down my dress so it fully covers my backside. Earlier tonight, Daisy played fairy godmother to my Cinderella. It's one of her favorite parlor tricks, turning boring me into a slutty princess for a night out.

"Any friend of Daisy's is a friend of mine."

He waves away our money for the cover and unfastens the rope to let us through. There are a few grumblings from the people at the front of the line, but Juan glares them into silent submission.

My excitement for the night fizzles as we step through the door to the first floor that houses the crowded main bar. Bodies are piled in together, people shouting to be heard against grating electronic beats. Male gazes creep over me, eyeing my expansive cleavage and exposed legs.

Now I remember why I hate going out.

"Okay, it's been super fun. Time to go home now!" I shout to Daisy.

"Oh no, you don't." Daisy catches my arm as I try to turn around to head back through the door. "You'll have at least one drink and dance with me."

"Everyone is staring," I hiss.

"We're fucking stunning, which is why everyone's staring."

I pull at my dress again. I don't have the wardrobe for clubbing. I favor neutral and dark colors, comfortable fit, and cozy fabrics. Daisy calls my style goth homesteader, so she convinced me to borrow one of the vintage dresses from her shop.

It's so lovely I couldn't resist. It's a swinging sheath of a dress that's low and tight across the chest and falls mid-thigh. Except when I'm walking or moving. Then, it falls higher. With my curves, I didn't think the style would work for me, but it's surprisingly flattering, if a little skimpy.

Maybe I should have more fun and take more risks with my wardrobe. I never had much time or money to spend on clothes and finding my personal style. But this summer is supposed to be about stepping out of my comfort zone.

Daisy pushes her way toward the front of the crowd.

She doesn't let go of my hand as she does her maneuvering, so I try my best to sidestep through the crowd with her. Wispy, delicate Daisy can breeze through tight spaces that my curves can't, while I feel like I'm molesting total strangers with my ass and boobs. The male strangers don't seem to mind.

When we finally make it to the bar, she catches the bartender's attention, calling, "Two old fashioneds!"

The bartender, a man with way too many tattoos for one person, stares her down.

"Lychee martinis?" she asks, twirling her hair.

"You need to go to the top floor if you want a froufrou drink. We only have the basics here," he growls, then folds his arms, waiting.

Daisy laughs. "Fine. How about two Red Bulls and vodka? But only the top-shelf vodka."

"Wait, no. I'll be up all night if I have an energy drink this late," I say.

The bartender thrums his fingers on the bar impatiently.

"Um. A gin and tonic?" I ask. "Really light on the gin." It seems like a safe choice.

The bartender just grunts and turns to make the drinks.

"Damn, I love a bad boy. And a challenge." Daisy eyes the disinterested bartender. She whips out her credit card. "I'm getting him tonight," she vows.

"Does he know that?"

"He will," she retorts with breezy confidence.

I try to hand her money for my drink, but she shakes her head.

"You can buy the next round."

"If there is another round," I mutter.

A few minutes later, we have our drinks, and after Daisy's done a little more flirting with the grumpy bartender, we clink our glasses.

"Cheers!" She takes a big gulp.

I wince at the strong alcohol taste. So much for light on the gin.

"So what happened to the bartender from Jack's?" Jack's is a dive bar two blocks down from my house. Daisy used to have a crush on the guy who worked Tuesdays and Thursdays, so she'd make Audrey and me go to their wing night specials. The wings were good; the warm beer was not.

"It was nice while it lasted." She shrugs. "Don't you just love a hot bartender? I think it's because they're so busy working, they mostly ignore me. I like a guy with an avoidant personality. It's like a personal challenge." Daisy winks at the bartender, who furrows his eyebrows and turns away. "See? He couldn't care less about me. It's a total aphrodisiac. He's probably madly in love with a girl who died. Or maybe he's working his way through seminary school, and he wants to give his heart to God."

I snort. "Maybe he's an asshole. Or just not that into you."

She shakes her head. "Hmm. Possible on the asshole part. But not that into me? Nah. He wants me even if he doesn't realize it yet. The main reason we're here, though, is because you need to find a man."

She hasn't said it, but I get the feeling that Daisy thinks my zoned-out behavior this week is because I'm missing Remington. I mean, I am. I do. I miss my friend so much it hurts, and every time I think of the way I put myself out there and he turned me down, I'm gutted.

Still, meeting Chase James helped. I realize that it's possible to feel a Remington-level crush on someone besides my pen pal. Sure, it's with another unavailable male, this time a ridiculously hot celebrity, but it's a start. Now, I just need to put myself out there with a non-famous, real-life guy.

Could that real-life guy be in this bar tonight? Doubtful.

"Hey." Daisy gives me a concerned look. "Are you okay?"

I take a deep breath and say with more conviction than I feel, "I will be."

"Exactly. We always will be. Eventually. And you know what helps?"

I tilt my head. "What?"

"Time," she says.

I nod in agreement. I learned that when Nanna died. Time didn't take away the pain, but it made it more bearable.

"Time and tequila," Daisy says with a wicked grin.

"No tequila. Besides, I have a drink." I look down at the glass in my hand and realize with surprise that it's empty. I was thirstier than I thought.

"You were saying? Come on. Being good at tequila takes practice," she wheedles.

In the end, she wears down my resolve by reminding me that Nanna would want me to take risks. And knowing Nanna, she would probably approve of tequila.

Daisy skips back to the bar for a few minutes, then appears with two tequila shots rimmed with salt and a wedge of lemon. I eye it warily. The truth is, I rarely do shots. I skipped over the whole turning twenty-one and drinking till I puked part of my youth. I'd had a drink here or there, but my birthday was the first time I'd ever been tipsy or drunk. My mother's history with alcohol has made me wary of it.

But I screw up the courage to lick the salt, throw back the tequila that burns its way down my throat, and bite the lemon. My face puckers, though it isn't terrible.

"Yasss, girl!" Daisy encourages. She finishes hers like the pro she is.

A Latin song with a strong beat comes on. Daisy grins, doing a twirl, her skirt flaring out. "And dancing! Dancing helps."

In spite of my self-consciousness, I sway my hips to the intoxicating rhythm.

My shake and shimmy are hesitant, but they must be somewhat effective because a tall, dark-haired guy standing near me who'd been watching as we did our shots meets my eye and grins. He's no Chase James, but he's kind of cute.

I lean into Daisy. "And boys? Do they help?"

She nods. "They're a very fun start."

"To fun, fresh starts!" I yell above the music.

She grins. "To smoking-hot, fresh starts!" she screams back.

And then we throw ourselves into the music. The beat pounds through me. The lights swirl. Cute guy moves in, settling his hands around my waist and dancing close. At first, I'm nervous, not wanting him to feel my not-so-flat stomach.

But something unravels in me. *Fuck it.*

I feel wild and free. I want to let go of my worries and insecurities and live. Starting tonight.

* * *

SEVERAL HOURS, a few more tequilas, and many songs later, I'm knee-deep in a fountain in the middle of a long-since-deserted park. This wouldn't be so alarming, except Daisy is swimming in the shallow fountain. In just her underwear.

Even more alarming? I'm also in the fountain in my bra and panties. I'm not sure how it all happened. One moment, we were giggling and walking arm in arm with a vague plan to hit up another bar, and the next moment, we were in the fountain *sans* clothes. I blame it on the tequila.

"This! Is! Awesome!" Daisy says, doing another shallow dive, and then drapes her dress over the nude male statue that's standing watch over us. "You're not allowed to look," she scolds the naked statue.

I try to float as best as I can in the water, my long hair streaming around me like seaweed. I look up into the night sky. I revel in the magic of the faint stars and city lights.

Until the police siren breaks through my reverie.

Shit. Cops.

Drunk Olivia is going to ruin my life, one bad decision at a time.

I splash to sit up and cover my ample breasts, clad only in a strapless bra. My wild eyes search the area for my dress, which has somehow gone missing. Flashlights train first on Daisy and then on me.

"What seems to be the problem, Officers?" Daisy asks flirtatiously, looking as enticing as a Botticelli babe.

"Ever hear of trespassing?"

The officer, unlike most men, does not seem at all affected by Daisy's brilliant smile and fit body. He looks irritated to be dealing with us. I don't blame him. Dealing with drunk girls swimming in fountains is probably super annoying.

"Or indecency? Or public intoxication?"

My heart is racing now.

"Step out of the fountain," the guy playing bad cop commands.

I look at the second officer with hope. Maybe he'll be the

good cop who lets us off on good behavior. But his glower causes that hope to crash and burn.

Daisy steps out of the fountain with grace, the water streaming down her shoulders and back, her pale-pink lace underwear nearly translucent. Bad cop tries to play it cool, but I see his eyes widen in admiration, which I imagine is Daisy's plan. Dazzle and charm them into letting us go.

I stumble out with far less finesse, trying to hide all my body parts. Luckily, the Spanx and bra I'm wearing cover me more than any bikini. It's still mortifying, though.

"I-I s-seem to have lost my dress," I stutter.

It's bad enough I'm about to be arrested. I have to add humiliation to the mix. I flash a pleading look to Daisy, who slips into her dress in one smooth motion.

She makes her eyes big and stares at me, while rummaging her hand into the purse she left on the edge of the fountain. I see her hand land on her phone. She tilts her head toward a nearby tree. I'm getting a little better at this subterfuge thing, and I think she's trying to tell me to distract the cops so she can call someone.

"Can you help me find my clothes? Please?" I beg the cops and point to the fountain.

Good cop and bad cop seem resigned to their fate as they flash their lights into the fountain. I turn to see Daisy dive into the shadows of the trees while texting madly on her phone.

We find the dress floating on the other side of the fountain, and by the time the cops turn back to Daisy, her phone is stashed away once again. She's looking calm for someone about to get arrested. Glad that makes one of us, I think as I hastily throw on the formerly beautiful dress, which has now shrunk to Barbie size.

Please, Daisy, I pray. *Use some of your magic to get us out of this spot.*

* * *

Hours later, I'm grumpy, exhausted, still wearing my doll-sized dress, and dead sober with the beginning of a pounding headache.

"Where's your sense of adventure?" Daisy asks me.

"Sorry, I don't consider spending the night in a police station and almost getting arrested to be an adventure," I shoot back.

But when I turn to Daisy, my annoyance fizzles just a bit. Despite her bravado, she's a flower wilting fast. Her small frame sags. Her normally sparkling eyes are dull, and even her curls droop under the harsh glare of the police station's ugly fluorescent lights. I give her a hug, and she hugs me back.

"I'm sorry," she says quietly, sounding contrite.

It's my turn to feel guilty. It isn't fair to blame her. There was no gun to my head when I took off my dress and jumped into the fountain. There was a lot of alcohol and the need to prove that I could take risks, but no gun. *Damn tequila. It's even worse than champagne.*

"It's not your fault. I went along with it willingly. And, until the police showed up, I had a great time. Plus, hanging out at the police station is good research for writing mysteries."

"Really?" she asks, a small glimmer in her eyes returning.

"Really," I say. "And you're right. We got off lightly with just a warning. I don't understand how."

"I can't imagine," Daisy says, her eyes innocent.

"Why weren't you more worried?"

She shrugs. "I made a call."

"To whom? Don't tell me one of your admirers is the chief of police?" Though it wouldn't surprise me. Not much about Daisy surprises me anymore.

I push open the station doors and breathe the fresh air. We step out into the early morning light. The sun is just rising, casting its soft glow over the street. Looking into the reflection of the large window fronting the police station, I'm glad it's so early and only a few people are in the streets to see me in my shrunken dress. My black hair hangs lankly against my skull. The bags under my eyes are as dark as Daisy's, and the makeup she put on me earlier is smudged beyond repair. All I want is a long, hot shower and bed.

I'm about to ask Daisy to call for a car because my phone died hours ago, when a long black sedan pulls up beside us.

I step aside, so I don't block the path of whoever is in the car, when the front window rolls down slowly.

Daisy leans into the open window. "Hey," she says to someone. "Are you the driver now?"

"Good morning, Miss Daisy. It's been a long time."

"So, is the big guy in the back?" She turns to look at me and winks while I gape.

The sternly handsome, dark-haired man in the driver's seat smiles fondly at her. "See for yourself. I heard you needed a ride."

"You just want to say you're driving Miss Daisy," she teases with a laugh. "Get it? It never gets old!" Daisy turns. "Ready to go?" She says it casually, as if getting picked up by a man in a strange car after spending the night at the police station is an everyday occurrence. Maybe it is for her. But me? Not so much.

"Erm, Daisy? What's going on? Are we getting abducted by the mafia as payback for them springing us from jail? 'Cause I have to call Audrey and tell her I can't come to work this week if that's the case." I know I sound cranky, but I'm tired and out of patience.

She flashes me a saucy look. "Are you ready for another adventure, Olivia?"

"No," I say with certainty. "Abso-freaking-lutely not."

"Too bad," Daisy retorts as the back door swings open, and she steps into the darkened interior.

"Wait! Daisy!" I hiss, trying to stop her. This is the thing about being a writer. My imagination presents me with all sorts of scenarios—being abducted and sold as a sex slave is currently topping the list. She ignores me, so I have no choice but to crawl in after her. It's the girl code.

Once in the car, I enter an alternate universe, one that's dark, cool, and luxurious. There's a bar in the corner with cut-glass decanters, and the scent of new leather and sandalwood engulfs my senses.

As my eyes adjust, I realize a man is sitting in the corner. My gaze shifts from large sneakers, up to long, strong legs encased in well-worn denim, and then to a wide, muscular chest emphasized by a dark gray T-shirt. I take in a strong jaw with a bristling of a five o'clock shadow, sensual lips, a straight, aquiline nose, and intense green eyes that burn over every part of my body.

Familiar eyes. Eyes I've been dreaming of this whole week.

"Wha-what are *you* doing here?"

CHAPTER 12

livia

CHASE JAMES LOOKS JUST as shocked as me.

He whips his head from me to Daisy and back to me. "What's going on? What are you doing here?" Chase asks in confusion. His gaze shifts to my body, gets snagged there, and then returns to my face.

I try to pull down my dress, but it doesn't help. It now has too little fabric for too much body. When I dreamed that I'd someday see Chase James again, I hadn't pictured this.

"Me?" I squeak as I swipe at my smudged eye makeup. "What are *you* doing here?" I repeat.

"Chase, meet my friend Olivia. Olivia, meet Chase James, my foster brother," Daisy says. "Though, for some interesting reason, it seems like the two of you are already acquainted." She tilts her head in question.

"You're Daisy's brother?"

"You're Daisy's friend?"

"Why didn't you tell me Chase was your brother, the other

day when I was—I, ah…never mind," I mumble in mortification, not wanting to out myself as having searched him online.

"When what?" Chase asks, his eyes bright with interest.

"It must have slipped my mind." Daisy stretches out her legs in the back of the car. "Maybe the same way it slipped your mind that you already knew Chase. And you still haven't said how you know him?"

I try to angle my knees demurely, in such a way that I don't flash anyone because of my teeny tiny dress, but I only succeed in brushing against Chase's knees in the tight space. "He, um…" Shit. Busted.

"I stopped for coffee a few times where she works. It's only a few blocks from the Heights," he explains smoothly, omitting our conversations and The Kiss.

"And you didn't stop by my house?" Daisy asks, sounding hurt.

"It was early in the morning, Daisy. I just stopped after a run. You wouldn't even have been awake. I called you last night, remember? I wanted to surprise you today with a visit. I had no idea you'd be calling me for a get-out-of-jail emergency."

"And you failed to mention this?" Daisy asks me pointedly.

"It didn't come up!"

Daisy snorts.

"Also, I thought he wouldn't want anyone to know. It didn't seem right to broadcast it," I defend. "And you didn't mention who your brother is either."

Chase runs a hand through his hair. "That's not Daisy's fault. We try to keep our foster-sibling relationship quiet."

"But why?" I ask.

Instead of answering, he looks at Daisy.

"The first reason is because Chase is insanely overprotective." Daisy rolls her eyes.

"With good reason," he shoots back.

"It's a long story," Daisy says to me, interrupting whatever else Chase was about to say. "Too long to get into now, but I promise I'll share it with you one day. Basically, the few times people have found out about our connection, they've tried to sell the story to the tabloids."

"That's terrible!" I exclaim. "But I would never do that."

Chase massages the back of his neck, bringing my attention to the veins on his forearms. How can forearms be so attractive? But when my eyes meet his, I feel guilty for getting distracted. His eyes are stormy. Clearly, this is a topic that upsets him.

"It's not just a matter of trusting someone's motives," he says, his brows drawing down in a frown. "If it accidentally gets out, or if I'm photographed with Daisy, her life will be splashed all over social media and the tabloids, with lies dragging her down. No one even knows my real background or that I was a foster kid in the system. So, if they found out about Daisy, the press will be all over the story, and she'll be caught in the crossfire."

"You can't protect everyone and everything, Chase," Daisy says. "I'm not afraid of the tabloids or rumors. I'm also not as young and stupid as I was that summer I stayed with you. What happened then never will again. I promise."

Chase snorts. "You're telling me I don't need to protect you anymore when I just kept you from being arrested? What the hell do you think you were doing? Do you know how many favors Duncan had to call in to get you out? These little stunts have got to stop, Daisy. And you're not to involve Olivia in them. Do you understand?"

I look from Daisy to Chase and back again, not knowing what to say. I'm a little worried that Daisy will get mad at Chase's heavy-handed reproach. Daisy, mad, is fearsome to behold.

But instead of getting angry, she surprises me by leaning over and hugging him tight. "I'm sorry, Chase. Thank you for rescuing us."

He stares at her, as if he's not sure whether to hug her back or to shake her. Finally, his tight posture relaxes and his lips quirk in an affectionate half-smile. He ruffles her hair and gives her a quick kiss to the top of her head.

"I missed you, Daisy, even though you're a menace."

"You love that I'm a menace."

His soft smile makes my stomach tilt. "Maybe. Sometimes," he says.

My heart warms at watching their obvious affection. I have so many questions. How long were they foster siblings? Was their bond formed in a loving family, or forged in the fire of pain and neglect? I pray it was the former but fear the latter. Daisy never speaks of her childhood or parents, but I've always had the sense there is trauma in her past.

I've been so focused on the drama in the back seat, I'm surprised when the car smoothly slows, and I realize we're in front of Daisy's store. She lives in the apartment above her vintage shop. I always assumed she was a renter. For the first time, though, I wonder if Chase owns the building, if he bought it for her. He must be a millionaire many times over.

"Thanks for the ride, big bro," Daisy says. She gives him a kiss on the cheek.

He returns the gesture with a quick hug. "I'll call you later so we can meet up before I have to head back to LA. I figure you'll probably need to catch up on sleep today, but I want to see what you've done with the store. I'm proud of you for sticking with it and building your business."

"You never said why you're in town." Daisy looks pleased with the compliment but tries to hide her smile and shifts the subject away from her.

"I had to take care of some business."

"You're being evasive. You do that thing with your eyes when you're hiding something."

Silence lengthens. She shakes her head and slides over to the door, opening it. "You're lucky I'm too tired to interrogate you further."

"Just get some rest, brat. I'll talk to you later." He shifts to me. "I'll drop you in front of your house, Olivia. I think you said you live on this block?" Chase's words halt me mid-scoot toward the car's door. I don't recall saying that, but maybe I did when we talked in the café.

"It's just a few houses down, and there aren't any other parking spaces free on the block," I point out as I try to step out of the car as gracefully as Daisy did while holding on to the hem of my dress so I don't flash a movie star.

I stumble onto the sidewalk. The wind is especially strong this morning, and I shiver, wishing for the hundredth time that I'd worn a coat last night. Hell, even a scarf would be nice.

"Here. You'll freeze," Chase says. I turn in surprise to see that he's slid out of the car also and is standing next to me, tall and protective. He drapes his jacket over my shoulders. Soft fabric that smells like cedar, spice, and heaven envelops me. His eyes are hot and hard, scanning my scantily covered body.

Our eyes hold. "Thank you," I manage to whisper.

I turn to see the large driver leaning against the SUV, his eyes roaming up and down the street, as if assessing it for hidden danger. Daisy, who has always been immune to the cold, stands on the steps of her house with a speculative look in her eye.

"Duncan," Chase says, "Slight change of plans. Since we're here, why don't you go in with Daisy and do a quick security assessment in her store and apartment now? See if she needs a new alarm system."

Daisy huffs out a breath. "I have an alarm, and it's fine, Chase. Stop being so overprotective."

"Humor me. I know you're tired, but it will only take a few minutes, and I'll sleep better knowing you're safe."

She sighs, but waves Duncan toward her house. "Come on,

big guy. You can come home with me. You coming too, Chase?" Daisy asks.

"In a few minutes," he says. I feel his gaze on me, and it makes me shiver even more than the wind. "I'll walk Olivia home first, make sure she gets there safe."

"Are you sure that's wise?" Duncan asks.

The neighborhood is quiet except for a lady walking her dog farther down the street and a few men waiting for the bus on the corner.

"I'll be quick."

Duncan nods, though with the hard set of his jaw, he does not seem pleased.

I suddenly feel shy. Flustered, I turn to Daisy to say goodbye.

She grins at me. "See you later, Olivia. Sorry again for, you know, the whole getting arrested thing."

"I should've known better." I laugh.

"Let's break up this party now," Duncan urges again, putting a hand at Daisy's back to move her forward.

She pulls keys out of her sparkly bag and opens the smaller door at the far side of her shop, which leads to her upstairs apartment. She says something to Duncan and laughs teasingly as he follows her in.

The door shuts behind them, and I'm acutely aware of Chase's commanding presence next to me. I clear my throat.

"My house is this way." I point to the end of the block. "But you really don't need to walk me home."

I can't figure out why he's still here. I pull his coat tighter around me. Why did he give it to me? He didn't put the coat on his sister, Daisy, even though she was dressed almost as scantily as me. I give him a side glance, my heart stuttering as I take in that famous profile.

"I want to," he says.

I follow him toward my house in bewildered excitement. His steps are slow, as if matching the stride of my shorter legs. I can't figure him out. Silence stretches as we walk side by side, arms almost touching. The click-clack of my heels is loud in the stillness of the street.

"Well, here's my place," I say when we get to the pale-pink Victorian.

I try to see the house I know and love so well through his eyes. It seems older, sadder. The sagging steps and chipped paint are like glaring scars on the once-elegant visage. He probably lives in some ultramodern palace with nothing out of place.

"It's beautiful," he says.

When I turn to him, he's looking at me and not the house.

"Just like I imagined," he murmurs, tearing his gaze from mine and taking in my childhood home, as if fascinated.

"Imagined?"

A car passes, and he turns his head, his arm coming up to block his face. It reminds me we're in the open, where anyone could walk by and snatch a photo.

But would that really be so bad?

"Well, I guess this is goodbye?" I don't know why I say it like a question. He's leaving tomorrow. This will be the last time I'll see him, unless you count on a movie screen or in a magazine. Sadness flickers at that thought.

A line forms between his eyes. "I guess it is." His voice, low and rough, skates over my nerve endings.

But instead of walking away, he closes the distance between us with a step. My pulse races. A gust of wind whips my hair into my face, but I don't move. I can't. I'm frozen by his intoxicating nearness and intent gaze. He leans down and pushes my hair back with gentle fingers, tucking the strands behind my ear.

I snuggle deeper into his jacket. It smells of him, as if I'm being wrapped in his embrace. I don't want to give it back. Ever.

The silence between us stretches like a band about to break.

Take a risk, Olivia. You won't get this chance again. Don't waste it. That thought whispers through my mind, as clear as if Nanna is standing next to me speaking it.

"You must be tired. Can I offer you a cup of coffee?" I say before I change my mind. "You can take it to-go. If I know Daisy, she doesn't have much more than a box of Pop-Tarts and maybe olives for martinis in her kitchen. It's the least I can do."

As embarrassed as I am at my forwardness, I'm also proud. There's a rush of freedom that flows through me. *I took a risk.*

He doesn't say anything for a long minute, as if debating my offer. My fledgling pride at my boldness starts to deflate. Gah. Risks are overrated.

"Never mind. You must be so busy."

"No, I mean yes—I'd love to. Duncan will be a while. And you're right. The odds that Daisy has coffee are not good." His gaze flicks over my abundant cleavage before returning to my face, and I self-consciously burrow myself into his jacket.

"Awesome! Great!" And then I panic, trying to remember if I tidied up before I left for the club last night. I'm generally neat. I actually enjoy keeping a clean house and find domestic chores relaxing. But even so, there is normal neat, and then there is entertaining-the-Sexiest-Man-Alive neat.

He follows me up the stairs, and I'm conscious of the drooping roses. No matter how hard I try, I don't have the green thumb Nanna did. And then my awareness shifts to something even more alarming. He's behind me while we walk up the stairs. Why the hell am I worrying about my gardening skills when Chase James is getting an up close and personal look at my cellulite in the light of day?

I tug my dress down with one hand while my other roots around my purse for keys. I come up empty. Finally, my fingers settle on a familiar metal shape in the corner of my bag.

"Hurrah!" I hold up the keys in triumph.

When Chase smirks like he is now, one side of his mouth curves higher than the other. It's so ridiculously sexy.

After I get the door open, I usher Chase into the house. Early morning light filters through the lace curtains in the bay window, settling a soft glow on my cluttered, cozy home.

Chase studies the photos that cover the wall of the entry hall. "You?" he asks, nodding toward a photo of a dark-haired girl reading a book.

I smile. "My brand was strong even from the beginning."

"Brand?"

"Quiet, bookish girl. Only thing I grew out of was the pigtails."

"I don't know. I think you'd look cute in pigtails."

His smile is warm, and when our eyes meet, all my thoughts flee.

He returns his attention to the pictures. A nude woman in shadow poses among sand dunes, juxtaposed against a tree. The light is like a blade, cutting sharply through the image with deep blacks and highlights. Another photo from the series that I'll probably need to sell next.

"My nanna," I say. "She was a model when she was younger, before she married my grandfather and became a photographer herself." I gesture to a series of photos on the wall. "After Granddad died, she went full circle and photographed male nudes. When I was young, I'd come home from school, and all the furniture in the living room would be rearranged and there'd be naked models posing, everything hanging out. She was scandalous," I say with a grin.

"And what about you? Do you have a scandalous side?" he asks, tilting his head as he assesses me.

I can't help but laugh. "Only in my imagination. I save that for the stories I write. I've been told I have an old soul. It's hard to be a badass when you're twenty-five going on eighty-five, you know?"

"You just swam in a fountain and almost got arrested. That's scandalous."

"That's all Daisy," I protest. But secretly, I'm a little pleased he sees me that way.

We're standing so close that if he leans down, and I stand on tiptoes, our lips will meet.

Don't jump him. Don't embarrass yourself.

He breaks the spell by stepping away and wanders over to three typewriters sitting in an orderly row on one of the floor-to-ceiling shelves that line the wall. He presses a key, then shoots me a glance. "Typewriters?"

"My mom was a writer, and she always wrote on a typewriter. She hated computers." I don't mention that she was a famous writer, a name most Americans would recognize immediately, even if they hadn't actually read a word she'd written.

"At one time, we had about ten typewriters. These are the last of them." I think about Remington. What would he say if I told him about Chase James being in my house? About the unexpected kiss?

I look down and spread my hands. "I don't know why I told you all that. I babble when I get nervous."

He frowns. "I wanted to know. I asked you about them, didn't I? Why are you nervous around me?"

"Are you kidding?" I laugh self-consciously. "I have a movie star in my living room, and we're talking about typewriters. It's been a weird night. And maybe an even weirder morning."

He runs a hand through his hair. "Could you ever see me as a regular guy, not a movie star?" he asks tightly, as if he's not really sure he wants to know the answer.

"Let's face it, you'll never be just a regular guy, even if you weren't famous. You're ridiculously beautiful." I slap a hand over my mouth. "Oh shit. Did I just say that out loud?" There's a five-alarm fire of a blush happening on my face.

He leans down so close that I can see golden flecks in his eyes. "You can't call a guy beautiful." His low rasp sends tingles down my spine. "And I'm glad you told me a little about your family. I wanted to know."

I try to ignore the feel of his breath against my cheek. I want to touch him. I want him to touch me. To kiss me. Everything about him draws me in, so I step away on shaky legs before I'm nothing but a pile of want at his feet.

I still don't understand why he's here. Why he's interested. "It's just… You ask a lot of questions. That's not a critique. But you can't possibly be that intrigued by my life."

"Why do you say that?"

I wave at him. "Because you're—"

"Don't say it again. Don't say 'Chase James' like that."

I shrug. "But you are."

"And you're a beautiful girl who I was damn lucky to kiss one morning."

Holy shit. "I thought you'd forgotten that."

"Did you forget it?"

"No! Of course not."

"Then why would I?"

"Because you're yo—"

"I know, I know. Back to that again. Because I'm Chase James." He sighs and looks out the window. "Can you pretend that I'm just some guy named Chase with a normal job?"

"Like a pizza maker? Or an orthodontist?"

One corner of his mouth turns up. "Or a hat salesman."

I think for a moment. "Maybe an elevator repairman."

"A basket weaver," he suggests.

I pretend to consider it. Then shake my head. "Nah. Can't do it. You're a star. Even if you never make another movie, it's embedded in your DNA and very hard to ignore."

"Stubborn girl." But the way he says it is like an endearment.

"Coffee!" I exclaim in desperation before I throw myself into his arms. With my heartbeat on accelerate, I wander into the kitchen in a daze. I say some calming mantras in my head, but that doesn't work either, so I pull out the tin with coffee in it and fill the well of the coffeemaker with water. The familiar action settles me a bit.

The normally bright and cheery kitchen is still a little dim, so I turn on a light. We never had the money to update the wood counters or the ancient appliances, but I'm glad. Everything is familiar, worn with years of love, from the blue-and-yellow curtains that Nanna said reminded her of a summer in Provence to the sunshine yellow walls I painted myself.

Chase is standing tall, again taking in every inch of the room with an odd intensity. My house couldn't be more opposite from glamorous Hollywood. But then again, I never did believe all that glitters is gold. Tarnish adds character.

We don't talk as the coffee brews, but it's not awkward now. There's ease in this quiet. When the coffee is ready, I pour him a cup.

"This is the way you like it, right? Black?"

He smiles. "You remember."

"You can take the girl out of the barista, but not the barista out of the girl, or something like that."

We take our coffee to the living room and sit on the couch together, watching as the morning sun moves a little higher and the streets begin to fill. I try not stare at him too awkwardly as we make idle chitchat. Mostly, he asks me questions and I answer the best I can, while trying to think of questions for him that don't feel too intrusive to his well-guarded privacy. But under our words there's an intensity, a weight, the silent refrain that this is goodbye.

I savor every glance he gives me, every smile, every gesture, storing them up so I can take them out when I'm old and gray and need something romantic to remember, when I want to think of the day I had a superstar's eyes lingering on me as if I was someone special.

Finally, he sets his cup down on the coffee table, and his long legs unfold as he stands. "I better go. Daisy must be wondering what happened to me, and my hat won't be much of a disguise now. I don't want to cause problems by being spotted leaving your house."

"Of course." I hop up.

"It's safer if you don't walk me out. I don't want anyone to see us on the street together."

"Oh! I'm still wearing your coat." I slip out of his jacket and hand it to him reluctantly, not wanting to part with this tangible connection of him. Our hands brush and I feel a jolt of electricity between us.

Even though he said not to see him out, I don't want to say goodbye just yet. So, I grab my favorite long gray cardigan from the coatrack and wrap myself up in it for modesty and warmth, then walk him to the door, opening it for him. Our footsteps slow as we stand framed in the large doorway. I'm running out of excuses to keep him with me.

It's a long shot, but suddenly, I'm gripped by the need for this not to be goodbye forever. "Will you be visiting San Francisco again soon?"

"No." Just that one word, and my hopes are rubble at my feet.

He swings his head toward the little park across the street. "Did you see that?" His eyes fix on something in the distance.

I crane my neck but don't see anything out of the ordinary. The park still looks peaceful at this early hour. "No? What?"

A cat jumps out of some bushes at the edge of the park and chases a squirrel up a tree.

Chase's posture relaxes. "It's nothing."

"So, um... I guess this is goodbye, then." My heart twists at the thought.

The thread connecting us pulls tight. I sway toward him as he leans down. We move like we're underwater, slow, with every motion exaggerated in a sea of longing and anticipation. My eyes close. His stubble brushes against my cheek, pinpricks of sensation shooting through me. My lips open a fraction in silent invitation. But his lips brush my cheek instead.

And then…nothing. Only cold air against my skin and a pit of loss in my stomach. My eyes pop open in confusion. He steps away, his face shuttered now.

"Goodbye," he says. And then, just like that, he walks down my steps and out of my life. Again.

* * *

"So, *Chase James* is your foster brother? You need to explain this. Now!"

I'm sitting in Daisy's boutique, drinking an extra-large coffee, something I desperately need to get through the day after the all-nighter we pulled at the police station. I'd been right about Daisy not having coffee, so we got to-go cups from Books & Buns.

We're curled up on a '70s-era velvet love seat at the back of the shop, surrounded by glamorous dresses. Though it's 2:00 p.m. on a weekday, Daisy's store sign reads "Closed" as we sip our coffee.

When Daisy just smiles, I try again. "Chase James is your brother."

"Yes, of course," she says with a delicate shrug. She readjusts what I think is a caftan, in a flowing gold-and-white material. Her hair is caught in a loose bun at the top of her head, with wild tendrils escaping and curling down her neck and back.

Her casual glamour makes me feel even more basic in my faded jeans and cozy sweater that's gotten stretched out and soft from years of washes.

"I'm just having a hard time wrapping my brain around it. How did you fail to tell me that your foster brother is one of the most famous men on the planet?"

Daisy sighs. "I know this is weird. But I'm not used to talking about Chase. You can't fully understand unless you know the whole story." She tilts her head, her gaze faraway.

"Well then," I say expectantly. "Tell me."

She snaps her head back to me. "Okay," she says, as if suddenly deciding something. "When I first met Chase, we were just kids. I was only six. He was a few years older than me when he was placed in my parents' house as my foster brother. I was my parents' only biological child, but they took in foster kids for the extra money. They should've never had any children, let alone foster ones. They were both messed up, both mean drunks and abusive in their own ways, but they were able to play the system for a long time."

"I'm so sorry, Daisy." I wish I could take the bad memories away.

She smiles, but it doesn't reach her eyes. "Everything changed for me when Chase came to live with us. I never had a family who cared about me. But the two of us, we became each other's family. He was my caretaker, my protector. He stole food for me when my mom was passed out and our cupboards were bare. He got me up for school, helped me with my homework, and even made up bedtime stories."

My stomach does a funny little dance at getting this glimpse into who Chase is. "He sounds like a great big brother," I say softly.

Her eyes are lost in the past. "He was, as long as he was allowed to be. It was just Chase and me against the world until, one night, a neighbor called the cops during one of my dad's drunken rages. I broke something, and my dad took his belt to me, hard. He'd been drinking even more at that point. Chase retaliated, and my dad went ballistic, beating him. The cops came and took my dad away. The next day, when I got home from school, Chase was gone. Social services sent him somewhere else.

"My mom moved us in with a boyfriend she'd had on the

side. My dad had started beating her more regularly, as well. I remember being distraught because I knew Chase would come back for me, and when he did, he wouldn't be able to find me. We moved around a lot after that. My mom had a lot of shit boyfriends, and it was more difficult than it had been before, maybe because after having someone to care for me, it was even harder to have no one again."

Daisy looks at me with a sad smile on her usually sunny face. "Chase was always my brother, even if we weren't blood."

"I'm glad you had him." I cover her hand with mine and squeeze. "You deserved so much more, Daisy." And in that moment, I'm so grateful for Nanna it hurts. I had her my whole life growing up. Other than those years with Chase, Daisy had no one to love her properly.

She flashes me a shaky grin. "And then one day, the craziest thing happened. I was at a convenience store, and there he was, on the cover of a tabloid. Chase, my brother. I recognized him immediately. This was just before the first *Wanderers* came out.

"I was sixteen, and my mom's shitty new boyfriend had started coming into my room at night. I'd managed to hold him off, but I needed somewhere else to go. Fast. So I researched some fan sites and found out where Chase lived. I snuck out, took several buses, and walked the rest of the way to his gate." She laughs. "It was a fancy estate in Malibu, and I managed to sneak past the guards, climbed a fence, and…"

"And what?" I lean forward.

"And the guards caught me, of course." She shakes her head. "It's a miracle I wasn't arrested. Chase came home, and I can't believe he still recognized me. I didn't look anything like the girl he'd known anymore. But he took me in that night, no hesitation, no questions asked."

My mind can't comprehend Daisy—shiny, happy, always smiling Daisy—going through all that.

"What happened next?"

"It gets worse before it gets better," she continues, her narrow shoulders slumping. "That whole summer, I stayed with Chase. I was too afraid to go to the authorities, too afraid to go home. I was broken and wild. Sebastian and Ryder treated me like a little sister as well."

"Sebastian. As in Sebastian Blake?"

She nods.

"And *Ryder*?" I cry. "You lived with Ryder Black? So, when you said you had a crush on him, you weren't talking about a fantasy crush. You actually know him."

Her wry smile dims. "He just thought of me as a kid, which made me mad because he wasn't much older than me. But they were all gentle and sweet with me, even though I was miserable and pushed everyone's buttons. I was so messed up after everything that had happened."

She averts her eyes, playing with the rim of her coffee cup. "I watched movies all day and didn't go out. Chase kept trying to get me to see a therapist. He said we had to make arrangements, that he couldn't hide me forever. He was right.

"Sebastian had these parties. Chase would always watch over me, make sure I didn't get into any trouble. And Ryder was just as protective as Chase. But one night, Chase was working late, and Ryder had a date with some model. They told me to stay in my room, but I didn't listen. I'd been crushing hard on Ryder all summer, so I was wild with jealousy. I got smashed and left with a random guy. All I wanted was someone to distract me so I didn't hurt anymore and prove that I wasn't the child Ryder thought of me as, but instead, I got into a bad situation. I called Chase in the middle of the night on set. He came and literally carried me out of some club. But we were photographed. The tabloids went crazy. The only blessing was they didn't get a clear picture of my face."

"I remember reading something about that," I say, shocked it was my friend. I didn't follow celebrities, so it must have been a scandal if even I heard about it.

She nods. "It was all over. They thought I was his new girlfriend. They called me ugly, a gold digger, a whore, a mess. I couldn't stop reading the comments and the fan sites. It was horrible and everything that was written just reinforced what I'd been hearing all my life from my dad, my mom, and the assholes she dated. I felt as if everything I touched went to hell."

"Daisy, none of that is true."

She inspects her manicure, refusing to meet my eyes. I can't imagine Daisy with low self-esteem. She's always been self-confidence personified. But maybe I'm not the only one who tries to hide. Maybe we just hide in different ways.

She takes a deep breath before continuing, "I was tired of being a burden, of hurting, of being such a mess. So, I...I found pills in one of the guest rooms that someone had left and swallowed them all."

"Daisy!" I hug her close to my side. I'm surprised at how small she feels, because she's got such a huge personality. I'm not sure how long we stay like that, but my eyes mist as I think about how much pain she must have been in to be that self-destructive.

She sniffs and pulls away with an awkward laugh, wiping tears from under her eyes. "I'm fine now. I don't think I truly wanted to die, but I wanted everything to stop for a while—all the confusion, all the hurt. They got me to the hospital and kept everything as hush-hush as they could.

"If it got out who I was, no one would believe the brother-sister story since we weren't technically related. An underage runaway staying with three megastars was bad enough, but add in a suicide attempt and drugs? It would be a PR nightmare. I don't know how they did it, but all three with their star power kept it quiet. It must have cost a fortune."

She looks at me through wet lashes. "I told you it wasn't a

pretty story. But it does get better. I don't know if it was almost dying or the therapy I got in the treatment center, but I turned my life around. Chase managed to arrange it so that I moved in with a nice family to finish high school, and I got accepted at the Art Institute, which is how I came to San Francisco. Unfortunately, I wasn't any better at college than I was at high school, so I started my vintage business with Chase's help."

"I-I don't even know what to say. I never could have imagined any of it."

Daisy laughs. "No one could. Which is good. All this secrecy, it's because Chase feels like he needs to protect me. He doesn't want to risk me being in the tabloids or getting attacked on social media again. And he fears that if we get photographed together, the story of that summer might finally come out. I think he's petrified that I'll have another breakdown if that happens. I keep trying to tell him that I'm stronger now." She grants me a wry smile. "So, you still want to be friends with this drama girl?"

"Daisy, you're amazing. Whatever happened in the past has made you the incredible person you are. This just makes me prouder to call you my friend."

"Right back at you," Daisy says with a watery laugh. "Now, it's your turn to explain what happened when you met Chase and why you didn't tell me about it."

I look away from her too-insightful gaze. "Nothing happened. He bought coffee. It wasn't a big deal."

She shoots me a skeptical look. "Olivia, I think there's more that you aren't telling me, but I won't pry. At least not right now because I'm too damn tired. But here's the thing about Chase. He may seem like he's got it all together, and he does. He's got money and success now. But in a lot of ways, he's still that foster kid who's afraid to trust. And his issues with fame make trusting even harder. After what happened with me, he's so afraid of letting people in and hurting them, losing them, even if he won't admit it. But he needs and deserves someone special in his life he *can* trust. More than he realizes."

I nod, my mind full of thoughts about Chase. My idea of him recalibrating with everything Daisy has said. "Daisy, I think you're imagining more between us than there is. I've only had a few brief conversations with him. Honestly, I'll probably never see him again."

Daisy smiles. "Hmmm. Well, I don't think that's precisely true."

I tilt my head. "What do you mean?"

"Want to do me a favor?"

"It depends on the favor," I say with a wry expression.

"Don't worry. It's one I think you'll like."

CHAPTER 13

livia

THE NEXT DAY, I stand at the door of Chase James's hotel room, carrying a box that contains a gift for him from Daisy and a tin of home-baked cookies from me. I've been standing here for way too long, but I can't quite force myself to knock.

Get it together, Olivia, I lecture myself.

I'm not some fan stalking the guy. I'm here on a Daisy-sent delivery mission. I'm doing my friend a favor.

Daisy asked me to deliver this gift to Chase because she had some sort of vintage-fashion emergency and had to leave town. She told me to apologize for her, and that she would be back in San Francisco in a few days and would call him then.

It occurs to me that she might be matchmaking, but that doesn't make sense. I'm a San Francisco girl who works in a bookstore. He's a Hollywood star. In what world could we ever make a good match? It's all a little odd. Though, admittedly, so is Daisy.

Regardless, I don't question the favor. I'm not stupid. Of

course, I jumped at the chance.

I consider this my risk for the day.

Before I left on my little "movie star errand," I baked him a batch of Nanna's famous chocolate chip cookies. It's the least I can do.

Yesterday afternoon, a crew came to my house, ready to install a fancy and way-too-complicated alarm system. I called Daisy and tried to tell her I didn't need an alarm and couldn't afford one even if I did, but she said Chase insisted on it.

I'm not sure why he'd care about my safety one way or another, but maybe that's just the kind of celebrity he is. Walking around gifting girls alarm systems and kisses. There's also the little matter of him keeping me from jail. It would be rude not to thank him properly, which means with baked goods.

That's the only reason I got up extra early to do my makeup and changed ten times before settling on just the right pair of broken-in skinny jeans, the only thing I own that's formfitting, and a white top that makes my breasts look great, if I do say so myself. So here I am, standing at his door, with mouthwatering cookies, looking as good as I can, and all I want to do is bolt.

This is my daily risk, I remind myself before knocking three times as decisively as I can.

After a few minutes and a few more tentative knocks, I'm equal parts relieved and disappointed that the door remains closed. I'm about to give up and leave a note when the door swings open.

My mind blanks. I try to speak, but when I open my mouth, there's nothing there.

"Olivia," Chase says, his voice even deeper and rougher than usual.

"Hi. You-you're, um…"

Shirtless. All he's wearing are loose sweats that ride low on that magnificent Hollywood body of his.

I gesture to his bare, broad chest, all gleaming skin and

muscles.

I'm so transfixed by his body, it takes a minute to realize he's just barely hanging on to the door handle. He sways on his feet, and I come out of my stupor long enough to notice that his gleaming chest matches his glistening face. For the hottest man alive, he looks a little green. Don't get me wrong; even looking like death is a good look for him, such is the power of his cheekbones, but he is definitely not well.

"Are you okay?" I ask. I reach up on my tiptoes to feel his forehead. "You're burning up!"

My worry outweighs my shyness. "You need to sit down."

I balance the box and cookies in one arm, grab him with my other, and pull us into his hotel suite. I manage to steer him toward the couch that has a pile of throw blankets on it. Half-filled glasses of various liquids clutter the side table. He looks as if he's been camped on the couch for a while.

I set my items on the glass coffee table, fluff a throw pillow, and pat the couch. Despite swaying, he remains standing.

"Why are you here?"

He doesn't sound annoyed, just confused.

"Daisy asked me to deliver a gift to you. I think it's a very hipster vintage jacket, but don't tell her I ruined the surprise," I babble. "She gave me your room number and a secret name to tell the reception so they'd let me up. Jay Gatsby, huh? Very literary. Anyway, she would have come herself, but she had to go to Santa Barbara for her store at the last minute. I also brought you cookies." I gesture to the tin. "I wanted to thank you for helping us not get arrested and for the alarm system. I didn't know how to repay you, and everyone likes cookies. They're chocolate chip." I taper off.

I clear my throat and start again. "Anyway. None of that's important right now. You have to sit down," I urge. "You're about to fall over. And you're way too big for me to drag off the floor if you collapse."

He looks ready to argue, but then he turns even paler. "Maybe I will sit down after all," he mutters and sinks to the couch, resting his head on the back of the cushion.

I fuss over him, pulling up the soft blanket. "Are you hot or cold?"

"Yes," he says through chattering teeth.

"That's an either-or question."

"Both. I'm sweating but freezing," he explains.

"Did you take any medicine to lower the fever?"

He shakes his head. "I tried, but it didn't stay down. I started to feel like shit after stopping at a food truck yesterday afternoon."

I groan. "Was it the food truck a few blocks away? By the flower shop?"

"I think?"

"Mexican fusion?"

"Yes."

"You didn't happen to get the seafood tacos?"

"Don't say the word seafood," he pleads.

"Oh no. Been there, done that. Pretty sure you have food poisoning. Can you hold anything down at all?"

"I haven't tried in a while."

"You need electrolytes. My grandma always gave me ginger ale when I was sick. Do you have anything like that, or maybe a sports drink?"

He shakes his head.

"What about someone who can take care of you?" It's none of my business. But I'm concerned.

"I don't need anyone. I'm a big boy, Olivia," he mumbles.

"Daisy's gone all weekend, so she can't come to help," I say, thinking. "What about Duncan? Can he take care of you?"

He makes a noise that might have been a snort. "Duncan's a bodyguard, not a nurse. He's not here, anyway. He has the day off."

I bite my lip. "What about your assistant? Don't all Hollywood stars have personal assistants?"

"Emma's in LA. And she'd be worse than Duncan. Not exactly the warm, fuzzy type," he mutters. "I need to close my eyes for a minute. The room won't stop spinning."

I watch him as he rests with his eyes closed, and I get lost in the masculine beauty of his features. I marvel that, despite his perfect appearance, he's human, fallible, sick.

His breathing turns deep and regular in just under a minute. I stand over him, unsure of what to do now. I know what I can't do. I can't just leave him here with no one to help if his fever spikes or he becomes dangerously dehydrated. There's nothing worse than being sick and not having anyone to care for you.

After Nanna died, I came down with the flu. I remember feeling so alone and longing to be a little girl again, to be fussed over with fresh-squeezed orange juice and lullabies. I wanted to be surprised with comic books and my favorite TV shows as I recovered.

None of that happened. Instead, I had to get to the doctor's office by myself, sick and feverish, and then once home, I managed on my own, dragging myself to the kitchen when I was hungry to scrounge up whatever I could. It was lonely and scary. I could have called Daisy or Audrey, but I hated bothering anyone. I hate asking for favors. And though they're friends, they aren't responsible for me.

I can't leave Chase like this, I decide. He may not like it, but I'm here regardless of what he says. It wouldn't be right to walk out the door when he's so sick, even if I'm worried about overstepping.

So I get busy—clearing the dirty dishes, straightening books and magazines. It surprises me how many books he has in the hotel room for this short trip. He hadn't been exaggerating when he said he loved reading. Why that makes me happy, I'm not going to analyze.

His hotel room, the penthouse suite, is unlike any I've ever been in. It's luxurious, spacious, and equipped with a stocked gourmet kitchen.

First things first. I need to get him some ginger ale and other foods he might be able to keep down. There's a small market half a block away. I look around and find a key card in a sleeve on the counter. I feel guilty taking it but justify that it's for his own good. Thirty minutes later, I'm back with a bag of provisions.

Chase is still sleeping deeply when I return. I put a ginger ale by his side, debating whether I should wake him to drink some, but he looks so peaceful, I decide against it. I get to work making chicken soup, Nanna's cure-all for whatever ails.

When the soup is simmering on low and the kitchen cleaned, I check on him again. His sleep is more restless now, and his skin is heated, so I take his temperature with the forehead thermometer I bought. It's high, but not alarmingly so, and I don't want to risk medicine upsetting his stomach. I wake him up long enough to get him to take more sips of ginger ale.

He falls back asleep immediately.

I kneel next to him and can't help watching as he sleeps. Shirtless, he's a revelation. All those bronzed muscles. His stubble softens his face, making him more approachable.

I sigh and lay a cool cloth on his forehead, my fingers running through his hair in a rhythmic, hopefully soothing, gesture. I'm not sure how long I stay like that with the cool cloth, my fingers stroking across his hair and face, but it's long enough for the light and shadows to shift across the slowly darkening suite.

Chase makes a soft sound, and I pull back my hand, afraid of being caught like a thief, stealing things that aren't mine to take.

I go back to the kitchen, looking for something else to do. Keeping my hands occupied will help me keep them off the sick man on the couch.

CHAPTER 14

hase

I WAKE TO A BURNING THROAT, a pounding headache, and an incredible smell wafting through the hotel suite. My eyes feel too heavy to open just yet. Do I smell…chicken soup? I open one eye, noting the twilight city skyline through the floor-to-ceiling windows.

Why am I asleep on the couch, and how long have I been out? Foggy memories come slowly into focus. Olivia. I answered the door, and she was here. With cookies. She looked worried and told me to rest. I try to hold on to the feeling that comes over me, something warm and hazy, but it's just beyond my grasp.

I tilt my head enough to see that Olivia's still here, curled up in a chair next to the couch, a throw blanket over her, reading one of my books. With her hair up in a haphazard bun and wearing her glasses, she looks beautiful in a natural, girl-next-door way.

I clear my throat, wincing at how raw it feels. She looks up.

"Oh! You're awake."

"You're still here," I croak out, ferociously thirsty all of a sudden. I sit up slowly, careful of the dizziness that slams into me and then recedes. I reach for the glass on the coffee table and take a cautious sip, remembering how just last night, a sip would start painful cramping and nausea. But my stomach thankfully accepts the cool liquid without protest. I try my voice again. "What time is it?"

She brushes her bangs out of her eyes, a gesture I'm coming to recognize as something she does when she feels nervous. "It's about midnight. You've been asleep all day. I hope you don't mind that I stayed. You were so sick. I didn't think it was right to leave you alone."

She unfolds herself from the chair. "Are you hungry?" she asks as she walks to the open-plan kitchen. "Do you think you can try eating? I made you chicken soup."

After a few minutes, she returns with a tray and bowl and sets them on the coffee table.

"You made me soup?" I ask, a lump forming, which I swallow away. It's being sick; that's what this feeling is from.

But I know the melting weakness is beyond fever and body aches. It has to do with this lovely girl who cared enough to spend the afternoon cooking for me. She took the time to make me a tray with soup, crackers, and a small bud vase with yellow daisies. Where had she gotten the flowers? Hell, where had she gotten the ingredients to make soup? She said she made it, not ordered it.

She shrugs and smiles shyly. "It's no big deal."

Has anyone ever made me homemade soup? I think my mother might have, before she died, but my memories of her are hazy. She was a single mom who worked every minute she could to help us survive. She probably didn't have much time for cooking.

So many people in my life take care of me—managers, assistants, drivers, bodyguards. But I pay them. Olivia did this because she wanted to, not because it's in her job description. And somehow, that makes all the difference to me.

"You didn't need to do that," I grind out, not knowing what to do with this tightness in my chest. I hate being dependent on others. I learned long ago that it's dangerous to be vulnerable. Dangerous to need.

Olivia's face falls. "I overstepped, didn't I? If you're not hungry or it doesn't sound good, you don't have to eat it. I won't be offended."

She's done something kind for me, and here I am being an ass.

She nervously runs her fingers over her bracelet. With a start, I realize it's the charm bracelet I sent to her the first Christmas we exchanged letters. She'd mentioned in a letter that she loved the idea of having a charm bracelet, with each charm representing her life, so I gave her one. The next Christmas, I had a miniature typewriter crafted for it, a Remington, but I never sent it. By then, we'd moved on from sending letters to texts, and it felt like breaking the rules to mail her another gift.

But every Christmas, I still buy her a new charm. I like imagining what she would like, which delicate trinket would mean something to her. I keep them in a box in my office and try not to think about why.

I lean over her now and touch her wrist, reveling in the spark that ignites. Her charm bracelet is empty. It's selfish of me, but I'm glad she's left it empty. I want to fill it myself. I vow to send her the charms I've bought. Someday.

"Don't you like chicken soup?" she asks, a line forming between her brow at my continued silence and my touch.

I shake my head. "No, sorry. It smells delicious, and I'm starved." My stomach growls.

I turn her hand over and trace the delicate lines of it,

reveling in her warmth. "I don't mean to sound ungrateful. It's just that I've been taking care of myself for a long time, and I'm not used to letting someone help. But I'm thankful," I admit.

I move my finger back to the bracelet. "This is pretty," I say lightly, my heart in my throat, wondering what she will say. Will she mention me—Remington?

"A friend gave it to me."

"Just a friend?"

Her smile seems wistful. "It's all he'd let us be."

I don't know what to do with all these feelings that I can't name.

The night descending around us creates an intimacy that feels dangerous in a different way now. Or it would be dangerous if I weren't weak and in desperate need of a shower.

She kneels down next to me and takes the spoon, dipping it into the bowl of broth. She holds it up and offers it to me.

"Are you going to feed me like a child now?" I ask, with a wry smile.

"You're sick," she says simply.

I want to balk at that. But something in her eyes, at her focus on my mouth, has me transfixed. So I open my lips, my eyes on hers, and sip the broth she's made me.

It should be awkward. Instead, it's intimate.

After a half dozen spoonfuls, she stops. "We better go easy," she says, her voice breathless, her cheeks as heated as mine. "We don't want to overdo it and risk having you sick again."

I want to argue, but a sudden wave of tiredness hits me.

"Lie down," she says, pushing me gently against the soft cushions. "You need to recover your strength."

I'll figure this all out after a short rest. When I wake, I'll tell her to go, for her own good.

Later, I think, before sleep overtakes me.

CHAPTER 15

livia

THAT NIGHT, I fall asleep in an overstuffed side chair next to the sofa, where Chase sleeps fitfully.

When I wake throughout the night, I check his fever. While checking, it's possible I stare at him a little too long, my hand brushing the soft strands of his hair out of his face.

It's no wonder, when I sleep, my dreams are full of Chase.

In the morning, consciousness comes slowly. I open my eyes, disoriented, staring at an unfamiliar ceiling, hovering on that precipice between sleep and reality. My lips tingle, my body is on fire, and *am I panting?* Trying to catch the thread of my dream, I lie still until I remember.

Oh, I remember.

Chase came to me in my sleep. His kiss was carnal and roamed everywhere on my body. I couldn't get enough of him or his wicked mouth.

For a fraction of a second, I wonder if it could have been real because I suspect my panties are wet. With eyes still closed, I pat my hands over the blanket covering me, and I assure myself that my jeans and shirt are still on. I'm fully clothed, still reclining in the chair where I fell asleep. My breath rushes out in relief—or is it disappointment?

I will my eyes to open. And stare straight into Chase's eyes.

"Ah!" I gasp in surprise to find him awake and looking at me with a mix of curiosity, amusement, and heat. That's when I recall something else about my dream. Chase's hands and mouth had me moaning. A lot. And not just generic moaning. I recall moaning his name over and over like a prayer, and—oh my God. *Had I been having a sex dream, saying Chase's name out loud?*

"I didn't—you didn't hear—um." My breath whooshes out.

"Good morning," Chase says in a sleep-roughened voice, ignoring my fumbling attempt to ask if he knew I was having a horny dream about him.

I'm sure I didn't moan out loud. The alternative would be too mortifying, so that's my story, and I'm sticking to it. A lifetime of practice avoiding reality comes in handy sometimes.

I sit up, smooth my hair, and rub sleep and rogue mascara from my eyes.

"Morning," I mumble-greet Chase, angling my head down as I panic about the state of my breath. I need the bathroom. Stat.

"You don't need to do that," Chase says and reaches over to stop my hand that's finger-combing the tangles from my hair. "You're cute all mussed."

In the night, I'd shifted my chair, so it was up against the sofa he slept on. I told myself it was so I could check on him without having to get up. But in reality, I loved being close.

Tingles spread from where he touches me, but he drops his hand all too soon. I try to let go of my self-consciousness and focus on Chase.

"You look better." I lean forward. His forehead thankfully feels cool to the touch.

He scans my face, a small smile playing on his lips. My hand falls from his forehead as I realize how intimate my gesture is. It's something you might do to a child or a loved one, not a casual acquaintance.

He was so sick last night that I became familiar with his body—a deceptive familiarity, I realize. It's not as if I gave him a naked sponge bath or anything—though that sounds like a fun idea—but I passed a good portion of last night memorizing every line and shadow of his face, the strength in his neck and shoulders and chest. But that was conditional on me playing nurse. It's not something I can continue, as tempting as it is.

"Sorry. Force of habit. You were really sick yesterday."

He brushes a wisp of hair away from my face in return.

My eyes widen at his touch, and my heartbeat speeds up. *Well, okay then.* I guess the familiarity works two ways.

"So, how long have you been awake?" I ask, breathless.

"Not long. A noise woke me," he says with a secretive smile.

I pray my blush isn't as bright red as it feels. *He couldn't have heard my sexy-time dream. I'll die.*

Deflection needed, I gaze out the window and at the rain that's still falling in buckets. "Wow. It's really coming down out there," I say, my words flying fast. "You probably don't remember, but it was storming all night."

He turns to look. I stand on shaky legs and wander over to the window to get some space. There are no cars or people on the street down below. The water pools onto the road, turning it into a shallow stream, and trees list to the side with the force of the wind. While the storm rages outside, the two of us are in a peace-filled bubble, with only the gray light of the rain-soaked day and the sound of the storm lashing against the windows to keep us company.

I sense his movement behind me, and I turn to him, worried.

"Are you sure you feel better?"

He nods. "The worst of it is gone. I'm just a little tired. And I'm desperate for a shower."

"Well, I should get going, then," I say, unsure of myself.

Now that he's better, there's no excuse for me to stay.

"Look at it out there. You won't get anywhere. The road is practically flooded." His eyebrows come together.

"But I can't stay here now that you're well. I don't want to bother you."

"You spent the night taking care of me." He smiles gently. "So, no, I'm not going to thank you for that by sending you out in the middle of a storm."

"It wasn't a big deal."

"Olivia, you're stuck with me until the rain stops, so you might as well get comfortable."

The look in his eyes, as if he likes what he sees, melts away any objections I might have. Not that I have many; his company is addictive, storm or no storm.

"Okay, Chase, you win." I can't help but grin back at him.

"You finally called me Chase." His smile grows even more devastating. "About time."

"Why wouldn't I call you Chase? It's your name."

"You usually call me by my full name. Not just Chase."

It's true. I still have a hard time seeing him as just a regular guy. He isn't regular—he's special. He's magnetic. His talent and face belong on film. They blind and disarm.

But watching him sick and vulnerable changed the way I view him.

I'm not sure how to explain that to him without sounding like a lovesick lunatic, though, so I go for a light, breezy change of subject. "So, *Chase*, what's on the agenda for today?"

"Well, Olivia, I can think of a few things," he murmurs.

Down, girl, I scold my overeager imagination.

"Such as?" I ask, pretending he doesn't affect me.

"We could play some games." His smile is mischievous, as if he knows what he's doing to me.

"I'm great at Scrabble." I force myself to say blandly.

"I'm thinking more along the lines of truth or dare." His mouth tilts up.

Is he flirting with me?

"Um, sure, 'kay," is all I manage.

"Great," he says. Our gazes hold.

He looks away first and clears his throat. "But before that, I really do need a shower. Do you want the bathroom first?"

"I'd love to freshen up," I say, hopping up.

"It's down the hall on the left."

I grin. "I've been here all night. I found it."

He laughs. "Right."

"I'm just going to…" I point my thumbs toward the hallway.

He watches my awkwardness with a raised eyebrow.

"There should be an extra toothbrush in there."

Does he keep extras for girls staying over?

"Don't look at me like that," he says. "It's from the hotel."

"Hey." I hold up my hands in innocence, as if I hadn't been thinking of how often he gets female visitors. "It's none of my business."

The truth is, I hate the thought of another woman being here, especially one who could freely explore his body. I'm his guest, but only by default. I have no right to the jealousy that's like acid in my belly.

I pad down the hall and into the plush bathroom, all marble and glass, with a few masculine grooming products lined neatly on the counter. Like a total creeper, I pick up his cologne, spray it, and close my eyes as the scent he uses fills the air.

I'm just looking for the extra toothbrush, at least I tell myself that as I open all the drawers under the counter. I find the toothbrush—and more.

Condoms. My emotions swing on a pendulum. Jealousy at

the thought of Chase using those condoms with another woman. Excitement at the thought of Chase using them with me.

It's embarrassing to be a virgin at twenty-five. I've never had a boyfriend long enough to do the deed. And casual sex is just not my thing. Sex is too intimate, too important, too exposing, for me to engage in with someone I don't trust implicitly. When I was younger, my virginity wasn't a big deal. I figured there'd be time to find the right guy. But as each year passes, it becomes more of a burden.

Now, even if I want to have sex just to get rid of my virginity, the V-card makes it harder. I don't want to be fumbling around clueless, in possible pain. Or worse—what if I bleed on the guy? Plus, whomever I choose to "deflower" me will probably think I've been saving myself for love and make it a bigger deal than it might otherwise be.

Maybe the romantic in me does want to wait for love, but the sensible part realizes that there won't be a prince coming to sweep me off my feet and divest me of my virginity anytime soon. Chase would be better than any prince, but my chances with him are probably just as far-fetched as with royalty.

After brushing my teeth, I stare at myself in the mirror. There isn't much I can do with my bangs that are sticking up at odd angles, but I smooth them as best as I can. My cheeks are full of color—I can thank Chase for that—and my eyes are bright with excitement. I bite my lips, wishing I had a touch of gloss, and stick out my tongue at my reflection.

Padding back down the quiet hall, I stop at the entrance of the living room. Chase is at the window, framed by the falling rain and looking every inch a movie star.

As if sensing my presence, he turns, smiling. The warmth in his eyes is my undoing. Setting aside my insecurities, I can't help smiling back at him like a lovesick girl.

"The bathroom is all yours. I found the condoms in the drawer."

Crap! Double crap!

"Toothbrush! I mean, I found the toothbrush!" I correct in a rush.

I should stop there. But Chase's smirk makes me even more nervous, and the horrifying word vomit just keeps coming.

"I found the condoms, too, but I didn't mean to tell you that. I didn't mean to snoop. It's none of my business. None. Please forget I said that," I plead and take a deep breath, hoping oxygen will eventually find my brain and make me shut up.

Chase says nothing, just strolls toward me like a jungle cat on the prowl. Even his smile feels predatory. I stand at the edge of the narrow hallway, frozen as he approaches me, his strong body brushing up against me.

My body catches fire with every part of him that touches every part of me. He pauses as we stand next to each other, flanked by the walls, my skin a live wire of nerves.

"There are some things I can't forget, Olivia." His breath is a breeze against my ear.

A dimple flashes in his cheek. I hold my breath until he oh-so slowly moves past me.

When he passes, I let out a long breath, sagging against the wall. It holds me up as I watch Chase stroll toward the bathroom, admiring his long legs, broad back, and that ass.

Damn that ass, I think. I scrub a hand in front of my face as the door shuts and then the shower turns on, and I imagine how he must look naked. It makes me whimper. I may not survive the day.

CHAPTER 16

hase

Being stuck in a hotel suite with Olivia is like being in heaven, while on a fast track to hell. The more time I spend with her, the guiltier I feel for lying by omission and not telling her about my double life as her pen pal.

But growing up on the streets, you learn to not throw away fleeting moments of grace. So today, I've decided to just enjoy it all and worry about the devil to pay tomorrow.

We call down to the front desk, and the concierge sends up a Scrabble set, which we plan on playing later, and enough snacks and junk food to last for weeks. Sometimes, it's good to be a movie star.

"It's your turn," I prompt.

We sit on the floor cross-legged, facing each other.

"Shh, I'm deciding." She leans over to steal a peanut M&M from the bag in front of me and pops it into her mouth.

I fixate on those lips for far longer than is appropriate before

I shake my head. "You've been *deciding* for five minutes. There needs to be a time limit."

"Fine," she says. "Truth."

"Do you have a boyfriend?" I'm pretty sure I know the answer. She's never talked to Remington about a guy in her life, so I've always assumed she doesn't have one, but I realize now that there's a lot she hasn't told him—me—so I'm questioning everything.

"No." She hesitates briefly, before saying with more decisiveness, "No boyfriend."

Relief flows through me. But something about the way she answers makes me feel like she isn't telling the whole truth.

"*Was* there someone?"

"That's two questions."

I wait patiently. Our staring contest stretches. Her eyes are beautiful, storm gray against her pale skin.

"Yes, maybe." She shrugs. "I don't know."

"Who?" I try not to glare, but I'm not successful.

My jaw clenches. She's not mine, I remind myself. She's just a long-distance friend that I have no claim over. And she doesn't even know she's that.

She looks out the window, watching the rain. "I thought maybe there was someone. The possibility of someone, at least. I liked him a lot. I imagined he might like me."

"And?" I urge, torn because I want to hear the story as much as I don't want to hear it.

She tilts her head. "I was wrong."

The stark way she says it has my chest constricting. Some asshole broke her heart. And I want to break his face. *Who was he?* In all the years of letters and texts, she never indicated that there was a boy she cared about.

"What happened?"

"In retrospect, he was just a friend, and that was all he'd ever be. I never even met him. Isn't that funny?"

Shit. She means Remington. She means me.

Her smile doesn't meet her eyes. "I didn't realize it was possible to fall for someone just through their words. We were pen pals. I know that sounds a little old-fashioned."

Relief that she doesn't have another guy and guilt that I'm the asshole who hurt her war within me. Guilt, as always, wins. *What am I doing?* Ironic that we're playing truth or dare because if she knew the truth, she'd hate me.

I should do the right thing and change the subject. But I don't. "And then?"

She hasn't mentioned Remington before this, except for the charm bracelet, so I was beginning to think all it took was a celebrity to forget the years of friendship between us.

"I liked him. A lot. Long story short, he friend-zoned me," she continues. "I sent him my photo, and he wasn't interested. I guess he didn't like what he saw," she mumbles, looking down.

Her words hit me like a blow to my core.

I got my answer. She does care. Instead of making me feel better, it guts me, because I'm responsible for her pain and insecurity. I tried to do the right thing, but it still hurt her.

I think of an alternate future, where if things weren't so complicated, if I were a normal guy, then we could have met and fallen for each other. I'd get to do all the things with her I dream of every night.

But that's not reality.

As she looks down, her hair falls like silk, partially shielding her face. "Daisy said it's for the best because I've been too hung up on a fantasy. But it's not as if any other guys are knocking down my door. It was the first time I ever put myself out there, and I guess it was a hit to my already less-than-stellar confidence. I mean, someone who I thought of as my best friend let me down easy after seeing my photo."

She covers her face with her hands and then peeks out at me, what looks suspiciously like tears shining in her eyes.

"I don't know why I dumped all that on you. This is so embarrassing."

Fuck it. I have to say something.

She believes Remington blew her off because she isn't enough. But that's bullshit. She's everything. And she needs to know it.

I grasp her hand. She's warm, exquisitely soft, and I want to run my fingers over every inch of her body, but I resign myself to whispering my thumb across the sensitive skin on her wrist.

When her questioning eyes meet my serious ones, I steel myself, determined to explain somehow. "Olivia, I-I can't tell you why this guy couldn't give you what you needed. But I know there's not a chance in hell it had anything to do with you, because you are absolutely, utterly, and completely beautiful, inside and out."

I can feel her pulse race at my rough, quick words. I lace my long fingers through hers. I need to make her understand just how special she is. I caused this, and I need to fix it. She must know that every part of her is deeply wanted.

"Any guy would be so fucking lucky to have you. To be *yours*. The only thing I know is, this guy…he doesn't deserve you. And I'm sure, wherever he is, he knows the value of what he lost. And that he's lost without you. Because who wouldn't be?"

Her mouth opens in surprise, eyes wide with a questioning stare.

I tilt my head back, and I watch her through slitted eyes. She leans toward me, and I inch toward her. Inch by infinitesimal inch. I'm obsessed with the way her top lip is almost as wide as her bottom. I have to have a taste.

Between us, my phone on the table rings.

She jumps back. "Aren't you going to answer it? It could be important," she asks tentatively when I let it ring.

Nothing is as important as she is. Not blockbusters or awards or supermodels calling. But a second more and I'm going to kiss her, and possibly hurt her worse than I already have. I want to build her up, give her back a little of the confidence I stole from her as Remington. And I can't do that if I selfishly take this further than friendship. There's no future in us for so many reasons. I don't want to risk her vulnerable heart for something so temporary.

I need to put distance between us.

So, as much as I hate it, I know this phone call is saving me from doing something stupid, something I've been trying to keep myself from, even as I want it with every atom in me.

I answer the call. "Hello?" I keep my attention on Olivia as she stands and walks toward the kitchen.

"Chase. I'm glad I caught you."

"What's up, Patrick?"

"Don't act like you don't know why I'm calling," my agent chides. "You're supposed to be in LA. Your meeting with the director is done, and you have a photo shoot scheduled for tomorrow. I've already rescheduled it twice. It's for a cover feature in the biggest men's magazine. It's not something you can just blow off again. And we need to discuss the rest of your week."

As I pretend to be interested in my agent going over a long list of appearances and meetings that are coming up, my brain is fixated on what almost happened. We almost kissed. I know what I need to do. I need to walk the line of making her feel like a beautiful, appreciated woman to undo some of the damage I did rejecting her as Remington, while keeping enough of a distance to not make things worse.

I can manage that. Maybe.

Just one more day with her. And possibly one more night.

CHAPTER 17

livia

I PUT on the kettle in the kitchen and try not to overanalyze what just happened. *Did Chase almost kiss me?*

I rummage through the cupboards and find, along with coffee and tea, a gourmet tin of hot chocolate, perfect for spending a rainy day with a movie star, I decide. When the hot chocolate is ready, I take two mugs back into the living room. Chase is still on the phone, but he catches my eye and smiles as I hold up his mug and set it on the coffee table.

I walk over to the large window, not wanting to appear to be eavesdropping, though, admittedly, I am.

"Send over the script and the schedule. Just don't book me for anything more until I've approved it. And tell the magazine I'll be there tomorrow to do the shoot with Cassidy."

The slow love song about rainy days and crushes playing in my head screeches to a halt. He'll be flying back to his glamorous life to do a photo shoot with Cassidy Reynolds, his incredibly beautiful costar.

But, a sneaky voice whispers, I already know he isn't mine. If I acknowledge that this is just for now, why can't I have fun? No questioning it, no second-guessing, no worry. Just living in the moment. Just taking risks, like I'm supposed to be doing.

Chase hangs up the phone and picks up his mug from the table.

He takes a tentative sip. "Hot chocolate? You know, I've never had hot chocolate before."

"No way!" I say, shelving my inner musings for some other time. "How is that possible?"

"I didn't have the typical childhood with hot chocolate and marshmallows."

"Mr. Hollywood, hot chocolate is a prerequisite for any kick-ass rainy day."

He sips the steaming drink, moaning a little when he tastes it, and I feel that sound reverberate through every nerve ending.

"Damn, this is good."

It's ridiculous how happy his simple compliment makes me. I try to contain my smile but fail.

"So, should we continue our game?" I ask.

He presses his lips together, as if debating. "Sure," he says, but more cautious now.

I hope I haven't brought down the vibe with my declarations. Did he just give me those compliments because he felt bad for me?

I set my insecurities aside. This is a once-in-a-lifetime experience. And I'm determined to enjoy it to the fullest.

"It's your turn, then." I get comfortable on the floor, my back against the couch. He shifts and our knees touch. Electricity flows between us. "Truth or dare?" I ask, my voice breathless.

"Dare," he says.

I'm a little disappointed that he didn't choose truth. I'm dying to ask him if he has a girlfriend, just as he asked me about a boyfriend.

I watch him, considering. I have no idea what to dare him to do. My mind is crowded with inappropriate dares I'd never have the guts to suggest, ones that involve being naked. I'm oh-so tempted to ask for a kiss, but I'd need something stronger than hot chocolate to throw myself at him in that way.

And then I have it. The dare. It's ballsy, but I'm supposed to take risks. My smile widens. He's going to think I'm nuts, but I have to do this. For all *The Wanderer* fangirls in the world, I'm taking one for the team.

"Olivia, your smile is making me nervous."

"Chase, it should. It really should. But before I tell you your dare, I want to make sure you're truly feeling better."

"Why? What are you going to make me do?"

"That's for me to know and you to find out. But I don't want you to have a relapse."

"I probably shouldn't admit this, but I'm fine," he grumbles. "Whatever it was seems to be all out of my system. So, what's the dare?" he asks warily.

I stand up and hold out a hand to him. "Come on. I'll show you."

He slips his hand into mine, and the feeling is as sweet as the hot chocolate.

I laugh, feeling younger and more carefree than I can remember. Maybe risks are fun after all. At least, this will be fun for me. Maybe not for him.

* * *

Fifteen minutes later, Chase glowers at me.

"Remind me again why we're doing this," he complains.

I grin at him. "Don't even think about backing out of this. You chose to take a dare."

"I promised, and I don't break promises. But for the record, you're evil." He raises his voice, but not in anger—at least, I hope not too much anger. We're standing under the overhang outside the hotel's revolving door, and he's yelling to be heard over the sound of the pounding rain.

Normally, the street we're on is packed with cars and pedestrians, but now, the road is deserted. The weather has calmed some, but it's still pouring. Everyone sane is inside, staying dry.

Wind whips rain toward us. I laugh in exhilaration at the cold shock, feeling more alive than I ever have.

"I'm sorry, but I have to do this. I mean, here we are, in a rainstorm. How could I pass up this opportunity? This is for all the girls everywhere!" I shout back to him, wanting to laugh at his expression, but fearing it will push him over the edge.

He lets out a long-suffering sigh and rips off his hoodie, one-handed. I watch in fascination as a white T-shirt and muscles appear from beneath the shapeless fabric. His shirt lifts a little with the sweatshirt, revealing a patch of smooth-looking skin, strong muscles, and a thin line of hair that I'm dying to explore.

"Lift your arms," he instructs.

"Why?" I tilt my head.

"So you can wear my sweatshirt," he says as if I'm a child.

"Oh, but you'll be cold."

"But you won't be, which is what's important."

"That's very gentlemanly of you." I try to hold back my pleased smile but can't.

"I *am* a gentleman. Even with evil girls and their evil plans," he teases.

I think about refusing his sweatshirt because I feel guilty for taking it, especially since he's probably still weak from being sick, but then I realize my shirt is so thin that it will be transparent if it gets wet. I'd rather it be his shirt that turns see-through than mine.

So, I lift my arms and luxuriate in the soft fabric that envelops me like a hug.

I can't believe I had the guts to make him do this.

"Ready?"

"As I'll ever be."

"Let's go!" I squeal and run out into the middle of the deserted city street. He follows me.

Rain beats down on us.

"It's cold!"

"And wet!" Chase yells.

I laugh, rain rushing over my face.

Chase shakes his head like a dog, streams of water flying at his gesture.

I hold up my arms, and he steps into my space. We embrace as if we're about to dance.

Because we are. About to dance, that is. I look up at him.

"This is ridiculous. Olivia Evans, you're impossible."

"Shut up and twirl me like you do in the movie."

The Wanderers is a sci-fi thriller with a group of time-jumping heroes. One of the movie's most iconic scenes is at the end of the film, after the bad guys are banished to the outer regions of space forever, Chase dances in the rain with Cassidy Reynolds and professes his undying love. The scene melted a million girls' hearts and catapulted Chase to maximum heart-throb status.

In that movie moment, every girl wanted to be Cassidy. And every girl wanted to be in Chase's arms, or at least his character's.

And here I am, reenacting it. The idea for the dare was one-third wish fulfillment, one-third mischievous glee, and one-third to give me the chance to be in his arms, any way I can.

He twirls me as demanded, and I tilt my head up toward the dark gray sky. He leans down, blocking the rain, gathers me in those muscled arms of his, and sways with me.

I'm short enough that I have to stand on my tiptoes and he has to bend down. I close my eyes and memorize every sensation. The cold slick of rain. The heat coming off Chase's body. It feels as if we're all alone in the world.

"Thank you," he says.

"For what?"

"For this," he says simply, and then his lips meet mine.

It's a sweeping brush of a kiss. A butterfly that touches down before flying away. It sends an electric wave through my body.

I long. Long for his lips to come back to me. Long for more than the briefest taste of heaven. But I already pushed myself so far out of my comfort zone, I don't dare ask for more. He tucks my head back into the safety of his chest and holds me as if I'm precious to him. As if he longs for me as well.

I sway in time with him and memorize the feel of his body, never wanting this to end.

But it's cold and wet, and we probably look crazy, so with a flourish, he twirls me one last time, and then we're running back under the awning of the hotel, laughing and dripping, his hand in mine.

His eyelashes gleam with water droplets, making his already-long lashes even more so. He grabs me and twirls me again, this time out of the rain. Our eyes hold, and something sweet and desperate cuts through me, the fierce desire to hold fast to this moment, as pointless as trying to catch the wind.

"Olivia," Chase rasps.

I shudder—not from the icy hand of San Francisco's weather, but from the sound of my name coming from this man.

"Shit, you're freezing," he says, his lips pressing tight. "We'd better go back inside."

Is it my imagination, or did he sound disappointed?

I gather my hair and wring it out, water streaming from the long strands.

"Are they going to let us back into the hotel?" I ask. "I mean, look at us, we're soaked."

"I am looking at you. And you look damn good from where I'm standing. Just walk in with confidence, and they won't say a word," Chase says, leaning in toward me to be heard over the rain. My pulse races at the way his warm breath tickles my ear. "They expect wild shit from actors. A little water in the lobby is tame, all things considered. It'll give them something to talk about today."

He grasps my hand and leads me with brash confidence through the doors of the hotel. The well-trained staff pretend to ignore us as we speed walk through the lobby to the elevator, sopping wet and laughing the entire way, but I see their furtive glances.

As we wait for the elevator, a maid approaches us. At first, I think she might be about to kick us out, but instead, she shyly offers us two towels. Chase gifts her with his signature grin and murmurs, "Thank you." Her eyes go so wide I fear they might pop from her head.

"Oh, sir," the pretty girl gushes. "We watched the two of you dancing in the street. It's just like your movie. We were all smiling and sighing. Even Ms. Ballister, who never smiles at anything." She turns to me. "You're so lucky," she says with a dreamy, lovestruck look in her eye.

The elevator dings. I thank the girl for the towel, trying my best to wipe away the water that clings to me. After drying himself quickly, Chase passes me his towel as well and wraps it around my shoulders.

When the door opens, we step into the elevator. The doors close with the maid and the rest of the lobby staff watching us with smiles.

On the long ride up, neither of us says anything, though I can't help sneaking sly glances at him, while he looks straight ahead. I'm acutely aware of the cold fabric sticking to my wet skin, the hot, constricted air of the enclosed space, and just how many fiery love scenes start, and sometimes end, in an elevator.

Don't jump him, don't jump him, I scold myself.

All too soon, the elevator door opens to his floor and the spell breaks.

Once back in the suite, he clears his throat, avoiding my eyes.

Suddenly, it's awkward. Maybe the breathless anticipation, me dying for him to kiss me again, was all one-sided. Maybe he was just being polite. It isn't his fault that every girl, including me, falls at his feet from just his smile.

"Fuck, I shouldn't have done that." His words confirm my fears.

"What? Why?" Is he talking about the dare? Or the kiss?

"I got caught up in the moment. It felt like we were alone out there in the rain, and the lobby was deserted when we left, but anyone could have gotten a photo. *Fuck.*"

"I-I'm sorry. I didn't mean to make things harder for you."

"I'm not worried about me. I'm worried about you. Don't you understand how it could affect you if this got out, if we got out?"

"We're a we?"

He doesn't answer, just stares at me with a mix of frustration and something more. Something tense and heated. The same something I thought I'd seen in his eyes before he gave me that fleeting kiss in the middle of the storm.

Finally, he looks away. "You should take a shower to warm up. I don't want you to get sick." He runs his hand through his hair, making the wet strands even wilder.

"I have no dry clothes."

He swallows hard. "The bathroom should have a robe. And if you want, you can borrow something of mine until your clothes are dry. I can send them out to housekeeping. Now, go," he says softly. "Your lips, tempting as they are, are turning blue."

He thinks my lips are tempting! I want to say something, a witty retort, an avowal of love, an entreaty to ravish me until the rain stops falling—hell, until the world stops spinning—but my brain and mouth aren't working at the moment.

I float my way to the bathroom. The shower soothes me, clearing my mind. The water jetting down from the fancy showerhead reminds me of the rain outside, only it's blissfully warm, and the fresh, woodsy smell of the shampoo reminds me of Chase. When I finish, I dry myself in another cloudlike towel and look around for the robe Chase said was here. But it's nowhere to be found.

Damn.

I wrap the towel as tight as it will go, trying to stretch the insufficient fabric. For a luxury hotel, their towels sure are on the small side. I quietly open the door and peek around the corner.

"Chase," I hiss. He doesn't answer. The door to the bedroom is closed, and I hear music coming from it.

"Chase!" I call louder.

Still nothing.

I swear silently and pull the towel tighter, feeling like a sausage in a too-small casing.

I walk to his room and clutch the towel with one hand and lift up my other arm to knock on the door. But as my hand is about to hit the door, it opens. The surprise of it knocks me off-balance, and I fall into a very tall, very large, very muscular body. Both my hands reach out to steady myself.

A shocked Chase drops the stack of clothes he's holding, presumably for me, and reaches out to keep me upright.

I realize too late that with my hands otherwise occupied on Chase's chest, there is nothing holding my towel up. In slow motion, my towel slips, then slips some more.

"Eeeep!" I squeak, trying to catch the falling fabric.

I catch it halfway down my body. My full breasts are out there—hanging wild and free and unencumbered, like two party girls.

I make a noise that's somewhere between a squeak and a squeal and jerk my towel back up.

He swallows audibly.

"Th-there was no robe," I stutter.

"Sorry." He pulls his gaze from my chest. "I was just coming to bring you this." He leans down and picks up the fallen clothes, which brings his head dangerously close to my almost bare bottom half. When he straightens, his breathing seems accelerated. He clears his throat. "A T-shirt and some shorts," he holds them out to me. "They'll probably be too big, but it's the best I can do."

"Thanks," I mumble. Can someone die of embarrassment? I fumble with the clothes, still holding the towel as best as I can.

"I'm just going to go back to the bathroom to change," I say, with as much dignity as I can muster.

"Okay." His gaze slides back to my body and snags on my chest again. He blows out a deep exhale and glances away abruptly. "I'll take a shower when you're done."

"I know it's a hotel and all, but I think I might have used up all the hot water."

He shakes his head, as if coming out of a trance. Something in the way he looks at me causes the heat of embarrassment to turn into heat of another kind. I'm acutely aware that I'm wearing nothing beneath this towel. I open my mouth, but there are no words. I lick my dry lips.

His smile is slow.

"It's okay. A cold shower sounds like a good idea," he says in a growly voice that I feel at the very center of me.

CHAPTER 18

livia

I'M HAVING one of those surreal moments. Where I stop, look at my life, and wonder how the heck I arrived here. What amalgamation of sliding doors, missed opportunities, and quirks of fate somehow added up to this here and now?

Because lying on a couch snuggled up to superstar, super-hot Chase James is just not in the context of a normal life. At least not my life.

We still haven't talked about the towel incident. I'm highly grateful for that.

We decided to watch a movie, which is how we ended up sharing a blanket on the couch, an uber-popular sci-fi flick on in the background. I hold the giant bowl of popcorn on my lap.

Chase and I keep making up alternate dialogue for the film.

This day has been all laughs and butterflies, which is a blessing and a curse, because no guy will live up to the standard Chase has set. The only one who's come close to making me fall this hard is Remington, but he doesn't count because I've never been able to couch-snuggle with him.

Chase and I are playing a drinking game with whiskey. Well, he's playing it with whiskey. I'm taking tentative sips of Bailey's, which is a little more my speed. Chase called down to the concierge, and miracle of movie-star-miracles, the bottles of alcohol arrived at his door twenty minutes later, along with what looks like really good champagne. Had I known his hotel was privy to this kind of service, I wouldn't have gone to the corner store for soup ingredients last night. I would have used the concierge fairy.

So we drink every time someone says, *"Transport,"* in the movie.

They say it a lot because it's the teleport command, which means we've been drinking constantly, and explains why it's such a popular game on college campuses. I've taken a lot of sips—not enough to get drunk, but enough to make me feel soft and fuzzy around the edges.

Chase nudges me. "You're not paying attention to this masterpiece of modern cinema."

"Oh, sorry. Am I missing something super good?" I ask dryly and throw a piece of popcorn that lands in his hair.

He takes the popcorn and pops it into his mouth.

"Ew." I laugh, lightly slapping him.

He grabs my hand, speeding up my heart rate.

We started out the night sitting next to each other on the couch, a respectable distance apart. But over the course of the movie, inch by agonizing inch, we got closer. A shift here, a move there, fingers closing the distance until they touch.

Eventually, we got so close that we give up the pretense of this being accidental. At least, I don't think it's accidental. Definitely not on my side.

"Watch. You're gonna miss the best part," he orders.

"And what part is that?" I ask.

"The kissing part," he murmurs into my ear.

The only sound is the movie—the romantic score, the sound of lips locking.

"She's pretty," I comment as casually as I can manage. It's an understatement. The actress is stunning and another woman rumored to have dated Chase. I learned that in my internet-stalking research.

I shift slightly, and as I move, my breasts brush against him. The contact only lasts a moment—it's there and gone, but I can't help letting out a little gasp. It's the fault of my sensitive nipples and braless state since my clothes still haven't arrived back from housekeeping. I'm in one of Chase's oversized T-shirts and a pair of his boxers, which hug my curves. His clothes smell like his detergent, and I never want to give them back. When he first saw me wearing them, he got all quiet, which I'm not sure how to interpret.

He clears his throat. "She's okay, I guess," he finally answers, his voice low and rough.

We both say nothing as the couple on the screen gets down to business. Moaning sounds fill the room. The two stars have evolved from kissing to getting naked. It's excruciating to watch with Chase so near. A cold sweat prickles my body.

"That must be fun for the actor—getting paid to kiss pretty girls," I say.

I feel his gaze on me instead of on the screen. "You'd think doing those scenes would be sexy, but it's just awkward," he says. "There are dozens of people watching, and you're worried about how your costar feels, getting so intimate with you. You're thinking about your lines, your angles, hitting your marks, making it look good. I've done more than a few now, and it's always uncomfortable as hell."

"But in *The Wanderers*, your romantic costar was your girlfriend, right? Or is? That had to make it easier." I can't help asking. *Subtle, Olivia.*

I need to know, though, because here I am on the couch with Chase, dreaming of him kissing me again, which I shouldn't be doing if he's another woman's man. He doesn't act like it, but then again, cheating in Hollywood is probably not as big of a deal as it is in the rest of the world.

"She was for a while."

Was. As in past tense. *Good.*

"What happened?" I glance at him. He's not watching the movie anymore. And I give up the pretense of it as well, focusing all my attention on him.

"We were young and in this weird bubble where we had no time for an outside life. We just filmed the movies and promoted them. We'd go from city to city on the tour, but we were mostly trapped in hotels. We had a lot of time alone together, and we helped each other through an experience that no one else could understand." He shrugs. "It was convenient, I guess, until it wasn't."

He looks away, so I turn back to the screen, relieved that the movie has moved on to a fight scene. I can't help my curiosity, though. Blame the nosy writer in me. "What changed to make it inconvenient?"

"Honestly? Dating me sucks. I wouldn't wish it on anyone I liked. Even someone as famous as Cassidy struggled with it, and she's been in the spotlight since before she could walk. Her social media turned into a bloodbath. Gossip blogs made up crazy lies and conspiracy theories, which kept getting picked up by the tabloids. Because we were also an on-screen couple, we had a lot of fans of our relationship who were obsessed with us. They still are. They trash any girl I'm even photographed next to."

He clenches his jaw. "It all got too much for Cassidy, and I don't blame her. Relationships aren't a good idea for me."

"So, you're just never going to be with anyone?" I shouldn't be so disappointed. It's not like we were going to walk off into the sunset together.

His smile doesn't reach his eyes. "Oh, I can be *with* someone. Just not in a relationship. And only with girls who know the way Hollywood works and can handle the life." His gaze shifts down. "I don't want someone I care about to get hurt because of me," he says softly.

Like Daisy did, I think.

I'm definitely not the Hollywood kind of girl he's talking about, the only kind he dates. My heart does another sad little flip. I need my heart to get a clue.

"It's a lonely way to live." An uncomfortable thought occurs to me—that hiding behind my writing and books, falling for unavailable men, is just as lonely.

He shrugs. "It is what it is, at least for now. And the few girls I reach that level with know this upfront." His eyes boldly meet mine.

Are his words a warning?

Or a promise?

Could I be a girl he's with, even just for a night? I don't meet the Hollywood standard, but I'm here with him now, and he isn't exactly running the other way.

A night with Chase, if I were lucky enough to have one, would be worth any pain that follows.

"Maybe when *The Wanderers* movies are done, your life will be a little less crazy? You just finished the last one, right?"

He hesitates, as if debating if he should say something. "I'm up for the role of Max Thunder." He looks away and runs a hand through his hair. "They want to go with a younger lead, do his origin story, for the next movies in the series."

I gasp. Legit gasp. That's how big that part is. Even I, whose favorite movies are black-and-white, know that. Max Thunder is the lead in the most famous spy thriller franchise of the last fifty years. It's an iconic role in cinema. If Chase is going to step into those shoes, he'll be at the very top of the A-list, even bigger than he is now, and on the cover of the tabloids forever.

"Wow. Congratulations," I say, trying to sound excited for him. And I am. It's the role of a lifetime. "That's amazing."

"It's not official," he says. "It's hush-hush, but they're getting close to a decision. It's between me and one other actor. They think he might be too old for the direction they're going, though, which is lucky for me. My agent thinks I'll get it."

He's so close to me, I can smell the whiskey on his breath and the familiar sandalwood of his cologne and something potent that is all Chase.

"Do you want to know a secret?" he asks.

I'm mesmerized by how handsome he looks sitting there on the couch, those famous cheekbones illuminated, his hair mussed, and his strong body showcased by his T-shirt.

"Yes," I say, my breath quickening at the fallen angel look he's giving me through slitted eyes.

"A part of me would be relieved if I don't get it. I haven't told anyone else that. Hell, I'm not even supposed to tell anyone I'm in the running for it."

"You wouldn't want to play Max Thunder?"

"It's not the kind of part anyone turns down. But if I get it, my life will become even more out of control."

"We only have one life, Chase. We have to live it in a way that makes us happy."

He leans down, picks up the whiskey bottle from the floor, and takes a swig straight from it.

"Easy," I say, staying his hand. "You've been sick. That will hit you hard."

"Maybe I want to get drunk," he says lightly.

"Why?" I pull the bottle from his grasp.

He runs a hand over his face. "Because it will keep me from thinking about leaving tomorrow. Keep me from thinking about what I want versus doing what's right."

I'm not sure whether he's reminding himself or reminding me. We have one night left, and then that's it. He'll disappear from my life as fast as he appeared in it. Something sharp twists in my chest.

He wraps his hand around mine, engulfing my fingers in his, making my nerve endings tingle all the way to my core. At first, I think he's trying to hold my hand, but he gently takes the bottle I hold and takes another deep swig of the whiskey, trapping my gaze while he drinks. I watch his throat work.

When he finally puts the bottle down, he asks, "Do you understand?"

My answer is barely audible. A soft "Yes" for only him to hear.

But it's a lie.

I don't understand. Not what he means. Not why, even though it's only drizzling now and I could have left hours ago, I'm still here. And especially not why someone as gorgeous and famous and rich as him is paying attention to an ordinary girl like me.

The delicious tension is laced with the promise of pain to come when he leaves tomorrow, because I know with the certainty of my next breath that he isn't coming back, at least not for me.

But I need his lips on mine.

I lean into him, shocked at my boldness. Despite all my insecurities, I force myself to move past the fear of rejection. I reach into myself for a lesson I'm trying to learn—that it's regret that hurts the most, not only of what you've done, but of what you haven't.

I don't want to live with the knowledge that I had this moment, and I squandered it. So, I lean into him, into that hard body, with my soft one.

I press my lips to his. It's soft and fleeting, more a question than a statement.

When it's over, I lift my head a fraction and stare into his eyes, trying to gauge his reaction, but his eyes are hooded. *Did he like it?*

"You don't want—" I say, embarrassed now.

"Oh, Olivia, but I do want," he murmurs silkily. "I want so much. It's fucking killing me to hold back." He raises an eyebrow, challenging me.

Our faces are still inches apart. Our mouths a breath away. I look down at his lips, so tempting, and then back at his eyes.

"Come on, Olivia," he gently mocks. "What are you waiting for?"

"I'm not sure what to do," I admit in a whisper.

"Whatever you feel like," he breathes back.

Whatever I feel like.

An elation I've never known flows through me. I close my eyes and let pure instinct and raw desire take over.

My lips press against his again, but this time firmer, deeper, as I memorize the shape, the softness, and the taste of him. His lips part, a whiskey-flavored invitation to all the best things.

He groans, and I realize just how much he'd been holding back. His hands pull me tight. One fists in my hair, the other molds my hips to his, and his mouth—oh, that wicked mouth—is sure and certain. Whereas my kisses were tentative, lips on lips, tongue barely tasting, his kisses claim and conquer. I open for him fully, luring him inside, and our tongues meet in long, luxurious strokes.

Our hips shift into each other in an aching approximation of what might come next. We're aligned in such a way that I'm left with no doubt that he wants this, wants me. I may be a virgin, but I'm not completely innocent. I've been kissed before, just never like this. I've never been kissed in a way that lights up my whole body, in a way that makes me ache and burn and feel like I'd die for the fire to come. After what may have been a minute or an hour, he breaks free, panting, his forehead resting on mine.

He brushes back my hair with reverence. "You're so damn lovely."

And maybe, in his eyes reflecting back at me, I can see a little of what he sees in me. His mouth descends on mine once again, this time gentler, just a brush of lips on lips. I want to cling to him, to force the kiss deeper, to feel his hands on every part of me, but he leans away once again, as if he knows the wild direction of my thoughts.

"I don't want to hurt you, Olivia." His brows knit. "I'm leaving," he reminds me again.

"Now?" I ask, confused, my blissed-out brain unable to process anything but him kissing me again.

He smiles, but it's bittersweet. "No, not now. Tomorrow. I have to go back to LA."

At this moment, I don't care about the future.

"I know this is just for tonight. But it's okay." My hand shakes as I touch his chest. "I want to be with you, if that's what you want. It's just that I don't know what to do," I say, feeling inept.

"Are you... You're not a ..." He doesn't finish, but I know what he's asking, and I wish I could avoid this conversation.

I blush deep and look away. "It's not a big deal." Feeling like a freak, I shift, putting a little space between us. "It's not like I'm saving myself or something. And I've done things, just never *that thing*. It seemed like something I'd do with a boyfriend, but I've never dated anyone for long enough to feel that comfortable. I know you're not my boyfriend," I rush out, not wanting him to think I'm clingy or deluded. "But it's way past time to get it over with." I shrug, trying for a casual smile and failing. "And I'd like it to be with you."

His expression scorches my nerve endings. "Olivia, it *is* a big deal," he insists. "Quick and casual is not who you are or what you deserve. Especially not for your first time."

"Thanks for telling me who I am. I wasn't sure," I mutter, annoyed now. "And thanks for mansplaining my virginity."

I want to argue further, insist it's my choice, but I've had enough rejection for one month. I'm not going to beg. I sit up and push my hair out of my face, straightening my clothes.

He reaches for me and pulls me back down to him. My breath comes out in a squeak, and I find myself face-to-face with a fierce-looking Chase. It's a good look for him. Let's be real; all his looks are good.

"Hi," I say.

"Hi." His lips quirk. "I don't want to do anything that will hurt you. But we were having a nice time. At least, I was. And I'm pretty sure you were. Let's just watch the movie and not worry about anything else."

"You want to watch the movie?" I ask dubiously.

"And...other things. Just not *that thing*." He flashes me a teasing grin as he echoes my earlier words.

"What kinds of other things?"

"Kissing things."

I nod slowly. "Any other things?"

He shakes his head. "Too dangerous. You're not good for my sanity or my control."

Heat blankets some of my annoyance. I love the idea that I might make him lose control because he does the exact thing to me. A naughty impulse inspires me to brush against him. He's still rock-hard, and I feel better about his rejection of *other things*. He's not lying about wanting me. My fingers want to linger there, feel the steely strength, but he grasps my hand and gently pulls me away from his cock. Fire burns in his eyes.

"Careful, love."

I melt at the word and the rough, desperate rasp of his voice.

"So, we just kiss?"

He nods. "Like in high school. Those long make-out sessions."

"I didn't really have them."

He thinks about it. "Actually, me neither."

I narrow my eyes. "Somehow, I can't believe you didn't make out with girls in high school."

"Oh, I didn't say that. Just that we weren't confined to kissing." His laugh is wicked.

I punch him, and he laughs harder, grabbing my hand. He pulls our joined hands up above me on the couch and twists us in one smooth move. I lie on the sofa, looking up at him, and he looms over me with a seductive promise.

"What are you waiting for?" I ask.

"You have to tell me what you want," he taunts.

I lick my lips and try to form the words.

"You," I murmur. "Only you."

This is the moment I know for sure that some risks are worth everything.

CHAPTER 19

hase

HIGH SCHOOL SUCKS.

Making out with Olivia is paradise, but stopping before we go too far? That's torture.

We're on the couch, the movie long since forgotten, kissing like the world will end tomorrow. We alternate between a desperate fusion of mouths, teeth clacking, tongues thrusting; and long, lazy, sensual explorations.

Younger me would say we make it somewhere between first and second base. Hell, I give her a damn hickey, something I don't think I've ever done, even as a teen. But I'm territorial about Olivia in a way I've never been about anyone else. I want to mark her, a brand to announce that she's mine.

I try to keep my hands in safe zones, but I can't help skimming her side, dipping into her cleavage, and when she begs me, I give us both relief by palming her full breasts and rubbing her nipples. I memorize the sweet sounds she makes when I touch them, my tongue in her mouth, my body covering hers. I want to worship at the altar of her curves. To suck, to lick, to tease, to do every dirty thing to them. I grind against her, my dick rock-hard, and she pushes back, assuaging the ache at the center of her. I've never been more turned on, and if we keep at this much longer, I'll embarrass myself in my jeans.

On fire, I exert all my will to wrench my hands to safer zones and ease off her. I'm dying to lick her until she screams and comes for me, to show her—graphically and often—just how good sex can be.

But she's not someone I can fuck and leave. I care about her. She's my best friend. And a damn virgin. She deserves more than I can give.

Panting, I close my eyes and breathe in and out, trying to remember a Shakespeare monologue my acting coach once made me memorize. When I'm in better control and my heartbeat has slowed, I roll over and tuck her onto my chest, thankful that the hotel's couch is wide enough to accommodate us.

The bed would be more comfortable, but far, far more dangerous. And I'm not ready to have her leave. Not yet. Even if we can't do more, we can still have this night together.

She makes a little huffing noise. "Why'd you stop?" Olivia asks, leaning up on me, her hair falling like a curtain on my chest.

I brush her hair back, reveling in the softness, then follow the line of her shoulder, up her neck, to the curve of her chin, over her full lips, where I rest. She closes her eyes and lets out a shuddering breath. I trace my thumb over her top lip, then her bottom. She reaches out and touches me with her tongue, and with that one gesture, I'm undone again.

"We have to stop. Sleep," I urge in desperation.

"I can't." She laughs. "I'm too…"

"Horny," I supply, grinning even through the frustration.

"Maybe."

"Same. You make me out of my mind. You're everything I

want." My words, soft and fierce, are wrenched from my chest. If there's one thing I can give her, I hope it's this understanding.

She smiles against my skin. "That's flattering, yet hard to believe."

I shift my hips until she moans, feeling my still massive hard-on against her thigh.

"Believe that," I growl.

She's quiet for a long time. "Chase?"

"Yeah?"

"If we're both so...keyed up, why can't we? I know I'm a virgin, but I told you, it's not a big deal. It's not like I'm guarding my virtue or took a vow of purity."

"We already talked about this. Because I'm leaving. And you're not a girl who someone fucks and leaves."

"That's ridiculous."

"You deserve your first time to be with a guy who can promise you more than one night." I want to tear down the world at the thought of her being with someone else. But she deserves love and happiness, even if it can't be me who gives it to her. "Never sell yourself short like that."

"But you don't do that. You have one-night stands, right?"

I frown, but I don't answer.

"So, why isn't it okay for me to have sex for just one night?" She narrows her eyes. Feisty Olivia is so damned hot.

"It's not the same thing."

"Double standard much?"

I don't answer her, just kiss the top of her head again. Her hair smells like my shampoo, and I find I like that. She sighs. It's a frustrated, discontented sound, like an annoyed cat.

The truth is, I'm dying to make her come, but my fear is that if I do, I won't stop there. I'm too aroused to trust my restraint. So instead, I say, "This is enough. This is everything."

"This *is* everything." She cuddles closer, deeper. "But it's not enough."

"It will have to be."

This time, she doesn't argue.

After a few minutes, I break the silence. "Olivia, after tonight, when we say goodbye tomorrow, I can't..." I halt, because what I have to say seems so wrong, but I need to be upfront. I'm hiding so much else. I can't lead her on.

She puts a finger to my mouth. Her eyes are somber. "Shh. I know, Chase. You've already made it more than clear. I'm a big girl. I don't expect you to call me. You've been honest. Brutally so," she says with a small laugh. "Despite my inexperience, I know how these things work."

The hell of it is, she is wrong, so damn wrong. She doesn't have a clue how I feel. How hard it will be to give her up in the morning.

I close my eyes, memorizing her every contour, her every breath. "Good night."

"G'night," she breathes.

And it has been. Despite it all, I relax completely with her in my arms, her weight a soft anchor against me. I close my eyes and know a sleep that's better, deeper, warmer, softer than I've ever had waits for me. Because it's with her.

When I wake the next morning, it's with Olivia in my arms and a deep comfort in my heart.

The wanting hasn't left in the night.

Olivia shifts. The soft early light falls over her face and curves like a caress. She rubs her curvy ass against me, and I'm not able to keep from shifting back into her. She lets out a breathy moan, but when I look down, she's still asleep with a blissful smile. I kiss the top of her head so as not to wake her.

I'd never been one for cuddling before.

On the rare occasions a woman stays in my bed all night, I'm up and out first thing, not wanting to give her false hope that anything will come of the night. I should do the same now.

Instead, I lie there, watching her, spending these precious

last few minutes memorizing her arched brows, her black-as-night hair. The curve of her cheek, the gentle jut of her chin. And down lower, to the gorgeous tits I'd trade my fortune to see again.

I want to cancel my flight and make love to her all day, but she deserves a boyfriend who can give her the regular, peaceful life she wants. Who can take her to the movies without having to sign autographs in line for popcorn, go out for dinner without drawing a crowd, walk down the street hand in hand without being chased by the paparazzi.

Just a few more minutes, and I'll say goodbye in real life. Hopefully, she'll once again allow me back into her life as her long-distance friend Remington. Because the best thing I can do for her is to not get too close. And I care about her enough to do just that.

CHAPTER 20

livia

I WAS RIGHT.

Chase James is a bitch to get over.

It's been two weeks since our magical weekend, and every moment is on repeat in my head, including our final goodbye when he left me to go back to his celebrity life.

But this can't be real heartbreak. We haven't known each other long enough.

The cynical side of me knows I was just another night in a long line of hookups as he jetted away.

At least I hadn't gone into whatever we were with stars in my eyes and hope in my heart that I was somehow special. I'm not Cinderella. He's not my Hollywood Prince Charming. He's the star. I'm the ordinary girl.

I only wish I had someone to process this all with, to break it down. But I can't exactly share my maybe kinda sorta heartbreak with Daisy. Chase is her brother. That would be weird.

And I miss Remington. So much.

I visited the shop where my phone was being fixed, and the supposed tech whiz said that he was waiting on a part, so it would be at least a week or more before he could recover my data. Every time I look at the fancy new phone that I'm still borrowing from Daisy, I ache to message Remington and I curse myself for not memorizing his number. But it will only be another week. And the truth is, I'm still embarrassed about the message and selfie I sent. Maybe a little space in our friendship is a good thing.

Besides, I'm not sure if I would have told him about Chase, even if I could. It would sound unbelievable. Remington might think I was making it all up just because he rejected me. That would be mortifying.

But I miss Remington's ability to make me laugh. I need it more than ever. Last night when I popped into the deli for broken-heart-therapy fudge brownie ice cream, Chase was all over the tabloid display at the checkout. He's shooting a new movie with Cassidy Reynolds in some far-off destination. Why are they always doing movies together? Are Hollywood directors playing matchmaker?

Intellectually, I know the weekend we shared is all we'll ever have. But late at night, when I can't sleep, I sometimes have this unreasonable fantasy that he'll call. Just to check on me. Or maybe to declare his eternal love. Whatever.

I should be glad for the tabloids. It's proof of just how unobtainable he truly is and how our lives couldn't be further apart.

Because, while he's frolicking in foreign locales with his maybe-ex, possible-girlfriend, I'm writing and working at the bookshop shilling coffee, restocking books, and eating delicious cinnamon buns—which is a fabulous comfort food for the lovelorn, by the way.

I'm also moving forward with my life by continuing to take a risk a day.

Today, Daisy is helping me over my fear of heights by taking me skydiving.

Sort of.

"Thank you for not forcing me to jump out of an airplane," I say when we get to the indoor skydiving venue.

Daisy grins. "I figured this would be risky enough for you. Baby steps. But maybe, after this experience, you'll work up to the real thing."

I look at the people floating around the air tunnel dubiously. I doubt this will ignite a new hobby. But floating around in a somewhat controlled environment is much better than dropping from ten thousand feet, so I'll take it.

"You're up." Daisy nudges me.

My hands get clammy and I freeze. "I was wrong. I'm scared of heights. I'll puke in the tunnel, and it'll get all over me. Or the wind won't be strong enough to pick me up," I say, quick and shrill. A hundred humiliating ideas of what could happen bombard my mind.

"Or you could do it, and it could be fun." She hugs me quick. "Now, go, before I kick your ass."

I know Daisy won't let me get away with backing out, so I make the cross symbol even though I haven't been to church in forever. And on shaky limbs, I force myself to walk to the tunnel.

The instructor is already in it, waiting for me. Earlier, I was briefed on hand signals and what to expect, but I could never have imagined the force of the air. Its strength steals my breath and pushes me up. All my senses are on overload as I attempt to recall the instructions on how to control my direction.

Floating madly, I lift my head against the pressure and look through the glass wall at Daisy, who's already chatting up the guy behind her in line. Only Daisy could get hit on while wearing an orange jumpsuit and large plastic goggles. She catches my eye, grins madly, and gives me two thumbs-up as I try not to take out the instructor with my flailing arms.

The instructor points up. My eyes bug out as the wind whips around me. I want to shake my head, but I force myself to take both his hands as he spins us around, and then there we are, spinning up, up, up to the top of the wind tunnel before he sends us plummeting back down to the bottom on a circle of death. It's scary, exhilarating, disorienting, and over too soon.

When I step out of the clear dome on unsteady legs, all I can do is laugh in sheer joy.

"You did it!" Daisy cries, taking my hands and bouncing up and down while I try to steady my heartbeat.

"I did it!" I can't wipe the grin off my face. I faced my fear of heights and won. I skydived—sort of. And it was fun.

"And?" she asks with a tilt of her head.

I say the words I never thought I'd speak. "When can I do it again?" In the overall scheme of risks, it's a small one, but I feel like I can tackle anything after this.

"Yes, Olivia! That's what I like to hear."

Half an hour later, we're out of the hideous jumpsuits and walking down the city street on our way to head home.

"Let's stop here." She points to a corner deli. "I need something to drink after all that wind," Daisy says.

At the deli, she loads up on drinks and snacks. I eye her growing basket, and she laughs. "What? It made me hungry, too."

When we get to the register, I purposefully keep my eyes forward, avoiding the tabloid display, afraid to see Cassidy and Chase again.

"Holy shit, Olivia!"

I turn. Daisy holds her basket in one hand, while the other grasps a magazine.

She pushes the magazine toward me. "What's this?" she asks in accusation. "What the hell, Olivia?"

I look at the grainy photo on the cover. At first, I think it's a still from *The Wanderers* movie. The famous scene where Chase dances with and kisses his costar in the rain. But the setting and clothes look all wrong. And then I realize that, though it's Chase in the photo—the girl kissing him...

It's me. My heart plummets.

Someone captured our rain-soaked kiss on camera. Maybe one of the hotel employees.

It's blurry, and the rain obscures a good part of my face, but that's unmistakably us. Still, I try to brazen it out.

"I don't know. Who do you think it is?" I ask weakly.

"Don't play me. You're a terrible liar, and I recognize you. That's your lips kissing my brother. And that's your hair he's burying his hands in. And your body he's..." Daisy doesn't continue that line of thought because, well, his hands had been wandering when we kissed, and the photo shows just how far they'd traveled. Daisy shakes her head, still looking at the magazine in disbelief. "Gross."

"I'm on the cover of a tabloid," I mutter in shock.

"Never mind the tabloid. I can't believe you hooked up with my brother."

"I didn't—" and then I stop. Because I kind of did. Not all the way, but still. "He's your *foster* brother," I correct.

"Like that matters. It is so ew."

"It is not ew. He's a sex symbol. You can't say ew."

"Yes, I can. When did this happen? Are you dating? Why didn't you tell me?" She fires the questions at me like a machine gun.

"What? No! We spent last weekend together. And it's your fault. You asked me to drop off that gift at his hotel. I thought maybe you were trying to play matchmaker. But it was just a temporary thing. He's a star, and he dates supermodels. He's not interested in me like that."

The cashier leans across the counter until he can see the

magazine Daisy's holding. "Holy shit, that is you," cash register dude exclaims in surprise.

"Damn, girl. Don't get down on yourself. You're hot, and you've got great tits." He zeroes in on my chest. "Some dudes like a little more to grab, if you know what I mean. Just keep giving him more of that there, and you'll be fine."

I glare at the cashier while he rings up our purchases. Daisy presses money into his hand. "Here, for the food, the magazine, and the relationship advice. Keep the change." She grabs my arm, leading us out of the store.

As we walk, I scan the magazine, speed-reading the article and flipping through the rest of the pages with increasing desperation.

They only got a few grainy shots. But my face is tilted up and at least partially recognizable. I read the salacious headline and then scan down to the first line when my heart stops cold.

I grab Daisy's arms. "They have my name and where I work. How did they find out? How'd they know?"

I go cold. Then hot. My legs shake, and my face breaks out in a sweat. Is this what going into shock feels like?

This is an international magazine, the most prominent tabloid in multiple countries. My face and name are plastered at magazine stands and cash registers around the world. This must be viral by now. Chase James kissing a girl is a major story.

"I need to sit down. I might be sick."

"Not on the street," Daisy says. "We'll get you home and figure this all out."

I'm grateful for Daisy's cool composure. She hails an Uber, though with my mind still spinning, I don't remember the ride. Daisy insists on coming home with me and makes us two cups of coffee.

I accept the drink, feeling grateful for her presence.

"It's good. Thank you," I say. I'm usually the coffee-maker, the caretaker. It's nice for someone else to take that role.

She sits down next to me. "Care to fill me in on what's going on?" she asks gently.

I take another sip, giving myself a minute. Daisy waits without saying anything.

"When I got to his hotel to deliver your gift to him, he was really sick."

"He should have called me! I was out of town, but I could have come back," Daisy says in dismay.

"He didn't want to bother anyone. He had food poisoning. I was worried and didn't want to leave him with such a high fever, so I stayed. Then he got better and…"

"And?" Daisy says with impatience.

"And I spent the weekend with him," I mumble into my coffee.

"You did what? Why didn't you tell me?" Daisy cries, as if she can't decide whether to be outraged or excited.

I gnaw on my lip. "I'm still trying to process it, honestly. Talking about it would make it feel real, and it was just this very temporary thing. I can't be hung up on a movie star."

"I suspected something might be between you. I thought it might even be good for you both. But maybe I was wrong. I'm going to kill Chase if he did anything to hurt you. I know you, Olivia. There's no way you are okay with a one-night hookup. He's a million times more experienced."

Hearing that makes my stomach churn, even if I know it's true. But this isn't his fault. I meet her gaze. "Don't be mad at him. It's also why I didn't tell you. He never made me any promises. I knew how it would be. He was sweet. He didn't take advantage of me. If anything, I threw myself at him."

She snorts. "I doubt that."

"It's true. At least, I wanted more, but he stopped us from…" I falter, embarrassed. "He put the brakes on things."

"Not on everything, by the looks of it," Daisy says, jiggling the magazine.

"Yeah, well, that was my fault, too. We were playing truth or dare in his hotel room, and I dared him to kiss me in a rainstorm. I thought it would be funny to make him reenact the scene from *The Wanderers*. It didn't even occur to me there could be paparazzi or that someone would get a picture."

"Chase's life is like that old movie, *The Truman Show*. You have to accept it if you want to be around him. And you might not have realized someone would take a picture, but Chase knew the risk."

"I'd accept his life. But he's not interested in giving me the opportunity. And now, we're on the cover of a magazine because of my dare," I say with a groan.

I wonder what Chase will think of the tabloid. Will he be upset?

Daisy stays with me as I work up the courage to do a search of myself and Chase on the internet. I need to know what's being said about us.

Horror shoots through me as I read the comments on my laptop. Brutal words dissect my every flaw. My vision clouds with tears. It's like middle school all over again, the year when I was bullied. Only this time, instead of a few nasty preteen kids, it's thousands of online trolls doing the hating.

Gross. Slut. My middle school bullies called me that because my breasts came in, fast and furious. It hadn't been long after my mom had died, and I retreated more firmly into my writing and the world of books, into that safe space of dreams and make-believe.

Back then, it felt as if the whole world was against me, but it had only been a small group of girls and boys, led by one boy in particular. Now, the world truly is looking at me, judging me, and tearing me to shreds. Nausea rolls through me.

Daisy must see it all on my face because she reaches over and shuts down my computer.

"I was afraid this would be a bad idea. You can't fight the

trolls. You can't control what they say. But you can control what *you* do. Don't give them power over you. Stay away from the online bullshit, especially the comments sections. You checked once, and now you never need to do it again. Promise me."

I promise her, praying my words are true, that I'll be strong enough not to seek out that vitriol.

But the damage is done. I'm shaking. I can't get it out of my head, the ugly words of strangers that have seeped into my cozy living room, creeping across my soft couch, winding their way through my home like insidious poison.

None of it is real, I remind myself. I'm not even on social media except for my bookish accounts. I barely watch television. I don't read tabloids. I just need to pretend that sick alternate world full of trolls and haters doesn't exist.

Despite her protests, I tell Daisy I need to be alone. Pretending to be okay is too hard right now. She nods, even though I can tell she wants to argue.

"Fine, I'll go," she says reluctantly. "Rest, and I'll be back first thing in the morning. Chase will fix this."

I nod with a weak smile and shut the door.

When she leaves, I lean against my door and close my eyes, relieved to be alone, relieved not to have to try to hold it together anymore. I mostly feel numb and just want to crawl into bed and sleep until I'm anonymous again.

Now, I understand what Chase told me about the dark side of fame. Why he was so adamant that he didn't want a relationship. If this was the public reaction to one photo, I can't imagine the hate a girlfriend would get.

I thought he was being high-handed. Or overreacting. Or just making excuses because he wasn't interested in me like that. But this small taste of dubious fame has shown me his scary reality. I had to experience it firsthand to truly understand. And he was right. It's daunting to think of withstanding that world for the long term.

Even worse, this is what Chase has to live with on a daily basis. He goes through it all alone. Who's there to comfort *him* when it gets too much? He worries about protecting others from this damaging force, but who protects him?

When I finally fall asleep, I dream fitfully and wake in the middle of the night.

I'm still floating in and out of wakefulness when I see something flicker at the edge of the room. I think it might be a trick of the light, but goose bumps erupt on my skin. "Hello?" I say, my voice coming out so tight and constricted, it's barely a whisper of fear.

I can't see the door. A glow of dense haze fills my room, illuminated by the streetlight filtering through my lace curtains.

My lungs fill with smoke, thick and acrid.

Smoke? How?

I cough uncontrollably, trying to draw in enough breath to scream, to do something, anything, before the black mist overcomes me and the world fades into a heavy blanket of nothingness.

CHAPTER 21

hase

It's been two weeks since I said goodbye to Olivia.

And I'm in hell.

First, because I miss her every damn day.

And second, because I think I'm in actual hell. I'm shooting a film in the Amazon, getting eaten by bugs the size of my fist, swimming in a crocodile-infested river, or, rather, a caiman-infested river, which is basically the same thing. I'm running from floodwaters and living off chicken breasts and air for every meal because, in the movie, I'm supposed to have zero body fat. All in the name of art.

We've been working long days and longer nights to get this shoot done as quickly as possible. We all have places we'd rather be, and every day, the production is bleeding money.

Working on this film is an unexpected whirlwind. I'd returned to LA, believing I'd have a month off with just some meetings and promotional tasks and way too much time thinking about Olivia. But I got a call to be a last-minute replacement for a supporting character in the Oscar-bait film of the year. The actor who was cast originally broke his leg a few days before shooting. His bad luck was my gain—from a movie perspective. Though, after filming here for two weeks, I'm beginning to believe the actor's freak accident was deliberate.

To avoid the insects, I think as I smack another mosquito. But mosquitoes are just a small part of it. They have bullet ants. And assassin bugs. And the feared Amazonian giant centipede. I shudder.

The other thing that sucks about shooting here is the lack of regular phone or internet.

Thankfully, I shoot my final scene today, and then I get to fly far, far away from this place.

"Hey, Chase."

I turn to Cassidy. She's also in this movie and suggested me for the part.

Cassidy has a genetic mutation that causes her to look incredible, even in the heat of the jungle. She's an Aussie, so maybe that's part of her secret. Her straight brown hair, bright blue eyes, and wide smile are as gorgeous as ever. And she doesn't even have one bug bite on her smooth, tanned legs.

At one time, I'd been infatuated with that beauty. She's also charming and fun, and we had a good time in the beginning. Our relationship felt shallow, though that probably wasn't all her fault. But despite our past, when I look at her now, I only feel vague nostalgia.

She sits down next to me, her hair falling over one shoulder. Now that she's closer, I can tell she's been in hair and makeup. Her look for the jungle is "natural," but it still takes hours to achieve that perfect glow and flawless no-makeup look. I know because I sit in the same chair every day, despite being a guy. We all need a little enhancement, especially when being filmed in high-definition.

"Hey, what's up?" I ask. "I haven't seen much of you since I arrived."

Though we ended things amicably years ago, it's still awkward. Before, we'd had a casual friendship—joking, laughing, and hanging out—now, not so much. Since I arrived, she's kept to herself, which surprises me because she suggested me for the part. But it's further proof that going from friends to lovers is a guaranteed way to lose a friendship. Something I need to remember.

She holds out her phone and points to it. "Did you check your phone lately?"

"Not since yesterday when I managed to get a few minutes of reception. Why?"

She chews on her bottom lip and blows out a breath. "So, you haven't seen it..."

"Seen what?"

"I'm not sure whether to show you this, but I thought you'd want to know." She passes me her phone. I glance at the picture of a couple standing in the rain, embracing. The photo on her screen is too small to make out details.

"Someone reenacting our scene again? So?" I ask. It's not unusual. Fans do that all the time, just like couples on a boat always do the famous *Titanic* pose.

"No, Chase. Look at it."

I look more carefully, and my stomach would have dropped to my shoes if I'd been wearing them. "Fuck."

In my life, I've rarely felt helpless.

Sure, I've been in plenty of shitty situations, one after the other, since the moment my mom died to today. Through all of it, I always had an unshakable certainty in my ability to manage, perhaps due to being challenged daily from a young age and surviving.

But that's only when I've had to worry about myself. Now, this isn't just about me.

Fear grips me, imagining how Olivia must be feeling, having the attention of the world—the haters, the trolls, the paparazzi, the unstable fans—all directed at her. And me being so fucking far away, I can't protect her. This is the beginning of all my worst-case scenarios.

I hold the phone so tight I think it might shatter.

"That's—"

"You," Cassidy supplies.

"And that's—"

"Not me," she says.

I scroll down the screen and read. *"Chase James and Mystery Girl Replay Famous Kissing Scene in the Rain.* Fuck." I scroll down farther to the subheading. *"The Hollywood Herald* can exclusively report that Chase James's mystery girl is Olivia Evans, who works at a small bookshop in Noe Valley."

My hand shakes. They know who she is. That means the full fury of all my obsessed fans and every tabloid in the world is about to rain down on her.

"Fuck," I repeat, weaker now. My insides feel hollow. "Olivia."

"So, who is she?" Cassidy asks, her face tightening.

"She's my best friend."

"It looks like she's more than that," her words echo my thoughts.

Cassidy observes me. "So is she the one?"

"The one who...?" I ask. My brain is far away—in San Francisco with Olivia.

"The girl you were hung up on when we dated."

"What are you talking about, Cassidy?"

"I always knew there was someone else. The way you were so preoccupied. The way you were always texting someone. I see how you're looking at this girl in the photo. It's obvious how you feel. Is it her?" She doesn't look mad, just curious.

I can't deal with this now.

"What are you talking about?" I say. "We broke up because you couldn't handle the media and fan scrutiny and their obsession with our relationship. After the death threats, you said you wanted a low-key romance."

She looks sad. "That was hard. But if you had really cared, it wouldn't have mattered. It seemed easier to blame the media. I'm not saying you cheated. But your heart was always somewhere else. If you looked at me even once like you're looking at this girl, all the crap and baggage would have been worth the trouble." She gently takes back her phone from me.

My phone vibrates in my pocket, surprising me. The screen reads, "Daisy." *Shit.*

I answer and don't bother with niceties. "Daisy. I just saw the photo. Are you and Olivia okay?"

"Ch-Chase, we have to talk." Her voice is trembling. My always-glib, always-unflappable sister sounds upset.

Whatever happened is bad. And I already know that it's all my fault.

CHAPTER 22

livia

IN YOUNG ADULT NOVELS, when there's a life-threatening crisis, one of two things always happens.

Either the hero comes crashing in and saves the day, or the heroine steps up, kicks ass, and saves herself, along with everyone else.

Yeah, that didn't happen when I was caught in a fire.

Clearly, if I was in some Nancy Drew girl gang, I'd be the one kicked out for sheer incompetence. Or poor lung functioning.

I passed out for only a minute or two. When I regained consciousness, survival instinct kicked in. I began crawling toward the stairs, but I grew weaker with each slow struggle forward.

Thankfully, several firefighters, who were called by a neighbor, arrived and saved me.

And now here I am, outside my somewhat charred house, gritty with exhaustion and soot, being philosophical about my lack of heroine potential. Obviously, I'm on the verge of losing it.

It's nearing five in the morning, and all I want is silence, a hot shower, and sleep. Maybe I should have let them take me in the ambulance.

I'd resisted because I can't afford another trip to the ER this month. But even with nurses poking and prodding me, at least the hospital would have been a more peaceful scene than my house, which is filled with official-looking people in uniforms.

I close my eyes and try to be thankful. The firefighters risked their lives to put the fire out. So, I can't complain or cry, even if the whiny, overtired child in my brain wants me to. I refuse to think about the damage to my home.

At least the damage isn't nearly as bad as it could have been. Most of the destruction is confined to the upstairs bathroom and the hallway outside my bedroom.

"Ma'am? Have you seen this?" a police officer asks.

The officer holds up a paper in his gloved hand. It's a handwritten note with an angry red scrawl.

Daisy, who'd shown up just after the firefighters arrived, peeks over my shoulder.

As I read the note, the hair on my arms stands up.

"Slut. You don't deserve him. Stay away from Chase." Is slashed on the page.

"Do you know what this is? We found the note sticking out of your mailbox."

I bite my lip, more than just the smoke inhalation making me feel queasy.

"I-I've never seen it before, but my picture was just published in the tabloids with a celebrity. Chase James," I admit.

One of the firefighters looks at me in surprise and maybe a little envy.

"Chase should know about this," Daisy says. "Most of his fans are great, but there are a few who are obsessed to the point of stalking and worse. A few have done some scary things. We need to take this seriously, Olivia."

The police officer frowns. "This note changes things. We could be looking at arson."

"But the fire started upstairs, didn't it? How could they have gotten in without your alarm going off? Didn't Chase just install one?" Daisy asks.

"The security system is really complicated, and I couldn't remember the code," I say sheepishly. "I didn't think I even needed security, so I never activated it."

Anxiety, thick and heavy as molasses, spreads through me. The house I love and my formerly peaceful life have just been torched. My brain can't process anything more, like the idea someone might be trying to kill me.

When the firefighters and police officers leave, Daisy leads me to her apartment, and I drag myself up her narrow stairs and go straight to her shower to scrub the soot and smoke from my body. Standing under the powerful jets—seriously, how does she have such a fabulous shower with these vintage pipes?—I let the water rain down on my exhausted body. I shampoo, condition, and scrub until the smoke smell has lessened and the panic of waking to a fire-filled house recedes a little. It's surreal, as if it happened in another world, to another me.

I'm not allowed back into my home. They said the structure has to be deemed safe first. I fear the worst. What had I lost in my bedroom? Nanna's photos? Remington's letters that were kept in a box under my bed? My birth certificate and important documents? All my clothes? Hell, I don't even have a toothbrush with me.

It's true that the fire was somewhat confined, but the firefighters warned me about the destructive potential of the smoke and water damage.

The only things I have on me are my purse and my laptop. Both were on the table by the door, which a kind firefighter had brought to me once the fire was extinguished. My wallet and new phone were thankfully still in my purse from earlier. I have the most important necessities. I'll figure the rest out.

Being run over by a bike messenger was nothing compared to this. They say bad things happen in threes. Hopefully, this is the third thing, as I can't even imagine what fate has in store for me next.

I wrap a towel around me and realize I have nothing to change into since all my clothes are at my house, possibly ruined. I'll need to borrow something from Daisy. That might be tough since I'm several sizes larger than waif. But it's either that or wander around the mall naked while browsing for new clothes.

I look in the mirror. Audrey told me recently that repeating positive affirmations can help in all sorts of situations. Sometimes she's a little overfond of the personal development section of the bookstore. I decide it can't hurt to try it. "This will all be okay," I say out loud, into the mirror. "I'm okay." I feel silly but repeat it until I almost sort of kind of believe it. Huh. Lying to yourself does work.

Feeling slightly better now, I walk out of the bathroom in my towel with a frown on my face but determination in my steps. That determination falters when I pass the living room to see Daisy sitting on one couch.

And Ryder Black sitting next to her.

Rock star Ryder. The musical genius who transitioned from boy-band heartthrob to full-fledged rock god years ago. A singing, guitar-strumming, piano-pounding god. Sitting in Daisy's living room.

My towel slips, but I catch it before I flash a second celebrity this month.

This time, though, I'm not mortified. Maybe it's that I'm getting used to being semi-naked around famous people. Or it might be the exhaustion, the fire, and the relief I'm not dead.

Basically, I'm out of fucks to give.

So, I stand there, looking from Ryder to Daisy. Each gives me a casual smile as if there isn't anything odd about this scenario. Ryder sips from a glass of what looks like water but could be vodka, knowing Ryder's reputation.

"Daisy?"

"Yes, Olivia?" she asks, head cocked.

"Why is Ryder Black sitting in your living room?"

"Really, Olivia, that's a rude question with him right here. I mean, he can hear you. Why shouldn't he be sitting here?"

"Is he also your long-lost foster brother?" I'm just teasing her since I know about her crush.

She snorts. "God no."

I turn to Ryder, who has one eyebrow arched. He and Chase do that amused eyebrow arch so well.

"Ryder, why are you sitting in Daisy's living room? Not that I have an objection to it. But just…why?"

Daisy's mild expression breaks, and she cracks up laughing. "Oh, Olivia, you should see your face. I thought you'd drop your towel again."

"When was the last time she dropped her towel?" Ryder asks, leaning forward with interest.

"She told me she dropped it in front of Chase. I think he liked what he saw, judging from the pictures of them making out," Daisy says.

I pull the fabric tighter and glare at Daisy. "I told you that in the strictest confidence. You might not want to be sharing any secrets, Daisy. I could let certain things I know slip out." I look meaningfully at Ryder.

Daisy narrows her eyes at me, but she wisely changes the subject. "Wow, you're a grumpy cat. I'll give you a pass because your house almost burned down. Anyway, to answer your question, Ryder is here to take us to Malibu."

I sink down on the edge of the couch, pulling at my towel. At least Daisy splurged on extra-large towels, unlike the hotel.

"Say again?"

"I called Chase about the fire and the threatening letter. He freaked and called Ryder to whisk us away since Chase is in the Amazon, and it will take him a day or two to get home, even with him leaving right away. So, Ryder's our official white knight and will fly us back with him, along with a gazillion bodyguards that Chase arranged. Isn't that kind?"

"White knight at your service." Ryder's dimples pop as he smiles.

"We're going to Malibu? With you? Where will we stay?" I hate being ten steps behind everyone else, but nothing makes sense right now, and all I feel is overwhelmingly tired, as if I could go to sleep for two weeks straight.

"We're going to Chase and Ryder's place," Daisy answers, her eyes sparkling with excitement. "Well, it's technically Sebastian's estate, but Chase and Ryder live there too."

"Chase doesn't want you to stay in San Francisco until they know who sent the letter and your place is inspected for structural damage," Ryder interjects. "After what happened, it's better to be somewhere with gates and security."

"But how did he know? How did you get here so fast? This all just happened."

"I called Chase as soon as I found out about the fire," Daisy says. "He called Ryder and arranged everything."

"I've never heard Chase so freaked out," Ryder says to me gently. "He wanted to be here himself, but he's catching the first flight out."

Butterflies invade my stomach at the thought of seeing Chase again. And staying at his place, seeing him in a Malibu mansion, in his own glamorous world. I try not to think about what it might mean that Chase is worried about me. I imagine he feels guilty if he thinks the fire could be linked to one of his fans.

Boring reality intrudes. "But what about our jobs? I can't leave Audrey with no notice. And you've got your shop. I also need to be here to sort out my house." I swallow down a hot lump of what could be tears at the last thought. Rock gods and movie stars aside, how can I leave my house and belongings in this condition?

"I've already called Audrey. She can cover your shifts, and she said to take all the time you need. Don't worry about your house either. Chase is sending his old assistant down to sort everything out. He'll need a key to your place, and you'll need to coordinate with the authorities by phone, but you don't have to be in San Francisco. Chase is worried about you, and so am I. Plus, you deserve a holiday. Ryder—rich, famous, hot Ryder…" She turns to him. "Sorry for objectifying you." She grins at him.

"Not a problem," he responds, taking another sip of his questionable water-vodka.

"Anyway, Ryder is offering to whisk us away in his label's private plane to romp around a Malibu mansion with three famous dudes, including your crush, Chase, who we all know you're hot for because we've got photographic evidence. And you're arguing about it? Really, Olivia, I didn't think you were this dumb."

Daisy has a valid point. Plus, I'm way too tired to argue.

"You're right." I shrug. "Thanks, Ryder. I accept your offer to rescue us."

"About fucking time," Daisy mutters. Then she hops up and takes my hand. "So, now that we've got introductions and explanations out of the way, we'll pack."

I head to Daisy's room to pack my nonexistent wardrobe.

This *is* turning into the summer of risk, after all. Scandals, fire, and a possible death threat. I'm not sure that's exactly what Nanna had in mind.

* * *

I don't recognize myself or my life anymore.

I've been in Malibu a little over twenty-four hours, and I'm lounging by a turquoise pool in a cute retro swimsuit and glamour-girl cover-up, with my laptop balancing on my lap and editing my fourth novel—for the fortieth time.

I never actually consider a manuscript finished enough to send out to agents or publishers. I just edit them incessantly until I can't stand to look at them, and then they go into my computer's folder of death named Old Novels, and then I start work on the next one. It may be why I'm not making headway on my dream career as author. Just a guess.

A team of professionals already came by the house to give Daisy and me a massage, pedicure, and blowout, all courtesy of Sebastian and Chase's fabulous assistant, Emma, who is a magical fairy godmother in pint-size Southern ballbuster form.

When we arrived yesterday in the early hours of the morning, Emma already knew about the fire and my lack of wardrobe. I inquired about the local Target, but Emma just laughed as if I'd made a hysterical joke, and an array of summer styles in my size arrived at the mansion. When I argued with Emma about accepting what must have cost a fortune, she rolled her eyes at me and said Chase would want to spoil us. In the end, there wasn't much I could do. All my clothes were back in my charred house. And, apparently, Chase gave strict instructions that we weren't to leave the estate. He's that worried about the threatening note and fire.

With time and distance, I begin to feel like we're overreacting. Surely this is all an awful coincidence. The note, while concerning, is probably an overzealous fan, and the fire could be the result of old wiring and nothing more.

But here I am, feeling like an extra on the set of *Mad Men* during its LA season. Nanna and I loved *Mad Men*.

Daisy rolls over. "I'm bored," she complains.

"Then do something," I say, reaching to take a sip of iced coffee through a straw, the ice having long since melted in the heat. Condensation pools on the glass, and I have to wipe my hands before I go back to typing on my keyboard.

Sounds of a guitar and male laughter carry to the pool from the open French doors that lead into the house.

Daisy picks up her camera and points it toward me. I hold my hand in front of my face.

She sticks out her tongue. "Spoilsport. Help a girl out, please. I need to update my Instagram."

"Daisy, we're here to hide. We can't post on social media. You're the one who keeps telling me how obsessed Chase's fans are. They'd somehow find that photo, recognize the freaking pool tiles or umbrella, and know where we are."

She sighs, pouting. "I hate it when you're right. But I want some fun. All the boys are busy working."

The boys are Ryder and his band, who've been working on Ryder's new album, alternating between the living room, kitchen, and converted studio he has set up in the basement. Sebastian was gone all morning, doing promo for a movie.

Unlike Daisy, I'm not bored. I've been writing. The words are suddenly flowing in this new environment, the change of scenery unlocking something in my brain, and plot points that were tripping me up for months have fallen into place, like finding the key piece to a puzzle. It helps that I write mysteries and feel like I've fallen into the pages of one myself.

Even with being occupied, though, I can see how this life, while the height of luxury, could feel like a gilded cage. I'm not used to having people always around me. I wonder how Chase handles it, but at least he's in the cottage next to the main house, so he has more privacy. Since his place is just one bedroom, Daisy and I are staying in the main mansion.

Ryder and Sebastian share the grand home, which was built

by Sebastian's grandmother, who was also a famous film star. It was renovated by his equally famous parents before their acrimonious divorce. Then there's Marie, the cook and maid, who reminds me of a house mom; and Emma, Sebastian's personal assistant, who also helps out Ryder and Chase when they need her. The women don't live on the premises, but they might as well, as they seem to be here around the clock. Finally, there's the security team who are in and out of the house and grounds all day and night, doing patrols.

The introvert in me hates the entourage, and I understand Chase's insistence at living in his peaceful white-shingled cottage, which, like the main house and pool, has a spectacular view of the cliffs and ocean below.

"So." I take another sip of my drink, "have you heard from Chase yet?" I ask, casual-like.

"He called earlier asking for a full update," Daisy says. "He's trying everything to get back as quickly as possible. His filming location is super remote, and there was a storm that delayed all flights out."

She turns to me, her blue eyes worried. "Chase is freaking out, wanting to make sure you're safe. I know there's something between you two. I love my brother, but he's not good with relationships. When he arrives, take it slow. I don't want you to get hurt."

I flush. "I know, Daisy. I'm not expecting anything."

A bronzed body flashes past us and does a cannonball into the water.

A fine spray of water hits me and the edge of my laptop, even though I'm a few feet back from the pool.

"Hey! Watch it!" Daisy cries. "Don't you dare get my camera wet, or Olivia's computer."

"Oh shit!" Sebastian says after his head breaks the surface. "Sorry."

"I didn't realize you were back." It's hard not to give Sebastian the fangirl stare. His eyes are impossibly blue against his dark features, and his abs are rock-hard. But despite admiring the eye candy that is Sebastian Blake, I have no butterflies or intense chemistry like I feel with Chase.

"The interviews finished early. Thank fuck. Sorry I almost got your *precious* wet, squirt," he says to Daisy, referring to her camera. "I'll tell you what. I'll make it up to you by letting you shoot nude photos of me." Sebastian waggles his eyebrows.

She laughs. "Maybe next time, hotshot."

"If you're not down for shooting *my* nude calendar, I'm sure you could ask Ryder to model for you," he says slyly.

Daisy blushes. Daisy is not the blushing type.

"I knew it!" Sebastian shouts, pointing to her. "You're into him. Ryder, oh, Ryder," he croons, making his pecs dance.

"Shut up, Sebastian," she says, amusement in her eyes, until her smile freezes.

Sebastian tilts his chin up. "Hey, man."

I look to see Ryder behind me, surveying the scene.

"I always knew you were hot for me, Blake," Ryder says.

"My secret's out," Sebastian responds dryly.

I notice that Ryder's eyes avoid Daisy, and now she's looking down, playing with the straw in her drink, appearing uncharacteristically shy. He slinks into a pool lounger. He's in his standard uniform of jeans and a black T-shirt, leather and silver bracelets on his wrist, with tats snaking up his lean but muscular forearms. His eyes are weary. He looks beyond exhausted, but there's something in his smile, in the way he's drumming his fingers against his well-worn jeans that radiates energy.

"You guys finish your session?" Daisy asks, a little breathless.

"Yeah. It took us the whole night, but we finally laid down a new track." With his wide smile, he's less jaded rock star and more excited little kid. I find myself warming to him. The truth is, everyone in this house intimidates the hell out of me, but the more I get to know them, the more I realize that despite their insane jobs and glamorous lives, they're just normal people, passionate about their careers, having fun with friends.

"That's dope." Sebastian jumps out of the water and grabs a towel before plopping down into the pool lounger next to Ryder. "I thought you were in a writing slump."

Ryder shrugs, his eyes briefly straying to Daisy before quickly looking away when her gaze lifts to his. "It's been years since the music just flowed."

"This is major," Sebastian says. "We need to celebrate."

"Yes! Can we? Please?" The prospect of a party shakes Daisy from her silence. "It doesn't have to be a big party."

"Daisy, last time…" Ryder says with a frown.

"This isn't last time," Daisy snaps. "Jesus. Can everyone forget that? I'm not a stupid sixteen-year-old now."

"Daisy. I found you after you—." He takes a deep breath. "I'm never going to forget. That was the scariest damn day of my life." Ryder's eyes light with intensity.

Daisy plays with the dials of her camera, but she doesn't answer him.

"Bro, we're not talking about a rager. We'll keep it chill," Sebastian says.

"Chase won't like it," Ryder warns darkly.

"Well, it's a good thing Chase isn't around, then." Sebastian grins. "He's still stuck somewhere. Right, Daisy?"

Daisy nods. "I think."

"So he won't be back for another day, at least. This place is like a morgue, and you writing new music deserves a celebration. We won't call it a party. It's just a few friends hanging out. It'll be fine. All in favor of a non-party, say aye," Sebastian says.

"Aye." I raise my hand. It's a risk, so that means it's something I have to do. Gotta listen to Nanna.

"Aye," Daisy says, her eyes shining with excitement.

"Fuck yeah," Sebastian says.

Ryder's eyes scan our eager faces. He sighs. "I know when I'm outnumbered. But no strangers. I don't care if they're supermodels, Sebastian. Only a few close friends hanging out. And I'm sticking to you girls like glue tonight. Call me Velcro. And you, Daisy, no trouble. Got it?"

"Yes, Daddy," Daisy says with a cheeky grin.

Even with shades, Ryder's glare is fierce.

"Relax," Sebastian says. "Uncle Sebastian's got it all under control."

CHAPTER 23

hase

I'VE BEEN IN JEEPS, boats, planes—big and small, and even a short trip on a bus trying to get home, and I'm bleary-eyed from exhaustion. I spent the car ride from the airport to Malibu on the phone with my security team, trying to figure out who the hell left Olivia that note and doing damage control with my publicist.

No one has new information on the fire or the letter left by the stalker, but at least my publicist has a plan. She suggests the best way to throw the world's attention off Olivia is to date someone else. Distract and deflect.

She throws out the names of a few fellow actresses. Her first choice is Cassidy since a significant portion of the fandom already believes we're dating, and it would be great for the franchise. Plus, the stalker likely ships Cassidy and Chase—otherwise known as Chassidy. Cassidy is back from Colombia in a few days, so I tentatively agree with the plan.

This whole situation is my nightmare come true. The pap

scrutiny surrounding Olivia is bad enough. But could a fan really have started a fire to try to kill her? Unfortunately, I know the potential exists. Over the years, I've had fans do some sick shit in the name of loving me. They've surprised me in various hotel rooms, usually naked in my bed. That may sound like a good thing, but the reality is unnerving. One woman, very early in my career, believed she was my wife and spent the entire weekend at my last house. I came home to her baking me a chocolate cake and wielding a kitchen knife.

That incident, combined with the desire to help Sebastian through his rehab, prompted me to move in to the guest cottage on Sebastian's estate. There's nowhere in Malibu or LA more secure or private.

But it's the girls I date who get the worst treatment. Fans have harassed and threatened every woman I've been linked to. Olivia nearly died, and it's my fault for not having the strength to keep away from her.

I try to remind myself she's safe at the estate. But as my car makes its way down the long driveway to the mansion, any thoughts of safety fly out of my head.

"What the fuck?" I snap, turning to Duncan in the front seat. "Did you know about this? What the hell is happening?"

"It appears to be a party. And no one invited me," he says lightly, but his expression I can see in the mirror is not pleased.

And neither am I. "You said you were on top of things. That they were secure. This is not fucking secure," I bark.

"I gave the guards strict instructions. But obviously, one of your housemates overrode them."

As we go through the gates, we pass cars lined up the driveway. I roll down the window to hear music blaring from the house and pool area.

The SUV slows to a stop, and I jump out, not worrying about my bags or Duncan, and stride up the wide staircase into the house. I don't need to open the door because it's already wide-open, which only pisses me off further.

Inside, I scan the room for Daisy or Olivia. I'm prepared for the worst, but rather than the raging party I fear, there are small groups of people scattered around, talking and drinking beer. I recognize all the faces, people we've known for years, and my heart rate slows, just a little.

A group of Ryder's bandmates congregates by the pool table.

"Hey, man," the guitar player, Kenji, says as I walk by. "You down to party? Ryder's finally writing music again. The next album is coming."

So that's what this is about. On a normal night, I'd be amped for Ryder. But now is not the time. "I'm looking for two girls. One has long black hair, and the other is short, blond."

"You mean Olivia and Daisy?"

I don't like Kenji's smile when he says their names. It seems far too appreciative. I decide maybe he's not so cool after all.

"Yes," I grate out.

"They're in the pool."

Feminine laughter and a squeal filter in through the row of French doors. I follow the sounds outside.

And there is Olivia, having climbed out of the water, standing backlit by the pool lights, water dripping from her gorgeous curves. Her pale skin is set off against a deep-blue bathing suit. It's not as revealing as the bikinis flaunted around the pool, but somehow that just makes it sexier. She throws her head back and laughs at something Sebastian says. Jealousy, hot and primal, rushes through my body. *Mine.* The fierce longing echoes inside me. I want to make her laugh. Make her smile. Every damn day.

I stride toward her, watching intently, waiting for the moment she sees me. When she does, her mouth opens in surprise.

"Chase." She gasps, pulling a fluffy white towel around her. I mourn the disappearance of all her creamy skin.

Is she breathless from laughing or from seeing me?

The proof that she's safe is right here before me. All I want is to wrap my arms around her and never let go. Vow to never leave her again. Yell at her for how worried I've been. I've been imagining the scenarios of our reunion in my head the entire trip home.

But it's not like any of that.

Now that I'm in front of her, all the adrenaline that had been carrying me, leaves. I'm awkward and unsure and shaky with relief.

"Olivia," is all I say. I don't complete my sentence. *Olivia, I'm so fucking glad you're here, you're safe.*

The last time I'd seen her, we'd spent the night in each other's arms. I thought we'd said goodbye forever. Now what the hell am I going to do?

She takes a hesitant step toward me, and I mirror the move. We stand a few feet apart, just taking each other in.

"I'm so damn sorry about the fire." My voice is hoarse with emotion.

"Stop. It isn't your fault," Olivia says softly.

"Are you sure you aren't hurt?" I scan every part of her body I can see, assessing any damage.

"No, I was lucky. I'm fine," she reassures me.

"When I think about what could have happened to you…"

"Chase!" Daisy runs over and throws herself into my arms, soaking body and all. She messes up my hair with wet hands.

I push away the frustration of being interrupted. The truth is, I don't know what I was going to say. I switch gears and smile down at Daisy. "Hey, kid."

"It's about time you got home," she says with a cheeky grin. "You had to send someone else to rescue us."

Sebastian swims up to the side of the pool. "Hey, man. You missed all the fun. Throw me a beer, will you?"

I ignore his request and walk over to him, kneeling down so that he can see I'm deadly serious.

"So, what part of *take care of Daisy and Olivia* did you not understand? You selfish prick. Olivia is getting threatening letters from one of my fans, and then her house catches fire. I doubt that's a coincidence. I asked Ryder to bring them here to keep them safe, and you throw a party? Do you not recall what happened before?" My voice is quiet, controlled, and sharp as a blade.

Daisy puts her hand on my shoulder. "It's not Sebastian's fault," she says. "I was bored and just wanted a little fun. They only invited close friends."

"It's not a party, dude. It's a gathering," Sebastian says, backing away from me in the pool, his hands held up in innocence. "Besides," he says, tilting his chin up, "I could be wrong here, but I think this is *my* place, *my* property, so I can do whatever the hell I want." He says it lightly, but I can read the challenge in his eyes.

And fuck, he's right. Ryder and I both stayed with Sebastian because he needed us to keep his old seedy entourage of druggies and users away, to keep him tethered and stable. He tends to unspool when left alone.

We continue to stay because it's secure, comfortable, easy. This may only be a place to rest my head in the short stints between movie gigs, but when I'm here, it feels a bit like family, something I know precious little about.

Maybe, though, I've been here too long. I insist on paying rent, which Sebastian donates to charity, yet this isn't really my place as I was just reminded. Perhaps it's time to find somewhere of my own. A place where I can set the rules.

Ryder swims up to Sebastian. "It's not just Sebastian's fault. We all voted on it. The girls haven't been out of our sight the whole time. We can't keep them locked up with just us, man. Daisy threatened to have a night out on the town if we didn't give them a little fun. I figured it was better to have something here than risk them sneaking out."

"Daisy, you just got here. Do you ever do a damn thing that you're supposed to?" I turn to her.

She shrugs and sits down next to me, letting her legs dangle in the pool. "Well, I didn't sneak out. I just said maybe it was a possibility."

Olivia walks over and sits next to Daisy.

I meet both girls' eyes. Affection and exasperation fill me. "Why am I the only one taking this seriously?"

Ryder holds up his hand. "I was about to fly to Europe when you asked me to get the girls. I've never missed a concert in my life, so no, you aren't the only one taking this seriously."

"Really?" Daisy asks. "You missed a concert for us?"

Ryder looks uncomfortable, probably at the hero worship in Daisy's eyes. "Uh, yeah. A small one."

I watch the two of them intently. Ryder is a good guy. Hell, a great one. But Daisy had a wicked crush on him that summer she stayed with us. Everyone knew it. I can only pray she's smarter this time. Ryder thinks of her as an honorary kid sister, as he should. That left her devastated before. I'd hate to see her heartbroken again.

I sigh. "Sebastian, I know this is your place and you get to make the rules, but as long as they stay with you, any party, even if it's a fucking tea party, needs to be approved by me and Duncan. If we can't agree to that, then Olivia, Daisy, and I need to go somewhere else. I don't want to leave, but I have to know everyone is safe until the stalker is caught. It's your call."

"Nah, no need to bail. The girls are safest here. Anyway, my agent's on my shit to live clean and get back into shape for my next movie," Sebastian says.

Daisy frowns. "Hey, I think you're all forgetting that Olivia's the only one who needs security, not me. I haven't been in any tabloids, and no one is threatening me. I'm just here to support my friend. Well, that and the free trip to LA."

"I don't want to be any trouble, guys," Olivia protests. "This is all really unnecessary."

"I think you need this, bro." Sebastian leans over to the large ice bucket, pulls out a beer, and throws it at me.

I catch it and only debate for a second before popping it open and taking a long drink.

"So, any updates?" Olivia asks hesitantly.

"I have good news, which is why you're all still alive after this party stunt."

"Gathering," Sebastian corrects.

Ryder slaps the back of Sebastian's head.

"Ow!" Sebastian rubs the spot and shoots Ryder a look of outrage. "What the hell?"

"Just keeping you from having Chase kick your ass, idiot."

"You have news?" Olivia prompts again.

"We have evidence linking the notes to a specific fan we've been keeping an eye on, based on the handwriting and the profile. And her family lives in San Francisco, so she could have gotten to you easily. If we're right, she thinks I'm her husband, and she hates any woman I'm associated with. She's done something similar before. Sending threatening letters. Not arson," I clarify.

"Man, is it the chick who lost it with that girl you dated?" Sebastian asks.

I nod grimly. "That's the one."

"What happened?" Daisy asks.

"I went on one date with an actress I knew. She started receiving similar letters at her home. At first, it was just regular fandom crap. Then the letters started to get more unhinged, and someone broke into her house. They slashed up her bed. The investigators I hired analyzed the notes, and hers are almost identical to the one you received."

"Why isn't the stalker in jail?" Olivia asked.

"The cops messed up the evidence, and the whole case fell apart. The PR team didn't want drama in the tabloids, so we let it go, provided the fan received psychiatric treatment. It seemed like she was better until now."

"I thought this was good news," Daisy says.

"The good news is that she's nowhere near here, and we have her under twenty-four-hour surveillance. I'll keep you safe, and I'll do everything I can to keep the tabloids off your trail. I promise, Olivia. This is all my fault, but I'm going to make it right." Our eyes lock and hold. Her gray eyes are the color of storm clouds in the low light of the poolside.

Daisy clears her throat. "Well, this has been fun, but I'm getting cold. I need to grab a towel." She hops up and looks pointedly at Sebastian and Ryder.

Ryder takes the hint and pushes himself out of the pool. "I need something more than beer. Gonna hit the kitchen. Sebastian?"

"I don't wanna go to the kitchen."

Ryder slaps Sebastian again.

"Oh shit. Fine, I'm going."

The three leave fast. It's awkward as fuck.

Olivia watches them go, her face flushed. "They aren't subtle, are they?"

I shake my head. I don't want to talk about them.

With Daisy gone, there's no one between us. Olivia's bare feet and legs dangle in the water. I kick off my shoes, roll up the jeans I wore on the plane, and sit next to her. The water is cool, but I can feel her heat.

She sucks in a breath, watching me. Like magnets, we lean closer. My eyes zero in on those lips. If her tongue peeps out, I'll be a goner.

Her eyes close, and she tilts her face toward me. I want to take what she's offering.

But I can't. If I've learned anything from this dangerous situation I've created, it's that. I shift away, and she jerks back as if burned.

"I didn't mean to—"

"I need to be clear—"

"You first," she says.

"I just hope...I hope we can be friends. Anything else would put you in more danger, and it would kill me if something happened to you."

The look in Olivia's eyes before she glances away guts me. Fuck, I hate this. But there's no other way.

She's silent for a long moment. I resist the urge to fill the space with more apologies.

"Friends, sure," she says. "Of course. It seems like you're back with Cassidy now."

The tabloids have been full of Cassidy and me, rumors from filming in the jungle, even if the gossip is baseless.

She shivers, and I resist the urge to pull her into my arms to warm her. I open my mouth to deny the rumors and then change my mind.

Maybe it's for the best that she thinks I'm with someone else. It's safer this way. It's on the tip of my tongue, but I can't say the lie. There are too many other untruths between us. So I just nod.

The silence lengthens and she jumps up before I can answer her. "Okay. Well, that was a good talk. I'm going to sleep now."

I think she's going to walk away, but she hesitates.

"Chase?"

"Yeah?" I watch her standing over me.

Bundled in a towel, with her long, wet hair sticking to her face and shoulders, she's everything I've ever wanted and won't let myself have.

"Thank you."

She says it softly, and the words compete with the music and laughter of the surrounding party, but it's all I can hear and the last thing I expect.

"For what?"

"For having us here. For trying to keep us safe. Don't worry about me. You've been honest from the start about what we are and what we aren't. I understand. You don't need to feel guilty."

My breath leaves me in a blow. I hurt her; I know I did. And what does she do? She thanks me. And calls me honest, when that's the last thing I am. With her, my Typewriter Girl. With myself. The lies just keep compounding. They're for her sake, but they still stack up in front of me like an accounting of my sins.

"Good night," I say.

Then I watch her walk away.

CHAPTER 24

livia

THE NEXT MORNING, I wake with the sun streaming through gauzy curtains in the all-white guest room. It overlooks the pool, and the sky and water are brilliant hues of blue. This whole stalker situation might be confusing, and I was just friend-zoned by the Sexiest Man Alive, but at least my room rocks.

There's something about the bright Malibu sunshine that makes me hop out of bed. Maybe it's also the possibility of seeing Chase around the kitchen table. It will hurt, but the pain will have a certain pleasure intertwined.

Breakfast at the mansion has become one of my favorite parts of the day in my short stay here. For the past few mornings, it's been an adventure to see who will show up in the enormous kitchen. Marie acts like a den mother for the guys and their friends, laying out a full breakfast spread each morning that must rival any five-star hotel.

I stumble in, looking for coffee, only to find Daisy, Sebastian, Emma, Ryder, and a handful of Ryder's music entourage sitting around the table. Relief and disappointment run through me because Chase is absent.

"Hey," I say shyly, pulling my hair up into a jaunty ponytail. I'd brushed my hair, my teeth, and dressed in an oversized T-shirt and leggings, both courtesy of Emma after I begged her for some actual comfy clothes. I even slicked on a little gloss. That's as fancy as I get before my first cup of coffee, celebrity roommates or not. Working in a café has got me addicted to caffeine. If I don't caffeinate soon, I'll get a killer headache.

"Speak of the devil!" Daisy greets me, looking like the epitome of a California girl in a mustard-yellow macramé bathing suit and a gauzy cover-up, her hair in braids. "We were just talking about you!"

The rest of the table mumbles greetings around mouthfuls of pancakes and eggs.

Marie fills a coffee cup for me, pouring in milk and foam from a large silver dish, along with two generous scoops of sugar, just the way I like it. Bless her.

"I love you, Marie." I moan as I take the first sip.

"You look tired today, Ms. Olivia. Make a plate. You need to eat." She fusses over me.

I smile at Marie in thanks, then turn to Daisy. "What are you saying about me?" I ask warily.

"I'm telling them about Nanna's letter. We're helping you come up with a list of risks."

"Um. Thank you?" I'm not sure how I feel about enlisting their "help," so I take a large gulp of coffee.

"We all agreed you should get laid."

I spit out my drink.

Everyone cracks up as I mop up the mess I've made with a napkin that Marie hands me. Even Marie is grinning, the traitor.

"Daisy, you're in time-out. We did not all say that," Ryder says with a laugh.

"Well, Sebastian suggested it," Daisy argues. "And I agreed it's a smashing idea."

"Thanks for your support," I say as I check my white shirt for coffee splatters. "But I doubt Nanna meant that when she said she wanted me to take risks." I wince that this group is talking about my sex life—or lack thereof. Now I'm grateful Chase isn't here.

"You never know. Nanna was a firecracker. I bet she'd approve."

Unfortunately, Daisy is right. I'm the lone prude in my family. My grandmother was far more adventurous than me. She was never shy about talking about anything with me, even sex. And my mom never met a risk—or a man—she didn't like, which eventually led to her death. I've read enough psychology books to know that my mom's history probably contributes to me living life vicariously through screens and books. It's safer that way.

"I can come up with my daily risks without your help," I say mildly.

"You clearly need it," Sebastian says, as if he's talking to a child. "We're the experts."

Daisy looks down at her notepad. "Here's what we've come up with so far. Number one: skinny-dipping. I didn't put that item on the list. Kenji did."

I glare at him.

"If that's the first one, I'm scared to know what else you've come up with," I say.

"I think it's awesome because you already have a water theme going with your risks. Also, a naked theme. So, it fits right in." Daisy looks pleased with herself.

I narrow my eyes. "What do you mean, naked water theme?"

I really shouldn't ask, though, because I'm not sure I want to know. Ignorance is bliss. It's my new motto.

"Well, there's skinny-dipping in the fountain. Naked, check. Water, check. Then there was you and the towel incident." Daisy leans closer to me and whispers, even though everyone can hear what she's saying. "That involved nudity after a shower."

"That was not a purposeful risk. It was an accident!" I protest.

Daisy shrugs. "Haven't you heard? There are no accidents. Regardless, you definitely have a naked water theme going on, so we must honor that. Plus, skinny-dipping is freeing. It's perfect, even if Kenji has less than pure motives suggesting it. Now, where was I? Oh, yes. Number two: learn to roller skate. I added that because I can't believe you don't know how. You were deprived as a kid."

I'm happy for Daisy to change the subject away from me getting naked. "I wasn't a coordinated child. Nor am I a coordinated adult. I prefer pastimes that involve being seated. Like reading. Or writing."

"Number three: swim with the sharks."

"That's my suggestion! It's sick." Sebastian pounds his muscular chest, proud of his contribution. I'm not caffeinated enough to be confronted with the prospect of sharks.

I take another large gulp of coffee and hold out my cup desperately as Marie comes by to top me up. I'm going to need all the help I can get to hold my own in this conversation. "No. Not gonna happen. I hate sharks. Man was not meant to swim with them." There's no way I'm getting in the water with anything that has that many teeth. I shudder just thinking about it.

"Interesting," Daisy says, taking a giant forkful of pancake, maple syrup dripping. She chews and then swallows. "I like how you didn't discount skinny-dipping. Okay. We can cross off swimming with sharks." She consults her list and looks back up, hope in her eyes. "Maybe snorkeling with dolphins?"

I shake my head. "I don't care how friendly they are. In the water, with that fin, they look too much like sharks." Another shudder.

"Fine." She sighs dramatically. "What about visiting an aquarium? We can do this in baby steps, just like the skydiving," Daisy suggests.

"How is visiting an aquarium a risk?" Sebastian cries. "I'm taking charge of this list, Olivia."

"No way, Sebastian!" I point to him. "You are officially off my risk-taking committee."

"Don't you worry, woman. I promise you'll love it," he says smoothly.

I open my mouth to argue, but Daisy holds up her hand.

"We'll table number three and revisit it later."

"Fine," Sebastian grumbles.

"Motion to table risk number three approved. Moving on to item number four: take up a sport."

"That's my suggestion," Emma pipes up. She's perched on a stool, the only one of us dressed for work in a polished suit and hair in a sleek bun. "Fitness is healthy for you and provides serotonin and a great ass. I left the sport up for you to decide, because I can be nice." She shoots Sebastian a look. "Despite what some people think."

"Thanks, Emma. I'm glad *someone* is letting me choose."

"Hey, you didn't thank me!" Sebastian complains.

"That's because your risk involved something that could eat me!"

Daisy slaps the table with her spoon, as if it's a gavel. "Come to order and stop interrupting. So, what sport should we choose?"

"Should *I* choose," I correct. If I'm the one who chooses, at least I can make sure it doesn't involve further nakedness or balancing on tiny wheels. I tilt my head, thinking. "Maybe running?" It's the first sport that pops into my head. I recall the way Chase looks all sweaty from a run. Maybe he can give me some pointers.

Emma's smile is sly. "I bet you could go running with Chase. He goes every morning."

I doubt he'll want us to run together, so I hedge. "I wouldn't want to bother him. And I'm completely out of shape. I'd only slow him down."

"You can discuss it with Chase later." Daisy waves away my objections. Again. "Moving on to number five: learn to pole dance."

"Why do these involve me in various states of undress?"

"Because there are a bunch of guys here who are hungover, horny, and want to watch you doing naked-ish things. Duh," Daisy retorts with a grin. "And now, number six is good. It's for you to go on a really romantic date. With a hot guy. I added the *hot guy* part."

"I can help with that," Kenji says. I've met the guitar player several times now, and he is always very flirty. He's hot in a tall, dark, bad-boy way.

"No, pick me!" another guy shouts. I laugh. I know it's all in good fun, so I don't take them seriously. The idea of these good-looking, talented musicians fighting for me is not a possibility. These guys have their pick of LA women.

"If Olivia needs help with her list, it will be me. Not any of you asses."

I swing my head to see Chase standing in the doorway in long shorts and a T-shirt, with a towel around his neck and a glower on his face. He must have come from a workout in the gym because sweat glistens on his defined muscles, making me weak.

"Ooh, someone's jealous," Daisy says.

Chase glares. "I'm not jealous, but I don't trust any of you to ensure Olivia's safety while she's swimming with sharks and going on dates." He almost chokes on the word *dates*.

Wow. Just how much of the conversation did he overhear?

This conversation is getting far, far away from me. "Excuse me. Hello? I'm here, in front of you all. There will be no sharks. And I haven't agreed to pole dancing."

"Notice how she still says nothing about skinny-dipping," Daisy whispers loudly to Emma. "She's totally down for the skinny-dipping."

I kinda was down for skinny-dipping. There's a beautiful pool out there, and every night, it calls to me. I wouldn't mind sneaking out and swimming under the stars, feeling that cool water over all parts of me. But I'm not about to tell any of them that because I don't want an audience joining me for that particular risk.

"We're all just trying to help you fulfill your grandma's wishes," Emma says. "And pole dancing is the best."

"Since when have you done pole dancing?" Sebastian asks Emma, not sounding happy about it. "Your dad's a minister."

Emma puts her hands on her hips. "Says who? Just because Daddy's a minister doesn't mean I can't dance. What is this? *Footloose?*"

"It's not just dancing. It's like strippers," Sebastian hisses.

"There's nothing wrong with being a stripper." Emma folds her arms over her chest and glares at Sebastian.

"Your dad's a minister?" Kenji asks. "That's cool."

"Her dad's great. But she's the meanest minister's daughter I've ever met," Sebastian elaborates.

"You know her dad?" I ask.

"That's how Sebastian and I met," Emma explains. "Daddy helped out at Sebastian's rehab center."

"Her dad suggested I hire Emma to babysit me when it was time to go back to LA. She wanted to ditch her small town. Her dad said she was perfect for the job because she was good at staying organized and keeping people from having fun." Sebastian smirks.

Rather than be offended, Emma nods, as if proud of that particular attribute. "Sometimes, you have to be cruel to be kind," she retorts. "You should thank me more. And my daddy."

"Ahem," I say to the group. All eyes turn to me. "Not that I'm not appreciative of your help, but I think I can handle making a list all on my own."

"Nope. We've decided this is our job to help you. You're stuck with us and this list," Emma says. "Cruel to be kind, remember?"

Chase plucks the list away from Daisy. "If Olivia needs help, I'll do it. And her list will not involve stripper poles, naked swimming, or dates. She doesn't do things like that."

I glare at Chase. "Why wouldn't I? Are you trying to tell me I'm not allowed to skinny-dip or date someone?" The idea that he thinks I'm too boring to take sexy risks makes me grumpy.

His mouth turns downward, but he seems to value his life because he doesn't answer.

"Last time I checked, you aren't my father." Actually, I never knew my father, but I do know it's not Chase.

"Good thing," Chase mumbles.

"And I'm not your responsibility. Why don't you go worry about Cassidy?" I huff. I saw another article about them online just this morning. It speculated on whether they were exclusive or just casual friends with benefits.

"Cassidy? Why would he worry about Cassidy?" Emma asks, looking at me in confusion.

"Daisy?" I say sweetly.

"Yes, Olivia?"

"We'll strike off swimming with the sharks. But the rest of the list is good. That will keep me busy this week," I say and stand up, snatching the list from Chase.

"Yes!" Daisy lifts her fist in jubilation.

"Yes!" The pervy drummer twirls his drumstick and gives me a slow appraisal, focusing most of his attention on my breasts.

Sebastian shakes his head sadly. "One day, you'll regret this opportunity. And then it might be too late to swim with the sharks."

"We haven't even gotten to the last dare. Lucky number seven," Daisy says wickedly.

I look down at the paper, and my mouth goes dry.

"Number seven is you have to get laid!" she exclaims.

"What the hell, Daisy? Olivia, are you serious about this?" Chase glowers at the rest of the group and snorts.

I stare at the list in my hand, and yup. Lucky number seven. Get laid. It's written in a purple glitter pen. There's even a heart and smiley face next to it, along with what looks suspiciously like the eggplant and peach emojis.

I want to lecture Daisy and the rest of them about boundaries. But after Chase put me firmly in the friends-without-benefits category, it doesn't sit right with me that he's trying to dictate whether I get laid or not. I tried to. With him. And he turned me down.

We glare at each other, but my gaze keeps straying to his muscular chest and arms, and I find myself distracted by how good he looks, standing there all sweaty and manly and growly-like.

Still, I try to keep up my righteous annoyance. He has no idea what I'm capable of. Maybe I don't even know what I'm capable of. That's the whole point of these risks.

One day, in the not-too-distant future, I'll have someone of my own. An ordinary someone like me. Someone who doesn't have fans and crazy stalkers or beautiful women chasing him. Someone with real potential for a real relationship.

And maybe this list will be a good place to start.

CHAPTER 25

livia

Four days—and nights—later, I'm about to tackle my fourth risk. Technically this risk is first on the list. But it's taken me a while to lead up to it because it requires a little more daring.

It also requires the least number of clothes.

As in, none.

Over the past few days, I've ticked off most of the list.

Three days ago, Emma, with her magical skills, got us all sparkly pink skates and turned the large foyer into a roller disco, complete with colored lights, Sebastian playing DJ, and a disco ball. Emma and Daisy skated circles around me as I clung to them before landing on my ass, over and over.

Ryder's band eventually joined us, but Chase was noticeably absent.

The next day, Emma arranged for a pole-dancing instructor to come to the mansion. The lady even brought her own stripper pole, which, with Sebastian's and Ryder's very enthusiastic support, she installed in their giant home gym.

Daisy and Emma took the lesson with me. We drew a small crowd of guys from Ryder's band watching until we kicked them out. The pole dancing went a little better than the rollerskating. I wasn't good because I'm so out of shape, but it was fun, and it's one sport where my full breasts are considered an asset, not a liability.

Again, Chase was missing. I worked up the courage to ask Emma where he was, as casually as possible, and she mumbled something about him having meetings. I pretend it doesn't matter. But the idea that he's purposefully staying away from his own home because of me hurts.

I shake my head and try to focus on my next risk. That's the thing about the list. It's a great distraction from obsessing over Chase.

It's two in the morning. The house is quiet, and I'm standing next to a pool with water as smooth as glass. A gentle breeze blows.

Even though no one is around, I'm achingly aware that I'm wearing nothing but a sarong wrap under my towel.

I take a deep breath, then drop my towel before making a clean dive into the pool.

"Balls!" I whisper-squeal as I come up for breath, the frigid water stinging my exposed skin.

Trying to ignore the icy bite against my skin, I swim for a moment, working up the courage to remove my final item of clothing. The sarong is of a semi-sheer fabric meant for swimming, and I'm tempted to leave it on. But that would be cheating.

"Fuck it" I whisper to myself, unwrapping it and setting it near the edge of the pool.

I'm not sure what I expected, but being naked outdoors is electric. It reminds me of the night in the fountain. Even the possibility that I could get caught adds to the energy coursing through me.

Not that there's much chance someone will come to investigate. At least, not at this hour. I purposely waited until Ryder's crew left and everyone else was finally in bed. The whole house is black as pitch, no piano music or guitar chords from the basement, no jovial arguments, loud laughter, or feminine giggles. No video games, beer pong, or pool games. Just peace and quiet.

I float on my back, acutely aware of my pale breasts in the moonlight, and look up at the stars. The stars are faint, but it's still magical to see them hanging above me in the inky sky.

Something brushes my foot.

"Gah!" I scream.

A dark figure moves past me under the water.

I splash furiously and then freeze. My imagination conjures up various scenarios. I wouldn't put it past Sebastian to arrange for a shark in the pool, so I'd have to do his risk. Not like a giant killer shark. But maybe a small one. Or a dolphin. It's one of those fancy saltwater pools. Could a baby shark survive in it?

There it is again. A splash in the water a few feet behind me, and I scream, "Ah! Shark!"

"Olivia, what the fuck are you doing?" a familiar voice floats to me.

Oh, hell no.

I'd rather deal with the shark.

"Chase!" I immediately sink deep and splash into the darkest corner of the pool.

"I'm swimming," I answer, while I huddle in the grotto with the fewest lights, praying he can't tell I'm naked. "What are you doing sneaking up on me? Are you trying to give me a heart attack?"

"I'm not sneaking up on you. I swim at night. *You* interrupted *me*."

"At two a.m.?"

"I get insomnia. Swimming helps. What are you doing in the pool now?"

"I, um… Well, you see… Yeah, insomnia too. Ha."

"Olivia?"

I pretend to ignore him, but he isn't deterred.

"Are you skinny-dipping?"

"What? No. It's none of your business."

"Damn Daisy and her damn ideas," Chase mutters.

"Hey, this isn't all on Daisy. Who would have thought anyone else would be swimming at this hour? Why do you keep seeing me naked? And Ryder, too."

"Ryder?" Chase advances toward me. "When did he see you naked?" Spotlighted by the pool light now, he looks menacing, with several days of scruff and all those wet, glistening muscles.

I try to concentrate on his question. "Ryder didn't see me naked, just naked-ish."

"Olivia," Chase says in warning.

"I was coming out of the bathroom in my towel, and he was in the living room at Daisy's apartment, and my towel slipped a little. So, it was innocent, and I don't think he actually saw anything. And I don't know why this keeps happening. My previous twenty-five years were towel-incident-free."

Chase's tightened expression relaxes a little. "You're very exasperating," he remarks.

"You're bossy. And obnoxious," I charge back. "You haven't been home all day, and suddenly, you go for a swim?"

"I've been playing catch-up on meetings I missed while I was filming." He pauses. "So. What do you think of the water?" He asks, his voice going husky.

"It's cold," I lie. Right now, cold is the last thing I feel. I'm warm and tingly in interesting places and aching in others. I move deeper into the dark, as if I can hide the evidence that just being near Chase turns me on. "You shouldn't be looking at me. Turn around."

"Olivia, I can't see a damn thing. You're just a shadow in the corner."

"Good." I tread water, feeling naked emotionally as well as physically. Even in the dark, it's as if everything in me is on display just for him. My annoying flaws, my deep hurts, and my obsessive crush.

"How...else does it make you feel?" he asks.

With each word spoken in his gravelly voice, he's drawn just a little closer. He isn't in touching distance yet, but I can make out the individual water beads on his strong neck. The droplets in his hair. The gold ring around those green eyes.

Vulnerable. That's the answer to his question. I think about lying again. But Nanna's advice echoes in me. Each time I take a risk, I break a little more of the hold fear has on me, and I'm led further into this adventure. There are no guarantees, no safety net.

And isn't that the greatest risk?

The risk of being seen.

The risk of showing someone who I am and having them reject me anyway.

But what's the other option?

To always stay hidden. In stories. In letters and texts. With the subterfuge of trying to be someone I'm not, to deny the things I feel.

I've been too afraid that my crush on Chase will show even more than it already has. I've been pretending everything is fine. That I'm the type of cool, casual girl who can hook up with a boy one weekend and then just be friends the next. No biggie, no aching heart. I've been lying to myself, and to Chase, too afraid to reveal the truth.

I'm not sure how I find my bravery, but I'm so done with hiding. With resolve that has me shaking, I slowly swim away from the shadows.

Toward Chase.

He's close enough that I can hear his gasp of indrawn breath.

"How does it make me feel? Scared. Excited. Seen," I whisper.

A few small movements, and I'm there before him. I'm still beneath the water, but in the silvery moonlight I wonder how much of me he can see now, if anything.

Only his gaze strays, flashing down my body briefly before shifting back up to meet my eyes. He swallows audibly.

We stay like that for I don't know how long, both floating in the light, facing each other, only our eyes connecting. The world narrows to just the beat of my heart, the sound of our breaths. I don't touch him; he doesn't touch me.

"You can touch, you know." His voice is a caress in all my most intimate places.

"What?" My heart stutters.

"Your feet can touch the bottom now. We're at the shallow end," he elaborates.

"Oh," I say, feeling stupid, my mind on a different kind of touching.

I stop treading water and realize he's right. It's still deep, but my tiptoes can touch the pool floor.

A breeze chills my skin.

I think he might bridge the distance and touch me, kiss me. I hold my breath, waiting, wanting, but instead he steps back into the shadows and the moment is gone.

Feeling exposed and foolish now for everything I was thinking, everything I was hoping, I look away and spot my wrap near me at the side of the pool. I grab it and cover myself. The mesh-like fabric doesn't hide everything, but it helps, giving me a layer of protection. *We're just friends*, I tell myself. *Friends swim together. Not usually naked, but still.*

"I can get used to this," I say, pretending a casualness I don't feel, pretending I hadn't just been wishing he would take me in his arms and kiss me.

"Used to what?" His voice sounds rough in the night.

My mouth tips into a wistful smile. If he had reached out to me, I would have said "you." Instead, I settle for another version of the truth. "This weather, this pool, this view, this estate. It's magical."

He turns away from me slowly, and looks around, taking in the place he calls home. His expression is tight, but when he speaks, his words are light. "I love this estate. It's another reason I've stayed here so long. Sebastian and Ryder are great, but living with them can get a little insane between Sebastian's parties and Ryder's late-night jam sessions, even if I have my own space."

"I heard that Gretta Blake built this house?" Sebastian's grandmother was a Hollywood icon and a pioneering feminist.

He nods. "Did you know she built my cottage for her hookups?"

I laugh, letting the tips of my fingers play with the water, creating wave patterns. "Go, Gretta."

"I read her biography when I first moved in. This estate was rocking back then."

"It's rocking now, I imagine."

"Sebastian helps keep up the rep," Chase says with a slow smile that sends a shiver down my spine. "So, how are you doing with your risks?"

"They're uncomfortable. But I've also gained some experiences I wouldn't have wanted to miss out on," I answer honestly. Tonight is one of them, even if I feel too exposed, like a live wire.

His smirk causes every part of me to tingle in the cold water. "Like skinny-dipping?"

At his rough murmur, my nipples pebble and heat rushes between my legs. He causes that response with just the skim of his eyes, the velvet reach of his voice, when he hasn't even lifted a finger to touch me.

"Like skinny-dipping," I confirm with a bemused smile, trying my best to ignore the sensations he raises in me. "I guess I've always been afraid to take risks. I like to take adventures in my imagination and in stories, not for real. It feels safer that way. My mom took too many risks. I became her opposite. And when my grandmother got sick when I was in high school, it reinforced all my natural tendencies to retreat from life."

I tilt my head back, letting myself just feel. The air on my face, the heat of my body beneath the water, the exquisite vulnerability of baring myself in more ways than one. "Have you ever felt like you've been sleepwalking through life?" I ask softly. "And worry that if you don't wake up, ten years will have gone by and you won't have much to show for it?"

When I turn back to Chase, he's watching me with an intense look I can't decipher. "It's probably just me. I mean, you've obviously got things figured out."

"No, I know exactly how that feels."

"Really?"

He gives me a ghost of a smile. "I'm human. Not some robot. I have feelings. Mostly I feel like I don't fit in anywhere."

"But everyone wants to be around you," I say, backing away a little. It's easier to concentrate on his words, easier to ignore the ever present pull I feel toward him, when there's more space between us.

He shakes his head. "People only want their projected image of me. The real me would disappoint them. They want the red-carpet version, but that's far from the reality."

"What's reality?"

"The reality is that I'm not so different from you. I stay home, probably way too much. I know you're going to roll your eyes at me when I say this, but I don't like attention."

I snort. "Yeah, right."

"No, really. I didn't get into this career because I wanted fame. I fell into it because I needed money."

"Well, what makes you stay? I imagine you have all the money you need now."

"I love telling a story, giving people something to connect to, somewhere to escape for a few hours." He smiles. "Don't get me wrong. I like the money. I just hate the fame that comes with it."

"Do you ever think about doing something behind the scenes, like directing?"

"Maybe. But in this industry, people put you in a box and don't want you to step out of it." He studies me. "I guess I'm like you. I need to step out of my comfort zone."

"You should, Chase. You can do anything you want. If you choose."

"I can say the same about you."

I sigh. "Lately, I've been thinking about my choices. It's like I'm scared to move on and find a life of my own. I live in my childhood home, which I love, but still. I've worked the same job since high school. I went to college just ten minutes away. And I write books that I'm too afraid to send to an agent or publisher. I'm hiding away from anything that truly makes me feel alive, anything that feels scary. That's what these risks are about."

"Did you always want to be a writer?" he asks.

I shake my head. "I started writing the year my mom died. It was a distraction, I guess. And catharsis."

"What happened to your mom?" he asks. "You've never said." And then he shakes his head. "Is that too personal?"

"A car accident."

"I'm so sorry."

I don't talk about my mom. But something about the way he's looking at me, as if he sees and accepts all of me, releases my words.

"My mom loved driving. She drank in the morning while she was writing. Said it helped her process, and then she'd go on these long drives, drunk. Sometimes, when she did, she'd take me. And when she did, she thought everything I did was wrong. I was too quiet. Too boring. Too shy." My smile is bittersweet. "You should have seen her. She was brilliant. She had red hair and this magnetic personality. And she was a famous writer."

I slant Chase a look. "You would know her if I tell you her name." I laugh, but it's a joyless sound. "She won all sorts of awards for her first book, a memoir about how much being a mom sucked. The critics loved it. And they loved her. Called her bold and honest. Meanwhile, I was mostly raised by Nanna.

"There I was, this shy girl who was terrified while my mom swerved all over the road. She loved driving fast. She scared me as much when she was manic like that as when she was depressed." The words are coming faster now, toppling over one another, as if once I've opened the dam, everything just floods out.

"One minute, we were flying down the coast in a convertible while I begged her to slow down, and the next thing I remember is waking up in the hospital. I spent a month there, but she escaped with just a broken arm that time. She didn't learn. She died a year later in another drinking and driving accident, this time with her married lover. Sometimes I think that's what she wanted."

"I'm sorry," he says quietly.

I look at him. "I've never talked to anyone about that."

"Thank you for telling me," he says, eyes somber.

He moves closer to me in the dark and takes my hand as if it's as natural as breathing and folds his fingers between mine, letting our joined hands rest on the surface of the water.

We're friends, I think. This is friendly hand-holding.

Chase makes my heart beat faster and my stomach do twists with just a look. But this feeling that spreads through my veins like warm honey is different. It's sweeter, deeper. It's not the butterflies I had when I first met him, an impossibly handsome movie star. This is about Chase, my friend, the man behind the image.

"What about your family?" I ask quietly. "Before the foster homes."

He's silent for so long, I think he's not going to answer,

and then he begins to speak. "My mom was young, a single mother. She worked several jobs. But she loved me. I remember her making up stories at bedtime about what we'd do and where we'd go when she could save up enough money."

"She sounds wonderful."

"I wish I remembered more." He takes a deep breath. "She died when I was seven. She was driving home one night, and she was killed in a car accident. A neighbor was babysitting me, and then a lady came to her house, told me my mom died, had me pack a bag, and took me to a foster home. And that was it. My whole life changed in that one night."

My heart turns over. He says it offhandedly, but I know the searing pain of the words, and I wish I could draw them into me, take some of his burden.

"Oh, Chase. I'm so sorry. I had Nanna. But you had no one."

"I'm glad you had her," he says with intensity. "That you were safe and loved."

"I can't imagine going through what I did without her. You were so young. You must have been so confused, missing your mom."

He plays with my hand, our fingers entwining. "I think the hardest part is that the memory of her fades a little more each year," he says.

He attempts what I think was supposed to be a careless smile, but it doesn't reach his eyes.

"It was a long time ago, and it feels good to talk about her. I knew what it was to be loved, at least for a little while. Daisy's asshole parents gave her nothing."

"But don't you see? You gave Daisy the stories, the care, the love. You filled that role for her, even if it wasn't long either."

He frowns. "I tried. But I did a damn poor job of protecting her."

"You were just a kid. She loves you like the older brother you are to her. You are each other's family. I know she'd like to spend more time with you," I say, probing gently.

He doesn't answer.

He takes my hand and presses a kiss into my wet palm. The gentleness of the gesture turns me inside out.

"You're cute when you're earnest." He lets go of my hand and traces my face with his long fingers before letting them fall back into the water. "You make it so hard to stay away. But I shouldn't be with you like this." There's an edge of desperation to his voice.

"Have you been avoiding me?" I ask, even though I fear I already know the answer.

He tilts his head up to the sky, the angle emphasizing his perfect profile. He blows out a breath and runs a hand through his wet hair. I wait, and when his eyes return to mine, they are dark and conflicted.

I'm wearing next to nothing, and he's close enough to reach out and touch my breast, touch every part of me, if he wants. And probably more significant, we both bared our souls to each other.

His gaze lingers on my lips and then shifts lower. And I wonder again just how much he can see through the water and the dark.

I'm pretty sure he's with his ex-girlfriend. He didn't say he wasn't.

As if he can hear the thoughts, he snaps his head back and puts distance between us with one large slice through the water.

"I'm sorry. I thought it would be better to not be here much."

That confirms what I suspected. He's been avoiding the house because of me.

"I'm not your responsibility," I say, disappointment clogging my throat. I've been desiring him, while he's been dodging me. I shiver in the dark, feeling a chill that's beyond the water. "I don't want my presence to make you feel uncomfortable."

He doesn't correct me, tell me I'm wrong. He says it all without saying a thing.

I yearn for connection, for someone to see all of me and who likes who I am. But I won't get that with Chase.

"It's getting cold." I move away with more speed than grace. "I'm getting out now. Close your eyes," I mumble, just wanting to be covered. I feel naked in so many ways.

"I can't see you," he says from somewhere in the shadows.

And he never will because he doesn't want to, no matter how much I wish it.

I slip from the water and wrap my body in a towel, wishing I could wrap my heart in armor as easily.

CHAPTER 26

livia

"Olivia, wake up," Chase calls.

Two days later, I wake to banging on my bedroom door. I roll over and pull the pillow over my head to block the sound.

More banging.

I rub my eyes and sit up.

What is Chase doing here before it's even light out? Especially after our pool session the other night where he basically told me he didn't want to be around me.

"Are you decent? I'm coming in," he calls through the door.

I barely have time to pull the covers up over my nightshirt before he strolls in, looking wide awake in workout shorts and a tank top. It isn't fair to short-circuit the few working brain cells I have this early in the morning.

"What are you doing here?"

"I'm taking you for a run. Isn't that on your list?"

I rub the sleep from my eyes. "Yeah, but I can run with Daisy or Emma. I don't need you."

Something in his eyes flares as he stalks closer to the bed. I touch my throat and swallow. I imagine him in bed with me, the crisp white linen surrounding his bronzed skin. I look into his face, and it's a good thing I'm not standing because I get weak at the slight laugh lines crinkling his eyes, those molded lips curving in amusement.

"Daisy and Emma don't run."

"Right. Well, maybe with Ryder or Sebastian."

Anyone but Chase. Chase, who all but admitted he's been hiding from me the past few days, but suddenly switches course and turns up here in my bedroom. Chase, whom I'd prefer to not see me sweat or pass out from running half a block.

He takes a step closer, his expression tight. "Kenji volunteered to run with you this morning, but I told him to go to hell. I don't trust the guy."

I let out a huff of irritation. "You were just warning me to stay away from you, and now here you are in my room. I'm getting whiplash from your mood swings," I say. "I can go running by myself or wait until I get back to San Francisco to start. It's not a big deal."

He runs a hand through his hair until it stands up on end, tousled as if he just emerged from a morning of hot sex. He studies me long enough that I start to fidget. Finally, he shakes his head. "Listen, I'm sorry about the other night. And I'm sorry I've been avoiding you. This is...complicated. But it's not your fault. It's all mine. I care about you, probably more than I should, and I don't want anything to hurt you, ever, including me. I'd really like us to be friends," he says with an earnestness that contracts my heart.

"That's the thing about life, Chase. Hurting is kind of unavoidable," I say in a small voice. "And yes, we're friends."

His eyes linger on me, and then he nods. "I'll meet you in front of the house in twenty minutes. I left you a cup of coffee with cream and two sugars. There's also some fruit and a granola bar on the counter. I don't want you to pass out on the run."

"You know how I take my coffee?" I ask.

"You'd be surprised what I know, Olivia."

"Oh," is all I manage, but that word stands for so much.

Oh my God. Oh, my heart. Oh, how in the ever-loving hell am I going to manage this ridiculous crush I have? And oh, why are you so damn confusing?

Fifteen minutes later, I open the large front door—seriously, why is this door so huge?—and walk out to the curved driveway. I'm wearing workout clothes, courtesy of Emma.

Chase is bent, stretching. He looks up at my approach and grins, and there it is again, my heart wobbling.

"Come stretch with me," he says.

I try to touch my toes but only make it to my knees. This is embarrassing.

"It's been a while since you worked out, huh?" His grin is so attractive, only half of me wants to smack him.

"I'll have you know that my fingers are very dexterous."

"Are they now?" he asks.

"I mean, from writing. Typing. Get your mind out of the gutter, Mr. James."

"I didn't say anything," he retorts, all innocence. "Here, stretch your hamstrings."

He demonstrates a series of movements, which I'm attentive to, mostly because of the things those stretches do to his muscles.

He's serious about his fitness, probably because of his job. He's not quite as buff as Sebastian, but he's taller, with wider shoulders, and every part of him is lean, hard, and strong. Or at least, every part I can see, and I imagine the parts hidden by clothes as well.

I attempt to copy him, and he adjusts my body with a large

hand on my waist. My breath catches, and the slow, steady pressure feels like a prelude to more.

He quickly lets go, but not before he gives me a look. It leaves me thinking that maybe, just maybe, he's at least a little affected by me, as I am by him.

"Here, like this." He shows me what I should be doing, and I fix my stance.

We go through the rest of the stretches like that—with him touching me in the most distracting of ways. He's so close, I can smell the shampoo in his hair, feel the calluses on his fingers. It seems like hours, but it's probably only been a few minutes.

When we're done, he steps away. "You should be warm by now."

"Oh, I'm warm all right," I mutter.

His mouth quirks up.

"Good," he says with a bland smile. Maybe I'm just imagining the heat in his eyes. "Let's get running."

Shit. While he was doing all that close touching, I almost forgot that the object of this is to run.

He must read my mind because he laughs. "Yes, Olivia, now we run."

"Do we have to?" I whine. It's not attractive, I know.

"Nothing worth doing is ever easy," he calls, jogging backward faster than I can jog forward.

I follow him with ungainly strides.

Ten thousand years later, I think I'm going to puke. My breath wheezes in and out like bellows. Sweat drips down my forehead. I don't even bother wiping it away because more sweat instantly takes its place. Nothing exists. Not birdsong or breeze, blue sky or trees. Not even Chase casually running next to me. There's only the relentless pavement that stretches endlessly and me trying not to die with the dragging lift and pound of each murderous step. I've never thought of myself as competitive, but I can't bear the shame of telling Chase I have to stop because of wimpy lungs and out-of-shape legs that feel like jelly.

He jogs alongside me, commenting on houses we pass and neighborhood features, while I contemplate how to fall down on purpose and break my leg, so I never have to run again.

And he isn't even out of breath. That's the worst part. This is a pity jog, the mildest of warm-ups for him. He'll probably run ten miles after he kills me with this light jog.

I stumble as a wave of dizziness crashes over me, my lungs trying to draw in enough oxygen to keep going. Maybe I'll get a broken leg after all.

"Hey," he says, stopping short, catching and steadying me. His touch makes me even dizzier.

He gently bends me over. I inhale beautiful, blessed oxygen in deep gulps. In this position, the sweat pours off the top of my head rather than going into my eyes, which is a nice change.

Chase rubs my back in soothing circles. "Breathe. Slow, deep breaths."

After a few minutes, my breathing does slow to manageable levels, and my heart rate calms. When the world rights itself, I stand and wipe my face with my soaking T-shirt. I'm a mess. I bet Cassidy Reynolds doesn't almost pass out from a short run. I bet she glows.

"Are you okay?" Chase asks, his eyebrows drawn together.

I nod, embarrassed. I know my face has to be tomato red from the exertion.

"You need to tell me when to stop, Olivia. We don't have to run miles on the first day."

"I'm embarrassed," I mumble. "I just wanted to keep up. I'm ridiculously out of shape."

His gaze drags up and down my body. It leaves a path of warm tingling.

"You look good to me."

I gulp back a laugh and kick out one leg, wincing as I do

because…running. "These legs are pasty and have no muscle tone."

His eyes are hot on me. He grazes my thigh with his finger, burning a path where he touches. "Your legs are smooth—pale, not pasty—and the perfect, curvy shape. I'm glad you want to get more exercise because it's healthy and good for you. But your body couldn't be more perfect, Olivia."

I clear my throat. Our faces are close. His hand falls away from my leg, and he takes a tight breath before stepping away. I blink at the loss of him.

"Ready to go back?" he asks smoothly.

His words chill me.

"Run back?" I whimper.

He throws his head back and laughs. "You should see your face right now. You look horrified. No, we can walk. You've done a mile, which is great."

"One mile? Are you sure? It felt like at least five."

He grins. "Positive. But that's awesome for your first time. You should be proud of yourself. We'll go a little farther each day."

I ignore his assumption that we'll do this again. That's insanity. But now that I can breathe again, I am beginning to appreciate my accomplishment. I'm also supremely grateful that I don't have to run anymore today.

We walk in silence for a while. The neighborhood feels like an oasis. The houses are mansions, but they are older, with lush gardens.

A patch of wild flowers grows beneath a large shade tree at the edge of one property.

Chase leans down and picks a few daisies. He places two in my hands and turns me to face him, gently sliding one behind my ear.

"Thank you," I say. "Daisies are my favorite flowers." My eyes sting at the unexpected sweetness of the gesture.

"I know," he says. "I-I mean, I'm not surprised."

We keep walking while I twirl the pretty but unassuming flower. "Nanna believed that the secret to happiness is appreciating the mundane pleasures of life, like picking wild flowers or reading in a park on a sunny day." I tilt my head to him, a quizzical smile on my face. "What? Why are you looking at me like that?"

"I used to read in the park all the time whenever I ran away from my foster homes, because I had nowhere else to go. Sometimes it's funny to think that in a lot of ways, I had more freedom back then."

"But when you're in a new city, don't you explore? You know, sight-see?"

"Not really. If I'm there for an event or to make a movie, it's big news. My hotel is usually surrounded. It's amazing, really, how little you ever have to interact with the real world when you're famous."

"Are you happy living this way?" I suspect he's not. Just like when I watched the video of him surrounded by paparazzi, I feel sad for him. For all his wealth and success, he's more trapped by circumstances than I am.

He shrugs. "It's just the way it is. Most people have far bigger problems than mine."

"But maybe you can do those things, regular things," I urge.

"I can, if I don't mind ending up on TMZ."

"But things have changed now, Chase. You're not new to this anymore."

"Life is about trade-offs. I'm rich enough that I never have to worry about money again, and I have a job I enjoy. I'd have to be a real asshole to complain about velvet ropes in clubs and parties in Cannes."

"True," I say. "I guess most people would prefer A-list parties and international holidays over reading in the park."

"But you wouldn't like that life?" he asks, his eyes sharp on me in a way that feels raw. "The jet-setting, the parties?"

I bite my lip, thinking about his question. "I wouldn't mind traveling. But I'm happier reading a book in front of the fire than partying all night. I'd be completely useless as an A-lister."

Our eyes connect. "And what if I say that your kind of day sounds better to me than mine?"

"I'd say it means you have discerning taste."

He laughs, his expression lightening. "Come on, slowpoke. We're not far from the house. We can run the rest of the way," he teases.

"Noooo," I say. "You go. I'll just lie down in that soft-looking patch of grass."

He pulls me along. His palm is warm and strong enveloping mine. And he doesn't let go for the rest of the walk home.

* * *

I HOBBLE out of my bedroom an hour earlier the next day, wanting to get fully caffeinated before I'm tortured by the hottest man alive again. Every muscle in my body hurts from yesterday's run, but maybe the pain means itty-bitty muscles are being formed, and that's not such a bad thing. So I've heard. Allegedly. As I reach up to grab a coffee cup from the white cabinet, I wince as my body protests the movement. Maybe I should have just stayed in bed. All day.

"What's wrong with you?"

I turn around, startled. Emma stands behind me, looking calm, cool, collected, and pain-free in her stilettos and pencil skirt. She's already clutching her giant mug of coffee, and for a brief moment, I kind of hate her.

"Exercise happened. Or, more specifically, running," I grumble, scooping a generous mound of sugar into my coffee, then topping it with enough milk to turn the drink a nice creamy color. I take a deep sip. Sweet, sweet elixir of the gods.

Daisy saunters into the kitchen.

"What are you doing up so early?" I ask.

"Couldn't sleep," she replies with a wide yawn. "Damn birds outside my window." She slides on a pair of sunglasses. "And the sun. So much sun."

Emma watches Daisy with narrowed eyes. "Aren't you the perky one? Isn't that part of your thing? Fun. Blond. Perky. A little zany."

Daisy rolls her eyes. "I am perky. But not before eight a.m. I need time to build up to greatness."

"So what you're saying is Daisy's a manic pixie dream girl?" I say to Emma with a snort.

"Well, we are in Hollywood." Emma gives a shrug. "We're all playing a part. For example, I'm the overachieving biatch. And I fully embrace the cliché." She kicks out her stilettos.

"I love a self-aware diva," Daisy says, filling her coffee cup from the large French press that Marie left on the stove.

"And I am…?" I ask, cringing a little.

"Girl next door," Emma and Daisy say in unison.

"Huh. I guess the girl next door could be worse."

"Now that we know what part we'd play in a movie of our lives, I just have to say you're looking mighty foxy, Miss Olivia, in a sporty way." Daisy eyes up my terry cloth shorts and V-neck T-shirt.

"Courtesy of Emma." I do a little twirl. I'm having fun with my new wardrobe, even the workout clothes. It's making me rethink my former fashion choices. I do miss my writerly T-shirts, though. Those make me happy, so I don't plan on leaving them behind anytime soon.

Emma shakes her head. "Courtesy of Chase."

"But you picked it out, right? And put the shopping bag on my bed yesterday."

"Nope," Emma says. "That was all Chase. He didn't do too bad, considering he's a man. Seems he got the sizes right. He must be *very* observant." She grins.

"But he bought me *sports bras*. Several." I gulp, mortified at the thought of Chase knowing my sizes. I'm not exactly an extra small like Daisy.

Emma cackles wickedly. "I am surprised."

"That he bought me sportswear? Me too."

"No, that he went shopping. He never goes shopping."

Daisy nods. "He always gets mobbed, so he never goes anywhere."

"We talked about that a little yesterday after our run," I say.

"Chase's fan base is extreme. He went from being unknown to one of the most famous people on the planet overnight. I don't think he's ever figured out how to handle it. He's never really recovered from the experience of all that sudden fame."

"But other celebrities do, right? They don't just hide away."

"Ryder and Sebastian go out," Daisy says. "All the time."

"Sebastian doesn't care about being photographed. He eats it up," Emma says. "But he's used to it. He was born famous."

"What about Ryder?"

"Ryder is good with disguises." Daisy grins.

"Ryder and his disguises. Bless his hot heart," Emma says, cracking up.

"He has an entire closet full of decoy outfits. He had some wardrobe consultant put it together when he was in the boy band. He even has prosthetics," Daisy elaborates.

"So why can't Chase do something like that? He just seems to have given up on the idea of a regular life."

Emma tilts her head. "Maybe we should do an intervention. Push him out into the world with a ball cap, wig, and shades."

I laugh. "I just want to do something for him."

Daisy smiles, but it doesn't reach her eyes. "You and Chase seem to be getting close."

"You don't need to worry about me," I say, avoiding her concerned gaze.

"I can't help it. I remember how heartbroken you were with Remington, and you didn't even know him in real life."

"Who's Remington?" Emma asks, leaning forward.

"This guy who catfished Olivia."

"He did not catfish me. You make it sound sordid. We were pen pals. You can't be sordid when you meet through a typewriter."

Daisy frowns. "Wait, what? What about a typewriter?"

"That's how we met. I sold one of Nanna's typewriters, a Remington, at the neighborhood antique shop. I included a note, and we started exchanging letters. We agreed to keep things anonymous, so I don't know his real name, but I do know he lives in LA."

"Fuck me," Daisy whispers.

Someone clears their throat.

Our heads swing up.

Chase stands in the kitchen in a sleeveless tank and running shorts. His gaze lands on mine before it slides down to check out my outfit, the outfit he picked out. His eyes light up, and I can tell he approves. Warmth suffuses my body like melting caramel.

"Morning glory," Emma drawls, waving with two hands. "Hello, earth to Chase."

He tears his gaze from me. "Uh, morning." He throws a brief smile to Daisy and Emma, then directs his gaze back to me. "Ready for our run?"

I groan. "Maybe?" My muscles may not be ready, but as I stare at the man before me, the rest of me is all in.

"Was I interrupting? You ladies looked like you were discussing something intense."

"Were you interrupting something?" Daisy answers with an arch look. "That's such an interesting question. Olivia here was just telling us about this pen pal she had and how they met when he bought her typewriter. A Remington."

He stiffens at her words, his head jerking back.

I turn to Daisy.

I don't want Chase to get the wrong idea and think I'm still hung up on Remington. I mean, I am, a little. I miss him with an ache in my heart and an emptiness in the parts of my life that used to be filled by him. The texts in the morning and the texts before bed and all of those in-between moments in my day. But that's over, at least for now.

Daisy wanted me to leave my online friendship behind, so why is she bringing it up now, and to Chase, of all people?

I look up at Chase. For a brief moment, I think I see panic in his eyes before his expression shutters.

He takes a deep breath. "Let's go," he murmurs before pinning Daisy with an intense look.

"Have a nice run," Daisy calls after us. "We'll talk later, Chase."

CHAPTER 27

hase

"When were you going to tell me?" Daisy bursts into my cottage later that afternoon, startling me as I stand in front of my refrigerator, debating which nutritionist-approved, premade dinner to choose, salmon or plain chicken breast.

"Nice of you to knock." I turn to her, resigned to my fate.

It took Daisy longer to confront me than I thought it would. But that might have been because I was hiding out in my cottage all day, like the coward I am.

"Why didn't you tell me?" Daisy repeats.

I can't avoid this conversation any longer.

"We'll talk. Do you want a drink?" I sure as hell do.

I pull out a cold beer and offer it to her. She grimaces. I shrug and open it for myself.

When we're both sitting at my wooden table, I take a long swig, fortifying myself.

"Why didn't you tell me about Olivia? The typewriter and

the letters, that you were 'Remington'?" she says, using air quotes.

"It has nothing to do with you."

"Except it does, Chase. I bought that typewriter and gave it to you. When Olivia finds out, she's going to think I knew this whole time."

She stares at me, at my eyes that keep sliding away, and then her eyes get big.

"You weren't going to tell her, were you?" She snorts in disgust. "Guys are such idiots. So tell me, big brother, what is your grand plan here?"

I run my hand through my hair and squeeze the back of my neck. "I never planned any of this, Daisy. I made a mistake visiting her in San Francisco and setting all this in motion, but she stopped texting me and I was worried. I just want to keep her from being hurt, and if I tell her, it *will* hurt her."

"And if you tell her, you won't be able to go back to being Remington again once the stalker and tabloids are under control," she says slowly. "*That's* your plan, isn't it? You're just going to wait this out and then go back to being Remington as if none of this has happened."

"I can't see another way," I admit.

"Or you could take a chance on love for once. Actually connect with someone, rather than pushing them away."

"It's not about love," I say. "Whether she knows it or not, she's my best friend. I want her happy and safe, and the best way to do that is to let her go."

She shakes her head. "You have to tell her, Chase. Or I will. It's not right or healthy what you're doing. She deserves to know the truth. And regardless, you can't go back as if none of this has happened. You won't be able to forget this all. Nothing will be the same."

Fuck. I close my eyes and know that she's right. I can't go

back to Remington. After being with Olivia in real life, anything else would be a pale approximation.

And once she knows I've been playing this double life, she's going to hate me, with good reason.

It's been wrong to lie to her for so long. I've been so caught up in being around her. So unhinged at being able to spend time with her, that I didn't just deceive her, I deceived me. There's only one way this can end. And that's badly. It's not rational. But then again, I haven't been rational since she sent me that text and her photo, telling me how she felt. I've barely been able to breathe.

I don't know what the hell to do about any of it. How can I go back to life pre-Olivia, pre-Typewriter Girl? I have to figure it out, though. Olivia will eventually return to her peaceful life. And I can't follow her there and drag the tabloids and trolls into her safe world.

I will tell her, to hell with the consequences, I promise myself. But I need more time with her before she inevitably hates me. And I need more time to keep her safe.

"I'll tell her," I vow to Daisy. "But not just yet."

"When, then?" Daisy says.

"When the threat to her life is gone. If she finds out now, she might be angry enough to leave, and she's safer here with me than she would be on her own in San Francisco." I look at Daisy with pleading eyes. "I couldn't live with myself if something happened to her." My voice cracks with emotion. "Please."

Daisy taps her long nails against the table. "Fine," she says. "But as soon as there's no more danger, she needs to know."

"Agreed," I say.

This is all coming to an end. At least I can build a few more memories and ensure she's protected before she leaves for good.

CHAPTER 28

livia

THERE ARE many things I never imagined. I never imagined making out with Chase James. Or living in a mansion full of hot celebrities. I also never imagined that the first time I met Cassidy Reynolds, I'd be facedown, ass-up, almost naked, getting massaged by a very tall woman named Helga.

Life. It's a constant surprise.

This is no luxury spa day. The massage is therapeutic because after all the running, roller-skating, and pole dancing, I can barely walk without tears. So, when Cassidy Reynolds saunters by, I'm lying on a massage table by the pool while Helga rubs my body all over until my aching muscles feel like jelly.

Helga gasps and pounds on my back a little too hard.

"Look! It is Cassidy Reynolds," she squeals. I didn't know a sound like that could come out of such a formidable body.

"What? Where?"

"There! Her legs! Her shoulders! Her perfect body alignment. I could give her a good massage." she sighs.

I look up from the massage table and get a glimpse of what might be Cassidy Reynolds's toned backside walking toward Chase's bungalow. She's wearing a white sundress and heels. The pleasure from my massage dissipates, and for the second time, I want to cry, this time not from muscle pain.

Helga pushes me back down, my face slamming into the little hole in the massage table. She enthusiastically goes to work on my other arm, rhapsodizing about the talented and beautiful Ms. Reynolds.

I shouldn't feel so shitty. I already assumed Chase and Cassidy got back together. But I've ignored that inconvenient thought as best as I could because, for the last week, Chase and I have been hanging out more and more. We start the mornings with a run and eat breakfast together after we cool down. Then, he goes off to do whatever it is that movie stars do during the day, while I write and hang out with Daisy, and Emma when she's on a break. But when he returns each night, whoever is around gets together to barbecue, have drinks, and hang out by the pool.

We even have a date night tonight. Not a real date, of course. He's just helping me with my list and still refuses to let anyone else take me out because of "security risks."

I'm not stupid; I don't argue.

The more I get to know him, the deeper my crush gets. Since that first run, when we're with the rest of the group, he's often next to me. And maybe it's my imagination, but even when we aren't physically close together, our eyes meet from across the room. He touches me often, and with each brush of his shoulder or pass of his hand, I break out in full-body shivers, remembering that one night we had back in San Francisco. Oh, I remember that night to the point of obsession, to the point of forgetting everything else, especially the role of Cassidy Reynolds in his life.

But here she is, and I can't ignore her presence any longer. I can't be jealous—well, I am, but I shouldn't be. And I can't help wonder if Cassidy knows that Chase is taking me out tonight. Maybe they are only back to casually dating, or maybe they have an open relationship. I'll never understand Hollywood. If Chase were mine, I'd never share.

An hour later, I'm done with my massage and having iced coffees at a poolside table with Daisy and Emma when Cassidy walks past again, returning from the path to Chase's cottage.

"Hi!" Cassidy says with a friendly wave as she approaches us.

The worse part is she seems nice.

Emma looks up from her laptop.

"Hey, Cassidy! I haven't seen you in forever!" Emma rises, and she and Cassidy do the LA air-kiss thing.

"Cassidy, this is Daisy and Olivia," Emma introduces.

Daisy smiles. "Hi! I loved you in *It Takes Two*. That was such a great movie."

"Thanks," Cassidy says, a warm smile lighting up her beautiful face. *Ugh. Why can't she be awful?*

"Chase has mentioned you both. It's so nice to finally meet you," the star says graciously, giving me a once-over.

He's mentioned me to Cassidy? I wish I could ask more, but there's no graceful way to insert that into the conversation.

Daisy and Cassidy exchange pleasantries while I paste a fake smile on my face and search for any flaws. But there aren't any. I'm gutted. She's nice, beautiful, and pretty much perfect for Chase.

"I wish I could stay longer, but I have a date I'm already late for," Cassidy says, looking at her watch with a frown.

Date what? Maybe she just means an appointment.

"Ooh, anyone interesting?" Emma asks before Cassidy turns to leave.

Bless you, Emma, you nosy wench.

"It's in the early days, and we're keeping it private, but he shows some promise. I've decided I need to get back out there. It's been too long."

"But—I thought you were back with Chase," I blurt out.

Cassidy tilts her head, frowning, her eyes speculative. "I'm not seeing Chase. At least, not for real, not for years. We still get photographed together and our publicists fan the flames, but that's just PR. I thought that—" She stops herself.

Daisy and Emma look from me to Cassidy, then back to me, as if they're watching a ping-pong match.

"But I heard… He said…" I trail off, trying to think.

What had he said when I brought up Cassidy being his girlfriend? Had he confirmed it, or had he been noncommittal and I just assumed?

"Trust me, the first lesson to learn in this crazy town is not to trust rumors. I'm helping Chase out with something right now, but you'll have to ask him about that yourself. It seems like he might be into someone else."

"Good to know," I say, my mind in a whirl.

After Cassidy saunters away, Emma turns to me. "Soooo, that was interesting."

"I don't understand. Chase led me to think he was back with Cassidy."

"Obviously, you misunderstood," Emma says. "Besides, you and Chase are going out on a date tonight. He would never take another girl out if he was with someone else. He's not the type to cheat. Hell, ever since that one girl sold her story about hooking up with him to the tabloids, he's hardly been with anyone."

Except for me. Except for San Francisco. I've never been more tempted to tell Daisy and Emma everything and ask what they think. They know that we kissed in San Francisco, but they don't know the details or the extent of it. I'm not experienced like they are, so I'm way out of my depth. I don't know the dos and don'ts of hookup etiquette.

I stay quiet, though. Saying anything would feel like a

betrayal of Chase's fragile trust, as if I were no better than the girl who ran to the press with her story. I know it's not the same, but he has so little privacy as it is.

"It's not romantic," I say instead. "We're just going as friends, so he can help me with my list."

"Two of Ryder's band members volunteered to go on the date with you, and Chase refused to allow it. He said he was the only guy who could take you out. He's awfully possessive of you. Doesn't sound like friends, sugar," Emma says.

Daisy's stare is dagger-sharp. "I have a serious question for you, Olivia. Now that you know he's not dating Cassidy, do you or do you not like Chase?"

"Yes, I like him. He's great." Nerves jangle down my spine.

"Do you like him as a girl likes a boy? As a woman likes a man? In a *sexual* way?" Emma asks with an eye roll.

What can I say? Of course I like him. But I'm scared to hope for more. It's not like I baby-stepped my way into this situation, hooking up with a few normal guys, gaining experience and confidence. If I even had a few friends-with-benefits situations, I might be less confused. But nope. I jumped straight into the dating pool with a movie star. I'm a mess.

Emma sighs at my silence. "Olivia, life is short. You've been taking risks, but not the ones that matter. Doing things like pretend skydiving or roller-skating are just baby steps to teach you it's okay to fall and that, sometimes, you'll fly. You've done those. Now, take a risk that means something. Do you or do you not like Chase?" she asks, her eyes flinty. Damn, she's tough. And dammit, she's right.

I take a deep breath and step out onto that ledge once again.

"Yes," I say.

"We can't hear you." Emma's mirth is evident in her wide grin.

Daisy's been uncharacteristically quiet during this conversation. She just watches me with a slight frown. Maybe it's weird for her to hear, what with the whole brother thing.

"Yes, I like him," I say with more force this time. "But he keeps giving me mixed signals," I can't help adding.

"Oh, honey, no guy knows what's good for him, especially not Chase. You have to show him," Emma says. "You can start showing him tonight."

"Just… Just be careful," Daisy says.

Daisy telling me to be careful is like being in the land of the opposites.

I still don't know why Chase let me believe he's with Cassidy. The most logical answer is he's trying to let me down easy. But Emma is right. I need to learn to be honest and go after what I want.

I'm tired of this back and forth. What I need is to have some straight talk with Chase. He keeps pulling me in, then letting me go. Tonight, we will talk. Tonight I will tell him what I want and find out once and for all what he wants. And what I want is Chase James. He's not just a fantasy or a crush anymore. This is real, at least for me, even if all we'll ever have is this short time during my summer of risk.

* * *

Later that afternoon, I wake from a blissful nap in groggy confusion. I can still feel the warm strength of being in Chase's arms. Only, in my dream, he doesn't stop our kisses or our wandering hands. I want to keep hold of the gossamer threads of the dream, but they disintegrate at the incessant ring of the phone, and all that's left is my body, hot and bothered.

Apparently, I can't get it in real life and can't even get it in a dream.

"Hello," I answer the phone, gravel-voiced and grumpy. I sit up in bed, pushing the cozy white throw off me.

"Olivia Evans?"

"Yes?" The stranger's voice sounds commanding and impatient. I brush my bangs back from my face. They haven't been cut since before we arrived in LA and are starting to annoy me.

"This is the fire inspector. I'm calling about the fire at your residence."

"Oh," I say, my stomach plummeting. "Do you have an update?"

A knock sounds on the door, and Emma pokes her head in.

I wave her in as I continue to listen to the man talking.

She looks down at her phone, typing furiously, as she waits for me to be finished. But I can't concentrate on her. The man on the phone has my entire attention. My breath whooshes out at his words.

"Th-thank you for letting me know," I say on a shaky breath. "Okay. Yes. I will. Goodbye."

I look up at Emma, trying to process what I just heard.

"Are you okay, Olivia?" Emma asks. "Any important news?"

"It wasn't arson," I mumble to myself, looking at Emma with wide, shocked eyes.

"What did you say, hon?"

I shake my head, as if to clear it. It's on the tip of my tongue to explain that the phone call was the fire inspector, and he just told me that the fire at my house wasn't arson. It was caused by old, faulty wiring in the bathroom.

I think of the burned socket in the upstairs bathroom and how my blow-dryer kept blowing a fuse. How I wanted to get the house rewired but could never quite afford it. I think Nanna had been planning on doing it before she got sick, but that was years ago. *Shit.*

That means that the threatening letters the police found were just a coincidence. A disgruntled fan may have been upset enough to send a nasty letter, but they didn't try to kill me.

I open my mouth to explain all that, but something stops me.

"Olivia?"

I don't answer Emma. All I can think of is that no one tried to kill me.

Now, normally, this would be a good thing.

But it also means there's no substantial threat.

Maybe there's a stalker. But there's no *deadly* stalker.

So, there's no need to be in this Malibu mansion with Chase and his crew.

No need to be with Chase at all.

And that is very, very bad.

Why can't someone want to kill me?

Just a little.

"Nothing. Just talking to myself. What is it, Emma?"

She tilts her head. I can tell from her sharp gaze that she doesn't believe it's nothing, but she doesn't press me.

"Chase wants you to meet him out front at eight for your date."

"Did he say where we're going?" I ask. "I'm not sure what to wear."

"Something cute and comfortable," Emma says. Then she grins wickedly. "With nice underwear."

I throw my pillow at her but miss. She laughs and saunters out the door with a wave of her hands.

As soon as she leaves, my mind goes back to the fire inspector's call and his unexpected findings.

Good Olivia knows I should tell everyone about the report.

But Bad Olivia, the one who's gotten addicted to taking risks, is asking if it's really so wrong to wait a few days, a week, hell, a lifetime, to tell everyone that I don't need to be here, that I'm in no need of protection after all? Because when I do, Chase might just put me on the first jet back to San Francisco, and I'm not ready for that yet.

I'm not asking for much. Just a little more time.

All things considered, I'm almost doing Chase a favor. He

needs to realize he shouldn't lock himself away on this property. I've vowed to help him. I can't leave before that job is done, can I?

My heart twists with the idea that I'll never see Chase in person again. And that's what will happen once I leave.

I walk over to the closet and pull out a few cute and comfortable options for our night tonight.

I'm just going to take this fire report and put a pin in it, as Nanna liked to say.

At least until we've gone on this date. Even if he is just doing me a favor. Even if he has been giving me mixed signals. Just for tonight, I'm not going to worry about right or wrong.

We'll just take this one last risk together, and then I'll tell him the truth.

CHAPTER 29

hase

I'M PALMS-SWEATING, heart-pounding, stomach-twisting nervous, like a teenager about to get laid for the first time.

But this is Olivia, and this is our first and only date, even if I haven't admitted to her that it's real, and not just for the sake of her list. Either way, I don't want to fuck it up.

We arranged to meet at the front of the mansion. I stand next to my car in jeans and a black sweater and try to tell myself to chill the fuck out.

But when she opens the door and descends the stairs, I realize that all my internal pep talks about staying calm were bullshit. There's nothing calm or settled about the way I feel about her. She slays me with each step closer.

"Damn," I mutter when she finally stands next to me, letting my gaze roam where it wants, which is everywhere on her.

"What? What's wrong?" she asks with a laugh. One hand goes to her hair, and the other smooths her dress. She looks down as if checking to see if something is out of place, which it's not.

I shake my head to clear it. "You. That dress," I say. "You're perfect."

And she is. By now, I know many of her strengths and weaknesses. I know she can't run for shit. I know when she gets nervous, she babbles. She prefers books to movies. Classics to modern. She's terrible at technology but feels most comfortable behind a screen. She says she was born in the wrong century, but I'm not sure if she could give up the innovation of cozy sweatshirts. She is clumsy and shy around strangers. But she's also loyal and funny and achingly sweet, and she's perfect —for me.

At my words, her smile lights up the early evening.

"Oh, this old thing?" she says cheekily. "One of Emma's purchases. Like Daisy, she has a fairy godmother complex."

The dress is ice blue, making her glacial eyes more blue than gray tonight; it shows off her creamy shoulders, a generous expanse of cleavage, then drapes down the curves of her hips, ending just above the knees.

I hold the door and usher her into the car. She slides in, and I walk around to the other side.

She looks at me, surprised. "You're driving."

I shoot her a wry glance. "I do drive."

"No. I mean, I know. I guess I always just imagine you with a driver. And a bodyguard."

The engine starts with a satisfying purr, and I pull out of the driveway, one hand on the wheel, the other on the stick shift. It feels good to be in control of all that power beneath me. I love the freedom of a fast car and a winding road.

"It's a nice car," she remarks. "What is it?"

"A Maserati. I bought it with my first big paycheck from *The Wanderers*. Whenever everything got too much, I'd find a way to get the paps off my trail and escape. It would make me feel like I could breathe again."

We reach the gates of the neighborhood, and I sense her nerves.

"Don't worry," I say as we pass through the safety of the gated community and pull out onto the road. "The windows have a special tint. No one can see in. And I don't drive this car often anymore, so they won't automatically know it's mine."

"But where are the photographers?" she asks, looking down the road. Normally, there are at least a few camped out in front of the guard house.

I smirk. "They're all chasing Sebastian."

"What? Why?"

"He's doing me a favor to create a distraction so we can leave undetected. He just kissed Emma in front of the photographers on their way out. They all know she's his longtime assistant, and a lot of people have speculated they are more. No photographer would wait around after that."

"They kissed? *Emma and Sebastian?*"

I shrug. "It was Sebastian's idea. I only wanted them to hug or something less definitive. But Sebastian said a kiss was the only thing that would work, and Emma went along with it."

"Wow," I say and shake my head. "Just wow."

He slants a look at me. "It probably isn't that big of a deal. Sebastian is a manwhore. I mean, who hasn't he kissed? Plus, it's just part of the job for actors."

"Like you and Cassidy?" she asks, her expression tight now.

I flex my jaw and concentrate on the road, unsure how to answer her.

The silence in the car lengthens. Finally, she lets out a gusty sigh. My concentration is on the winding road, but I can sense her attention on me.

"I'm just going to come out and say this. Chase, you gave me the impression that you and Cassidy are dating, but she told me earlier today that you aren't."

Damn, well, that was quick. She didn't waste any time calling me on my shit. I can't put this off any longer.

"I know," I admit. "She called me after she talked to you. Cassidy is a friend. I care about her, just not in that way."

Inside the car, we're sealed in our own bubble, with lights and buildings and trees flying by. Like the car, our conversation is also hurtling us into new territory. I don't know the direction we're moving toward, but it feels closer and closer to the point of no return, the place from which there's no going back.

I dare a quick glance at her. She's looking out the window now, ostensibly watching the scenery.

"So, why did you make me think you two were an item?" Her voice is hushed, threaded through with vulnerability. "It's not just my imagination, is it? You deliberately gave me that impression."

She sounds hurt. I made her feel that way. Again.

We come to a stop sign, and I take my eyes off the road to find her looking straight ahead, her hands in tight fists in her lap, worrying the beads on her little purse.

What I say next will matter. Matter deeply to her and to me.

But fuck if I can find the right words. I don't know if there's enough time in eternity to find the right words.

"Chase," she says with increased strength. "If we're going to be…friends…you need to really talk to me. Be straight with me. I deserve that."

A car horn honks behind me. I start driving again.

"I'm sorry," I say in a ragged breath. "You do. When we get to where we're going, we'll talk properly. I promise. There is an explanation."

I can't resist reaching over with one hand and brushing the curve of her cheek. Her face briefly leans into my palm. The things she does to me with a simple touch.

"Deal?" I ask, my eyes sweeping over her.

"Deal," she says after a long minute. But her eyes are still hesitant.

No photographers follow, so we drive along the coast until the city lights are beyond us, with the music blaring, and the wind flowing through the open windows of the car that we'd rolled down once we were clear of town.

All I want is to keep driving until we're as far away as we can get from the pressures of life.

As I drive, I wonder, *What if I do what Olivia has been doing? A risk at a time. Tonight can be my first.*

But it isn't me I fear hurting.

I'd risk my heart every moment of every day for her.

But it's her heart, her life, I'm playing with. Not just mine.

CHAPTER 30

livia

"WE'RE GOING TO THIS HOUSE?" I ask when we drive down a long, winding road that leads to a small home perched above the sea.

Chase hops out and comes around to open my door. He grasps my hand and helps me out of the low-slung car.

"Not the house. There." He points to a small strip of sand amid rocky boulders.

"Is that what I think it is?" I ask in wonder.

"A picnic."

"A candlelight picnic on the beach. And twinkly lights! This is insane."

"I can't take all the credit. Emma did the organizing, and the guards set it up."

"When you say guards, do you mean bodyguards?"

"They prefer 'close protection officers,'" Chase says with a smile.

Here, I've been giddy, thinking it's just the two of us. I

should've known Chase wouldn't let us go out alone. I look around but don't see anyone.

"This place is remote, and we weren't followed. Duncan would have called me if we had been. But the bodyguards are still a necessity, Olivia."

I look down at the scene below. It's straight out of a romantic movie. A checkered picnic blanket set with a basket and place settings is illuminated by dozens of candles. Twinkle lights wind through the surrounding trees.

"This is incredible, Chase. The nicest thing anyone's ever done for me," I admit.

His face cracks into a boyish, pleased smile. "Be glad I took control of this risk. Kenji wanted to take you to see *Murder Cult 5*. He says horror movies are good for getting laid because the girl will be too scared to sleep by herself."

"I am glad it's you," I say simply.

There's so much more I want to say, so much I want to ask, but the words clog in my throat. Maybe he has a bottle of wine down there that will give me the liquid courage to get the answers I crave.

I bend down and untie my sandals. His gaze follows my movement. When my shoes are off, I hold them in one hand. He takes my other hand as we walk, steadying me. I'm sure holding my hand is more practical than romantic, with us clambering down the narrow path to the sea. But with his fingers clasped in mine and the wide ocean before us, I don't care.

Nothing else matters but the wind whipping around me that tastes like freedom and the touch of Chase's skin that feels like joy. I've never felt more alive. Or grateful to be just where I am.

I turn to look at him, only to find him intently staring.

"Your smile," he says.

"What about my smile?"

"It's so beautiful, it hurts."

Instead of accepting the compliment gracefully, I say, "Oh. No. I'm definitely not beautiful."

Then I trip over a rock.

He laughs, and he snakes his arm around my waist to catch me before I fall. His strong arm is still around me when our feet hit the sand.

It's the picnic of every girl's dreams. There are blankets and pillows, and a wicker basket filled with food next to a tray of two champagne flutes and champagne on ice.

I shyly look up at him. With the dramatic shadows in the dark, he appears older and even more intimidating than usual.

"You like?" His voice is a husky murmur.

"I like."

His smile widens. "Are you hungry?"

"Starving."

Another benefit of crowding onto a blanket is proximity. Our legs touch as we stretch out to get comfortable.

The picnic basket is bewitched. Out of it comes a seemingly endless array of sandwiches, grapes, cheese, crackers, and pastel-colored cookies.

"I love macarons!" I give a soft squeal.

"I know," he answers, pleased with himself.

I narrow my eyes. "I never told you that. How did you know?"

His smile falters. After a beat, he says, "I have my ways."

I unwrap a tea sandwich and take a bite. The bread is perfectly soft, and it's filled with a thin layer of chicken, herbs, and Brie. All my favorites. I close my eyes. "Bliss."

He pulls out a bag of chips.

My eyes widen. "Salt and vinegar? Also my favorite."

He's nailing this picnic, like some sort of mind-reading wizard.

He smiles at me. "I pay attention to what matters."

My stomach does a funny little flip at his words.

He reaches over and steals a chip from the package I've commandeered as my own. I slap his hand, and he laughs.

"Don't be stealing my chips," I say.

"Oh, they're yours, are they?"

"It's your fault. You picked the only ones I can't share. I'm greedy about them."

He leans over, his face so close to mine that I can see the green-gold swirl of his eyes. "I'm greedy too," he says with a husky voice. "I don't like to share when something is mine."

I swallow my chip with an audible gulp.

"You okay there?" he asks.

"No," I cough out, gasping as the chip sticks in my throat. When the coughing subsides, I fake-glare at him. "It's your fault. You did that sexy-smolder thing. You need to prepare me for it."

"And did it work?"

My eyes meet Chase's. I promised myself that I would be honest, even if it makes me vulnerable.

"Yes. Everything you do works for me, Chase. That's part of the problem."

He draws in a breath and looks away, focusing on opening the champagne bottle. The cork pops in the night, blending with the sound of the rhythmic surf.

"So, we're celebrating more than just your risk with this champagne," he says, sounding hesitant.

"We are?"

He fills a glass and passes it to me. Our hands brush, and there it is—the electricity when we touch.

"We're celebrating that the tabloids have finally moved on from us."

He says it so casually, raising his glass.

"They have? Why? How?"

"I've been working with my public relations team to get the tabloids away from you and focused on another story."

I stare at him blankly.

"Another girl. With me," he says meaningfully.

It takes a few minutes to connect his words.

"Cassidy," I say.

He nods. "Cassidy."

"So, when Cassidy was over at your house yesterday..."

"She made it very evident that she was visiting me. It's all over social media. The fan sites and comment boards aren't even mentioning you anymore, and everyone is chasing the story of Cassidy and me reunited. We'll arrange to get photographed together a few more times, and you'll be forgotten." He flashes me a grim smile. "Your fifteen minutes of fame have officially ended."

My stomach clenches. Will Chase forget me along with the fans?

"Cassidy doesn't mind?" I ask. "I thought you broke up because she hated all the attention your relationship created."

"Cassidy's up for a huge movie role, so her PR team wants the extra publicity. When all this is over, we'll both put out statements saying we're just good friends, and everything will go back to normal."

I bite my lip and wonder if maybe Cassidy's motivation might also be getting to spend more time with Chase, despite what she said. Perhaps she regrets the breakup and misses their relationship. Fake dating is the perfect strategy if she wants to get him back.

"What about the stalker? Isn't this putting her in danger now?"

"Cassidy has great security, much more than she had when we dated. She's not concerned."

He rubs the nape of his neck. "This is just one step closer to getting you home and back to your real life. All we're waiting for is the fire report, which should be coming in any day."

My gut twists with guilt over the lie about the fire report. But even worse is the knowledge that Chase seems to be in a rush to get me out of Malibu and back home. I take a sip of the champagne, but it's ash in my mouth now. Suddenly, the picnic, this romantic setting, everything seems wrong.

"So, that's it?" I say.

"That's it." He nods, looking at the ocean.

I watch him, willing him to say something, anything that will ease the ache taking up residence in my gut.

Every time I open my heart, he shows me he doesn't want it.

I know I should just gracefully accept his friendship. The girl I was before would go back to her safe, small life without putting herself on the line. But that was before Nanna reached out from beyond the grave to kick me in the ass, daring me to start taking risks.

I'm learning that making myself open and vulnerable is a strength, not a weakness. It hasn't been an easy, comfortable journey, but it's led me here, to a secluded beach with the guy of my dreams. I'm not going to waste this. There are twinkly lights, for fuck's sake.

I might not end up with the guy. But I can at least be the heroine in my own story. I'm not going to be ashamed of my feelings. I'm going to be brave enough to tell the truth. At least about this.

"I get it, Chase." I give him a sad but determined smile. "You warn me away from you, are deliberately vague about having a girlfriend, and toast me going home with champagne." I tilt my head. "You draw me in and then push me away. And no matter all that, I'm still here, barely able to breathe every time you look at me. You may confuse the hell out of me, but I see you, Chase. I see the real you when I suspect almost no one does. I see the loneliness behind your fame. I see the pain in your childhood and how you give quietly to those in need. How you support Daisy and care about your friends. How you turned your life around to protect me. I know you're keeping me at a distance, but I also know that you've opened up to me in ways that are rare for you. I just want to do the same. If only you'd let me. If only you'd want me," I say, my voice ragged and fierce.

"You don't get it at all."

"Pot, meet kettle."

In one quick motion he shifts forward, cradles the back of my head, and pulls me closer until his forehead meets mine, until we're just breathing each other in.

"I want you," he forces out. "So damn bad I can't breathe either." He pulls back slightly. "But not at the expense of your life or happiness."

He closes his eyes, and when he opens them, they are clear. Determined.

"That's why I let you think I had a girlfriend. I could have told you about Cassidy's real role in all this. But I didn't because I don't trust myself with you. I needed something to keep you away. Every time you look at me… Christ, Olivia."

With a gentle, shaking hand, he traces my eyebrow, my cheek, down to my jaw. I hold so still; I forget to breathe.

"You look at me with those big gray eyes like I'm the sun and the moon, and I don't deserve it. My life will fuck you up. I mean, look at what's already happened. You could have been killed."

"I wasn't. That had nothing to do with you," I interject.

He ignores my protest. "You could have died because I've been too weak to keep away from you. So, when you assumed that Cassidy and I were an item again, it was easier to let you think that. I'm sorry for misleading you."

"You don't have to protect me, Chase. And I'm tired of you making decisions for me in the name of keeping me safe. I can make my own decisions. I *have* made my own decisions. I'm here, with you. You keep telling me what you *should* do. But what do you *want*?" I ask in an urgent, impassioned rasp, our faces close.

I wait for his answer as he gazes at me with a closed-off

ferocity I can't read. And then his face shifts. A shake of his head and a small smile, like the sun in a storm-filled sky. "*You.* I only ever want *you.*"

His mouth descends on mine in a long, drugging kiss, and all my questions, all my doubts, all my fears of not being enough fly out of my head.

When we finally come up for breath, he pulls away a fraction. I make a mewl of dissatisfaction. He quirks his lips at the disgruntled sound.

"I need you to understand that being with me isn't easy. We're here, on the beach, because it's beautiful. But I can't take you to dinner or to the movies without a crowd forming and us running from photographers."

I wave a hand. "I don't care about all that. Though I think we can get creative if you want to be incognito in public. I was talking to Emma and Daisy, and they had great ideas about costumes."

He laughs. "Lord save me," he says wryly. He presses his lips softly to mine, and my eyes flutter shut again. "I'll hear about their ideas later," he says, pulling away slightly. "For now, I have a great idea."

"What?" I have some great ideas as well. They involve his lips back on mine.

"Remember, one of your risks is skinny-dipping."

I smile, butterflies in my heart. "I already checked that off the list, Chase."

"It doesn't count in the pool. It has to be in the ocean, Olivia."

"Says who?"

"Says me." He downs the rest of his glass of champagne, stands up, and offers me his hand.

Of course I take it.

He pulls me up. I wish I could say I was smooth and graceful, but I stumble in the sand as we race to the edge of the water together. We laugh as the cool wind whips my hair around my shoulders and face.

He discards his shirt. His jeans go next until he stands before me, clad only in boxers. At first, I think he might take those off too, but sadly, he keeps them on.

He steps behind me and extends his arms, blocking me. I look back at him in question.

"So there aren't any prying eyes. The guards are watching. They're not close, and they probably can't see much in the dark. But I don't want to take the chance. Your body is for my eyes only."

"Are the guards why you're still wearing your boxers? It's not skinny-dipping without getting naked."

He raises an eyebrow. "I'm trying to be a gentleman. But just say the word, and I'll be happy to take them off."

"Hmm. I'll think about it," I tease.

The interesting thing about risks is, the more you take, the better you get at them. At least, that's the only explanation I have for how easy it is to shed my dress and stand before Chase in just my underwear. It helps that it's dark enough to feel a layer of protection from my insecurities.

If I thought his gaze was hot before, it scorches me now. "Pretty girl," he whispers, his breath caressing my ear, as we step into the surf hand in hand, Chase just behind me.

The moment is magical. It's perfect.

It's—

"Gah! Cold!" I squeal as a small wave slaps at my legs.

Chase laughs. "You wimp."

"I'm not a wimp. I'm sane. This is freezing."

He makes a clean dive into the deeper water. "It's only cold for the first minute. After that, it's awesome. Refreshing."

"Refreshing, my ass."

"Your ass is spectacular."

That makes me move toward Chase's magnetic, possessive

gaze. I mentally swear like a sailor the deeper I get, but Chase is right. It's refreshing, especially when he catches me around my waist.

"There're no sharks in here, right?" I eye the dark water with suspicion.

"Maybe. This could be Sebastian's dastardly plan to get you to swim with them."

I hit Chase.

"Ow!" he says, rubbing his shoulder. "For a girl who can't run, you sure hit hard."

"Don't you forget that." I soothe the area I just smacked. And then, unable to resist, I stroke down his chest, his arms, following muscle and skin that are so much hotter than the water.

He growls—legit growls—and pulls me tighter to him. I can feel his erection, and on instinct, I wrap my legs around him. The movement lines up all our most intimate parts.

"You're playing with fire," he warns.

"I like it hot. I'm yours now. So, what are you going to do with me?" I taunt. I can't believe I'm speaking so confidently. Around anyone else, except maybe Remington online, I'm too shy to say the things that come into my head, so I hold myself back. But with Chase, it's different. This man gives me the courage to be myself.

He kisses me, and everything is wet and wanting. Our bodies fuse together. Only his thin boxers and my even thinner panties keep us apart. He kisses me as if my mouth is his lifeline, his oxygen. He traces the fabric of my bra strap with his other hand until he's playing with the edge of the peekaboo lace. We do have an audience, even if we're probably just silhouettes in the water. Somehow, that just makes things feel hotter, wilder. Maybe I have a little voyeur in my inexperienced heart.

As if he can read my mind, he turns so that his large body blocks the view from the beach and shifts me up so that my breasts are on full display to him. His fingers play back and forth over my bra, as he watches my nipples harden through the see-through lace. He takes in a ragged breath when my hips move forward in a rhythm against his hardness. His hand goes to the front closure of my bra and hovers over it.

My eyes close as I whisper, "Kiss me. Chase. Please." I'm not too proud to beg. I want his lips more than my next breath.

His mouth crashes down on mine. Our kiss is as wild as a storm at sea. This is no sweet seduction. It's a mad melding of bodies as my hands grasp everywhere I can reach, and he brands me with his hot mouth and burning touch. I grind against him, dying for relief that only he can bring. As hot as it was in the hotel in San Francisco, this is even more.

He kisses his way down to my breasts that are on full display in my soaked bra, my nipples hard as pebbles. He unsnaps the front closure and sweeps aside the wet fabric, sucking first one nipple, then the other.

"God, your body, Olivia. Your tits are perfect. I've been dying to do this for so long," he groans.

I've never felt confident in my body before. But with the way he looks at me, the way he kisses me, and his rock-hard length pressing against me, for the first time, I feel the full power of being a woman. It's heady. It's hard to be an average girl with curves in a world that glorifies skinny. Until now. I see in his eyes just how much he loves my full breasts and hourglass figure.

We make out like that for I don't know how long. Long enough for me to get lost in his drugging kisses, his hand straying down to my underwear, and for my hand to get bold and desperate enough to stroke his length. Long enough for me to know that if we continue, I'll shatter right here in the sea, with bodyguards in the dark distance.

"Enough." Chase wrenches our mouths apart. His face turns

up to the moonlight, panting. "Fuck, Olivia. I didn't mean to go this far. You make me lose my mind."

I can barely make out his perfect features. What I do see mirrors my feelings, the passion and the longing. Yet he's still fighting it.

I'm achingly aware that there is no future in this, in us. He'll end up with a woman who can navigate his fame with grace. He's already told me this.

It's been fun to play at this life for a while, to let Emma dress me and get dolled up. But I'm a tumble-down Victorian, and he's a Malibu mansion. I'm shabby, light on the chic. He's a designer's dream. I'm all about the bookish life, and he's jet-set.

But despite all that, I still want him. When we're done, he'll go back to his life and I'll go back to mine, but at least I'll have this. Maybe someday I'll find that forever kind of love I've always wanted. Like what I hoped to have with Remington, only reciprocated, only real. Or what I'd like with Chase, only longer than a few hot summer weeks.

But until then, I want this night.

I open my mouth to tell him just that, but a distant ringing reaches us through the dark.

"Is that a phone?" I ask, confused.

He pulls away from me. "I'm sorry. It might be Duncan. I have to answer," he says, snapping my bra, taking my hand, and leading me through the water, blocking me from any eyes that might be looking from the rocks above.

He tosses me one of the towels that he left by the water and takes one for himself. He throws the towel over his shoulder, passing me my dress and rummaging in his pants pocket that he discarded on the beach. As he answers the phone with a growl, I towel off quickly and put the dress on, saying a silent apology to the delicate fabric for the saltwater bath it gets from my wet undergarments and still streaming hair.

"Duncan, I told you not to call unless there was an emergency. What? Are you sure? Fuck. How did this happen?" He listens without saying anything. "No. We're okay. We can stay at Ronan's, at the beach house. It's safer. Fine. Keep me updated."

He hangs up, and, shoulders hunched, looks at me with a dark expression.

"What's going on?" I ask, my palms sweating at the way he's staring at me. I rub my arm, feeling uncomfortably sticky from the salt water. His jaw clenches as he watches me. Nerves dance in my stomach at his intensity. Does he know I've been keeping the fire report quiet?

I laugh self-consciously as the silence draws out. "You're making me scared now. What was the call about?"

"It's about your stalker. The guards found another threatening letter from her. It was left with some packages at the guard gate. She obviously knows you're staying with me. We had a tail on her, but he lost her. It's not safe to go home."

"But—" I almost tell him the truth. The stalker may be a stalker, but she's not necessarily a danger. She didn't set fire to my house. I did that all by myself by not updating the electrical system.

"We'll stay overnight at Ronan's beach house. It's small. There's only one bedroom. But we can manage for one night. And tomorrow, we'll figure something out."

He turns and points to the small bungalow on the bluff above us.

"That's Ronan's house?"

"Yes. It's how I know about this place, and that it's private."

"As in your costar Ronan Masters? We're staying at his house?"

Chase nods. I can see his face tense in the moonlight.

"There's only one bedroom?" I breathe out. *Only one...bed?*

I may write mysteries, not romance, but I've seen enough rom-coms to know how that could end.

I try to wipe the smile from my mouth. This is supposed to

be a concerning situation. Even in the dim glow of moonlight and twinkle lights, I can tell that Chase doesn't look happy. Not at all. He looks stressed and worried.

But I'm jubilant. I only have a short time left with Chase. This is like a gift from the gods. And you can't deny a gift from the gods. It would be impolite. Blasphemous, even.

My guilty conscience says to tell Chase about the fire report. That he needs all the information. That it's not right keeping it from him. But if he knows, he might not think we need to stay in the bungalow for the night. The bungalow that only has one bedroom. Quite possibly only one bed.

It's just one night.

What's the harm in keeping it secret for one more night?

I'll tell him first thing in the morning.

CHAPTER 31

hase

WE MAKE our way up the path to the weathered cottage overlooking the beach. We walk in silence, hand in hand, except at the narrow portions where I follow her. She pulls down her dress self-consciously, and I want to tell her to stop hiding that luscious ass.

The cottage is small and quaint, completely hidden from the road, surrounded by craggy trees and rocks. Wind chimes greet us, and large shells line a handmade bench and a macramé hammock that looks like the perfect place to read a book. A row of surfboards gives the white-shingled cottage a surfer vibe. It's not what anyone would imagine Ronan Masters's house to look like. If not for the million-dollar view, the house could belong to an aging hippie or surfer.

"Pretty humble place for a movie star," she says, taking it all in. "Though he does look like he surfs, with that long blond hair and all those golden muscles." She gives a little sigh, as if imagining my costar's attributes.

I just grunt. It's obvious she approves of his muscles, and as much as I work out, I'll never compete with Ronan in sheer size. He's a giant, a Nordic god of an action star. His muscles have muscles.

I try to remember that I actually like Ronan. He's a good friend, or as much of a friend as two insanely private coworkers can be. But I don't like that smile Olivia has when she talks about him.

I reach into a potted plant and come up with the key.

Olivia tilts her head. "This is where you're taking me to be safe?"

"No one knows about this cottage. It's in the middle of nowhere with no neighbors. Ronan's owned it for years, and no paparazzi have found him here. Despite its looks, it also has a high-tech alarm system."

"Clearly," she says. "That key in the planter must fool all the crooks."

I put the key in the lock, and the door falls open. "The alarm system isn't for when the cottage is empty. It's for when Ronan is here. I'll alarm it once we're locked in. And the guards will be watching the house and grounds the entire time we're here."

I unlock the door, and she steps into the cozy room. The outside may show its humble origins, but the inside is meticulously renovated, with fresh paint, gleaming appliances, and simple yet expensive-looking furnishings in varying shades of white and beige.

I throw the key onto a sideboard that features more shells.

Olivia turns to me, hugging herself.

"Are you cold?" I ask.

"A little," she admits shyly. Her dress is soaked through.

I pull off my mostly dry sweater and hand it to her. "Here. Put this on. But take off your wet clothes first." I look down. "*All your wet clothes*," I say meaningfully. "The bathroom is through there." I point to a door off the living room.

She nods, staring at my chest in the slightly damp T-shirt I'd worn under my sweater.

"While you change, I'll get you something to drink," I continue, needing something to occupy my hands before I reach for her.

I find a bottle of chilled white wine in the fridge and wineglasses on a low bar. I try not to think of her stripping off her wet dress, bra, and underwear. When I return to the living room, she's opened the sliding door and is looking comfortable, curled up on a large, pillow-strewn daybed on the porch facing the jagged cliffs and expansive ocean. The wind is cool, and the only sound is the waves crashing in the dark depths below.

My sweater engulfs her. She's pulled it down to cover her knees. I can't help but focus on how the fabric stretches over her generous breasts, her nipples pebbled. I drag my gaze lower. Did she do as I advised and remove all her clothes? I harden, thinking about her naked in just my sweater.

I hand her the wine and sit next to her. Olivia takes a sip, and then she does something completely unexpected. She lays her head on my shoulder and gives a soft sigh.

This peaceful moment comes as a sweet surprise. I'm uncomfortably aware of her. But after the wild kisses in the water, and my wild imaginings just now, we settle into something that feels like contentment. With an intense yearning, I wish that I could hold her and this peace in my heart for always.

Her soft gray eyes meet mine. She squeezes my hand, and I squeeze hers back. She smiles, and my cold heart melts.

She looks out at the water below, and when she speaks, her voice is shy. "I still want you to be my first."

I don't answer her, just blow out a slow breath.

"You're helping me with my risks, right?" She continues, "Well, I have *that* on my list."

"You deserve—"

"What I deserve is to have good sex with someone I like. I

never meant to be a virgin at this age. I didn't have a boyfriend in high school because I was shy, and then when Nanna got sick, I got so busy trying to juggle work, classes, and taking care of her that I didn't have time. It didn't help that I was stuck on someone who was completely unavailable—"

"You're talking about your online friend," I rasp out. "The one you told me about." More reasons to stay away.

She fiddles with the sleeve of my sweater. "Yes. Remington."

My heart feels too big for my chest. "And you wanted to do *that*." I don't say fuck. She must be rubbing off on me. "With him."

She licks her lips, as if they're suddenly dry. And I imagine her tongue sliding over my dick.

"I always dreamed my first time would be special, or at least with someone I cared about. And he was the only guy I'd ever had those feelings for. Until you," she says the last part softly, hesitantly.

"Olivia." I'm in an impossible situation.

She takes a large swig of wine and then sets it back on the coffee table.

"I'm so awkward at this. See, this is why I'm still a freaking virgin. I have no game and no moves, and I don't know how to do this. I just don't want to be a fifty-year-old virgin and to look back with regret because I didn't tell you exactly what I want."

Her hair is a mess from the wind and water, and I brush the strands behind her ear. She leans toward my hand until I cup her cheek, savoring the soft, silky texture of her skin.

"First, you aren't going to be a fifty-year-old virgin," I scoff. But something acidic washes through my blood. I don't want to imagine her with someone else. Ever. And especially not this first time, when it means so much, when it could be with me.

I move my index finger from stroking her jaw up to her mouth. That plump, succulent pink mouth that begs to be kissed. What I want to do to that mouth. "And second, it's not that I don't want to. I'm dying to be inside you so fucking bad, just like I was dying for you in San Francisco and I was dying for you on the beach." I take her hand and move it to my jeans.

"This is what you do to me, Olivia. Every time you're near me, I want you. With your lush body and your pretty face. With your contrary mind and your old soul. Don't ever imagine that I don't want you because it's never going to be true."

With every breath, the need to take her mounts until it's a tension-filled force.

But I've lied to her on so many levels. I can't be with her with the lies between us.

I tell myself that, even as I can't stop touching her. One hand strokes her hair. She shivers in response, and I know she's feeling everything I am.

I should just be honest, to hell with the consequences. I open my mouth but find the words won't come. There's too much fear. Fear that if I tell her the truth, I'll lose her like I've lost almost everyone I cared about, over and over. Fear that if I squander this one precious moment, it will never come around again.

"Chase, it doesn't have to be forever. It can just be one night."

But that's the thing she doesn't understand. The thing I should never tell her. If I could have one wish, it's that I'd have that one night last forever.

CHAPTER 32

livia

HE TIPS his head back and closes his eyes for a moment, his stubble accentuating the pure lines of his face. Something about his beard and the bruised circles under his eyes makes him a little less perfect, but ironically, that just makes him more appealing. He's rugged and raw and so familiar, like a dream I can't shake.

I recognize something in him. A loneliness. A yearning. I know it's in him because I feel it in myself. Everything turns over in me.

I raise my hand and give in to trace his contoured lips with a finger.

His hand falls away and I feel him moving back, and I can't stand it. I can't stand for him to leave now, knowing this could be the end of whatever is between us.

I reach up, and it's my turn to brush his hair back, to whisper my skin against his in a caress, feeling over those famous cheekbones, that chiseled jaw, the one that journalists write odes to and cinematographers worship.

He's just a guy, not some god, I tell myself. *Just a guy. And I'm just a girl. I can do this.*

"I want it to be you, Chase. I don't think you're suddenly going to fall in love with me and get down on one knee and declare your everlasting love." Though it would be nice, I think.

His jaw under my hand flexes.

Chase closes his eyes. I can feel his turmoil, but I don't understand it. I'm offering him no-strings sex, every guy's dream. My mind starts to spiral in unwelcome and soul-destroying directions until he opens his eyes.

And there it is. I see that I'm not alone in this. It may mean more to me, but I'm not imagining our heat, our connection.

"No-strings sex? Yay?" I say, trying for jovial and failing. I blow out a breath. "I chose you. Now it's your turn to choose me, Chase."

"Oh hell, Olivia." And he kisses me. Swoops down and just kisses the shit out of me. He ravishes me, takes me hostage—not that I'm putting up a fight.

I want every hot, panting second of it.

Thanks, Nanna.

When we come up for air, his voice is ragged. "You have no clue how much I want you. But there's more I need to tell you."

I shake my head to clear it, but only one thought keeps repeating. "Later," I say.

He lowers his head, resting his forehead against mine, and our breaths meld. Everything about him overwhelms me. His hard arms engulf me. I want to dissolve into his embrace until we aren't two separate people, until my atoms and his atoms combine.

What I feel is raw, overpowering. It scares me, how much I can feel with just one embrace from him, not even a kiss. Only one other person had the power to make me yearn like this, but that man hadn't even been real. Remington only lived in my imagination. Chase is a flesh-and-blood man, and I'm ready to surrender.

I shift my hands from his face to his shoulders and down to his jeans. I rest my fingers on the button for a moment before lifting his T-shirt. His skin is hot, firm underneath. My hands continue their journey up, this time unencumbered by cloth, nothing standing in the way between me and his strong muscles and smooth skin, just a sprinkling of hair as I reach his chest.

"You need to kiss me. And you need to keep kissing me." The insecure, tentative parts of me have left the building, and all that's left are instinct and want.

I press my mouth to his. He freezes for a few seconds, seconds where my boldness almost collapses. Almost. But somewhere, I gather the courage to open my mouth on his, and my tongue slicks across his bottom lip, to suck and gently bite it.

His reaction is immediate. He gives a rough groan, and it's as if his control is a dam that reached its limit and cracked apart. Suddenly, everything shifts, and his self-control crumbles to rubble as we both get swept away in the current of sheer desire.

With a muffled, "Fuck it. We'll talk in the morning," he takes charge of the kiss, his tongue invading, plundering, capturing.

I make some sort of noise, an assent that I can't hold back.

It may have been the word *yes*. It may have been his name. Or it may have just been a sigh. All I can do is hold on to him as waves of feeling crash through me, dragging me underwater where it's just him and me and this explosive thing between us.

We devour each other, and then suddenly, I'm lifted into his arms. He continues to kiss me as he walks me into the house and into the bedroom.

He sets me gently on my feet as we stand in front of the bed.

He looks down at me with such intensity. Hair hangs in his

face as he breathes heavily, and my heart skips a beat. This beautiful man is mine, at least for the night.

He reaches for the sweater he gave me earlier. He pulls it up and over me. I reflexively hide myself with my arms, my dark hair a black shroud against the milky skin of my breasts.

He pulls my arms away from my body until they rest at my sides.

"Look at me," he commands.

I look up, and that gaze makes everything else fall away.

"You." He takes a step toclose the distance between us. "Are." He walks us backward another step. "Beautiful."

He gently pushes, and my knees buckle against the bed and I fall onto it, hair splaying around me, everything bared to him.

My breath comes out in a gasp at the hard planes and muscles of his chest and his full six-pack of abs. I give him a thorough perusal.

His body is both familiar yet achingly new. I've seen this chest. I know his smile. The whole world does. But up close, there's so much more.

There are the sensory details. The sound of his breath. The contrast between his smooth skin and rough hair. And then there are the surprises. He has a mole on his side, under his left arm. He has laugh lines that only crinkle when he's really amused at something. They don't activate in his Hollywood smile, and I'm so utterly grateful about that.

When I rub my hand on the side of his waist, he flinches, and the way he grimaces, I realize something else. Something that's just for me, not for those other million women.

"You're ticklish," I say in wonder.

"No, I'm not." He frowns.

I caress the same spot, and there it is. The flinch. The face.

"You are."

And then I launch a full-scale attack to get him to admit it, and he launches a counterattack, and we're rolling and wrestling.

I end up under him, laughing, until I'm not laughing anymore. We both pant as he hovers over me, his hands holding mine above my head, our bodies aligned perfectly so I feel his hard-on through his jeans, and again that liquid heat pools between my legs.

He moves. Just a little. And, oh shit, I need more.

He leans over me, arms bracing on either side, taking me in.

"You are so lovely. I wish you could see yourself as I see you."

He reaches out and plays with a strand of hair that rests against my breast, teasing it across my nipple. I squirm. Every part of me is on fire. At that moment, I feel lovely. And powerful.

He captures my mouth again, and we kiss like that for long minutes, alternating between soft and gentle and sweet to frenzied and back again. Even as our kisses remind me of that night we made out in his hotel room, it's also completely different.

Our hands are everywhere. There's a purpose to this, but he's letting me set the pace, holding back even now. I know, without him saying it, that it's up to me to take this further, that if I don't, he'll kiss me all night until our lips bruise from it.

But he already knows I want him.

I awkwardly undo the first button of his jeans.

He exhales sharply.

My breath is ragged. Chase overwhelms me in every way possible. His words, his kisses, his gentleness target that soft center of me and turn me inside out.

I unzip his pants as our mouths claim each other.

He makes his way to my breast, sucking on my nipple long and deep, nipping it and causing me to gasp before lavishing attention on my other breast.

I grind myself against the huge, hard ridge of him. I can't get close enough.

"I want to make you come."

"Yay," is all I can manage. I mean, does the man expect me to argue?

I lie there, bare to him, proof that I had indeed gotten rid of my wet underwear earlier.

One talented finger slowly teases my clit until my hips are moving against his hand.

"You're torturing me," I moan, shifting restlessly. Sweat breaks out on my forehead.

"You know how many times I've pleasured myself, imagining you like this?"

I can't answer because just thinking about him with his dick in his hand short-circuits my brain and takes me even higher.

His mouth tracks down my body, kissing each nipple, and then down to my stomach and continuing on. If I weren't so mad with lust, I'd stop him. The act seems too intimate, embarrassing even, to have a man tasting me, smelling me, feeling the evidence of just how wet I am.

But the way he whispers my name with such reverence and hunger and licks me like I'm his favorite flavor of ice cream is incredible. I'm dissolving into pure sensation.

My hands go to his hair, pulling at the strands, pulling him closer.

He licks and sucks until I go higher and higher, until it's all too much, and I explode.

Shattered, I finally settle back into the world. He's there next to me. It's cute how proud he looks. He brushes the hair out of my eyes as I try to get my breathing under control, aftershocks still working their way through my body. I smile shyly back, feeling my full body blush.

"Um...thank you?" I say.

"My pleasure," he murmurs.

I shake my head. "I'm not so sure about that."

"I fucking loved eating you out. Your taste makes me crazy."

He grasps my hand and tugs it down to the front of his jeans. "Proof I enjoyed it."

Warmth flows through me at the feel of him. I cup him through his jeans, dying to feel him naked.

"God, you feel so good," he whispers.

"*You* do," I whisper back. "I want to feel you naked."

I drag the zipper down. It surprises me he isn't wearing underwear, and I wonder when he removed his own wet boxers. I'm so glad not to have one more thing between him and me. He's silk and steel, but the sheer size of him intimidates me. I gently hold him, brushing my fingers against his length.

He gasps in response.

"Was that okay?" I ask, unsure of how to touch him, wishing I had more experience, feeling like a student showing up at a midterm without studying.

He laughs. "So much better than okay. You're killing me, Olivia. In the best way possible."

"I've never done this," I admit. "I know the women you're with are experienced." I falter.

He watches my hand slowly stroke him, but at my words, his hot eyes meet mine.

"I'm like a teenager with you," he says. "Trying my best not to embarrass myself the second you touch me. I love that no other man has had you. That I'm the first."

I laugh. "It sounds like you're staking your claim in a new land. Are you going to plant your flag? That Chase James was here?"

"Damn right."

I can't help the big, silly grin on my face.

He grins back at me.

He has dozens of ways to smile. I've seen them in person and on the big screen.

But this smile, I've never seen before. It's dorky and sweet and sexy, all rolled into one, and it mirrors my dazzled one. I'm the human equivalent of the heart-eyes emoji, and I'm too happy to even care that I'm showing him my entire hand. It's all there for him to see.

We lazily explore each other's bodies, and I shiver, wondering how it's possible to be turned on again after that explosive orgasm.

We play with each other until we're gasping.

"Baby, stop, or I'll come all over you."

"Same," I breathe.

I play with the moisture leaking from his tip, and he moans. Warmth blossoms in my chest that I have so much power over someone so amazing. And then it's my turn to groan when he retaliates by dipping a finger inside me, fucking me in long, slow, deep strokes.

"I need more, Chase," I beg, writhing on his finger as he moves it in and out in a rhythm that makes me mindless with need. "I need this," I say, squeezing his dick in my hand, and then stroking faster.

"You're so damn wet."

That makes me blush.

He grins. "Wet isn't a bad thing, you know."

He looks so self-satisfied that I push him. "You don't have to look so smug. Maybe I'm just easily aroused."

He's still smiling, but the smile is a little less playful, a little darker. "Not by anyone else but me," he says.

I lean over him. "No one else," I admit.

My dark hair hangs down as I kiss above his eyes. "Just you have this power." I move on to his high cheekbones, his strong chin. Then those lips. First the top and then the bottom. And back to the top one more time. I feel his lips curve in a smile against mine, and my stomach dips in reaction, butterflies unleashed.

He sweeps back my hair that brushes his face, neck, and chest. He follows the strands down to where they block my pale breasts. I'm soft everywhere—probably too soft, I know—but he doesn't seem to mind. He strokes the curve of my breasts, then he moves his hand lower.

"Stop making me lose my mind. It's my turn to explore," I say.

I look at him, so large and powerful below me. Even his dick is beautiful, because of course it is. So I lean and take a tentative lick, like the first taste of a lollipop. His answer is a deep moan, and his cock jerks.

I look up. "Is that okay?"

"*Very* okay."

"Good, then. Just checking." I laugh, and he laughs also. It's so surprising that while we're doing this intimate thing, we can be giggling like kids. I never imagined there would be jokes or talking or that I would feel as comfortable as I do with him.

I trust him.

I realize that's the difference. I've always been nervous around guys, afraid of saying or doing the wrong thing. You would have thought that, with Chase, I would be even more nervous. But from the beginning, there was something about him that just seemed familiar, like I could be myself and he would be okay with that. Maybe him being off-limits and so far out of my league took the pressure off.

I take him deeper into my mouth, and he moans louder, longer.

That's the way I learn to give my first blow job, by gauging his moans. I experiment, alternate rhythms, pressure, licking, stroking, and sucking. And he's not the only one who likes it. Getting him excited gets me excited. Pleasuring him is hot—tasting him, that feeling of power that this magnificent man is at my mercy and nearly mad with desire. That I can take him higher and higher until he gives it all to me.

I'm addicted to his taste and the sounds he's making as I take him into my mouth in a deep, wet, sucking rhythm. He attempts to pull me off him with a gentle tug and a warning. "Olivia, I'm going to—"

I've read enough books, heard enough talk about spitting or swallowing, and I want every last bit of him. I want to stay with him till the end.

When he comes with a curse, I swallow it like a good girl. When he finally settles, he pulls me up to kiss the top of my head and tucks me into that perfect crook between his arm and chest. And all I can think is, *God, who knew I'd enjoy giving blow jobs this much?*

I'm tempted to ask him if this means we won't make love. I'm not exactly up on male anatomy, but I've read enough to suspect that it will take a while to do *that* again. At least for him. For me, all my parts are awake and alert. My nipples are still pebbles, something he discovers as he palms them.

"I love your tits," he says, leaning down and taking one nipple into his mouth. I moan his name. He lavishes his attention on the next one, his hand roaming downward.

"Are you? Can we—" I ask.

"Shh, this is for you," he says. He plays with me in a way that has me gasping. "Tell me what you want."

When I don't say anything, he grows more insistent.

"Tell me," he repeats in a demanding tone that works for me. But still, I'm embarrassed. I don't know how to talk dirty.

"It's part of your education," he says in a more amused tone.

I snort. "What? Are you some sort of professor of sex?"

He does something particularly amazing with his fingers and, at the same time, slaps my ass lightly, and I moan and almost come.

"Okay, maybe you are," I admit to him. "Do that again," I practically beg, panting.

"This?" he asks. "Or this?" he teases, repeating them both.

"Any of it. All of it." I'm past talking, past thinking. All I can do is feel and let him do what he wants.

Thankfully, he takes orders better than I do because he does all of it to me and more, and soon, I'm splitting apart in the second most intense orgasm I've ever had in my life.

I might have blacked out.

He cuddles me back into the crook of his arm. It's the best place ever to rest my head. I've never been so content. It's scary, this feeling, because I know that this is all just temporary, and now that I know how good it is, how will I ever go without? And I'm not just talking about the mind-blowing sexy time. I mean the rest of it. The soft kisses, the crook, the cuddling.

And then I wonder if he cuddles with the other girls. I push that thought aside and concentrate on how good it feels to be in his arms. His cock is hard against me.

I want him so badly. Will he finally take me? I thought we'd have sex by now, but though I've had two more firsts, he hasn't taken my virginity. That needy place between my legs wonders.

He starts kissing down my body, whispering kisses along every inch of me, all the way down. I want to ask him, but I lose my train of thought when his talented tongue licks me.

I'm breathless and shaking. And that's the last thinking I do for a long while.

CHAPTER 33

hase

I WAKE AT DAWN, when light is at its softest, bathing Olivia in a muted glow of delicate pinks and purples.

Her eyes open, and she smiles at me, groggy.

"Hello."

I smile back.

"Hi." I dive in for a kiss.

She squeaks and puts a hand up to her face. "I haven't brushed my teeth."

I roll my eyes. "That's what you're worried about?"

"Yes. Fresh breath is very important," she mumbles behind her hand.

She's adorable. I want to explore every part of her again, but we need to talk. I put it off last night, letting myself be selfish, letting myself live in the moment for this one time, but I can't anymore. I need to tell Olivia about Remington. She may never want to see me again, but Daisy is right. I can't keep lying to her.

"Be right back," she says and drags the white sheet around her, wrapping up like a mummy.

While she's in the bathroom, I go in search of a coffee machine. If I'm going to have this conversation with her, she needs caffeine.

"Bless Ronan," I say when I spot an espresso machine and a basket filled with pods. There's even creamer in the fridge. It's some kind of vegan faux-creamer, but it will do.

The coffees are ready when Olivia emerges from the bathroom. She's dressed, wearing last night's dress, but she's still wearing the bedsheet like a wrap.

"Here," I say.

She takes her coffee and makes that sweet sigh she always does at the first sip. I love that sound.

We wander out to the porch, with its incredible view of the water. It's where we started before our night, and now here we are again.

At least I didn't take her virginity. I wavered more than a few times last night, but I couldn't be with her in that way and have lies between us. Even if she said she only wanted one night, she deserves my honesty.

I'm ready to give it to her. I can only pray she doesn't hate me.

I open my mouth, trying to find the words.

"I lied to you," Olivia says in a rush.

"W-what?" I say, for a moment, wondering if those words came out of my mouth and not Olivia's.

"I can't take the guilt. I have you here under false pretenses. I lied to you." Her eyes are somber.

"Okay," I drawl out.

She taps her nails against the coffee cup. "I'm just going to get it all out at once. Rip it off, like a bandage. There's no stalker."

"What?" I ask, looking at her like she's lost her goddamn mind.

"I mean, I guess there kind of is. Yes, one of your obsessed fans wrote mean letters to me. But she didn't start the fire. The arson investigator concluded that the fire started from faulty wiring. So, all this really wasn't necessary." She waves her hand. "The guards, staying here overnight, staying with you in Malibu, even."

"When did you find out?" I ask. Nothing is making sense.

"Yesterday, before we came on our date. But I was afraid if you knew, then we wouldn't have a date, that you'd leave or send me back to San Francisco right away, and I just really, really wanted to have one last night with you. I'm so sorry I lied and didn't respect your choices enough to tell the truth." She watches me with sad eyes. "I can't regret what happened last night, but I wish I'd told you before. It wasn't right of me to keep things from you."

She is sorry she didn't respect my choices enough to tell the truth. How ironic.

Those words rip into me like a serrated blade.

"You could still be in danger," I insist.

She shrugs. "Maybe. But doubtful. There's a big leap between sending nasty notes and trying to murder someone."

"You could have told me, Olivia. Worrying about you, thinking someone was trying to kill you, it was like my worst fear coming to life."

Guilt chases me. I have no room to chide her for hiding something from me. She's feeling guilty about a small lie that she quickly came clean about. While I've been lying to her ever since I walked into her café, longer even.

"Ijustwantedtospendmoretimewithyou."

"What?"

"I just wanted to spend more time with you," she repeats, slowly this time. "To give us a chance to be more."

"Olivia."

"I know, I know. You don't have to say anything. It's embarrassing enough to have to admit that I have this one-sided crush."

"It's not one-sided. If you recall last night."

"I know I should have told you as soon as I got the call. It was really stupid. I'll make arrangements to leave first thing tomorrow."

"Hey." I take her hand. "I don't want you to leave, at least not like this. You didn't need to hide something from me to stay. I love having you around. Too much. I love seeing you at the kitchen table every morning around coffee. I love running with you and watching that sweet ass of yours when you stretch. I love skinny-dipping with you, and I more than loved last night."

I need her to know that this time has meant something to me.

As if she can read my mind, she watches me warily. "But..." she says.

"But I need to show you something," I say.

"What? Where?" she asks.

"We need to go back home, to Malibu."

CHAPTER 34

livia

CHASE DRIVES me back to Malibu in distracted silence. I want to ask so many questions, but it's like he's shuttered behind glass, so I sit and try not to worry.

When he leads me into his cottage, for a fleeting second, I think it might be to go to his bedroom, that what he has to show me is in his pants and he's just being extra dramatic about it all.

But all I see is a lovely room with a huge desk and wall-to-wall bookshelves.

I turn to Chase in silent inquiry.

"It's my office," he says. As if that explains what we're doing here.

I walk farther into the room. Admiring the floor-to-ceiling bookcases.

Despite my unease, I allow myself to be distracted. Bookcases say so much about a person, and every little scrap of knowledge about Chase is like a precious gem. I collect them like a jewel thief on the prowl.

I run my hand over the smooth, whitewashed wood that holds a plethora of titles, a cornucopia of choice, from ancient Chinese philosophy to the history of cowboys. I wonder if that title was for the role of a Montana rancher he played last year. One section holds a collection of classic pulp fiction titles and spy thrillers, including the entire collection of Ian Fleming's James Bond. Hmm, I wonder if that's his genre of choice. Like Remington, I can't help thinking.

"Why are we here?" I ask. "What do you have to show me?"

He doesn't say anything. He's leaning against the wall next to the desk, his head bowed, as if bracing for something.

My eyes dart to his desk, and that's when I see it.

A Remington.

It sits near the middle of the desk, just above his laptop, and is surrounded by a few stacks of paper.

I walk over to the old machine. It's not just any Remington.

I know this typewriter.

I touch the T, where the letter is worn down and barely visible. I run my hands over the familiar chip on the N in Remington. I know every scratch and scrape on this typewriter because it used to be mine.

It's my pen pal's now.

So, how is it here?

It's like looking through the viewfinder of one of Nanna's cameras. Everything is blurry, and then with a few adjustments, suddenly, it all comes into focus. That's how the idea, the inkling, the bone-deep knowing hits me. It comes rushing in all at once and clear as the margin bell on this typewriter.

He's Remington, that voice inside me says.

But still, I look for evidence.

And there it is, in a stack of familiar letters, letters I wrote.

I riffle through them, reading, my face burning at how the breezy tone of my first few letters turns increasingly friendly, laced with intimacy and admissions about my life, my feelings.

Desperately lonely, needing a friend and confidant, I shared my soul in these letters.

To a mysterious stranger.

I'd had no fucking clue.

Anger, confusion, shock rise up in me.

My Remington, my best friend for years, is Chase James. Has always been Chase James.

And he's been lying to me this entire time.

Was this his idea of a joke?

Nausea overtakes me, and I feel like puking.

Remington—Chase—is the one who got me through Nanna's illness and death. The person in whom I'd confided some of my darkest fears, the worries, and also the small, funny parts of my day.

I'd never known who he was, though I always suspected his world was more rarefied, more glamorous than mine, but I could never have imagined the truth.

I thought, at most, he might be some minor celebrity's personal assistant.

My vision tilts just thinking of it. But it's there on Chase's face. The guilt of it. He swallows visibly.

"Now you know." He lets out a shaky exhale. "What are you thinking?"

"How did this start? How'd you get my typewriter?" I ask raggedly.

He shakes his head. "Daisy sent it to me."

My heart stops. "Daisy? She knows? She never said a word. I thought she was a friend," I whisper at the betrayal. Has everyone been laughing at me? Am I the stupid girl who was fooled so easily? I feel my knees get weak as my perspective on my world realigns into something I don't recognize.

"Hey, steady." It takes two of his long steps to reach me, and he's leading me to the couch. I'm too frozen to object. I sink into it. He kneels in front of me; his eyes are pleading. Chase leans over to touch my knee but then pulls away, as if thinking better of it.

"Tell me," I demand, my brain clicking rustily into place.

"Daisy had no clue it was your typewriter. She always sent me little gifts, things to make my house a home. She sent me the Remington, said she found it in the window of an antique shop when she was walking around her new neighborhood and it reminded her of me. I found the letter in the typewriter and wrote to you. I never told her about it, or about becoming pen pals. I wanted to keep what we had just between us."

"I didn't tell her either, for the same reasons," I admit quietly. "I told her I had a pen pal, but the story about the typewriter just seemed too personal. That was our story, not for anyone else."

He gives a small half-smile. "I felt the same way."

"But why did Daisy send you a typewriter, of all things?"

"I always loved to write. When I lived with Daisy, our next-door neighbor had a Remington. She was an older lady without kids. She felt bad for us. We spent a lot of time at her house. I would type the stories I made up and read them to Daisy at bedtime. I even illustrated them. *Poorly.*"

"So Daisy bought you a Remington like the one you used to use."

He nods. "She wanted me to get back to telling stories, said that I was happiest when I wrote."

"I remember," I say, a memory niggling at me. "You told me your sister sent you gifts because she said your style was sad and boring. You were talking about Daisy." All his past letters and the details are recalibrating in my mind. It's disorienting.

"When I wrote to you as Remington, you may not have known every detail, but the essence was all true. I tried my best not to lie, Olivia. You know more about me than anyone in the world except possibly Daisy. I have a hard time trusting people. You have to believe that as much as you didn't know about my life in Hollywood, you knew me better than anyone else. Remington is closer to who I really am than the movie star Chase James."

I gaze at him with his pleading eyes, his face now so familiar. He's become Chase to me, not just Chase James, movie star.

But he's more. He's also Remington.

And I suddenly see him for the first time, all the parts of him. My best friend and pen pal, the funny, sweet, vulnerable guy who comforted me when I most needed it. The letters were our personal diaries that only we got to read.

As I think back to what he wrote, I realize that he tried to tell me about himself. He told me about his emotions. About feeling overwhelmed. About panic attacks. About nights in different cities surrounded by people who didn't know him. Though I hadn't known the specifics, I had known his heart.

I examine my hands. "I just feel so stupid," I say in a small voice. "Like I should have guessed."

He threads our fingers together. Despite everything, his touch sends a frisson of excitement through me. He never fails to affect me, even when I'm spinning.

"Writing you was the only thing that kept me sane some days. The things I told you were real. When I said I hated coming back to dark hotel rooms, it was the truth."

I snort. "I wasn't exactly imagining suites at the Ritz."

His strong jaw clenches. "I'm not trying to act like, poor me, 'cause that's bullshit. I won't pretend that it's not better to have money than not. I know what it's like to think you have no future, and I will always be grateful for the opportunities this life brought me. But what's beneath the glamour and money is never knowing if someone is with you because of the fame or fortune, and not the person you are."

"Is that what you're worried about with me? That if I knew who you really were, I'd become one of those people who just cared that you were a movie star?"

He looks away. "Maybe," he admits.

I suck in a breath, stung.

He swears. "When you didn't know who I was, that was the only time in my life someone chose just me, not what I could do for them. When I was a foster kid, I was completely invisible. And then I got famous, and suddenly, everyone wanted me. It wasn't you I didn't trust. I couldn't believe anyone could care for the real me."

My eyes search his face, looking for evidence that he's been playing me for the past month, letting me get to know him and care for him, and never telling me that we'd been writing each other for years. But all I see is aching regret and more insecurity than I ever thought possible. The ice of his betrayal that froze my heart begins to thaw.

Who would I have been if I hadn't had Nanna to care for me after my mom died? He never had someone tell him that he was safe, that he was loved, that he was enough. And then to go from sleeping in the streets, unwanted by society, to a few years later having millions of eyes on his every move, adoring, desiring, fanatical. The fact that he got through all that without spiraling out of control is a testament to his strength and character.

I can see why he valued being anonymous. It doesn't excuse the lies, but I can understand a little better why he feared telling me.

"Do you hate me?" he asks in a ragged rasp.

The glacier melts down further. All I want is to reassure him. I'm weak.

"I don't hate you," I whisper. I'm confused, confounded, hurt, angry, but there's no hate. "I just wish you trusted me more earlier."

"I never meant for it to go this far. I came to San Francisco to make sure you were okay. When you ghosted me—"

"But I didn't!" I interrupt.

"You disappeared and didn't answer my calls or texts. I was

worried. I didn't know if you were hurt, lying in a hospital bed"—a frown cuts deep grooves into his otherwise perfect complexion—"or worse."

I flinch. "I kind of was. In a hospital, I mean."

His head whips up. "What do you mean, you were in the hospital?"

"I was fine," I soothe. "It wasn't a big deal. But my phone was damaged when I kinda got run over by a bike messenger in the street. I hit my head, blacked out for a minute, and my phone was smashed in the road. I realized I didn't have your number written anywhere else."

"You were hurt, and I had no idea." He looks stricken. "You didn't tell me."

"Well, to be fair, I had no idea when I met Chase James that he might be interested in my little concussion story. I'm fine. I just spent a few nights in the hospital. It was my phone that had the most collateral damage, though maybe I should thank that bike messenger and the car. It brought you looking for me." At that admission, I hold my breath.

"Does that mean you forgive me?"

I can't cave this easily. I just can't.

"You saw I was okay after the first café visit. Why'd you come back?" I ask.

Now is my time for answers, and I intend on collecting each one.

"I shouldn't have." He slants me a look. "At least, that's what I told myself. Look at what happened when we were photographed together."

I have to acknowledge he has a point. His fears are real.

He leans closer and caresses a lock of my hair.

"I wanted to see you one more time and swore it would be the last. Then Daisy called and asked me to pick her up from the police station, and there you were. Then you showed up at my hotel room when I was sick. I felt guilty as hell, but at that point,

I just couldn't keep pushing you away. I wanted to be near you, even if I knew it was for a short time."

"But you did push me away. If it hadn't been for the tabloids and the fire, would you have ever told me who you really were? Were you just going to resume texting me when I got my phone back? Even after those nights in your hotel suite?" My voice gains heat.

He looks away. "If I were being honorable, yes. It would be the safest, best thing for you. But as much as I'd like to think I'd do the right thing—"

"That's not the right thing. You're making a decision for both of us and not giving me a choice."

"That's because you can't understand. You can't know unless you've truly lived it."

"I've seen enough. Fans and trolls have been calling me liar, slut, whore, ugly—"

"Fuck, Olivia. Don't you see? I can't live with it, knowing that you're dragged into that toxic underworld just because you're with me. You're proving my point."

"It's my choice too," I say stubbornly. And then something else occurs to me. It bubbles up from that insecure place where all my doubts reside. "But maybe you're just using that as an excuse. I don't fit in. My favorite thing is to stay home and read. I'm a total nerd. Hell, I'm a virgin. I'm not like the other girls you've dated."

"Hey." He touches my chin, tilting my face up to his. I open my eyes, and I'm transfixed by how close he is. "I love that you nerd out on books and movies, because I do too. I love that your favorite thing is staying in, because it's mine too. And I certainly love that no other man has touched you like I have, like I want to. I love everything about you, whether you're Olivia Evans or Typewriter Girl."

My stomach flips. "As a friend," I say softly, more to myself than him.

"As everything," he growls, then dives into a deep, drugging kiss.

* * *

I'm not sure what finally does it.

Was it learning the many facets of Chase and what each version of him means to me?

Was it knowing how perfect it feels to be held in his arms all night?

Was it his infuriating but sweet concern for my safety and happiness?

Was it knowing that it was Chase who stayed up all night texting with me every night for a week after Nanna died?

Whatever it was that dealt the final blow, it's happened. I've fallen in love with him.

I wish I could say this is a happy realization. It isn't, even while I'm being kissed silly by the object of my adoration.

It has heartbreak typed all over it.

We're both panting as he pulls back, as if gauging my reaction.

"I've told you the truth now," he says in a velvet whisper.

"And you said once you told me the truth, you'd very agreeably fuck me like I asked," I say archly. My vagina, damn traitor, is already all on board.

"Make love," he corrects. "If you still want me."

I want him.

But the small, certain core of me, that inner voice to which I've learned to listen, isn't so certain. Before I knew I loved him, before I knew that the out-of-reach celebrity I wanted to have one fabulous night with was the same guy I'd spent my days and nights writing to for years, I thought I could give him my virginity and then go back to my regular life.

But now, I'm sure that just one night would never be

enough, and reaching heaven and then having it yanked away would break me.

He's so worried about a few trolls and photographers hurting me, when he has far greater power to devastate me than any stranger.

But maybe there's hope. Perhaps the lies were the final barrier, and now we can finally be together and see where it leads.

"I need to know first. Is this very generous offer of sex for just one night? Or are you telling me we can be together, date?"

"I don't date," he hedges, which, in my current frame of mind, pisses me off.

"Hang out. Friends with benefits. Be my boyfriend. Whatever you want to call it. Are you willing to give this thing a try, or are you just offering your dick for the night?"

He flinches.

And I see it in his face. I do. Even after all this, after all the secret sharing, the intimacy, the truth-telling, he still only wants to give me a small, temporary part of him.

And, I realize, that's just not enough for me. Not anymore.

So, this is it. One last try to reach him. One last truth-telling. And that's it.

"You know, Chase. I learned a lot since Nanna encouraged me to start taking risks. I never thought I could go for what I want. I was always too scared to show anyone who I really was, tell them my needs and my desires. And a big part of that growth is from you. You as Chase and you as Remington. I won't ever forget any of who you've been to me. But I just realized that I deserve more than a fantasy crush or long-distance friend. I want a real relationship. I want to love and be loved for who I really am, and to give the same back to someone else."

I take a deep breath, then forge ahead. "So, this is my final risk, Chase. And news flash, it's not to lose my virginity."

He watches me, waiting.

"I love you," I say. "I love you, Chase James, and I love you, Remington." I'm balancing on a live wire, but my voice comes out surprisingly steady. "I want to be with you for more than just a night or two. I know it's not what I've been saying, but you're right. I do deserve more. I deserve you, all of you."

His eyes flare. He doesn't say anything, just looks away.

I let the words hang in the air.

"Olivia," Chase says, "you don't know what you're asking. I don't know how to be in a relationship. To love. I've never known the kind of life you deserve. I didn't see any of that growing up. I'd only hurt you. I don't have what you really want."

I swallow back the tears and attempt to breathe past the ache in my chest.

"You're not just afraid of hurting me, Chase. You've come up with all these reasons why we can't be together. But I think the real reason is because you're afraid. It's safer to stay in your VIP life behind velvet ropes, to never take a chance on something real."

He doesn't answer. Not then or when I turn and walk out of the cottage.

That's when the tears do start. I cry all the way through packing. All the way to the airport. And the entire flight to San Francisco.

I'm traveling light on the outside, with just a backpack and a purse.

On the inside, though, I have more baggage than I ever anticipated.

I'm arriving home from Malibu with a broken heart.

CHAPTER 35

hase

Olivia left. It was inevitable. It was what needed to happen. But not yet. Not until I could make sure she was safe.

And now I have a group of pissed off friends staring at me, looking for answers.

"Chase, why did Olivia get on a plane to San Francisco?" Daisy holds up her phone. "She just texted me goodbye and apologized. She said she would explain later. What did you do?" Daisy gives me her death glare. It's the same one she gave the boy next door who called her Rags because her clothes were dirty and torn.

I want to rage at the thought of Olivia on her own without protection. I called in every favor to get a team of bodyguards to meet her plane as soon as she landed. Subtly of course.

"You two went on a date, stayed out all night, and she comes back here, packs her bags, and leaves."

"Dude, how bad was the sex?" Sebastian asks with a yawn, wearing a black silk smoking jacket, Hugh Hefner-style.

It is 4:00 p.m., and he's obviously just gotten up. On a normal day, I might tease him about his lounge attire, but this isn't a normal day.

"Our little Olivia flew the coop after spending the night with you." He slaps me on the back. "That doesn't bode well for your technique, my friend. I know someone you can hire. She teaches tantric sex and gives an advanced class on foreplay."

"I don't need a sex class," I growl. "This is serious. I know the media has died down now that they think I'm dating Cassidy. But what if the paparazzi decide Olivia's still a story? What if the fire investigator was wrong, and the fire wasn't started by faulty wiring? What if the fan who sent her those letters *is* dangerous?"

"You're being dramatic, Chase. The tabloids don't care about her anymore. You made sure they're too busy chasing Chassidy. And I doubt the fire investigator is wrong. Olivia is a full-grown adult and could leave, so she left. She wasn't kidnapped and held in a house full of celebrities," Emma says.

"Ha!" Sebastian says. "That would make an awesome script."

"I saw her on her way out. She looked pretty upset," Emma says.

"What did she say?" My stomach drops.

Emma shakes her head. "Nothing. Just said she was sorry she had to go, but it was for the best."

Sebastian slaps his hand against the counter in triumph. "I told you. Bad sex."

"It wasn't bad!" I snarl.

"I knew it! You had sex!" Daisy cries, pointing an accusing finger at me.

"No! We didn't. Not that." I cross my arms over my chest. "This is none of your business."

"Well, you made it our business when your little bedroom antics led to my friend bolting for the airport," Daisy retorts.

"Dude, we're not dumb," Sebastian says. "She had a massive

crush on you. Anyone could see it. If you didn't bang her, then what happened? Did you turn her down? Shatter her dreams?"

"I didn't turn her down." I close my eyes. "Well, kind of. But I was trying to protect her."

"Did you tell her the truth? Is that why she left?" Daisy chews her lip. "Was she mad? At both of us?"

"I told her, but that's not why she left. She didn't understand why it could never work between us."

"Chase, you are a first-class idiot sometimes," Daisy says. "You have this false belief that you have to protect people from being in your life. You don't let anyone get close. Yes, you have a fucked-up life. Fame does that. Plenty of people are fighting all kinds of obstacles but still find love."

"Hey, I'm famous, but I'm not fucked up," Sebastian says.

"You are *so* fucked up," Emma says. "But Daisy has a point."

"I love you, Chase," Daisy continues. "I'm so grateful to have you as a brother. But if it weren't for the stalker, I wouldn't be here with you because you wouldn't let me be. You call me. You support me. But you keep me at arm's length. You're so afraid of what happened that summer happening again, but it won't. I was young and hurting. You weren't to blame. And neither was your fame."

Guilt twists in my gut, churning up black memories of how unresponsive she'd been. Waiting in the hospital, not knowing if she'd survive. The pain of possibly losing someone else I dared to love.

"I was supposed to protect you that summer, be your safe haven, and you were trashed in public and almost died."

"It. Is. Not. Your. Fault," Daisy enunciates. "And you shouldn't have kept me at a distance for so long because of it. Don't you see? You're doing the same thing to Olivia that you've been doing to me all these years."

"Well, I hope not the exact same things." Sebastian snickers.

"Shut it, Sebastian," Daisy says, then turns back to me.

"You need to let the people who care about you make up their own minds about whether they want to be in your life," Daisy says. "If you like Olivia like I think you do, let her decide. She's not a child. And if she believes she can handle your fame and all that comes with it, let her have that choice." She tilts her head. "Unless that's just an excuse, and you don't want to be with her. In which case, you're even more idiotic than I thought."

"Of course I want her," I say. "But it's not that easy. Look, maybe the fire wasn't started by a stalker. This time. But those people are out there. What about that chick who broke into the cottage six months ago?"

"That was an isolated incident. We fired the security team."

"It's happened before. It's going to happen again. I can't count the number of times I've come back to a hotel room with a fan inside."

"That's what I call a perk," Sebastian says.

I shoot him a dirty look. "What can I give her? She wants a normal life. I can't do normal. This life would never work for her."

"Did she tell you that?" Sebastian asks.

"She didn't need to tell me. I can't tear her apart like that. Even on a low-key day with bodyguards following us, we couldn't have a peaceful afternoon. If she were different, I'd think about it. I'm not pretending I don't have a lot to offer a girl who wants an A-list life. But that's not Olivia. It wouldn't make her happy."

"So what do you want? It doesn't seem like that A-list life is making you happy either," Daisy retorts. "This is an intervention, Chase. This isn't only about Olivia. It's about how you want to live, because right now, it seems to me that you aren't in control of anything."

I shake my head. "If this were all ending with this last movie, it would be different. But it's not. My life is going to be even crazier." I snap my mouth shut. I haven't told them about the offer yet. I just got it myself.

"Because you officially got the offer for Max Thunder?" Sebastian asks.

"How do you know about that?"

"Eh. We told you before. Privacy's a myth."

My eyes do a slow sweep of the room, and no one looks surprised.

"No one in the industry would turn it down," I say, running my hand through my hair. "What would you do, Sebastian?" I'm asking Sebastian for advice. I'm truly at rock bottom.

Sebastian laughs. "I'd be on that role so fucking fast, everyone's head would spin. I'd lock that shit up. But, dude, I'm not you. You gotta do what you want. Agents, fans, studios will tell us how we should run our business and careers, but it's not their life. It's ours."

"You've never turned down a big role," I scoff.

"The hell I haven't," Sebastian says. "No one believed I could get another job after I had my public meltdown at eighteen. Instead, I had the biggest offer of my career from a director who loved a wild child. I was a walking disaster, but the only thing Hollywood cared about was how much money I'd make for them, and the only thing fans cared about was what movie I'd do next. Something told me that if I did that movie, I'd end up dead. I walked away, checked myself in to rehab, and disappeared for a year. It was the best decision I ever made. Everyone wants what you can do for them. That's why you have to figure out what you want and have the balls to make it happen, to hell with the industry and the rest of the world."

I think about what Sebastian said. Taking the movie deal and becoming an even bigger star is a guarantee that I would become even more restricted, even more hunted, even more alone. The money and fame would push me farther away from friends and family. I'd be whisked from hotel to movie sets enclosed in cars and private jets, never having to interact with regular life.

"Much as I hate to say it, Sebastian's right," Ryder says. "You need to decide what you want. You're smart and loaded. If you want the girl and she wants you, figure out a way to make it happen."

"You're scared." Daisy's words are an arrow, shooting straight and true. "You're scared of loving someone and losing them. So you don't let anyone get too close."

I flinch at her accusation, at the bone-deep truth of it.

I have so many reasons for not being with Olivia. Good ones. Valid ones. But in the end, they are all an excuse because I'm scared to try for something real.

Scared to lose. Scared to love.

But I already fell in love with Olivia, I admit to myself. And I've already lost her.

"It's simple. Do what makes you happy, dude," Sebastian says.

"Happy, huh?" I rub my jaw.

I'm not sure about much of anything. But I know I'm most happy when I'm with Olivia.

CHAPTER 36

livia

IT'S BEEN two weeks since I got back to San Francisco. Two weeks since I first walked into my house again. The house looks like new. Thanks to Chase, the damage was repaired, as if the fire had never happened. Even the roof is fixed, the crumbling steps like new, the entire house gleaming with a fresh coat of paint inside and out.

I don't know how he did it in such a short amount of time. It must have cost a fortune; one I can't pay back. I should be mad that he took it upon himself. But every time I look at the house, all I feel is relief and a warmth that he cared enough about me to care for something that I love.

Luckily, I didn't lose too many personal possessions in the fire since it was mostly confined to the upstairs bathroom and hallway. I did have to replace many of my clothes and buy a new mattress and comforter because I couldn't remove the smoke smell. But at least I'm having fun playing with my style now, and

I seem to be leaning more towards retro romance and away from goth homesteader.

Since I've been back from Malibu, so much has changed. Despite my heartbreak—or perhaps because of it—I have clarity. The distance gave me a renewed perspective on my life, and I didn't like a lot of what I saw.

The last two weeks have been about making changes, subtle shifts of my life's landscape. I turned down my friend's offer to be a technical writer. Yes, it was a steady job I could use to keep up my house and ease the bills. But every time I thought of going to work for them, my heart contracted.

If I took a job like that, I'd likely give up on my dreams of being a published author. I also took a hard look at myself. Though I've spent the last eight years writing novels, I've never had the guts to try for publication, fearing rejection. If I didn't try, no one could say no. Earlier today, I submitted my current manuscript to a list of agents. It's scary but liberating to move forward.

I wish I could move forward from my broken heart as easily. I ache for Chase. It's like walking around with a gaping hole in my chest, as if my heart is outside of me and I'll never be complete without him.

Three days ago, I got my broken phone back. The tech guy performed a miracle and fixed it. And there on that little screen was Remington's number and all our thousands of texts. I also read his increasingly upset messages from when I first ghosted him.

The first night back with my phone, I went to bed, reading over the years of messages. Reading them through a new lens. And what came through was just how much Remington—Chase—had needed me throughout all those years, just as I had needed him. Even while he was catapulting to movie stardom, he needed a friend as much as I did.

And then there's Daisy. She arrived back from Los Angeles a few days ago, and now she's in my living room.

"I swear, Olivia, I didn't know." Daisy leans toward me across the coffee table, her hands out, beseeching me.

I look at the smooth wood of the table and spread my hands out on it, anchoring myself with something that is solid, not the smoke-and-mirrors deception I'd unknowingly been part of.

"Do you believe me?" Daisy asks.

"I do," I say with assurance. Daisy isn't the type to keep a secret. If she'd known, I would have too.

"He should have told you the truth. I know that. But he's scared," Daisy says. "He pushes everyone who will love him away, myself included."

"It's okay. You don't have to defend him. I'm not mad. I'm just sad."

"I want to explain. Did you know he got placed into a good family right before mine? He was there a year, and they promised they'd adopt him. But then the lady got pregnant, and they changed their minds about Chase. That's when he ended up with us. Loss is all he's ever known. Every person he's ever loved has been taken from him. When I tried to kill myself, and he blamed himself, I think it made him terrified to try again. Sure, he gets all this so-called love thrown at him now, but it's a selfish, twisted, obsessive kind of love. Everyone wants a piece of him, or they project an image of who they want him to be. But when he was—"

"But when he was Remington, he could just be himself," I finish.

Daisy nods. "I think it was the first time he truly felt safe, felt seen and loved for himself. I think he was just scared to lose that, even if it was to reach for something more."

My phone beeps an alert. I pick it up and look at the screen. My breath catches and my heartbeat races.

"What is it?" She leans over to look at my screen in curiosity.

"A text. It's from him," I say shakily.

She smiles. "About damn time. What does he say?"

Tears pool in my eyes. I can't read it. I'm too scared of what it might say. What it might mean. I hand her the phone. "You read it."

"Are you sure?" she asks, taking it.

I nod, running my hand over the bracelet that Remington gave me like a talisman. Every time I look at it, I think of him, but I still wear it.

She reads his text message in a soft, sure voice.

REMINGTON:

Dear Typewriter Girl, You left, and you took all the light in my life. When I got too deep into the lies, I wanted to tell the truth, but you were right, I was scared. I told myself that if I kept up the Remington lie, I'd at least always have you as Typewriter Girl. I hadn't had any luck keeping people around until I became Remington. I didn't want to risk losing you as well. Forever yours, Chase

When she's done, she looks at me.

"He signed it Chase," I say around the lump in my throat. "I wanted to give him that gift. I wanted him to know that he can count on people. That he can be loved." I wipe at the tears that fall. "But he didn't want me."

"Are you going to respond?"

I shrug. "I'm not sure there's anything left to say. We can't go back to being just friends, to texting, not after everything."

Daisy reaches out and grabs one of my hands. She squeezes. "Don't give up on him."

I smile sadly. "I gave him my last risk."

"Well, maybe it's his turn to give you his," she says.

CHAPTER 37

livia

IT'S BEEN SEVEN DAYS, and I've had seven messages from Chase. Unlike the first message, they haven't been deep or serious. They are what Remington would have texted, but he signs each one with his own name, Chase.

On Monday, he messaged me an anecdote about a fight between his stylist and a photographer.

On Tuesday, he sent me a photo of a sign he'd seen. Typewriter Girl and Remington had always collected funny signs. He usually had the most because of his constant traveling.

On Wednesday, he said he missed me.

On Thursday, he told me he sent his script, the one he'd written years ago, to a director he admired.

On Friday, he sent me two messages. One wishing me a good morning, and another a good night. He said I was the first person he thought of in the morning, and the last person he thought of at night.

On Saturday, he said he'd gone to a park, sat under a big

shade tree, and read a book. He said he had to wear a hoodie, hat, and shades, but no one bothered him for two hours. At the end, two giggling tweens came over and he signed their T-shirts, and then he went home.

And today is Sunday.

He hasn't sent me a message, yet. Maybe he's given up since I haven't messaged him back.

I think the messages are his way of making amends, of getting back to being just friends, but I'm not sure my broken heart can handle being just friends with Chase. It hurts too much.

I stand in my kitchen, looking out the window at my little garden. There are herbs in the window box and roses beginning to bloom. Okay, the basil is a little wilty, but the rosemary is doing well. I even bought a tomato plant that has one tiny green tomato on it and a small planter with strawberries. I'm probably never going to be the gardener that Nanna was, but I don't need to be. I can find my own way. I know that now. I can take the best of what was in the past and spin it for myself.

That's what tonight is all about. Ella Fitzgerald plays in the background, and laughter filters in from the dining room. It's my first dinner party. We're celebrating the end of summer and the sale of the Adam Reynolds, what Daisy refers to as Naked Nanna. It collected a tidy sum, enough to pay the tax bill and make a dent in my student loans.

I don't need to spend the money fixing up the house anymore, thanks to Chase. Daisy convinced me to accept the gift of the repairs, though I was tempted to send him a big check to pay him back. But in the end, I decided he didn't deserve Nanna's naked money, not after refusing to take a chance on us. The confusing messages, notwithstanding.

So, yes, all isn't quite right with my world, but if there's anything I learned this summer, it's to live each day to the fullest, perfect or not. And this is a good night.

"Get your ass in here, Olivia. We want to make a toast," Daisy calls.

I walk out carrying a big platter and see all these faces I love around the large butcher block table. There's Daisy and Audrey, Mr. Jensen and his friend Mrs. Maple, who's arrived from Los Angeles, and Rose from the bakery down the block.

I place the roast chicken on the table with pride. I'm more of a baker than an accomplished cook, so this is the very first dinner I've made entirely on my own. It looks a little burned on the top, but otherwise, I think I did okay. The chicken is surrounded by lemons and potatoes that were in the bottom of the pan, soaking up the juices. Sprigs of rosemary from the garden decorate the top. I hope someone knows how to carve a chicken, because I have no idea.

Everyone claps, and the stress of preparing this meal and worrying that we'd have to order pizza melts away in a glow of love for my friends.

Daisy stands and raises her glass of wine. "You know I'm not one for speeches."

I roll my eyes, because she so is one for speeches.

She continues, "But I'm happy that your grandma was such a hot, rocking babe and modeled for that photo because it saved the day by paying for your property taxes and kept you in my 'hood. You're my girl, and no other neighbor would do. To Naked Nanna saving the day!"

"To Naked Nanna!" Everyone raises their glasses and clinks them.

I shake my head but laugh. Nanna would approve.

We dig into the food. Everyone contributed to the feast, which is good, because cooking a chicken was my culinary limit for the day. There's fresh bread from baker Rose that's probably the most divine thing I've ever tasted. Mr. Jensen brought a salad. Mrs. Maple brought two bottles of Napa wine. And Daisy brought fancy cupcakes for dessert. Designer cupcakes are her thing.

My phone dings. My heart constricts when I see the name on the phone.

"I have to…" I snatch the phone and push back from the table, speed walking to the kitchen.

"Are you okay?" Daisy asks my back.

I wave vaguely. "Just checking on…dessert." Which makes no sense, because the only dessert is the cupcakes Daisy brought.

I lean over the counter, and my hands shake as I open the message.

His messages are sucking me back into him, which isn't healthy. I swear to myself I'll tell him to stop messaging. Stop playing with my heart. Soon.

A burst of laughter filters into the kitchen, and that sound of joy bolsters me. This heartbreak is still fresh, but each cut taught me something, let the light into the dark spaces.

"My Typewriter Girl." I read the words on the screen out loud, but I can imagine his voice saying the words. It's so clear.

"I want to make new rules with you," Chase's voice continues. Really, it's his voice that continues.

I swing around.

Chase fills the doorway of my kitchen.

"You're here?" It's half statement, half question.

I'm not sure he's real, looking impossibly handsome in a forest-green T-shirt that matches his eyes and well-worn jeans that mold to his muscles and large frame. His hair is an artful mess as usual, and his face, oh that face, is beloved. Though his warm smile doesn't match his eyes, which are full of uncertainty.

He takes a step closer to me. "Only real names this time. Only real life."

Nothing is making sense.

"Read it," he says with a nod at my phone. I frown and look at the words on the screen.

> REMINGTON:
>
> My Typewriter Girl,
>
> I want to make new rules with you.
>
> Only real names this time.
>
> Only real life.
>
> And maybe the occasional dick pic (your choice).

A sound between a laugh and a gasp escapes me. My hand flies to my heart, as if steadying it, as if warning it to calm down.

He's rewritten our letter. Those first rules we lived by for all those years. Those rules that kept us only on the screen.

One more step, and he's directly in front of me. He takes my chin and gently tilts it back up to him, away from the screen.

"Does this mean...?" I can't say it. Can't dare to hope. So I tilt my head and latch on to the first thing that comes to mind. "No dick pics, ever. You'd get hacked, and your dick would go viral."

He laughs, and the sound is so welcome. That's when he says the last line on the screen. I know, because I'm a fast reader and I read ahead. So sue me, I like spoilers.

"I love you."

He says it softly, as if he's as surprised and overwhelmed as I am at the words.

I open my mouth to say something, I don't even know what, and he puts a finger over my lips. Like some Pavlovian response, my tongue reaches out and touches his finger for a taste. I feel his indrawn breath in tandem with mine at the spark of that small, sensual tongue-to-skin touch.

He clears his throat. "Before you tell me to get the hell out of here, that I'm too late, or any of the thousand things I'm afraid of but probably deserve, let me just say this. Let me explain," he says in a rush. He reluctantly draws his finger away from my mouth, as he brushes the hair back from my face.

I have to will myself not to nestle into that big, callused hand. His touch feels amazing. I missed it so much. I missed him.

"I'm sorry, Olivia. I'm so fucking sorry that I was such an idiot for so long. You were the strong one. God, you humble me with your ability to put yourself out there. You risked your heart with me. You were willing to put up with me and all my baggage. But I was too afraid to take the most beautiful gift I've ever been given. I was afraid to trust it. After my mom died, I tried to trust in other people, trust in love, but each time, I was left crushed. I guess I started to feel that there was something broken in me, that I didn't deserve love. I was afraid to hope that it was something I'd ever have because it hurt so fucking much when it was ripped away. And then when all that shit went down with Daisy, I just decided that opening myself up wasn't worth it, that it would only lead to hurting myself and the people I cared about."

He cups his hands around my face, and his eyes burn into mine, passionate, sincere, and I've never felt more loved, more seen. It's as if he can see into the whole of me and he miraculously likes it all, the good and bad and insecure and uncertain, and it's all fine. And I feel the same. He's opening his heart, and I can see all the parts of him, the incredibly charismatic movie star whose mere presence ignites the world, but I can also see Remington, the lonely, quirky, funny guy who gets my nerdy jokes and who needed someone to reach out to him as much as I did.

And I can see the beautiful, complex man I've gotten to know here in San Francisco and Los Angeles, the man who is kind and gives his jacket to a homeless man without making him feel lesser. The man who tries to protect the people he loves, even if he thinks it means giving them up. The loyal friend and the caring brother. He has a painful past that makes him a little broken and a turbulent life that makes him a little jaded. He isn't perfect, but I'm glad of that, because I'm not perfect myself.

I'm not cut out for the glamorous, fucked-up world of super celebrity he occupies, but I suspect he's not either. So maybe, together, we can figure it out.

"What about all your reasons for staying away? What about the new project? And the fans? And the travel? All those things that you swore meant we would never work." I have to ask, because if I let the walls back down and he does another 180 on me, I'm not sure I can survive it.

"I turned down Max Thunder."

I gasp. "W-what? You can't do that, Chase! That's the biggest job in Hollywood. Even I know that no one would say no to something so iconic."

"I can and did."

"What job did he turn down?" I recognize Mr. Jensen's voice. I look up and see my dinner party crowding around the kitchen doorway, their heads sticking in, watching us like we're a K-drama on television.

"He was supposed to be the next Max Thunder," Daisy says to the rest of the audience.

"And he turned it down for Olivia!" Audrey exclaims.

"How romantic." Mrs. Maples sighs.

"Max Thunder! Olivia Evans, did you make this young man turn down Max Thunder?" Mr. Jensen glares in accusation.

"Wow. I've never seen you fired up before, Mr. J. You must really like those movies," Daisy says.

"Everyone likes those movies!" Mr. Jensen exclaims. "You can't make him turn it down."

"I didn't make him turn it down!" I shoot Chase a fierce

glance. "We need to talk. In private," I say pointedly to my dinner guests.

I take a small step away from Chase just so I can think, but he grabs my hand and twines his fingers with mine. Warmth shoots up from where our skin touches.

"Okay, everyone, back to the table," I shoo everyone toward the dining room with my hands. "We'll be back when we're done talking." I look at Chase. "My room?" I ask. He raises an eyebrow but nods.

"Sure, talking," Daisy says with a wicked grin before she herds the rest of my friends back to the dining room.

"Oh, young love," Mrs. Maple says. "I remember all that talking I'd do with Mr. Maple when we were first dating." She cackles wickedly.

"They're not coming back, are they?" Mr. Jensen asks mournfully. He shakes his head. "I never thought I'd get the chance to meet Max Thunder."

"It just means more dessert for me," Audrey says, grabbing the tray of cupcakes from the counter.

I shake my head at my friends' antics and usher Chase up the stairs to my room. We walk silently, hand in hand, me leading the way.

He closes my bedroom door with a firm thud. He looks around my room, missing nothing. His perusal unnerves me, and I'm suddenly aware of the evidence that I'm still in my childhood bedroom. There's my favorite stuffed bear, Porridge, on the bookshelf, along with my collection of Winnie the Pooh books, which I have to admit I still reread occasionally. Porridge still smells a little smokey, but I couldn't get rid of him.

Chase grins and picks up a book.

"Pooh is my philosophical guru. Nothing bothers him. He accepts life as it is. He's very Zen," I say with a blush.

I snatch the book from Chase's hand and place it gently back on the shelf.

Chase picks up my bear next. "I'm not judging," he says with a laugh. "Is this the bear you told me about? The one named Oatmeal?" Chase teases.

"You know very well he's Porridge." I glare at Chase.

And that's when I realize I've confided to Remington about my ridiculously named favorite stuffie, and, when we texted into the night, told him about the four-poster bed with the romantic netting I put up when I was sixteen and went through my *Out of Africa* phase. He even knows I added the twinkly lights on my bed frame one Christmas, and I just never took them down.

He knows it all, even if he didn't know my name.

My legs feel weak, and I sink onto the bed.

He stands in front of me, looking down. I crane my neck to see him better, and he kneels.

"Did you mean it?"

He doesn't ask what I mean.

"Every word," he vows.

"Even—"

"Especially the part when I said I love you." He traces a line down my nose and ends at my lips. Everywhere he touches burns. All I want is to kiss him, but this is too important.

"You can't turn down the movie role, Chase. This is your career. I can't ruin it for you. What if you resent me?"

"I'm not turning it down because of you, Olivia. Or, if I am, it's only because you've inspired me to take control and figure out what I want from my life, to risk the status quo that's not working for me. If it's a question between some movie role and you, I'll choose you every time."

My heart flips, but I still need to make him understand. "But that's just it. You don't have to choose. We can figure this out. I don't want you to sacrifice your career or who you are. That's not love. I want the man I'm with to be better because of me."

"This *is* what I want. I love movies, but I want to be involved with stories that matter to me. The director I sent my screenplay to loved it. He wants to make it. It will be a long road, but it's a start. Just like you predicted when you read it years ago." He looks down, a tinge of red appearing on his cheeks, and I'm charmed by that tell of insecurity in such a strong, brilliant man.

"*The Forgotten Ones*," I say on a breath. It was the screenplay Remington had sent to me. "Oh, Chase, I'm so happy for you. It's so good. So raw and beautiful, and I know it's going to be amazing on screen." I throw myself at him, almost toppling him, and hug him, quick and fierce.

He pulls us both up to standing and hugs me back, and he feels like home.

I shift away just enough to look at him. "The main characters are runaways. It's about you. Your experiences."

"Loosely. But yes, I drew from my childhood. There are so many kids discarded by society. I was the lucky one, so I need to give back. I want to tell their stories because I want kids like I was to know they matter."

He says it with passion, and I realize that he never spoke about his movie career like that before. He didn't seem to mind his job, except for the fame part. But he never had a fire for it. Not like this.

"My agent and manager want me to keep racking up the big roles to line their pockets. My PR company wants me to keep the fame up, because that's their job. I always just assumed that's what you did. You got on this roller coaster, you felt grateful they wanted you, and you never left unless they kicked you off. I was just along for the ride, but you helped me realize that's not what I want." He leans back to look at me.

"I want to do work that matters to me. Max Thunder isn't it. Thanks to *The Wanderers*, I have more money than I can spend in a lifetime. I don't want a yacht or an island somewhere. I want the freedom to choose work that interests me and to not be chased by paparazzi."

He smiles at me, and the joy in his face echoes the joy in my heart at his words.

"I want to be able to live wherever I want," he says. "I want to date the girl of my dreams and show her that, despite the lies we started with, what we have is very real, and I can be trusted with her heart."

The heart he refers to is beating overtime. "So, that other place you want to live?" I ask.

He scratches his chin. "I wouldn't mind San Francisco."

I tilt my head. "I kind of like Malibu, at least for part of the year. The weather is pretty nice in the summer. And that girl you want to date?"

"Her name is Olivia. Sometimes she goes by Typewriter Girl."

"Hmm. Typewriters? That's kind of old-fashioned."

"I'm an old-fashioned guy."

"Well, it beats texting. Texts are temporary. But letters are forever. Mr. Jensen reminded me of that at the beginning of the summer." I grin. "Speaking of Mr. Jensen, should we rejoin everyone? They might be waiting for us, and I am the host." I say it, but the truth is, I don't want to go downstairs. I want to stay right here in my bedroom with Chase, possibly forever.

His eyes are warm. "I vote no on going downstairs. I want you right where I have you, and I'm not letting go anymore," he says teasingly, but his expression is serious. "What I want with you isn't temporary. It's forever."

He bends down and captures my mouth. I'm shaking from the relief of kissing him, when I thought I'd never feel this again.

I lean in, standing on my toes. He backs me up to the wall and lifts me until we're lined up as he settles between my legs.

He moans into my mouth as he grinds against me. We go from rated G to R in the span of a minute, but I can't get enough of him, of the feel of his body against me. He cups my face in his hands.

"God, I missed you," he says when we take a break to breathe. He traces his finger over my face, my lips. I reach out and touch my tongue to his finger and revel in his taste. But his hand is on the move, down to the edge of my lavender dress.

I love this dress; it's cute and quirky, a little retro. I bought it last week in my experiment to find my style. But right now, I want it off, especially when he dips his fingers below the material, pulling it down to expose my plain bra. I wish I'd also bought a matching set of sexy lingerie.

The look on Chase's face tells me he doesn't care. He's not comparing me with the women he's been with in the past. His eyes are hot, his gaze covetous, as if the beige cotton bra were black silk and lace.

His fingers make me tremble as they edge closer to my nipple. It's an extended bud now, straining to be closer to him.

"Hey! What are you doing in there? We're hungry! Should we wait for you two or start eating?" Mrs. Maple calls from behind the bedroom door.

"What if they kick us out? I want that roast chicken. It looks amazing." I hear Audrey say.

"If they kick us out, I'm taking back my cupcakes," Daisy threatens in a loud voice.

I bite my lip, debating, because I know I'm weak, and if Chase pushes even a bit—hell, if he so much as touches me again—we'll be staying in this room forever.

He must sense my torn thoughts, because he gives me a pained smile and sets me back on my feet, my body sliding down his with every inch. He taps me on my nose. "When we do this, I don't want any distractions. I can eat really, really fast," he says, his voice rough with desire.

I smile slowly. "So can I."

He shakes his head. "The timing could be better, but come

on, Typewriter Girl, let's host our very first dinner party together."

I grin up at him.

We walk out of the bedroom and are greeted by Daisy, Audrey, and Mrs. Maple lounging in the hallway.

"Did we interrupt something?" Mrs. Maple asks innocently.

"Damn, Olivia bagged a movie star," Audrey says.

"How many times do I have to remind people? He's not a movie star, he's my brother. I don't want to think of her bagging him," Daisy says.

We follow them down the stairs, and the doorbell rings.

"Are we expecting anyone else?" Mrs. Maple asks.

"Oh shit, I forgot." Chase winces. "Is there room for a few more?"

"A few more?" I ask, glaring at him. So much for eating quickly and rushing back upstairs.

"I, uh, had some moral support for this trip. Sebastian insisted on coming with me, and Ryder flew us in his plane. I told them to wait in the car and leave if I didn't come back out, but they're shit at following directions."

"Sebastian? Ryder?" Audrey looks as if she will faint. "As in Sebastian Blake and Ryder Black? Here? Now?"

"Yes," I say.

"Audrey, stop being such a fangirl," Daisy says.

But I notice Daisy is fluffing her hair and licking her lips. She's not above fangirling a little over Ryder.

The doorbell rings again, followed by a pounding sound. "Yo!" Sebastian's unmistakable voice calls. "Are you banging in there? Let us in! We're getting bored in the Rover!"

"Yup, that's them," Chase says.

He grabs my hand, and together, we make our way to the door.

Old friends are seated around my table. New friends are here. And I'm walking hand in hand with someone I love.

We open the door to find Ryder and Sebastian with matching wide grins. Sebastian holds out a framed portrait.

"Yo, your grandma was hot."

"The Adam Reynolds!" I gasp, grasping the precious photograph. I never thought I'd see the original again.

"But—how? Mr. Jensen's friend sold it. I got the money!"

"She did. She sold it to me," Chase says. He cocks his head. "And now I'm giving it back to you. Do you like it?"

He looks like a little boy, asking if he did well on a test.

"I love it."

I stand on tiptoes, and he leans down to meet me in a sweet kiss. I almost drop the framed photo as we cling to each other.

Someone clears their throat. Loudly.

Chase kisses my forehead and smiles down at me, totally ignoring our new guests. "I'm glad. I was going to keep it in the car and give it to you later, but I guess the guys had other ideas."

I know how much this cost him, and I hate that he spent that much money on me. Just as it had been hard to accept that he did so many repairs on my house.

But Daisy's words come back to me. She'd said that when someone gives you something with an open heart, as I know Chase has, then you should accept in the same spirit. He's new to showing his love. I don't want to reject it, in any way, even his ridiculously generous gifts.

"Thank you," I say in his ear, with a soft kiss to his cheek.

His smile makes me thankful for Daisy's wisdom.

I look down at the photo of Nanna. When I was young, it embarrassed me, because who had a naked photo of their grandmother in their house? But now, all I see is a woman living life fully. She took the biggest risk, showed the world who she was without artifice, without a mask, without adornment.

What a beautiful gift it is to see and be seen, to be accepted for who you are. And to be loved for it.

I take Chase's hand.

When we all gather in the dining room, making room and setting plates for our new guests, the only thing I see is our friends blended, varying ages, varying wisdom, all laughing, passing food, crowding around a big table.

I've finally done it. I filled the vacant table, the empty house, the lonely parts of me, with love. With Chase by my side. I know that we have so much more to do, so much more to conquer, and it won't all be easy.

We have to figure out the right balance between real life and celebrity, LA and San Francisco. We have to navigate career pressures and fame, and the regular problems that come with two people making a life together. But with Chase's hand in mine and people who are happy to be in our corner, I'm filled with a certainty that we can make it.

It feels like hope. It feels like joy. It feels a lot like love.

He leans down and whispers into my ear, "This is taking too long. I can't wait. On a scale of one to ten, how devastated would you be if we didn't taste your roast chicken?" he asks.

I tilt my head. "Well, I am rather hungry."

"I can fill you up, babe."

I laugh. "I don't doubt it."

He kisses that sensitive part under my ear, and with just one brush of skin against skin, I'm a puddle of longing.

"I think I overcooked the chicken anyway."

"They won't even miss us." He brushes another kiss a little lower on my neck.

"They can see themselves out," I murmur.

He pulls away from me, looking me in the eye. "Let's go."

We stand in tandem and all but run out of the room, like naughty children escaping detention.

"It's about damn time!" Daisy yells at our departing backs.

"Bro, give her some good loving!" Sebastian calls out.

"Would you like more rolls, Mrs. Maple?" I hear Audrey ask,

taking over the role of hostess. She does it better than I do anyway.

I giggle as we rush up the stairs. We finally reach my bedroom, and Chase grabs me, pulling me toward him, and slams the door of my childhood room behind us.

"Finally," he says with satisfaction. "Alone."

CHAPTER 38

livia

I REACH FOR HIM, and there's a desperation to our movements.

"I want you, Chase," I mumble through long, drawn-out, drugging kisses. "Make love to me. Be my first."

We draw apart now. Our foreheads touching, deep, labored breaths mingling. His eyes are on mine, trying to read my mind. "Are you sure?"

"More than anything in the world. I love you, Chase James."

He closes his eyes, as if hearing the words is too much for him. When he opens them, his eyes burn into mine in heated tenderness.

In one swift motion, he lifts me like I'm made of feathers. I make a surprised sound at the unexpected gesture and hold on as he carries me across the room, kissing me the entire time.

When we reach my bed, I slide down his body, and we stand there, just staring at each other. I feel the weight of the moment.

Chase's hand trembles as he brushes it over my collarbone. He bends and kisses that patch of exposed skin, and gooseflesh breaks out. My whole body trembles like his hand, from excitement, from anticipation, from nerves.

A gust of laughter breaks out from the party below, and we look at each other. It makes our act seem more illicit, which ratchets up the nerves and excitement.

His half-smile sends longing coursing through me. God, what it does to me. It's sexy and secretive and naughty, and it focuses my gaze back on his lips. I tiptoe up and kiss him until he takes my mouth and gives me the kiss back tenfold.

His hands mark every part of me, a little desperate, a little clumsy. And I love that he's not being practiced and smooth, because as I stand there being worshipped, I acknowledge I have no idea what I'm doing. I'm desperate to get his shirt off. I feel his hard abs and smooth skin and strong chest, and I don't want clothes between us. I don't want anything between us. Skin-to-skin and heart-to-heart. My soul is his.

He walks me backward a step, and I fall to the bed as he stands over me, like a conquering god. His eyes are full of want for me. I'm humbled. And slick with desire.

Our minds must be on the same track because he murmurs, "I need your clothes off. Now."

That's when it hits me. This whole sex thing means I need to get naked in front of one of the most beautiful people on the planet.

I've been there before, but damn, it's bright in here.

When we walked into the room, Chase flipped the light switch.

"Um. Okay. But can we turn off the lights?" I mumble.

"I want to see you, Olivia."

"I just need some mood lighting here, Chase. Work with me. Overhead lights off. Twinkly lights on? Or candles?" I ask.

"I need more than candlelight to appreciate your body properly," he murmurs. "You have no idea how beautiful you are."

"I'm even more beautiful by twinkly light," I assure him.

He shakes his head. "You're beautiful always."

"Stop distracting me and turn off the lights."

He rolls his eyes and walks to the light switch. He turns the lock while he's there. Good move. I admire his rangy muscles and tight ass. I successfully removed his shirt, so I have a lot to admire there as well. Until the room goes dark.

Damn. Maybe I didn't think this through.

A second later, my twinkle lights turn on, and the room is bathed in a soft glow. He's disconcertingly good at navigating a girl's bedroom.

He climbs onto the bed and stretches out next to me. He shifts to his side, his head in one hand. I roll over to face him, mirroring his pose.

"Hi," I say.

There's that smile. "Hey. You're right."

"I know." I grin. "About what?"

"You're gorgeous by twinkle light."

"Told you so." I make a goofy face.

"Be serious. We're having a moment."

"I hope we have more than a moment."

"Really? The virgin is making stamina jokes?"

"Shh, don't say the V-word." I push him.

"Why? It's part of you. I like that you've saved yourself for me." He's teasing, but there's truth in it.

"I kind of was."

He cocks his head. "What do you mean?" He traces my collarbone with his hand, edging to my bra.

"Every time I met a guy, I'd compare him to Remington, and he would come up short. I had a crush on my pen pal. It didn't feel right to be with another guy."

"Does it make me a jerk that I'm glad?" He kisses my neck, and I shiver.

"Kind of," I whisper. "Being my pen pal didn't stop you from hooking up with other girls."

"No matter who I tried to distract myself with, it never felt right to be with anyone else. You were the one I wanted."

He roams his hand up to my breast, covering it, lightly caressing. "I've been dying to do this since that first morning I saw you. Actually, since that selfie you sent to me. I love your tits. I need to see them. Now."

He lifts my dress, and I help him drag it from my body. When it's off, I'm only in my bra and underwear and I'm tempted to cover myself, but the hunger and admiration in his expression stop me. He doesn't see my imperfections. He loves what he sees, and through his gaze, I can reimagine my image of myself. Where I see extra flesh, he sees lush curves. It's heady.

"Gorgeous," he whispers.

He pulls aside the cotton of my bra, bending over me to draw first one nipple, then the other, into his mouth. It's both too much yet not enough. I writhe under him, trying to touch every part of his chest, stomach, raking my hands over him. As he sucks at me, his hand goes lower until he skims up my thigh. I'm quivering beneath him, filled with longing. He plays with the seam of my underwear, and I whimper. He skitters a finger over that place that's just concentrated want, tickling, teasing, making me gasp and writhe.

"Please," I beg.

With his other hand, he finds my bra clasp and worships my bare breasts. But still, he holds back, teasing me over my underwear.

"I like it when you beg for me." His voice is sandpaper rough.

I want him to beg for me also, so I drag my fingers over the front of his jeans, feeling his erection. He sucks in a breath as I rub up and down in a slow rhythm. When his breathing is rough, I drag his zipper down and touch him through the space I've made. He's wearing boxers, but I feel his dick through the thin material and relish his gasp.

"You make me crazy for you."

"Ditto," I whisper.

With one smooth move, he pushes me down on the bed. He stares at me, and my gut response is to cover myself, but he takes my wrists and pushes them back against the bed, raising himself above me.

Everything but overwhelming desire falls away.

He leans down and places a kiss on my soft belly. I shudder at the sensation, anticipation and nerves warring. He lands a kiss lower, and then lower, one at a time, until he's at my panties. He looks up, his gorgeous face full of heat, a wicked smile playing at his lips.

He takes a finger and dips inside to the curls beneath. I realize that, just as before, I have no girl prep going on down there. I'm sure most of the girls he's been with have been completely smooth or maybe with designer pussies. I read an article once about all the styles you can create.

"I'm an all-natural girl," I say, not sure how to put it.

"It works for me." He's practically panting. So I choose to believe him.

He drags my underwear off and gets up close and personal with me.

I kinda want to die. Excitement and shyness mix together.

"Relax," he croons. "Just feel."

We've done this before, but it feels more intimate now. Maybe it's because the room is brighter with the twinkle lights so we can see more of each other, or maybe because we've told each other how we feel.

Then he licks me, and any self-consciousness flies out of my head. One long, smooth lick at my center, and my hips shoot up. It's wet and decadent and, *God*, so good.

He licks me slow and languorous, as if he wants to savor each drop. He teases me, tortures me. I lose any sense of myself, any shame or fear or insecurity until I finally explode. He rides my orgasm, raining soft licks and kisses down on me until the aftershocks fade and I'm a boneless, satisfied mess.

I sigh when I can draw breath, feeling shy again. "That's... Yeah. Wow," I say. He fried my brain.

"We'll be doing it often, because I can't get enough of you." He brushes my hair back from my face. I look at him, at the need in his eyes. I realize again how one-sided this is. I want him as wild as I just was.

My hand shifts down. I feel just boxers. Sometime, during all that, he took his jeans off. I push his underwear down, and he kicks them off. We're both naked now. I grasp him and have evidence that he did, indeed, like going down on me. I rub the moisture I find at his tip, and he draws in a breath.

I play with him, exploring the satin-smooth hardness, exploring his shape, texture. He gives himself over to me, and I revel in it. He's big, worryingly big, and now that it's about to happen, I'm not sure how it's possible for us to fit together, but I'm willing to give it a try.

It's my turn to lean over him, and I kiss down his ripped stomach. I recall how he'd kissed my soft belly, but his body is so different from mine; where I'm soft, he's hard. I count his abs. A six-pack has nothing on him. His dick is standing at attention for me, and I give him a lick. He jerks like I jolted him with electricity. I draw back. "I'm sorry, did that hurt?"

He laughs, a deep, husky sound. "It felt too good."

"There's no such thing as too good."

"There is, if you want me to last. I've been dreaming about this forever."

I smile. I'm glad it's something we've both wanted, both dreamed about.

"Hush, I'm concentrating." I taste him again. Excitement thrums through me. This gorgeous man who's wanted by millions is laid out before me, all mine.

"I still don't know what I'm doing," I admit.

"You're a natural," he rasps out and then moans as I sink my mouth down on him, taking him to the back of my throat. He's too large to take him all in at once, so I settle a hand at his base and let instinct take over, listening to his response, going slow and fast, experimenting like he's my favorite science project. Just as I find a rhythm that drives him mad, he pulls me away.

"Enough. You're killing me. And I don't want this to end before it begins."

"I think we already began," I say. I lick my lips, savoring him on me, and he makes a guttural sound.

I watch him with wicked merriment, feeling proud of myself and a little relieved. I've had a niggling worry that I wouldn't be enough for him—not experienced enough, not sexy enough, not naughty enough. That I was too much of a good girl.

But I'm realizing that I am enough. I love every part of him and want to make him happy and satisfied, and he wants the same for me. It's about our connection, not fancy tricks. We'll learn and teach each other all we need to know together.

He reaches down and strokes me, and I moan.

"God, you're wet."

He rubs me until I'm wild for him again, dipping a finger in, then two, stretching me as my hips follow his rhythm, drawing in and out.

He stops and I whimper. His half-grin is sexy and full of promise as he reaches for his jeans and pulls out a condom.

"So, you planned this. Is this a booty call?" I tease.

"If by planned, you mean hoped and prayed and begged God, then yes."

I feel him between us, putting on the condom.

And then he's there, at my entrance. Our eyes meet. He's serious, almost reverent. There's a question in his eyes.

"I want you to be my first," I assure him. I want him to be my last, as well, but I'm not sure if we're ready to say that.

"I love you, Olivia Evans."

"I love you," I whisper. Tears pool in my eyes. I've felt so alone. And now I'm not.

"Hey, don't cry."

"They're good tears. Does it seem too fast to feel this much?" I ask.

"It's not fast, Typewriter Girl," he says.

And then he's pushing. There's pressure and tightness and a tearing burn, and he's there inside me, filling me, and despite any lingering pain, it's everything I've ever wanted.

I'm full of him as our bodies mate and our mouths meld and our hands are everywhere. I'm drowning in Chase and he's drowning in me until we're no longer separate anymore, until we become one.

He sets a slow and steady pace that has me crazy. My body has mostly adjusted to the fullness. The pleasure-pain of it makes me cry out as he draws in and out, driving me mad. He adjusts his hips in a way that hits something in me, something that makes me gasp.

"More. Just like that," I order. And he does.

He reaches between us and rubs my most sensitive spot, and the sensations, the friction, are all too much. "Come for me, Olivia." His command is dragged out of him. "Come because I can't last much longer."

It's his rhythm, his restraint, his desperation that pull me over the edge, and I reach that peak again, feeling it everywhere this time, inside and out. My body's climax sets him off, and he drives deeper into me until he stills.

Our eyes lock, bodies entwined, as we fall over the precipice together.

I come back to reality first.

I did it.

We did it.

I'm no longer a virgin.

And even more important, Chase is in my body and my heart.

I close my eyes, savoring the satisfied languor in my limbs, even savoring the full soreness between my legs, knowing I feel it because the man I love was there.

Yep. Falling in love makes me a sappy dork.

"Hey." Chase kisses my shoulder and brushes my hair out of my face. I pop my eyes open to see him smiling above me. He looks younger, happier than I've ever seen before. I've done that. Me! And I'm awed all over again.

"Hey," I say.

"Are you okay? Did I hurt you?"

"I'm more than okay."

"Did you like it?" he asks uncertainly, which only makes me fall in love with him more.

I laugh. "You mean you couldn't tell?"

He gives me that slow smile I love. "Well, it seemed like you enjoyed yourself, but I don't want to presume. It's supposed to be painful, isn't it?"

I can't believe we're talking about this. "It was a little when you... But then you... And then it was incredible." I shrug. I'll let him fill in the blanks.

"You're adorable."

"You're hot as hell."

"You're that as well. And so damn pretty. You don't know what these big gray eyes do to me." He strokes a finger over my eyelashes. "Or these lips." He draws his finger down my face to settle on my lips. "Or your incredible tits." His finger follows the line of my neck and chest to circle my nipple. "I could spend forever worshipping them."

I wriggle a little, unable to believe I'm turned on again. He looks up at me, his eyes hot. It's as if he can read my mind and feel my growing excitement.

His hand glides down to my clit and finds it, circles it once, then twice. I draw in a breath and raise my hips to his hand.

"How sore are you?" he asks.

"Don't worry about that," I say.

"Hold that thought." He jumps up and struts to the bathroom. I admire the view. He comes back a few minutes later, still unapologetically naked. He's big all over, with hard, rangy muscles, his body moving with unconscious, lithe grace. *And he's mine.*

He has a wet washcloth.

I covered myself with the white sheet for modesty's sake. He rips off the sheet, eyes raking over my nakedness, and then he touches me with the warm, damp cloth, gently wiping away any traces of blood there.

"We won't make love again," he says with authority.

I cock my head. "Ever?"

"Oh, I'm going to fuck you every way you can imagine. Just not again tonight."

"That's disappointing," I remark. I'm planning on seducing him, so I don't believe what he says.

"Don't be. I'll take care of you in other ways."

"What ways?" I ask, fully on board now.

"How about a warm bath and I show you?"

I grin. "The other bathroom has a bathtub. I'm here to learn from you," I say. I can't wait to introduce him to my beloved claw-foot tub.

"And I'm here to love you," he says. "But first, I have something to give you."

He reaches over to his discarded jeans again.

"Another condom? Oh, yes please." I laugh.

His mouth quirks. "Something else. Something I've had for a long time."

He pulls out a small velvet pouch.

"Hold out your wrist," he instructs.

I offer my left wrist.

"The other one."

I do as commanded and give him my right wrist, palm up. My bracelet jingles.

He empties the small turquoise bag into my hand. A series of the most delicately carved charms fall like raindrops into my hand, each one more exquisite than the last.

"How—why?"

His eyes glint. "I've been collecting these since I sent you the charm bracelet that first Christmas, one for each year of your birthday. But we stopped writing and started texting, so it seemed like breaking the rules to send them to you. But I couldn't stop buying them."

"A typewriter." I smile. "It's perfect. It's a Remington," I say in awe.

"Two typewriters," he says. He picks up another charm.

"It's my Smith Corona! It's even teal."

He places the two typewriters together on the same link. That small gesture brings tears to my eyes.

I hold up my arm, admiring the way they shine. Then I move on to the next treasure.

"A heart," I say, touching the platinum heart edged in what looks like rubies.

"Mine." He swallows.

I lean over and kiss him, just a gentle thanks, but the kiss heats.

I manage to pull myself away. "Stop distracting me from my gift. What's next? Oh, Chase, it's my house! How did you know?"

"You described it so many times in your texts."

I look at the next one. "A camera," I say, looking at him. "For Nanna?"

He nods. I swallow back tears at the care that went into selecting each treasure.

The last charm is an intricately designed book.

"For all the books you will publish one day. Soon."

I smile wistfully. "I sent my manuscript to several agents. It was scary. But I did it."

"I'm glad," he says. "You're so damn talented. And I know that because I've read your work. It's about time you listened," he grumbles.

"It took me a while, but I did it."

He places the book on a link, and now all the charms are there, all representing different facets of me.

I wrap my arms around his neck, loving the jingle of the bracelet.

"I love you, Remington."

"I love you, Typewriter Girl."

"So about breaking the rules. How do you *really* feel about dick pics?" I giggle.

"Don't even think about it."

"Hmm," I say. "Maybe that's a risk too far."

ACKNOWLEDGMENTS

You always remember your first. That's what this book is for me. Not the first novel I ever started. But it's the first I ever completed. This book is proof that it's never too late to take risks and live life fully. That's the lesson Olivia learns in Star-Crossed Letters, and it's a lesson I continue to learn every day.

Writing and publishing takes a village. Thank you to all my fellow writers who answered my million and one questions. Thank you to all the amazing professionals who helped along the way: my fabulous editors, proofreaders, beta readers, cover designer, and public relations and promo team. The mistakes are all mine.

Thank you to my husband and my family for always encouraging me to chase my dreams.

And most of all, thanks to you, my readers.

ABOUT THE AUTHOR

Sarah Deeham is the author of sexy slow-burn romance novels to make readers smile and swoon. With a master's degree in writing and publishing, she got her start in writing as a freelance journalist, communications director, and an editorial director for a public relations agency. She is an American expat living overseas and currently makes her home in Kuala Lumpur with her husband, two children, and lazy golden retriever. When not reading or writing, Sarah can usually be found with a camera in hand, traveling the world, or dreaming up stories in a cafe.

GET A FREE BOOK AT
WWW.SARAHDEEHAM.COM

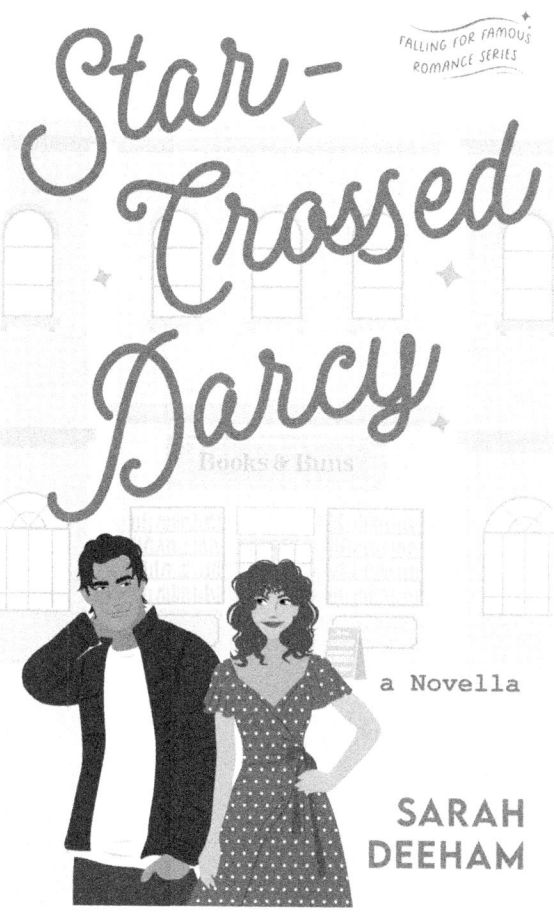

Sign up for my newsletter and you'll get Star-Crossed Darcy, a free standalone novella in the Falling for Famous series. You'll also get updates and romance book news, cute golden retriever photos, and giveaways.

ALSO BY SARAH DEEHAM

In the Falling for Famous Series

Ronan & Poppy's Story is available from October 2023

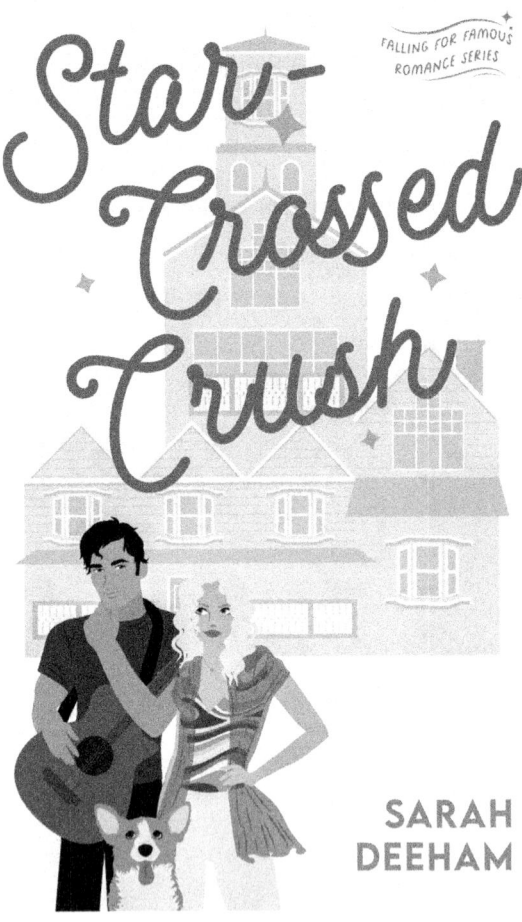

Ryder & Daisy's Story is coming soon